The Drums of Winter

The Drums of Winter

Sandra Paretti

Translated by Sophie Wilkins

M Evans
Lanham • New York • Boulder • Toronto • Plymouth, UK

M. Evans
An imprint of The Rowman & Littlefield Publishing Group, Inc.
4501 Forbes Boulevard, Suite 200, Lanham, Maryland 20706
http://www.rlpgtrade.com

10 Thornbury Road, Plymouth PL6 7PP, United Kingdom

Distributed by National Book Network

First Rowman & Littlefield paperback edition 2014

Library of Congress Cataloging-in-Publication Data Available

ISBN 13: 978-1-59077-458-8 (pbk: alk. paper)

The paper used in this publication meets the minimum requirements of American National Standard for Information Sciences—Permanence of Paper for Printed Library Materials, ANSI/NISO Z39.48-1992.

Printed in the United States of America

If buttercups buzzed
after the bee
If boats were on land
churches on sea
If ponies rode men
and if grass ate the cows
If cats should be chased
into holes by the mouse
If the mammas sold their babies
To gypsies for half a crown
If summer were winter
and the other way round
Then all the world would be
upside down

—*Stanza from 'The World Turned Upside Down,' a popular song during The American Revolutionary War, 1775-1783.*

BOOK ONE

The Deserter

> Almost every week there'd be new frightening stories of captured deserters, who, no matter how cunningly they had disguised themselves as sailors or tradesmen or even women, or hidden themselves in tuns or barrels or whatever, had been caught just the same. Then we had to watch while they were made to run the gauntlet, eight times or more, through a corridor of two hundred men, until they collapsed, unable to draw another breath—only to have to go through it again the next day.
>
> *From* The Life Story of the Poor Man of Tockenburg, *Zurich, 1789*

1

The cherry trees bloomed for the second time that year, and it seemed the summer would never end. The barns could hardly hold the harvest, but the earth seemed far from tired; the winter wheat grew so fast the farmers began to yearn for an early frost, to bring this strange miracle to an end.

The sheer abundance of the year 1775 made everyone uneasy. The sky seemed too blue, the sun too warm, and it was more than people could accept. They weren't used to being given anything at all; they knew that everything they had—property, freedom, life—was theirs only on loan, and could be taken away at any time, without warning. It was a fact they could hardly forget, living as they did at the foot of a fortress that was both barracks and prison in one.

It rose steeply above the gently rolling land. The gray cone of its tower cast a pall on the brightest day and cut a dark, threatening gash in the blue of the sky. To live near it was to be aware of it at all times, if only because of its great wandering shadow that was always cheating some part of the land out of its share of sunlight.

The Hessian tenant farmers on their way to the Haynow estate had Ramswood Fortress at their backs. They moved in single file across the meadow, walking on the grass parallel to the road to keep their shoes from getting dusty. Every man wore his Sunday best—the dark country jacket with massive lead buttons, black neckerchief, black wide-brimmed hat. Far ahead they could see the stone entrance gate of Haynow, large enough to admit even high-piled hay wagons. The torch brackets on either side still held large bouquets of wheat stalks from the recent harvest festival, one from each tenant farmer. Each had once been a small landowner, but over the years more and more small farms had been absorbed by the big Haynow estate, and it was only a matter of time till the last of the local freeholders became so deeply in debt to Gottfried Haynow that he lost house and land and became a Haynow tenant farmer.

They took off their hats when they reached the gate. Ahead of them stretched the long driveway, flanked by oak trees. Set back away from the drive, on either side, lay the outbuildings. At the end of the driveway, where the sun made a golden haze in the autumn trees, stood the Haynow residence, a handsome two-story main house flanked by long, low parterre wings. It had long been known as Haynow House, though it had originally been left to Haynow's wife by her uncle, and Haynow had acquired it through marriage. Its tall French windows glittered in the sun.

They listened to the sounds coming from the various utility buildings—a mixture of children's voices, chickens squawking, the clang of a hammer. They were the sounds of any farmyard, the same sounds they heard at home, and suddenly it seemed foolish to be so timid. It was a beautiful day, the kind of day a man should breathe deep and walk proud. Maybe their errand wasn't hopeless after all; maybe they wouldn't be sent away empty-handed.

They were starting through the gate when someone shouted at the rear of the column. They stopped and turned. A puff of white smoke was rising from the walls of the fortress. They watched the smoke roll up into a cloud, its soft edges billowing lazily out, trailing little cottony puffs. Behind this island of foaming white, the sky seemed even bluer than before.

They knew what such a smoke signal over the eastern outworks of the fortress meant, but they could hardly believe their eyes. If a man was going to desert from the Hessian army, the time to do it was in spring and summer, not in the fall when the fields were a bare stubble. Soldiers who risked it in November were likely to share the fate of the rabbits that were being slaughtered in their hundreds by hunters everywhere.

The sounds coming from the outbuildings had stopped. Silence crept across the estate grounds. The seconds stretched away, until finally the smoke signal was followed by the sound of the alarm cannon, rolling like thunder across the landscape, followed by three overlapping echoes.

The tenants avoided each other's eyes. Only one of them refused to be cowed. Felbing, a broad-shouldered man with white hair and a red beard, rapped the ground with his gnarled stick. "You should be used to that kind of music by now," he said. "Damn it, the man they're playing that tune for's got more grit in his little finger than all of you put together. I'll tell you one thing. Anybody that deserts this time of year knows exactly what he's doing. He's got people to help him, and I hope for his sake they're made of better stuff than you are. You haven't even got what it takes to help yourselves."

"We'd better turn back," the dairy farmer said.

"Turn back right at the gate?!"

"You know how the Elector's gendarmes are. They think we're hand-in-glove with the deserters anyway."

Felbing stood with both hands gripping the top of the stick, looking hard at the others. "When did a gendarme ever help any of you drive off those wild pigs? Or have you forgotten why we walked all the way over here in the first place?"

The others shifted their feet, slumped dejectedly, as if carrying an invisible load.

"Well, you can do what you want," Felbing said. "I'll go see Haynow by myself. Just don't expect me to fight your battles, too." He looked up toward the fortress. The first cloud had begun to dissipate; like a burst pillow, with feathers streaming, it drove before the west wind. A new plume of smoke was already rising over the walls. Again a cloud formed and swelled to full size before the thunder of the alarm cannon followed. "I wish I had half the gunpowder they're wasting up there," Felbing said. "I'd know what to do with it." He turned and went through the gate.

The others followed hesitantly, but after a few feet they stopped again. A rider had appeared at the far end of the driveway: a man wearing the green uniform of the First Hessian Guards regiment, riding a high-stepping sorrel. The shimmering sunlight under the trees seemed to part like a gold curtain to let him through.

The tenants stepped to the side of the road, to make way for their landlord's son. Claus Haynow pulled up abruptly, and the sorrel snorted and reared. The stamping hooves threw sand against their legs. Standing in a cloud of dust, they murmured their greetings.

Claus Haynow patted his horse's neck. He had very delicate features, the face of a man who had spent a long time in a childhood sickbed. Even his posture still showed traces of a lifelong fear of paralysis. He held himself inflexibly straight. He glanced over the men, his father's tenants. He hardly knew them, couldn't come up with one name apart from Felbing's, that old troublemaker who couldn't forget he'd once been a freeholder and was always demanding his so-called rights.

Felbing stepped forward. "We've come to see your father."

"You've picked a bad time for it," Claus said curtly.

"It's about the wild pigs." Felbing was undeterred. "They're destroying the fields before the crops can even come up. There's no controlling them."

Claus was counting the men. There were twelve of them. If he added the grooms from the stables, the coachmen, the hunters, he'd have thirty-six—enough for a posse to go after the deserter.

"Shouting won't keep those pigs off our crops." Felbing said. "Neither will clubs. We need guns." Whatever else he said was drowned out by the third boom of the alarm cannon.

"Wait here." Claus turned his horse around. "I'll bring you some horses. If we catch the deserter, I'll see you're paid for it." He rode off up the driveway and disappeared into the stableyard. They could hear him shouting orders.

Felbing swore under his breath. "Just our rotten luck to run into him. Robert Haynow at least would have heard us out."

"I wouldn't give you two cents for the difference between them," the dairy man said. "Even if Robert is only Haynow's stepson."

"I can talk to Robert like he was my own son."

"We're all just dirt to them."

"What's the matter, don't like you like the tobacco Robert brought you from Holland?"

"Piss on his tobacco. I'd rather he kept away from my daughter."

"The question is, who should keep away from whom. I never heard Robert Haynow had to lift a finger to get any girl he wanted. I know all about it, there's womenfolk aplenty on my place."

There was the sudden hiss of a riding whip cutting the air. A dozen horses came crowding out of the stables; it was all the grooms could do to hang onto the reins. Again Claus Haynow cracked the whip. "Come on. Mount up, all of you. Hurry, or the man'll be gone before we get started."

"We'll go on guard duty as soon as we get home," Felbing said quietly.

"Are you resisting my orders?" Furious, Claus Haynow rose in his stirrups. "You know the Elector's orders. Any man caught evading the search for a deserter is subject to the same penalties as a deserter's accomplice."

The tenants silently did as they were told. Claus sensed their reluctance, and regretted his promise to pay them. There was no need to buy or reward their obedience. He could barely look at them squatting lumplike in the saddle, an insult to his horses. But the horses would run like the devil anyway, hunters he had trained himself.

A fourth alarm cannon was fired up on the fortress. The tenants looked up; the harsh galloping echo drummed in their ears again, but this time their reaction was different. They exchanged a quick look. They knew now it was no common soldier, none of their own kind, who had escaped. A common soldier rated only three shots; five were fired for an officer.

"An officer," Felbing murmured, and flicked a sneering side glance at Claus.

Another group of riders came out of the stableyard. Claus waved them forward. "You bring up the rear," he said to the tenants. "And keep it closed up."

He gave his sorrel the spurs and moved out in front. They rode out of the gate at a gallop, Claus leaning over the outstretched neck of the sorrel. He was seized by a fever, a wild determination. Neither the town militia nor Commandant Rall's troops were going to capture this deserter. This one was going to be his. The wind, blowing his hair back from his forehead, was cool on his face, but he felt as though his skin were on fire.

2

The reeds bent under the pressure of the explosion. For a matter of seconds it was no mere bank of reeds but a forest of sharp hammered silver blades that fringed Heron Island in the midst of the river. As the blades straightened again, the air shimmered. The thunder of the alarm cannon and its echoes died away; the air ceased its trembling. Soon the reeds were still again. Only the heart of the heron Robert Haynow held in his hands was still beating hard. With wings and long neck held close to its body, the bird pressed tightly against him for protection, holding its long, scaly legs stiffly outstretched before it. The right leg was banded with a thin strip of linen above the foot.

Robert pushed his blond hair back from his forehead. A long-drawn flock of fleecy clouds moved eastward high in the blue sky. Behind them rose the white puff of smoke that had preceded the fifth blast of the alarm cannon. From this distance the banners on the turrets of Ramswood Fortress looked like weather vanes.

In his childhood Robert's favorite plaything had been a toy

model of Ramswood Fortress. It had been gathering dust somewhere in the attic for years now, but he still remembered every embrasure, every side door, every staircase. Which way out had the deserter chosen, he wondered. More soldiers than prisoners escaped from Ramswood, which was half prison, half barracks. But the chances of a prisoner making good his escape were better, oddly enough, as if in this country only the rogues helped each other.

Robert stroked the heron's back. It was a year-old bird. The grays of its top feathers blended into a blackish blue. He had found the bird in the reed-bank, its leg nearly broken, the first day of his return from Holland. He opened his hand—the bird's heartbeat had gone back to normal. The heron hesitantly pulled away, put its good leg down first, then the wounded one. It shook out its feathers, started to spread its wings, then drew them in again. Robert watched it intently. He would have given anything to have a pair of wings now. How quickly he would have known, then, where to find the deserter, and how to help him. Slowly he straightened up and hurried away through the reeds.

The ferryman's landing stage lay on the north side of the island. Robert slipped through under the low-hanging branches, leaped over moss-covered tree trunks. He moved swiftly and silently, himself a part of the green-golden wilderness, of the ringing stillness that surrounded him.

He drew a horn whistle out of his pocket and twice in succession blew three quick blasts on it, the signal for the ferryman. Soon afterward he reached the landing stage. While waiting, he looked up toward the fortress again. Its eastern outworks, where the alarm cannon was mounted, now looked deserted; there was no sign of the cannoneers' blue coats. The manhunt had started. Hundreds of men were already swarming through the woods below the fortress, patrolling every road, every path, every crossing and bridge. He could visualize it all: the women who had been washing clothes on the riverbanks were hurrying home with baskets full of wet wash. Guards were bolting the town gates of Ramswood. Two drummers were marching through the town, summoning the citizens to guard duty, followed by yelling children who regarded the sudden excitement of their elders as a kind of festival. When Robert was a boy, the thunder of the alarm had excited him too, much the same way as the arrival of a traveling circus at fair time. The words "deserter" and "running the gauntlet" had had the same adventurous sound as "bear trainer" and "tightrope dancer." Until the day he had slipped away from home and run up to the fortress, a five-year-old aflame with curiosity. Now, eighteen years later, the hissing of those hazel switches cutting the air as they came down to rip the deserter's bloodied back was still in his ears. It still felt as though each blow had hit his own back.

The slap of oars on the river roused him from his reverie. He stepped onto the tiny landing stage, which consisted of just two posts and a broad plank. The boat came sliding through the reeds. The ferryman had shipped oars and was poling the boat toward the landing.

Ludolf was a lanky man of middle height. He wore high boots reaching above the knee, gray-green canvas trousers, and a thick brown woolen lumber jacket winter and summer. He also wore a gold ring in his left earlobe: a talisman against disease, he said.

"You made good time," Robert called out to him.

"I was already in midstream when you signaled."

The boat had reached the landing. The two men exchanged a look. "Give me the pole," Robert said. In his gray-green eyes there was a glint of something a stranger would have called a smile, but Ludolf knew Robert better than that. The ferryman sat down and picked up his oars. Obedient as a toy, the boat turned outward.

The reeds parted with a rustling sound. Swarms of fish fled aside before the prow of the boat, their scales shimmering in all the colors of the rainbow. Robert looked upriver, where the reflection of the fortress hovered on the water, a trembling shadow broken by waves and slivers of light in constant motion.

"You'd think an officer would have hundreds of other ways to desert," he said. "What do you think of his chances?"

"Depends on whether he can manage to keep out of their clutches till dark." Ludolf rowed expertly, leaning far forward and pulling back strongly at each stroke, his sinewy body a powerhouse of energy.

Robert gave him a glance. "I'd rather not know how many men you've helped across the river already."

Ludolf rowed on steadily. "There's not so much doing lately, compared to the way it used to be. Rall's a tough commanding officer. Running the gauntlet's not just a beating the way he sets it up; it's an execution. Even the bravest men think twice before they take the chance." The boat docked with a crunch, and Robert leaped out.

Dragging his fishnets behind him, Ludolf followed him onto the landing. They walked along the sloping riverbank to the ferryman's house. Ludolf had known Robert's real father, the alchemist Robert Skelnik, and had known Robert since childhood. He knew what was going on in Robert's mind. He threw his nets to the ground. "Might be a good thing you don't have a horse here. You should be glad enough to let things be; it's none of your concern." He bent over, and started to untangle the nets. "Isn't that why you chose to become a businessman like your stepfather, instead of an army officer like your half brother? You'd never have stuck it as a soldier." He straightened up and looked past Robert to the river. "You're the kind of man who can obey no one but himself."

"That's what my mother says when she's displeased with me."

From the road to Kassel, about eighty yards to the north of them, there came the rattle of wheels, though there was nothing to see as yet. The bushes lining the road were as impenetrable as a wall in places. Finally a wagon came into view.

"You see that?" Robert said. "There's my horse. All I have to do is want something hard enough, and I get it."

"To judge by the sound of the hooves I'd have guessed at a team of oxen. That's no local outfit."

Robert studied the high-wheeled wagon covered in bright green canvas. He crossed the meadow to the road. Ludolf was right, this had to be an outlander. No one in the whole region drove anything like this, part peddler's cart, part circus wagon. The man on the driver's seat would suit either one. Under his open coachman's cape he wore colorful foreign clothes. But the horse drew Robert's attention even more than man or wagon. It seemed to have slats for bones, and hempen rope for muscles. Its hide, too, was the color and the rough texture of uncombed hemp. The painful, hobbling gait with which it was pulling the wagon looked like the fastest pace it was capable of. Robert stepped into the road in front of the vehicle.

"What do you want?" the man called from his perch. "Why do you get in my way? My papers are in order." He fished up a document out of his carpetbag. "There, the Hessian customs stamp isn't dry on it yet. I'm Balthasar Ploetz, glover from Anif in Salzburg County."

"If your gloves are as good as your horse, they must all be missing their thumbs," Robert said with a laugh.

The driver was still uncertainly holding out his documents. "Don't you like my horse? She limps a little, that's true, but she makes up for it. Too bad I have to use her to pull the wagon; she's a joy to ride. Believe it or not, she'll outrun any other horse in a gallop, swims like the devil. . . ." The glover leaped up in his box seat. "What do you think you're doing?"

With a few quick movements, Robert had freed the horse from its harness.

"But how will I get to Kassel? . . ." the glover cried, and fell silent. The harness lay on the road.

Robert mounted his horse. He pointed westward from the road. "Just keep going in that direction, till you get to Haynow Manor. Ask for the lady of the house. Tell her I sent you."

"But who are you?" the glover cried, staring helplessly after him.

3

Robert turned off the road and crossed the fields in the direction of the fortress, staying close to the trees and bushes and keeping a lookout as best he could. He had no clear plan of action. When he had passed the narrow defile on the western side of the fortress hill, he stopped his horse. By this time she responded to the lightest pressure from his thighs. Hidden in the shade of the trees, he listened.

He had heard right—there was a troop of riders nearby. He peered through the trees; near the end of the pass something hovered like a strip of mist. Then he saw a horse appear. The rider wore a green coat. In a cloud of dust, the cavalcade came closer.

Robert rode his mare behind the broad trunk of an old maple tree. Hidden behind its purplish leaves he could see everything. The troop was less than fifty yards away, its leader some distance ahead of it, and when he turned his head, tossing the hair off his forehead, Robert recognized him.

It took him by surprise—his half brother Claus was not due back home from the capital till this evening. He took a deep breath, feeling as if he were somehow at a game of cards or dice.

Crouched over his horse, Claus rode past him less than three yards away, followed by his men. In a sudden impulse, Robert swung himself up into the tree. One of the lower branches reached far over the defile.

The riders passed swiftly on beneath him, one after the other, all bondsmen, coachmen, hunters from Haynow Manor. He had counted twenty so far, and with each additional man his gambler's excitement rose with the stake. One against twenty-one, against twenty-two. . . . Finally the tenant farmers came. They rode by without looking left or right. The deserter could have sat in full view by the roadside; they'd have passed him by without flicking an eyelash.

Robert listened as the horses trotted off into the distance. One against thirty-two. The other posses didn't count. The game was between him and his brother.

He jumped to the ground. The mare obediently positioned herself for him to mount. He patted her rough hide. She might even turn out to be a white horse under all that dirt, after some proper grooming and currying.

The following hour, he was everywhere and nowhere. He turned up briefly with the militia in Hawkswood, a little later at Wolf's Meadow with Commandant Rall's special search patrol. After the encounter with Robert the militia separated into two groups, one turning toward the coal piles, the other in the direction of the mine. Commandant Rall, on the other hand, was moved by a few of Robert's casual remarks to surround Hawkswood. After Robert had also sent the regular mounted police on a wild goose chase and made sure that the pursuers would be kept busy in all the wrong places until dark, he turned toward home.

Glowing from the reckless riding of the last hour and the inner tension over the outcome of his game, he trotted through the woods, thinking about the game of billiards he would play with Claus that evening, the hour of conversation he would enjoy with his mother in the darkening living room, lit only by the fire in the fireplace.

A clearing lay ahead, the light of the sinking sun falling in long streaks through the trees. Suddenly a shadow passed through the light and into the brush. The hunter in Robert came instantly awake, and he rode straight at where he'd seen the man disappear. Then he recognized Klemm, the odd-jobs man who had his cottage nearby.

"You about scared me to death," the man said. He was a runt of a man with a face like a piece of tanbark, clothes that seemed too large for him, and a weathered old cap sporting a jay's feather. Beside him stood his handcart piled high with hazel switches, all two yards long, finger-thick. They had been freshly cut.

Robert pointed to the load. "Weren't you getting a bit ahead of yourself? If they don't catch the deserter, they can't have their fun making him run the gauntlet, either."

The handyman dropped the hand holding the curved knife. "Rall wants them fresh," he said. "So they can be soaked in salt water long enough. If I don't cut them, somebody else will. There was a time my wife wouldn't touch the money, wouldn't speak to me for a whole day afterward. But since she started havin' the trouble with her legs and can't do her work as a laundress, she doesn't object anymore."

"I didn't mean it that way," Robert said.

"Nobody means it that way," Klemm said. He gave his handcart a kick so that it rolled as far as the low door of his cottage and slowly followed behind it. "But they all treat me like an outcast, just the same. I don't get anything for free, you know, I've got to get by the best I can, I can't pick and choose." He opened the shed under the overhang of the cottage roof. "I've got those rabbits you ordered before your trip to Holland." He disappeared inside the shed for a moment, and emerged with two green boxes. "White ones with red eyes, the kind you asked for. Both from the same litter. Four weeks old."

Robert pulled one of the rabbits from its box. Ears close to the head and round-backed, it cowered in his hand, sniffing at it.

"Who are they for?" Klemm asked.

"Louis, the wheelwright's boy."

"The little devil. I'd like to know how he does it. In the spring he always starts out with the smallest herd, and in the fall his goats are the biggest and fattest anywhere. He'll have a dozen out of these two rabbits in no time."

"What do I owe you?" Robert asked.

"Not a thing," the man said abruptly, as if his feelings were hurt.

Robert handed him two talers. "For your grandchildren. When Dr. Crusius visits our house next time, I'll send him to see your wife. You know the old game beater on our place? He could hardly move any more. Now he can run like a deer."

Klemm mumbled something and turned quickly away.

The two boxes with the rabbits hung to the right and left of the horse's rump. The mare had resigned herself after some resistance to slowing down from a gallop. Robert's gaze wandered over the meadows to the blue mountain ranges in the distance, surrendering to the enchantment of the fading day. He enjoyed riding along the paths he had known since boyhood, lazing away the days, wearing his old patched moss-green jacket. But after three weeks of this kind of country life the same restless instinct that had drawn him home drove him back again to the tea and tobacco auctions in Amsterdam and London.

Where the ground dipped ahead the bell tower of the wheelwright's shop came into view. Slowly the whole farmstead became visible: its shingled rooftops, small windows, the long barn sheathed in its trellised grapevine reaching all the way up to the roofing, the dovecote next to the living quarters. It was a familiar scene—but seemed different, somehow. It was the total silence that made it strange—ordinarily the wheelwright's establishment rang with noise, all that busy hammering, sawing, planing of wood, the hiss of water into which the iron hoops were dipped red-hot from the anvil.

Robert rode toward the front gate. Two men were standing there with their backs to him, guns in hand. They wheeled about at the sound of his approach. Then they recognized him, dropped their guns in relief, and made way. The courtyard was surrounded. A man was posted at every door, under every window. Claus Haynow, on horseback, was directing his men with gestures and low-voiced orders.

When Claus caught sight of his half brother, a defensive, uneasy expression crossed his face. The lame, disreputable-looking mare his brother was riding, the rabbit hutches on either side of it, the worn old calfskin boots with bits of sedge and bark sticking to them, the much-mended moss-green jacket—the whole getup felt like a personal insult to him. Especially because he couldn't ignore the wave of affection rising toward his half brother among his own men. It was always and everywhere the same, beginning with the love of his mother and father, which Robert seemed to have preempted as if he, Claus, were the bastard. It was Robert who was the son of the alchemist swindler, Skelnik, an adventurer who had deceived and robbed the Elector, and had left behind his young wife, carrying his unborn child, when he fled with the Elector's gold. Claus was ashamed of his thoughts, but he couldn't stifle them; they sprang from some source stronger than reason, stronger than his sense of fairness and family affection.

Their horses now stood facing each other. Robert had grasped the situation at a glance. Still, he felt as if he had been taken unaware. He hadn't counted on something like this in his gamble for the deserter. For a moment he wavered in his resolution to go on with it.

"This *is* a surprise," he said, with unaffected honesty, "but if you can use an extra man, I'm at your service."

"You show up looking like a gypsy!" Claus said.

Robert looked down at his clothes and smiled. "I didn't know you'd be coming back from Kassel this afternoon." He glanced into the courtyard. "I seem to have arrived just in time."

"Thanks. I can manage without your help."

From the barn came a loud cry: "We've got him! Bring a ladder, quick! He must be in here."

At a signal from Claus, six men ran into the barn. The others readied their guns. There was the low clicking of flintlock hammers being drawn back. All eyes were turned upon the shed. The left wing of the barn door had swung shut again; only the right half was open. Along the whole length of the barn there were round air holes, half shaded by the roof overhang, spaced about two yards apart, some of them covered by the grapevine. Dark blue grapes hung among the yellow leaves.

Robert listened intently to the sounds inside the barn, trying to guess what was going on there. Suddenly the shouting of the men inside stopped. There was only the crackling and rustling of the hay in which they were rummaging. The open side of the door rattled on its hinges. Suddenly, like a storm breaking, an avalanche of hay cascaded down, and a cloud of gray-green dust billowed out of the open door.

No one paid any attention to the boy who just then slipped from the barn. Louis was tall for his thirteen years; his face, framed by dark blond hair, looked intelligent beyond his age. His eyes searched the courtyard. Suddenly he ran toward Robert and did a little dance around the horse, running happily from one rabbit hutch to the other. "You didn't forget!" He stood on tiptoe to look inside the boxes. "I'll take them now," he said eagerly, arms outstretched.

Robert dismounted and draped the hempen rope connecting the two boxes around the boy's shoulders. The boy clutched the rope, lifting up the boxes for another look. "White with red eyes, just the way I wanted them," he murmured.

"Have you got a place to keep them?" Robert asked.

Claus had been observing this scene with increasing annoyance. "Clear out!" he shouted at the boy. "Right now, or you'll wish you had."

Louis put his arms protectively around his boxes. "I think I have a special place for them," he said to Robert. "Let me show you."

Inside the shed something came rumbling down. "That's right, let's throw all the ladders down," a man shouted. "He can't stay up under the roof beams forever."

The boy touched Robert's sleeve and led him across the court to the coach house where the carriages were kept for repairs. After a slight hesitation, he drew Robert inside the half-open sliding doors.

"Call that a good place for your rabbits?" Robert looked around in the large coach house. "The place is too drafty. They'll never last in here."

The boy pointed to one of the carriages. His face glowed with excitement. He was about to speak, but stopped, because one of the workmen who had been standing guard in the courtyard suddenly appeared at the half-open door of the coach house, gun in hand. It was Valentine, the coach painter, and he made no effort to pretend he liked taking part in this manhunt. The way he held his gun showed he had no intention of using it. When he saw the rabbit hutches, he grinned. Claus shouted something from the courtyard, and Valentine went back out.

"The carriage," the boy whispered. "Look inside."

There was something in the boy's voice that put Robert on the alert. He stretched out his hand to the silvered doorknob of the carriage, aware that his throat had tightened. He looked back at the boy, who nodded silently.

His eyes seemed to take unusually long to adjust to the dark. Slowly they registered the red velvet of the upholstery inside the carriage. Just beneath the high little window opposite sat a man. A dim ray of light picked up the part in his light brown hair. His face was immobile, eyes calmly meeting Robert's, without a flicker of surprise or alarm. The deserter sat there like a traveler confidently awaiting the scheduled departure of his postcoach.

Steps came near. Robert shut the coach door. "Cats just love to snuggle in a coach, don't they?" he said to the boy.

It was Valentine who stood in the doorway. "Well, sir, how do you like the coat of arms on the door?"

Robert stepped back a pace. What he saw on the carriage door was indeed the new Haynow coat of arms, recently conferred on his stepfather by patent of nobility: a silver wheel, the spokes of which were formed by two crossed swords, on a dark red ground.

Valentine leaned his gun against the wall and opened wide the sliding doors of the coach house. "It has to be seen in the light, you know. It was a chore, I'll tell you. The old coat of lacquer on that coach was meant to last forever. Still, it had to come off —it never would have done to paint over it." He circled the coach, studying his handiwork with satisfaction. "If you don't put the right base under silver, it turns black inside a week. Silver needs a grounding of red clay, you know, to give it the right kind of gleam." He rubbed the ball of his thumb over the coat of arms. "When the sun hits it, it's more beautiful than gold." He caught himself, with sudden embarrassment. "May I congratulate you, sir, incidentally?" He held out his hand to Robert. "All of us are pleased about it. A funny thing about a title, it's almost like a little of the glory rubs off on the rest of us here. They're making bets, in fact, about the Haynow family's chances of rising even higher."

"It doesn't make that much real difference to being a Haynow," Robert said. He was thinking hard about getting Valentine away from the coach. There was only one way, which was to move off from it himself, though he felt as if he were lashed to it with ropes. Finally he sauntered toward the open door. Valentine followed. There they stopped, looking out into the courtyard. The men had disappeared; Claus had apparently sent them all into the barn. He was sitting ramrod-straight on his horse, which nervously capered in place under him.

"I need two horses," Robert said to Valentine.

"For the carriage? You want to drive it to Haynow yourself? Already? . . ."

"You're worried about the enameling?"

"Three coats, each of them dried for twelve hours, just like on a ship."

"Then get me the horses."

Valentine, who had insisted on doing the harnessing himself, was taking an irritatingly long time about it. But Robert made no move to hurry him along. Now that his decision had been made he felt as he did at the gambling table just before uncovering his trumps and still not quite certain they would see him through.

Valentine handed him the reins and bent down to remove the brakeshoes from the wheels.

"Tie the horse I rode coming over here on behind, will you," Robert said. Slowly he drove the coach out into the courtyard. He had to repress a strong desire to look back into the coach. All he could remember of the man was the eyes, the fearless, direct glance of those eyes.

He could hear the men in the barn still searching through those mountains of hay. Outside the barn, its huge doors now wide open, stood a semicircle of about eight men.

Claus had resolved not to let Robert distract him again. He forgot that decision as soon as he saw Robert driving the coach across the courtyard. "What's the idea?" he said between his teeth, pale with anger.

Robert stopped the horses. "Surely you don't mind my making the maiden trip in her? Father'll be pleased to see the carriage today, sooner than he expected."

As usual, Claus was disarmed by Robert's easy unconcern. "Anyone of the wheelwright's men could have taken it to him," he said tensely.

"Get home early, so we can play some billiards before dinner."

Claus couldn't resist Robert's smile. "I'll do my best."

By this time Valentine had attached the mare's leads to the back of the coach. "All set," he said.

Robert slapped the reins lightly on the horses' backs and, with a friendly nod to Claus, drove the carriage out of the gate.

4

The lights in the windows of the ferryman's cottage blinked through the twilight. Fishnets hanging out to dry festooned the alder trees around the little cottage and its vegetable patch. The smoke rising from the chimney carried the smell of charcoal and grilled fish over the riverbank.

Robert drove the coach off the road and down the grassy incline. It bounded wildly over holes and bumps in the wake of the galloping horses.

The ferryman had prepared for the eventuality of Robert's return—a bundle of clothing and a food package were ready in a safe hiding place—but, still, when he saw the coach, he was startled. He hurried over as Robert braked the coach to a stop. "At least try to put her in under the trees. Everybody'll recognize your new coach. A blind man could see that coat of arms."

"So much the better. Three dozen men saw me driving it away from the wheelwright's. One of them was my brother Claus. Now do you still think I'm too reckless?"

"You're crazy, that's all. One of these days you'll go too far. You mean to tell me you took him right from under your brother's nose?"

Robert fastened the reins to a post. "Tell me instead what kind of fish you've got in your frying pan tonight."

"Barbels. And two big trout in the cellar."

"Ask our guest which he prefers."

The ferryman hesitated, then stepped quickly to the coach door. Robert sat on the coach-box, eyes straight ahead, and listened. He could hear nothing but the beating of his own heart.

"I should have known you were pulling my leg," he heard the ferryman say. "I always fall for your practical jokes, don't I?"

Robert leaped off the box. He pushed Ludolf away from the open coach door and peered inside, staring at the red velvet seat. He stepped inside the coach; it was empty. Finally he sat down on the footboard, as if stunned. Abruptly he burst out laughing. "You know how fast I drive, Ludolf. Would you dare jump out of a coach while I was in the driver's seat?" He stood up, turned, pointed inside the coach. "He was sitting right there, the man they're all looking for. The deserter. They had him trapped, and I drove him out of the wheelwright's, right from under their noses. But he didn't trust me either. I never slowed up for a second,

I drove from the wheelwright's right to your door—but he managed to jump out anyway."

The ferryman slammed the door shut. He shook his head. "This coat of arms by itself should have put some sense into your head."

"Well, we can say the coach has had its baptism by fire. Get me some water and rags, and help me clean her up."

The ferryman stayed where he was, absorbed in the new coat of arms. "Your stepfather has risen in the world, hasn't he? Baron Haynow. Makes you a member of the nobility, too."

"You make it sound like a disease."

"And then you pull this stunt in the new coach, of all things. You'll never change."

"Should I?"

The ferryman gazed at Robert thoughtfully. "If you knew how like your father you look. A while ago, when you burst out laughing—I thought I was hearing him. It makes me fear for you, that it does."

"I never cooked anything on my father's chemical burner but my tea and bacon with eggs. I'll never make gold, you can depend on it."

"That's not what I meant."

The ferryman went inside for water, rags, and brushes. The two men began to clean the coach. After a while Robert stopped. "Did you help my father get away?"

The ferryman looked up. "He had Soerman to help him. There were two of them. They didn't need anybody else."

"But their boat was found on the island, across the river. Somebody must have taken it back there."

"I would have taken it back, just to give them a head start, if your father had asked me. But I guess he didn't trust me."

"Maybe he didn't want you implicated."

The ferryman tossed his rag into the pail. "Too late to ask him about it now. In the end it makes no difference. Probably it was lucky for me he didn't trust me, just as it's lucky for you the deserter has dissolved into thin air."

Robert went back to cleaning the coach, but his thoughts

circled around the past as if sucked into a whirlpool. Where he was standing now, his father had once stood, bantering with the ferryman, just as he was doing now. Strange, the way that man had suddenly appeared from nowhere, with those eyes, that face.

Until this moment the father he had never known had been no more than a name, Robert Skelnik, and the brief chronicle of an adventurous life. The fact that his father was dead had been the answer to all his questions; more than that, it had simply kept questions from arising. Now, all of a sudden, death was no longer an answer. His gaze wandered over the water to Heron Island. "When he disappeared from the island it was November, too, wasn't it?"

Ludolf nodded and kept on with his polishing.

"That's enough. It'll do," Robert said. "Tell me what really happened? You've never told me all of it."

"You never asked me." The ferryman stepped hesitantly back from the coach. "It was a bad year. A rainy summer, a poor harvest. And a freezing cold that November, but no snow. The ground got hard as rock, and the winter crops froze." The ferryman rolled down the sleeves of his woolen jacket. "Your father left the night it began to snow. He must have had a premonition, because he left the island before the snow fell, so there were no tracks anywhere. His boat was tied up at the landing stage, looking like it had been sprinkled with sugar." Ludolf fell silent for a while, as if to give the past time to resurrect itself. "The day of the first snow, the wind was blowing from the southwest. I could tell by the thin trail of smoke over the island, where his laboratory was. It was there all that day and night. Next morning there wasn't any smoke. I paid no mind to that, because he let the fire go out sometimes for a few hours. But when there was no sign of it by evening, I started to wonder. Later, they found a funny kind of sediment in the oven. The authorities from the capital said he'd tricked us all. They said the fire had quietly gone on burning for forty-eight hours before it finally burned itself out."

"Did you ever believe he could make gold?"

Ludolf shrugged. "I don't know whether your father was a swindler, or whether he thought he had a way to make people's dreams come true. The old Elector, the father of this one, brought Robert Skelnik to Kassel. All the princes were having a go at making gold in those days, it was like a fever. But our old ruler was a fox. He picked Robert Skelnik not because he believed in miracles: your father had found a way to melt coins down and make four gold pieces out of one, and you couldn't tell it by looking at them or even by their weight. He was supposed to turn sixty thousand gold pieces into four times as many for the Elector. That's why they built him a laboratory on Heron Island. But your father had a better idea: he took all the gold and cleared out. The Elector managed to hush it all up. It wasn't until after his death that the story gradually leaked out."

"Sixty thousand gold pieces. Quite a bit of extra weight for a man on the run."

"The gold was on the island for quite a while before that. Your father had enough time to make his arrangements. By the time he left, I bet he had nothing more on him than he needed for the trip. Everything else must have been sent on ahead. There are still a few old women who think the devil took both him and his gold."

"Who was that fellow Soerman?"

"Oh, he came from somewhere up north, Sweden or Norway. The story was that he'd wandered all over the map with some troops, a soldier brat. He was barely fifteen when he came here, but he spoke about a dozen languages. With your father he spoke only Polish. The spring after they left, word came that they had drowned. They'd boarded an American ship, the *Thetis,* at Bremerlehe, and it went down off Newfoundland."

The ferryman's eyes, resting on the river below where the mists were rising, seemed to see beyond it. "I don't think your father knew, when he left, what he was leaving behind. He should never have left your mother. That was his mistake. His luck deserted him right there."

Robert listened to the ferryman's voice as if its message held both past and future. This man, who had nothing in the world besides his little reed-thatched cottage, his garden, his one boat and fishing nets, had been his childhood teacher. It was Ludolf who had whittled his first flute from a willow wand, had showed him his first cricket nest, the spawning ground of the trout, the garlands of caterpillars in the pupa stage where the great oak had been split by lightning. He had taught him to distinguish the various bird cries, and how to make fire without flint. And there was another thing he had taught him: that a man could be poor and still be freer than all other men.

The ferryman swept the air with his hand. "Gnats, so late in November. That means a mild winter."

Robert turned to mount the coach. "If you hear or see anything of my lost passenger, let me know."

"What's he look like?"

"I saw him for just a second myself, not long enough to give any kind of description. But you'd know him at once. He has the most fearless eyes I've ever seen."

"I'll leave my door open tonight." Ludolf collected all the rags and tossed them into the pail. "Be sure to give your mother my congratulations."

"I will, thanks."

Robert went to the coach. When he turned once more, the ferryman was gone. The mists rising from the river and billowing up toward the cottage had swallowed him up.

5

As was her daily custom, Anna Haynow went through the house at twilight to light the lamps and wind the clocks. She was accompanied, as she had been each day for twenty-four years, by her housekeeper, Mrs. Retz, who watched as her mistress poured oil from the brass can into a narrow-necked lamp. Everything about Anna Haynow was like her hands, delicate but strong, self-assured. She wore a maize-colored gown with pale-green piping at the collar and sleeves. Her hair looked black in the twilight, as did her eyes that were too large and too far apart for her narrow face. Her mouth, too, was a bit too full-lipped. And yet all these flaws somehow added up to a face of such charm as to make any perfect beauty look insipid beside her.

As the oil quietly bubbled into the lamp, a fragrance of oranges and lemons rose up. This was a time of day especially dear to Mrs. Retz, when she and her mistress walked from room to room together, accompanied by the fragrance of candles and oil. She was always welcome to bring problems to her mistress at any time, but it was for this hour of the day that she saved those concerns that were closest to her heart.

"I always thought of Steward Lange as a reasonable man," she said, "but ever since we were raised to noble rank he seems possessed. One footman to see to the candles, another for the oil, another for the clocks, another for the silver—that's the way he thinks it's going to be now."

Anna Haynow set the oil can back on the tray and picked up the flint. "I know, he's been to see me about it already."

Mrs. Retz took a deep breath. She was as tall as a grenadier of the Guards regiment, and indignation added to her height and gave her cheeks the shiny glow of a baked apple.

"You listened to him? To think he dares to trouble you with his nonsense. Did he tell you he wants new liveries for the footmen who serve at table?"

"He ordered the tailor for tomorrow, in fact."

"What did you say?"

"I asked him to rescind the order."

Mrs. Retz nodded, and looked appeased. "Lange is out of his head. Imagine, two pages, just for standing on the backboard of the coach. An extra pastry cook *and* a confectioner for the kitchen. All he talks about is the social functions we shall be giving."

The two women had stepped out into the gallery. The tall windows shimmered in dark blue. The park, a distant silhouette in the daytime, had moved close up, become a series of separately framed scenes, every contour sharply etched on the dark glass.

Anna replaced the burnt-out candles in the candelabra with fresh ones. "Well, Lange takes pride in being, at long last, house steward in an aristocratic establishment."

"But the man is impossible. He is going to stick a French accent on the final *e* of his good German name. Have you ever heard of anything so ridiculous? Any new help must be able to speak French, he says, especially for our residence in Kassel. But Gilbert really let him have it: 'I learned my trade in the kitchens of the Bishop of Strasbourg, he said, and I earned my diploma as a master chef from the Cook's Guild of Strasbourg; tell me, Lange, where did you learn to be a steward, and where is your diploma?' Gilbert talks as well as he cooks, you know. And he'll never come around demanding that you double the kitchen budget. When Gilbert asks for anything, there's always a good reason for it. The wonderful things he's done with the old kitchen!"

"You didn't always think so." Anna smiled. Her smile was no more than a slight parting of the lips, a light in her eyes, that brought a touch of mischievousness to her face, and made her look very young. But it was with this smile that she ruled the house. All the little disagreements among the staff, the jealousies, feuds, and gossip, were dissipated by that smile.

"Well, everybody was startled at the time," Mrs. Retz said. "Until then, one kitchen had been quite sufficient, it was hard to see why he suddenly had to have three separate arrangements for cold, sweet, and hot food. But now that it's done I could wander around in it by the hour, watching him at work. And his idea to add a kitchen yard—since then, you never notice the smells of food in the house. Oh, before I forget, Gilbert wants to see you about supper."

The women had now reached the center of the gallery where it opened onto a semicircular landing. A broad staircase descended to the ground floor vestibule. Anna put the nippers with which she had been trimming the candlewicks back on the tray. The part of the gallery they had just passed through was now illumined by candlelight; the other still lay in semidarkness.

There were no mirrors or elaborately draped hangings at Haynow House. The five-armed candelabra were neither of silver or gold but bronzed wrought iron. The stands on which they were placed were solid enough to be pushed together as tables for the cold buffet on social occasions. The floorboards had the reddish-brown golden tone of much-polished and waxed old oakwood.

The linen curtains, once the color of rosewood, had faded with the years. Nothing else had changed since the day her uncle had taken her into the house, a nine-year-old, after her parents had died in the smallpox epidemic of 1742. It was here in the gallery, with the help of a French manual, that she had taught herself dance steps in preparation for her first ball. There, at the center window of the gallery, she had seen Robert Skelnik for the first time. It was on these very stairs that she had walked toward him on their wedding day. It was up these same stairs that the old Elector had climbed to call her to account for her husband's crime, and to confiscate all she had.

Anna moved toward the stairs now. Suddenly, on the first step, she stood still. "No," she said, extending her arms as if to embrace everything before her. "We shall not make a palace out of this house."

She stood between light and shadow, a woman flawlessly made, with the kind of appealing beauty that comes to certain faces only with the little lines at the corners of eyes and mouth. At that moment Mrs. Retz saw her differently. She saw instead the nineteen-year-old girl who had just been told that her husband had vanished with his assistant from Heron Island, and with them the Elector's sixty thousand gold pieces. That day, when the officials charged with the investigation had left, she had made the same gesture, as if to put her arms around the house, because there was nothing else for her to hold on to.

That moment had impressed itself indelibly on Mrs. Retz's memory, and just as deeply rooted was her fear that such a thing might occur again one day. What had happened then was only a beginning, the first act of a drama that must be followed sooner or later by a second act. There were laws of destiny to which all human beings were subject, even those who seemed stronger than their fates. The woman who stood there had risen where others would have slipped; she had kept her youth where others had aged. It was as if she had a special pact with fortune; but every pact ran out in time. Mrs. Retz was horrified by her own thoughts, and yet a certain terrible curiosity remained with her, an itch to see these nightmarish intuitions become reality.

It was her own house, but when Anna Haynow wanted to visit the kitchen she had to pull a bellcord first. Here Gilbert ruled. His ingenious justifications for keeping the kitchen as well-guarded as a treasure vault ranged from dramatic descriptions of how a delicate yeasting dough would collapse at the mere hint of a draft, to the most circumstantial analogies between a cook's confections and an elaborately dressed beauty: neither could possibly inspire ecstasy in anyone who had watched the preparations.

Gilbert himself appeared behind the peephole in the door. Silently he admitted his mistress and led her into the "sweet kitchen," a rather small, charming, cozy room. He offered her a chair, but she stepped to the table where cake molds of every size were piled up in a pyramid. "More new ones?" She reached for a little mold of brown glazed china.

"Madame, I try not to trouble you except in cases of extreme necessity."

Anna replaced the mold on the table and turned to him. "What is it, Gilbert?"

"A catastrophe, putting it mildly, and on this day of all days. Madame, I have to consult with you. The first course. . . ."

"I thought we had agreed on the burbot."

Gilbert nodded. "This miserable deserter has upset everything. There wasn't anybody left to catch the burbot for us, everybody was conscripted to hunt the deserter. If I could have foreseen such a thing, I'd have risked catching them earlier in the day. But, you know that his Excellency, the Baron, can sniff every extra hour in the cooler on a fish, and I can only agree: fish and lobsters should come directly from the water to the table. My last hope was Mr. Robert, who knows the best spots for catching them, but he disappeared without a trace."

"I'm sure you'll find a way."

"I'm too depressed to be able to think."

"Perhaps I'll think of something if you'll let me have a cup of bouillon."

Gilbert didn't know whether to feel flattered or insulted. How like a woman, to think of bouillon at a moment like this. Of course women thought of a menu as simply a series of courses.

There were very few who understood that it was a poem, where every syllable, every rhyme, mattered supremely in relation to everything else. He opened the door to the "hot foods kitchen." "A cup of clear bouillon for Madame!" he said. A minute later a kitchen boy appeared with an oval tray on which stood, besides the cup of soup, two shell saucers, one holding minced chives, the other ground nutmeg.

Gilbert kept his eyes down, waiting.

"How about leek soup?" she said.

Leek soup. Gilbert gazed into space, concentrating, like a general visualizing a new way of reorganizing an army on the point of being routed. His face brightened. "That's it, of course. Marvelous! Thank you, Madame. I just couldn't think. Leek soup is the Baron's favorite appetizer, and it's an ideal course to precede the roast young boar."

"I am only your disciple, Gilbert. Of course, there are times I would very much like to learn to cook properly. But in my youth they couldn't have beaten me into a kitchen with a whip."

"If I may say so, Madame, this was no kitchen then, it was more like a smithy. My first professional kitchen in Strasbourg was no bigger than an alcove, but the whole city used to talk about it. My second kitchen was the size of a boudoir, the third that of a salon. A kitchen should never be larger than that, however. A kitchen is a kind of study, if it's too large, inspiration is dissipated. What an excellent idea, leek soup with cream; that will do very well."

"Tomorrow morning at ten I shall expect you to bring me your menus for the next fourteen days."

Gilbert made a slight bow, and conducted her to the door. Outside, she heard him shoot both bolts. She smiled.

In the laundry room there was a fragrance as of lavender flourishing on a meadow in the noonday sun. Mrs. Retz came forward from behind an open closet door. "Which table linen shall we use tonight, the lily or the rose set? I thought you'd never get away from Gilbert today."

Anna opened the closet where all the lengths of fabrics were kept, ready to be made up into whatever was needed in the household. "Do you think this might make Steward Lange feel better?" She handed Mrs. Retz an embroidered piece of goods the size of a napkin. "Look at it as closely and critically as if it came from the best workshop in Kassel."

Mrs. Retz raised the napkin to her nearsighted eyes. "It's your coat of arms! You embroidered it yourself?" She slid the tip of her little finger over the design. "When on earth did you find time to do it?"

"This morning, between my morning ride and breakfast."

"I couldn't even thread a needle that early in the day. Did you design this yourself?"

"Claus helped me with that. The whole thing was his idea. He sent to a heraldry specialist for the model. Incidentally, is Claus back yet?" She noticed Mrs. Retz pressing her lips together, but it was too late; the poor woman could not hold back her tears.

"Please forgive me," she murmured, "I ought to have more self-control, but I've been fighting this all afternoon. The manhunt after that deserter. . . . I simply can't help remembering how it was with my son. Three times they made him run the gauntlet." She hesitated, but she had to come out with it—as she had again and again in the last twelve years—or it would choke her to death. "Since it happened, I haven't been able to pray," she said between clenched teeth. "I try, I want to, but then I remember how he looked when they brought him home the last time, nothing left of him but a mass of bleeding flesh."

Anna listened in silence. It had been Mrs. Retz's only son. He had deserted from the fortress three times, and the third time had cost him his life. He had died in this very house. She laid a hand gently on the mother's arm. "I know how you feel. I wouldn't be able to forget, either."

Mrs. Retz picked up the table linen, and the two women silently left the laundry. They were halfway to the dining room when they heard the coach rattling into the yard. There was the sound of horses' hooves on the cobblestones, the grinding of brakes, men's voices and laughter.

Anna stopped to listen. "That sounds like Robert to me."

"I'll get everything ready, don't worry," Mrs. Retz said. "It's time you started to dress for dinner." She started to leave, but turned around once more. "If Mr. Claus comes back without having caught the deserter—don't let him go out again after him, please?"

Anna nodded. She gathered in her skirt and went up the stairs.

As she hurried along the gallery to where her rooms lay, she heard her eldest son laughing outside. His laugh always reminded her of his father, Robert Skelnik. His tall figure, his eyes that were now blue, now green, depending on the light, his hair that was more golden than blond—it was more than a resemblance. The son was a perfect copy of his father, feature for feature. He ran his heels down at the same place; despite every effort to cure him of it, he kept his left hand under the table at meal times; he slept in the same position, slightly turned to the right, one leg straight, the other slightly bent at the knee, like a man on the run even in his sleep. She had observed this uncanny likeness for twenty-three years now, never ceasing to be mystified by it, a mystery that made her happy and fearful at the same time.

The candle-flames on the wall sconces gently flickered in the breeze of her passing. Her long skirt rustled over the floor. Her reflection accompanied her along the gallery, surfacing and vanishing in the polished glass of the tall windows. She had not yet decided what to wear this evening. In any case, she had not ordered a new dress for today. She would have to go through plenty of fittings in the next few weeks, as it was. The Court functions she would have to attend at the capital this winter would necessitate a radical overhauling of her wardrobe; the most elegant gowns she had were too simple, too middle-class. Even the men would have to get new dress clothes. Society at the Court of Kassel had keen eyes and even keener tongues when it came to judging a newly ennobled family.

She opened the door to her rooms, looking first toward the large armchair beside the fireplace which had always been the favorite of both Robert and Claus. It was empty. She walked to the table where she had left her game of solitaire laid out and scooped the cards into a pile. Something about the bowl of fruit on the table caught her eye—hadn't there been a pear at the top of the pyramid? Then she heard a sound in the next room, the barely discernible clicking of clothes hangers being moved about. She opened the door to her dressing room. The large wardrobe stood open. Even before the man stepped forward from behind it, she had caught sight of him in the tall mirror nearby.

He stepped into the room as calmly as if he were the one who lived here and Anna the intruder. "I hope you are still as fearless as you used to be," he said, bowing lightly. "It didn't seem like a good idea to announce my arrival beforehand, you see." He spoke as casually as he moved. Only the torn sleeve of his jacket indicated that he had probably not entered by the main staircase, nor the front door. His boots were muddy, his thick, light-brown hair clotted with dust.

Nothing about him had remained as Anna remembered him, except for the eyes. His eyes had lost nothing of their fearlessness.

"Soerman!" She moved toward him, her hand raised as if to touch him, to make certain that he was really flesh and blood. It was unbelievable. The man who stood before her was supposed to be dead.

"May I close the door of your sitting room?" He was obviously not inexperienced at getting inside strange houses, at hiding, escaping. "Is there another door to be concerned about?"

"No."

"Thank you for taking it all so calmly." His smile somehow emphasized the melancholy irony in the natural set of his face. "I would rather have spared you the shock, but my choice was limited to either you or your sons. One of them was doing his best to return me to the fortress, the other. . . ."

"*You* are the deserter they've all been looking for? *You* are an officer at the fortress? How? You were reported dead . . . it's been over twenty years. . . ."

"I cost the Elector five salvos of gunpowder today. And as I said, one of your sons came very close to getting a medal on my account. The other one, though, seemed inclined toward running the gauntlet with me, as a deserter's accomplice. I chose to evade both of them and to ask for your help instead. I wasn't sure how much your sons knew of the past."

So it really was Soerman, whom for twenty-three years she had believed to be dead. Twenty-three years ago she had been told that Robert Skelnik and Freder Soerman had lost their lives on the American ship *Thetis* in a storm off Newfoundland. If Freder Soerman was alive, then . . . her mind was behaving like a horse suddenly shying away from a hurdle. She took a half step forward toward Soerman. "What happened to Robert Skelnik?"

"Better draw the curtains," Soerman said.

Now she, too, became aware of the noise in the courtyard. She went to the window. Lights were flitting about under the trees below. A troop of riders came up the driveway, making for the stables. Above the confused sounds of voices and the dull thud of horses' hooves rose the shrill barking of a dog. A single rider broke away from the troop and came trotting toward the house. It was Claus. She waited for him to lift his face toward her window; for once, he did not. She drew the curtains. She had to hide Freder Soerman from Claus. Then she remembered Robert, and suddenly she could think of no place in her house that was safe enough. For his own sake, Robert must never encounter the past in the form of Soerman.

6

In the light of the storm lanterns the avenue of oak trees looked like a subterranean tunnel. The figures emerging from it seemed to move with a strange slowness and uncertainty, as if horse and rider were blind.

"Your vest, sir," the tall young valet behind Robert said for the second time. Without leaving the window, Robert stretched his arms backward so that Adrian could slip the vest on over them. Robert's window was better placed than his mother's for observing the returning riders. He had the corner room in the left wing of the main building, which commanded a good view of the entire front lawn, the driveway, and the stableyard. "You may go now," Robert said over his shoulder.

"Will you be staying at Haynow a while this time, sir?"

"If you're trying to remind me of my promise—yes, I'll take you with me when you reach eighteen."

"Sir, I'm already taller than most eighteen-year-olds."

"I want to take you along as my secretary, not as a servant."

"I've been handling your father's French business correspondence for weeks now."

"We'll talk about it again when you're doing as well in English and bookkeeping."

"What if I can do both before my eighteenth birthday?"

"Clearly you've nothing left to learn about driving a hard bargain, Adrian." Without turning his head Robert knew that the boy was grinning now, a half-impudent, half-embarrassed grin. The considerable number of his "foundlings"—stray dogs, kittens, tame nightingales—had been rounded out about three years ago when he found Adrian, a runaway schoolboy, half-starved and nearly frozen to death, on a road near Utrecht.

"You'll find everything ready, sir," Adrian said.

Robert nodded and buttoned his vest. Riders kept emerging from the darkness. Claus was among the last to arrive. Beside his horse ran a pack of bloodhounds that suddenly began to bark furiously.

Claus rode toward the house. The coach Robert had driven away from the wheelwright's stood in the circle of light shed by the candelabra at the front door. Claus leaped from the saddle, and a groom came forward to take the horse's reins. For a moment Claus hesitated, then he stepped toward the coach and opened the door.

Robert watched intently from above. That Claus had failed to catch his prey even in the last two hours was plainly apparent from the way his troop had drifted back. So the game was still on. And why not? Though when it occurred to him that the deserter might have dropped something in the coach, something that Claus could find, he had misgivings. What if the whole thing turned out to be more than a game, after all? He reproached himself for not searching the coach while he had the chance.

Claus shut the coach door and walked toward the house. He

seemed to be dragging one leg a little; it was only when he was extremely tired or disappointed that his old knee wound became so noticeable.

Robert stepped back from the window. He was determined to find out whether Claus had seen anything suspicious in the coach.

Two footmen dragged basketfuls of applewood logs into the dining room. When the folding doors were opened, Robert saw Steward Lange, in his silver-gray livery and white powdered wig giving orders in his high, nasal voice. Behind another door Mrs. Retz was in command. No sound came from the billiards room, but he was certain he would find Claus in there. He stepped into the dimly lit room. On the green baize of the table, the balls lay thickly clustered together.

Claus, cue in hand, looked up. "How elegant," he said sarcastically. "Rust red and plum blue. This season's Paris fashion. Have you suddenly discovered a nose for fashion, or is this the influence of some beauty you found in Holland?"

Robert felt relieved. Claus had apparently found nothing in the coach. Complicated though he could be, this kind of dissimulation was not in his line; had he known something. he'd have come right out with it. Robert smiled. "I merely took your criticism this morning to heart and decided to mend my ways."

"Since when do you spend so much on your tailor?"

"I didn't. I was collecting gambling debts from the head of the Amsterdam Tailors' Guild. He ran out of cash, so I had to let him make me some clothes instead. I'm completely outfitted for the next five years, shoes and hose included."

"You never lose, do you?"

"Winning is more fun. So far, anyway."

Claus glared bitterly down at the table. Robert was suddenly sorry he had spirited the deserter out of the wheelwright's. After all it had only been a game where he was concerned; for Claus it was a serious matter. Maybe a man had to be healthy to take life as he did. Maybe all the things that baffled him about Claus—his irritability, his vulnerability, his ambition—grew out of his physical handicaps. Something to have remembered at the time. Even if he hadn't liked what Claus was doing, he hadn't played fair. "You going out again after dinner?" Robert asked.

"I would have changed, otherwise."

"Father won't like that. It's a very special day for him. He'll want the whole family present."

"As long as you're there, he'll hardly notice I'm gone."

In the low lamplight, Robert saw only his half brother's hands holding the cue. The hands were still, but the cue was trembling. He moved over to the rack and chose a cue for himself.

"What stakes?" Claus broke the silence.

"I'll make you a proposal: if you win, I'll go out on your manhunt with you."

Claus stared at the table. He arranged the balls, his face under the light for a moment. When he chalked his cue, the bit of chalk crumbled in his hands.

For a while there was only the sound of balls clicking, chalk crunching on cue tips. Gradually Claus relaxed, as the natural intimacy of childhood returned to them. They had shared everything, done everything together—until the day Robert had discovered Heron Island and taken possession of it. Outside the dogs began to bark again.

"Do you think we have a chance to catch him at night?" Robert asked.

"I was a fool to take those tenants along. They stand around, blind as moles, unless you give them a push. And then they're only looking for a way to help the deserter."

"I thought you almost had him, back at the wheelwright's." Neither of them knew what the other was thinking. They were like strangers jockeying for position, uncertain whether or not they would be enemies the next moment.

"They tricked me," Claus said. "The deserter was never in the barn. It's a lesson I'm going to remember. On the way home I met Commandant Rall, and I borrowed his bloodhounds. They have the deserter's scent."

Robert knocked at the edge of the table with his cue. "Your turn."

Claus couldn't concentrate, though he tried. After the third round the balls were so badly distributed he missed his next shot. "Looks like your game."

"But we've just started."

Claus watched his half brother move casually around the table, the cue light in his hand, hitting the ball gently but with infallible accuracy, and winning one point after the other. His old admiration for Robert was gaining the upper hand. "If we'd gone after him together, we'd have him by now."

Robert said nothing. He quickened the pace of his game, but his winning streak continued.

His big brother, who was better at everything—as long as Claus could remember, all of his life had been a ceaseless effort to be like Robert. As a boy he couldn't wait until he, too, had his own pony. After that he rode as if possessed, until his bones ached; it was not enough to be as good in the saddle as Robert, he had to be better. He practiced in secret, setting up hurdles in the meadow, increasing his own handicaps. That was when he'd hurt his leg, when the horse had fallen on him. His right knee joint had never regained its flexibility after that. Six months of bed rest. Robert had sat at his bedside every day, reading to him, inventing new games they could play together. Claus remembered it as the happiest time of his childhood, when he no longer had to keep up with Robert. Afterward, it was worse than before. To compare himself with Robert, to compete with Robert, had become the motive power of everything he did.

Robert bent over the table, the cue balanced between the middle and index fingers of his left hand. Slowly, the ball rolled across the green surface, touched the cushion, grazed the red ball, and rolled to a stop.

Claus frowned. "Since when do you miss such easy shots?"

"Whenever I'm thirty points ahead."

Claus moved around the table, looking for a favorable point of attack.

"Who's the deserter?" he heard Robert asking. "Does anyone know?"

"Remember the ambush there was such a fuss about, in the woods between Loehlbach and Treysa? A gang of thieves attacked the Jew, Veitl Lesser, with his wife and servant, and got away with twenty-five hundred big gold pieces. They tied the three of them up, tossed them on the wagon, and drove the horses off into the woods."

"What's all that got to do with the deserter?"

"The Jew recognized one of the gang at the blacksmith's in Ramswood a few days later. The blacksmith hates Jews, though. He decided he wouldn't testify against the man, he'd sell him to the recruiters and make money on the deal instead. You know how they fix that kind of thing up. The recruiters at the Black Bear tavern in Ramswood swore the man had been playing cards with them at the time of the robbery, and with that, he was theirs. He was the kind they could get an officer's commission for—worth more money when they sold him to Commandant Rall." Claus stepped back from the table. "I give up. My hands are numb from holding the reins all day." He pulled off his jacket and tossed it on a chair.

"This is no time to quit. Your last ball was a good one. You're only ten points behind, come on now. . . ." Robert turned to the door.

Gottfried Haynow had come into the room, quietly as always. A giant of a man in a violet-blue dinner coat, he stood there, hands grasping his lapels, from head to toe the landowner, on familiar terms with his tenants, always careful to let them underestimate his wealth and consider him a more harmless person than he was. He had played this part for so many years it had become second nature; he could not drop it now even in his own home.

"How's it going?" he asked.

"Robert's winning."

Haynow laid his hand on Claus's arm. "Haven't I told you over and over you can't win against Robert? He's a born gambler, lucky to his fingertips. In any case, I want to talk with both of you after dinner." He opened the door to the dining room. The beam of light that fell on him from the door was too narrow to encompass the whole man, so that for a moment he seemed too wide and massive to go through the door.

Robert had remained near the billiard table. "Let's finish the game. If you make just ten points in one turn you'll be even with me."

Claus returned to the game.

"Only six more," Robert said after a while.

Claus moved around the table. There was no sign of a limp now. Robert had noticed this often; it was as though Claus's disability was not so much physical as psychological. Cue-tip and ball collided, and he scored.

"Did Rall mention the deserter's name?" Robert said.

Claus did not look up. He had hit his stride and did not want to break the rhythm. "I can't play and entertain you at the same time," he said gruffly. "Rall suspects the man gave a false name to the recruiters. 'Troops of mixed nationality,' they call that riff-raff stationed at the fortress. We get all the dubious types shoved over the border by other countries—bankrupt merchants, cashiered postmen, clerks who got caught with their hands in the till. Worthless trash, all of them. This fellow calls himself Soerman, but his name's probably as false as the recruiters' loyalty oath."

Soerman. Robert stood as if under a spell. Soerman. He tried to curb his imagination, to be sensible, but it was no use. Time rolled back and showed him men he had never actually seen; his father stood clearly before him, a man made to live and get what he wanted, not a man to die halfway to his goal. A man who had merely used death as a mask to shake off pursuers. A man who had begun a new life, with a new name in a new world. . . .

Claus tossed his cue on the table. "You win."

"Win?"

"By one point. You got me all mixed up with your endless questions."

Anna Haynow appeared in the dining room door, wearing a gown of dark red silk. "Aren't any of you hungry this evening?"

Robert followed her with his eyes as she turned back to the dining room. There was something about her that troubled him, though he couldn't tell what it was. A strange premonition overtook him. Something was in the air. The festive glitter of the dinner table, the aroma of the food, the warmth from the fireplace, all told him he was wrong; the deserter and the curious reflections he had aroused meant no more than a missed billiard ball. And yet he crossed the threshold to the dining room uneasily, as though setting foot on shaky ground.

7

Gottfried Haynow's rise from a minor court official to Hessia's greatest landowner and entrepeneur was more than a rags-to-riches story. Just as there was in Haynow House no ostentatious display of his new wealth, there was absolutely nothing in Gottfried Haynow's conduct to suggest his humble origins. He moved always with the self-assurance of a man born to affluence. There was nothing indecisive about him; his serenity was no mere pose, though it had very little to do with simple good nature.

Haynow nevertheless valued the appearance of good nature, and had quite deliberately added twenty extra pounds to achieve it, though twenty pounds could hardly make that much difference in a man over six feet tall. It was just enough to erase that lean and hungry look from a face with a prominent hooked nose, a square bony chin, and jutting brows—that look that might tell too much about the years of poverty endured, and the hardness of which such a man was capable. These twenty extra pounds, which were always threatening to evaporate, had made Gottfried Haynow into a gourmet.

The dining table now had a chaotic, after-dinner look. Dishes and table silver had been removed, the drinking glasses stood in unordered clusters among the mounds of crumpled napkins. Conversation had become desultory as well.

Robert reached for a mint. He had no idea what he was eating nor what he had eaten, whether the wine he was drinking happened to be white or red. Still, he wished he could postpone the end of dinner indefinitely, though he wasn't sure what it would bring. An invisible guest had sat down at the table with him: the past. It mesmerized him with the eyes of the stranger in the coach, it bore his name, it set him questions he had never before asked but which now would not let him go.

Anna Haynow, at her end of the table, looked pale. Robert wondered what was hiding behind her smile, what she was thinking behind the words she spoke. She was his mother, but what did he really know about her? She was of noble birth, but she had married an alchemist, a man hired to make gold, a Polish adventurer. One year after his disappearance she had married a second time to Gottfried Haynow, the man charged by the Elector to see to the confiscation of her estate. Was it thanks to Haynow that the confiscation had been rescinded? Was this the reason she had married him? What sort of a marriage had it been for her, and how would she take the news that one of the two men believed to be dead was alive? Soerman. He longed to blurt out these questions, and yet he was glad to put them off. Claus would soon ride out into the night again with his bloodhounds; Robert's instinct told him the stranger's tracks would not be found out there in the night. . . . *I must be crazy,* Robert thought. *My imagination is playing tricks on me.* He caught his mother's eyes on his face and wondered why she dropped them so suddenly, almost guiltily, when his own met hers.

Anna placed the cover on the plate of sweets with such an air of haste and absentmindedness that her husband said, "Are you trying to get rid of us?"

"You mentioned, before dinner, that you wanted to talk with Robert and Claus."

"Is that absolutely necessary?" Claus said. He reached for the wine bottle.

Haynow tried to read his wife's expression. There was something in her voice that puzzled him. Had she rather spent the evening alone with him? "You're spoiling these two," he said. "They're like purring cats around you, too comfortable to move. Your sons are going to have difficulty finding a wife who'll treat them like this."

"I think the matter is simpler than that," Anna said. "The reason they're still unmarried is not because they haven't found a woman they've liked, but because they've found too many."

"Nobody ever tells me anything about that," Haynow said. "But one thing is certain—I plan to have a say in any marriages being planned around here."

"Marriage is not so easy," Claus said, "considering the size of the dowry you would accept."

"I've only tried to point out to you now and then that it's possible to fall in love with a rich girl as well as a poor one. The simple truth is that a rich wife costs a man less. One has to be accustomed to money, to know how to handle it." He turned to his wife. "Excuse us, please." He pushed back his chair.

Anna rose, as if she had been impatiently waiting for this moment. "Shall I order your coffee served in the library?"

Again, there was an undertone to her voice that puzzled Haynow. "If you don't mind, I'd like to take coffee with you, a little later," he said.

"Fine. Let me know when you want it."

Robert found her evasive, her smile forced. At the door, he looked back at her. She was standing beside the table, absently folding a napkin; the expression on her face frightened him. He closed the door gently behind him.

Robert felt haunted by his mother's image. This house, which he knew so well, seemed suddenly full of secrets known only to her. He was dimly aware of his father and brother walking at his side, but his mind was still back there with her.

"Asleep on your feet already?" Haynow said, taking Robert's arm affectionately.

From outside the front door came the muffled sound of voices, a murmuring, shouts. Steward Lange's voice rose sharply above the rest.

Haynow left his sons, went to the front door, and tore it open. His tenant farmers were crowded together outside; they fell silent at the sight of him.

"What's going on?" he snapped at the steward. "Since when is my door closed to my tenants?" He ordered Lange back into the house, and then waded out into the crowd of farmers. "Don't you know you can see me any time? Here's the door; it's open to you as long as I'm master of Haynow. But you might pick a better hour next time. What brings you here so late at night?"

"It was broad daylight when we got here," their spokesman said.

"Well, if you let my steward turn you away like beggars, it's your own fault. You don't need permission to see me."

"It was your son, Claus. We had to ride off with him, after the deserter."

Haynow chose not to discuss this. "Well, speak up. I still have no idea what it's all about."

"We came to see you about the wild pigs, sir. There are more of them this year than ever; they're destroying the crops as soon as they're planted. Without a winter harvest, how can we pay next year's rentals?" The man was shouting now. "They didn't think of that in Kassel with their bloody decree. They were supposed to change it but all they did was change the words. It used to be 'forbidden' to kill the beasts; not it's 'not allowed.' Why don't they just order us to fatten the pigs up, so their lordships have even better game to hunt? It amounts to the same thing. We need guns, and permission to use them. The decree must be changed."

"You know I'll do anything for you that's in my power, but I can't change that decree. As far as the Elector is concerned, I'm just another farmer."

"This is your land. And now that you've been given noble rank. . . ."

"I can't give you that permission," Haynow said firmly. "But I'll give you some advice. Tonight you're on guard duty, with guns in your hands. If you think you see the deserter and accidentally kill a pig instead, I don't think anyone'll hold it against you. Where's your meeting place tonight?"

"At the wheelwright's."

"I'll send Claus over to you. With better guns than you get from the militia." From the stables came the sound of dogs barking. "Are those your dogs that have been making all that racket?"

"Master Claus borrowed Commandant Rall's bloodhounds."

There was a moment of silence. The men lowered their eyes,

but Haynow lost his temper only when it served his purpose to do so. "It's the only advice I can give you. Make of it what you like. I give you my word about the guns, and you can leave the sale of the pigs killed to me." He gave the nearest man a friendly pat on the shoulder and turned back to the house.

Haynow knew his sons didn't enjoy this kind of a scene, but what he had to say to the steward would make a welcome introduction to what he wanted to speak with them about. The steward had stopped inside the door of the counting room. Under his powdered wig, which went down too low on his forehead, Lange's face, with the chin buried in his tall stiff collar, seemed to consist chiefly of his broad, upturned duck's beak of a nose. He had all the appearance of a large shivering bird.

"Tell me, Lange, when did I issue any instructions to turn my tenant farmers away at the door?"

"These peasants have to be taught who is the master here," Lange said with assurance.

Haynow frowned, but his voice remained even. "It seems to me you're the one who has something to learn. I'm the one who makes the rules in this house, and none of our ways are going to change just because of a certain addition to my name. That'll be all."

The steward bowed stiffly and withdrew.

Haynow turned up the wick in the desk lamp. He was giving his sons time to react.

"I don't share your attitude," Claus said. "It's a mistake to treat those peasants as equals. They don't know how to take it. Did you hear them starting in on the question of their rents? That's the way rebellions get started."

"Your great-grandfather was a peasant, a cottager, no more. It might not be a bad idea for you to remember that from time to time. My father was a pit-boy in the copper mines near Treysa, one of the kids who dragged the ore to the surface. Luckily for him the press gang got him and recruited him into the military, because one of the officers taught him to read and write, a little math and Latin. After he lost a leg and the army couldn't use him any more, he became an outstanding teacher. I've made it a little further along than he did, and you'll advance yourself further still. But if you think you can achieve distinction by hunting deserters, you're mistaken. Dirty work will leave you with dirty hands—that's all. If you want to rise in the military, you'll need better ideas than that."

"Just give me a proper war," Claus said, "and you'll see how far I can go."

"That's another mistake. War just increases the chances of dying. There are better and more peaceable ways to succeed. In France, one marshal out of two owes his rank not to his bravery but to the beauty of his wife, or his daughter."

"You always think like a shopkeeper. That's fine for tea and tobacco, but not for men."

Haynow wasn't annoyed at Claus's back talk. It was, in fact, his way of educating his sons, always challenging them to test their temperament and aggressiveness on him. "Life is a shopkeeper's account," he said, "plus or minus, debit and credit, for each of us, no more. The sooner you grasp that, the better. You borrowed Commandant Rall's bloodhounds. I can't imagine what you thought you were doing. At the moment, all eyes are upon us; most of them can't wait to find some reason to make us look ridiculous. You ought to be too proud to court this kind of notoriety. You will leave those dogs in the kennel. That is not advice, it's an order. Come along, we can talk more comfortably in my office."

Haynow's office was as simply furnished as the rest of the house, with a certain old-fashioned austerity. There was a fire in the fireplace, and oil lamps giving a golden-yellow light. An English clock, the only new object in the room, was ticking away on the mantelpiece. Haynow had placed it there so conspicuously to please Robert, who had given it to him as a fiftieth-birthday present. Otherwise, he preferred to leave things unchanged. For years he had been stubbornly opposing Anna's attempt to have the old leather armchairs reupholstered, to replace his plain old desk with a more elegant piece of furniture. He couldn't even bring himself to replace the green felt blotter on his desk, which had turned almost black from countless inkblots and blottings. That blotter held, side by side, the sweeping signature of the Elector, and the clumsy mark of an illiterate tenant farmer, both men having signed their IOUs to him here. That piece of felt had become, with time, a kind of chronicle of his success.

He seated himself behind his desk. Claus leaned against the mantelpiece, and Robert dropped into a leather armchair. Before mention of the deserter Robert's attention had wandered. His stepfather had expressed his own attitude exactly—but he wondered if he had a special reason for forbidding Claus to use the bloodhounds. Had he already learned the deserter's name, too?

"You want it understood just how much our new social status is costing us, is that it?" Claus was saying.

"If you like. Bluntly, the Elector didn't give me this barony because he loves me but because he wants to borrow more money from me. It's strictly business, and with the risk all on my side. His Grace's carefree spending is leading him straight to bankruptcy, but his creditors can't afford to let him go bankrupt; it'd wreck the whole country. Still, this new title can be worth more to us than the payment of all his present debts—even with interest and interest on the interest. It can be a form of security, unlimited insurance, if we use it right." He opened his cigar box. "But it can be a road to ruin as well if we take it like so many new aristocrats do, who give up a profitable business so it won't tarnish their new social status. I know, Claus, this is what you call my shopkeeper's philosophy. But even if you become a general your salary will never keep you in the kind of horses you're accustomed to riding. And I can tell from your tailor's bills how much you enjoy luxury. So you'd better let me and Robert worry about providing the money to pay your bills on time. For a commoner, poverty is no disgrace; it can be death for an aristocrat."

What was all this leading up to? Robert wondered, knowing his stepfather was not a man to make speeches for the sake of hearing himself talk. Haynow had left his desk chair and walked over to the huge cabinet that contained the built-in fireproof safe where he kept cash and his most important documents. He opened and locked several drawers, then returned to his desk with two black folders and a small jewel case. He opened the folder on top.

"I've read your report and checked the figures, Robert. My

compliments. A very profitable trip. You've done brilliant work."

"I was a little uneasy doing it. Your orders to liquidate our van Notten account and use it all to buy tobacco made me nervous. And you call me a gambler."

"I'm sure we won't regret it. My information comes from Prime Minister Schlieffen, and he's always proved reliable. For a couple of years now, he's talked about the possibility of rebellion in the British colonies of North America. As the Elector's right-hand man, his sources are the best. It was on his advice I opened that account with van Notten in Amsterdam. It was through him that I first became interested in the New World. That country is a fountain of riches—for England. All their exports go out via the mother country, tariff-free, at throwaway prices: lumber, indigo, rice, tobacco. But the colonists have to buy everything overpriced and overtaxed, from England. The King of England treats his colonies like penal camps. His punitive laws, taxation, and stamp acts have gradually infuriated them. It was only a question of time for the inevitable reaction, the outbreak of revolt. Now they've dumped the cargo of three English tea ships into Boston harbor and announced they're all through paying the King's taxes. They've stopped trading with the mother country. That was a declaration of war, in a way, and George III has taken them up on it."

Haynow noticed Claus's mocking smile, but he went on. "Since that Boston rising, not one shipload of tobacco has left America. The longer the blockade lasts, the higher the price of tobacco will rise." He turned to Robert. "I couldn't explain this in my letter to Amsterdam, in case it fell into the wrong hands."

"I more or less pieced it together by myself," Robert said. "The English papers were reporting the first skirmishes between colonists and British soldiers. It didn't seem too serious, though."

"The English have every reason to hush the story up." Haynow bent over the lists of Robert's purchases. "Seven hundred bales of brown Virginia long-leaf, seven hundred bales of yellow Maryland, five hundred bales of medium grade Swicutt, five hundred of top grade Swicutt, four hundred fine Lux, three hundred fine yellow Maryland, and three hundred bales of York River Swicutt.

Those last two grades were quoted at three dollars a pound as long as two years ago. All in all, you did so well, what with discounts for buying in quantity, that if this war lasts just one more year, we stand to make a profit of sixty to eighty percent."

Claus could no longer restrain himself. "What war? Nobody's taking it seriously. The Boston rabble tossing a few sacks of tea into the harbor; a few malcontents and a few madmen waving guns around—there's your whole war. The English troops in Boston watched the whole 'tea party' without lifting a finger. Not one shot'll be fired in this war of yours. There are malcontents everywhere; just look at your own tenant farmers. Best pay no attention to them."

"If Claus is right about this," Robert said, "we ought to sell as soon as possible. As long as there's at least a rumor of war."

"Schlieffen is a very sober observer," Haynow said evenly. "I trust his information and his instinct."

"It takes a ship four to six weeks to cross the Atlantic," Claus said angrily. "Schlieffen's information stinks like dead fish by the time he gets it."

"Suppose we stick to the facts," Robert said. "It's months since an American ship unloaded in London harbor, and I think the chances are against one coming up the Thames in the next few weeks. It was the same in Amsterdam. Not a single ship, except for a few smugglers." He stood up. "I'm in favor of holding on to our goods."

Haynow's thoughts slipped away from the tobacco trade and turned to his sons. When they were growing up, he had tended to see Claus as the future merchant, and Robert as an army officer. But it had turned out exactly the opposite. Robert had the knack for money, the instinct a man needed if he was to transcend the shopkeeper stage, as well as the drop of adventurer's blood that would make him seize his fate in his own hands if necessary. It was odd, but his stepson was far more like himself than Claus. His own son was a mystery to him. He might, for example, quit the army as suddenly as had decided to join it. Basically he was not made to be a soldier. At bottom, he was far too sensitive a man for that profession. But before he could realize that himself, he would have to overcome his resentment of his father. Haynow was not blind: his son Claus rejected him. Had he been a poor man, Claus would probably have hated him outright; because he had succeeded in becoming rich, he merely despised him. Maybe it was for the best, maybe it was necessary for a son to feel superior to his father in order to rise, to realize himself in the world. A pity that love between father and son usually came too late. It had been so in his own case; he was able to do justice to his own father today as he had not in his youth. Perhaps a father had to die before a son could clearly see his true worth.

These reflections always ended with comparisons between his sons. Robert was quite as sensitive a man as Claus, but his sensitivity did not make him unsure of himself; it was more like the tension in a fine watch, that kept it in balance. Or was it simply that he could judge Robert more fairly because he was not his own flesh and blood? It was impossible to be sure. Still—Robert did feel more at ease in his own skin, in his own life, than Claus did, no doubt of that. Maybe if Claus found the right woman, became a father of a family himself, it would all straighten out.

In the course of these thoughts he had been adding figures on scraps of paper, figuring percentages, pursuing calculations. The part of his brain that did figures worked independently of the rest. Finally, he crumpled the paper. "I find I agree with Robert. We will hold the tobacco. Now to my second point. Do we sell our tobacco to Zagriani, or shall we try to take over the tobacco concession for Hessia-Kassel ourselves?" He drew a letter from one of the folders. "Zagriani's already told me his terms. Four installments, beginning in March, the final installment to be paid in March the following year, at a fixed price."

"March '77, then?" Claus said.

"If the price of tobacco doubles in a year, Zagriani'll be raking it in. And we'll be kicking ourselves for not taking him up on it." Robert stepped to the desk and moved the lamp aside. "Why don't we take the whole thing over?"

"We'd have to make a quick decision then. Zagriani's payment to the Elector for the renewal of his concession falls due the end of December. Forty thousand guilders. We could edge him out."

"I'll never agree to that," Claus broke in. "Not even the Jews will touch this kind of money-making. Just a few minutes ago you said this is no time for us to expose ourselves to public criticism. Well, if the people hate anybody, it's the concessionaires, those foreign robber barons who suck the country's blood with their indirect taxes, tariffs, and duties. Do you seriously mean to put yourself on the same level with that kind of foreign riffraff? Like this fellow Zagriani, with his self-appointed title?"

"I respect your indignation, but it's beside the point. Once Zagriani's daughters are old enough for him to slip them into the Elector's bed, he'll get a real title, too. I happen to like the man. Possible because I, too, had to build my own ladder upward, rung by rung, with my own hands. Which is the reason I would hesitate to do anything to undermine his position."

"How much more would we have to pay the Elector for the tobacco concession?" Robert was interested in figures.

"I'd pay for two years in advance."

"Eighty-thousand . . ." Claus murmured as if to himself. "I thought you'd put all the cash into tobacco."

"Only what we had in the van Notten account in Amsterdam."

For a moment Claus felt stunned. The sums that had been under such casual discussion in the last quarter hour far exceeded what he had supposed his father's fortune to be.

"I'm sure his Grace will accept my offer," he heard his father saying calmly. "His treasury is emptier than ever. Which doesn't keep him from spending more every day."

Robert was playing with a piece of sealing wax he had picked up from the desk. "If you want to know what I think, I'd rather we keep out of this. I'm sure lots of people would be delighted to see a foreigner like Zagriani booted out, but I'm inclined to agree with Claus; it could raise a lot of hackles against us. Your tactic has always been to wait for the Elector to come to you. Those sycophants at court offer him money before he needs it. He's always come to you of his own accord."

"Agreed," said Haynow, who had listened serenely. "We're safe in assuming there are lots of people interested in prolonging this tea war. War is an open sesame to money-making, after all. Let's wait and see then." He closed the top folder, laid it aside, and opened the second black folder. "Tomorrow morning at ten we have the hearing with regard to Heron Island."

"What's happening with my island?"

"The surveyor's reports and all the old deeds are with the magistrate in Ramswood already. According to them, half of the island belongs to the Sonsfelds and the other half to your mother."

Robert interrupted again. "The Sonfelds have never done anything w'th that island. There wouldn't even be a usable landing place on their side if Ludolf hadn't kept it in repair. According to common law, they've lost any claim to the island."

"I'd have bought up their share long ago," Haynow said, "if Sonsfeld were a man one could reason with. To settle the question once and for all, I've called on the magistrate to arbitrate the matter. We've settled on a value of five hundred guilders for the disputed property. I've already deposited that amount with the judge. If Sonsfeld raises no objections by tomorrow morning or fails to bring in the same amount, the island is ours."

"Why all the fuss? Why now all of a sudden?"

"The Elector is coming down here to hunt the heron. Please don't look at me as if the whole thing were my idea."

"It's been years since anyone thought about hunting these heron. Is he so low on funds he has to give his ladies heron feathers instead of jewels?"

"His Grace has never had any inhibitions about using foreign currency when his own runs out." Haynow released the catch on the enameled jewel box he had brought out of the safe. Inside, a brooch of sapphires and diamonds gleamed on white silk.

"Paris?" Robert asked.

"No, Frankfurt, but that Derenda fellow's prices are no lower than those of the Paris jewelers."

"And for whom is this little gift intended?"

Haynow paused eloquently. "For Christina Sonsfeld—from the Elector."

The two brothers' eyes met. Robert was the first to regain the power of speech. "Christina? But she's still a child."

"Girls are like that. They can bloom overnight."

"So now she's to save the family from ruin?"

"I believe her mother will consider herself lucky if she gets a marriage-of-convenience out of it."

Robert examined the brooch. "I hope she has a good eye for jewels. In her place, I'd return the thing to the Elector. Not one of these stones is more than a quarter karat. It might be a suitable gift for a fly-by-night *affaire,* but certainly not for ushering in the reign of a mistress at court."

Claus, who had been standing silently by the fireplace, whirled around. "You'd sell your own sister."

Robert looked up in surprise. "Has little Christina turned into such a pretty girl you'd begrudge her to the old Betelchewer in Kassel? I'll have to take a look at her."

"You're the one who was always bringing her presents from abroad."

"Only because I enjoyed making her mother nervous. I never had any other reason. Last time, about a year ago, I think, the girl was all skinny arms and legs and a dress that didn't fit."

"You wouldn't recognize her, then," Claus said. "She really did blossom overnight."

Haynow had been listening intently to his sons' conversation; he needed to know how they felt about the girl. "I can understand how a girl might do anything to escape that moldly family castle and the depressing circumstances they live in," he said casually. "And one can only hope she's not as innocent as she looks. Only the seasoned operator succeeds in this line of endeavor.

"Who thought up the idea, I wonder?" Robert said.

"Schlieffen ordered the pin from me."

"Is there any pie he hasn't got a finger in?"

"The more pies he's got his fingers in, the better for us."

"I don't care for your Schlieffen," Claus said.

"He's the most powerful man at Court."

"He's a totally corrupt human being masquerading as a pillar of society."

Haynow shook his head. "You ought to keep an eye on him, you might learn something. He knows how to keep his hands clean and let others do the work." He returned the jewel box and snapped it shut. "In any case, now you both know what kind of a hunting expedition it's going to be." He took the folders and the jewel case back to the huge cabinet.

Robert idly watched his father replacing the things in the open cabinet, where the iron safe was that held all the documents of his acquisitions and his rise in the world. There lay the papers, notarized and sealed, that gave Gottfried Haynow title to all the the properties he had acquired over the years. Almost everything that had once belonged to the Sonsfeld family—except for the one castle which was their last refuge—now belonged to him, including nearly a dozen farms, a porcelain factory, a wool-weavers' workshop that had once belonged to a Huguenot family, and three town houses in Kassel.

When Robert had reached his majority, his stepfather had shown him all the documents; each property had been acquired in impeccably legal fashion, step by step, contract by contract. Everything was accounted for, verifiable, correct beyond the shadow of a doubt. Even Robert's adoption papers lay in one of the drawers, inside a black folder containing legal notification of the death of Robert Skelnik, alchemist. Suddenly, he was assailed by doubt: was that notification authentic? Or was it just another commercial document, part of a carefully laid scheme to enable Gottfried Haynow to take over the property of the supposedly widowed Anna Skelnik? It was a hideous thought; he recoiled from it. He hoped his stepfather would not turn around; he wasn't sure he could keep from blurting out those questions. Half in a daze, he headed for the door.

8

He stood in the dark outside and stared up at the night sky. He felt an urge to run to the stables, leap on a horse, and ride off. It didn't matter where, so long as it was away from this house. To stretch out on the grass somewhere, fall asleep, hear the sounds of his horse in his dream, wake with dew on his face.

He could see the light from the windows of the estate manager's house behind the trees. The riders who were to accompany Claus were waiting in front of the stables. He heard steps in the vestibule. The front door opened, and Claus came out, carrying four heavy hunting rifles wrapped in canvas.

"Are you coming after all?" Claus asked.

"I'm afraid I'd fall asleep in the saddle."

A groom brought Claus's horse and held the stirrup for him. "Will you be leading the dogs yourself, sir?" he asked.

"We're leaving the dogs here. Everyone ready?"

"Yes, sir."

"The weather's holding," Robert said.

Claus laid the four rifles across the front of his saddle and buttoned his tunic. The other riders trotted forward to join him. Claus touched spurs to his horse, and the troop moved off.

Robert watched them out of sight in the dark of the driveway. He could hear hoofbeats long after they had been swallowed up by the darkness. The bell tower of the estate manager's house rang the quarter hour.

This was home, he thought: here he had been born, here he had grown up. But now he knew that someday he might leave it all behind and never come back. It was a new feeling, and it came over him like a wave. He had never known this kind of yearning. For the first time in his life, he wanted to flee—off to some world where every tree, every pathway, every little island, was not somebody's sealed, notarized property; where one man's riches had not been acquired at the expense of so many other men's poverty; where the earth still belonged to all the people.

He heard the tall grandfather clock in the vestibule chiming. The next moment he rammed his shoulder against the front door and raced up the staircase inside.

He had not expected to find his mother's door locked, but he was surprised to find it open. There was smoke billowing from the fireplace; fresh logs must have just been laid and had not yet begun to burn properly.

Anna Haynow sat in the window nook, a piece of embroidery

on her lap. Robert took one of the candelabra from the mantelpiece and put it on her sewing table.

She lifted a hand to shade her eyes against the sudden light. Her little sewing basket with the spools of silk thread had not been opened. There was no thread in any of the needles stuck in the green velvet pincushion, no needle in the embroidery.

She folded the embroidery and rose. "I thought your conference would take longer than this." She moved over to the fire, warming her hands at it. "Are Father and Claus coming up?"

"Claus has gone out on another expedition."

The logs had caught fire now, and the flames rose up, casting a wave of flaring brightness to flood the room, rise up the walls, then ebb away again. "I'd hoped your father would talk him out of it," she said. "What was all that business with the tenants?"

"They were complaining about the wild pigs, a real plague this year. Ludolf thinks it'll be a mild winter."

She looked up. "You were on Heron Island today? Is it still the same?"

Robert looked at his mother. Would her face remain this calm and controlled if he revealed his thoughts? "You haven't been there in a long time," he said. "Sometimes I think you're avoiding the island. Are your memories that painful?"

She turned her face away from him. "Shall I send for coffee?"

The fact that she was being evasive somehow made it easier for him. Only a moment ago he hadn't dared—now suddenly he wondered what had made him hesitate, and he asked the question which had obsessed him for hours: "Who is Soerman?"

His mother wasn't even startled. "I might have known Mrs. Retz would let you in on it."

Robert stared at her. "What has Mrs. Retz to do with it? What's going on here? How long have you known that Soerman is alive? How long have you kept it from me? Say something, for God's sake."

"You're asking a great deal all at once."

She tried to turn away, but he held her fast. "It seems I haven't asked enough questions in the last twenty years."

She looked up at him. In her dark eyes—those eyes that had

filled his life with warmth, tenderness, and smiles—there was something savage. "These twenty years were longer for me, harder for me, than they were for you."

He let go her arm. She did not move away.

"Ask your questions, then," she said.

He hesitated, not knowing how to begin. He was afraid of hurting her. Maybe she'd had to lie, to keep her property. Maybe she'd had to lie, just be be able to go on living. Still, he had to know. "What you told me about my father—my real father—was it the truth?"

"It happened just the way I told you. Your father was a man who—how shall I put it ?—he couldn't stand it that the world was already divided up, owned by somebody else, that everything you looked at already had somebody's No Trespassing sign on it. Do you understand me? To a woman, that's not important, but to a man—especially a man like him, who needed freedom the way the rest of us need air to breathe—he couldn't bear it, this tight little country, this tight little world, it was insufferable. The more he heard of the New World, the more he knew he had to go there, or he'd suffocate. I was pregnant with you then, too far along to go with him. So we agreed I'd follow him there as soon as you were big enough to travel. But before that could happen the news came that he was dead."

Robert had forgotten what he had asked; he merely had the dim feeling that she was answering some other question. "And Soerman? What has he to do with Mrs. Retz?"

"He's with her, in hiding, right this minute."

Again he had the dreamlike feeling that he and his mother were talking past each other, and about two different people. "The deserter is with Mrs. Retz? The man who was my father's assistant?"

"Yes, Freder Soerman."

"Since when?"

"When I came up here before dinner, he was in my dressing room."

He tried to take it in, get it straight. He had begun with the vague notion that he was tracking down a secret, that apart from being difficult and dangerous, it would all be hugely complicated. Instead, it was simplicity itself. Which made it all the harder to be sure he understood. "He's here, inside the house? You mean the whole time, while we were having dinner and? . . ." Again he put both hands on her shoulders, but this time tenderly, as if to shield her. "So that's why you seemed so different."

"Was it noticeable?"

"Only to me, I'm sure." It struck him suddenly that the woman who stood before him was someone new: no longer the familiar wife of Gottfried Haynow, but the wife of the alchemist Robert Skelnik, his true father. This woman was someone he had never known, before this minute. "Do you realize what you were risking? Claus brought Rall's bloodhounds with him."

"I heard them barking. Soerman heard them, too. But he's perfectly safe in Mrs. Retz's rooms."

"He can't stay here. You should have told me the moment you found him."

She turned her head sideways, shyly, one hand to her hair, a familiar gesture that seemed new and strange now, like so much else.

"I couldn't tell you about it until after I'd managed to take it in myself, don't you see? For twenty-three years I thought Freder Soerman was dead, and suddenly he was right here in front of me." She paced across the room and stopped behind the high-backed chair. "Back then, when the news came of your father's death, I didn't believe it—I waited, day after day, night after night, for word from him; my things were all packed, I was ready to leave this house at a moment's notice. You've wondered how I always know exactly what time you get home at night. It's only that ever since that time I've been a very light sleeper; I know all the night noises of the house by heart, the crackling of the bricks in the fireplace when they cool, the creaking of the furniture, the rattling of the shutters when a bat leaves its bed. For a whole year I did nothing but wait, and listen. I was so sure, so sure. . . ."

She fell silent and resumed her pacing of the floor. Robert, watching her, could see the young woman who had waited through the nights, after the lamps were out, the only light coming from the fireplace, pacing the room with her light step, sometimes bending over the crib to look at her baby, finally dozing off on a sofa or chair some time in the early hours.

His mother's voice came out of the darkened room somewhere. "I simply couldn't believe I'd never see him again. Strange, when Soerman suddenly stood before me, I wasn't the least bit startled. I guess I've still been waiting."

"What about my father? Is he alive?"

She took a deep breath. "My instinct was right about that. The death notice was untrue. Soerman says that the moment your father landed at Staten Island he mailed a letter to me by way of an outbound ship. Every ship bound for Europe carried a letter for me that first year, and the next one, too."

"And you never received one?"

"Not a single one—and he never had an answer."

"Where's my father now?"

"Soerman came back to Europe five years ago, and they'd lost touch even before that."

"Why did he leave America?"

"I never asked him. I wanted to know about Robert. . . ." She broke off, struck by the naturalness with which the name had passed her lips, how little difference twenty-three years had made, how immediate everything seemed to her.

Robert guessed what was going on in her thoughts. It was as though their feelings and thoughts sprang from the same roots, grew in the same direction. "His letters can't all have been lost. Someone must have intercepted them."

She did not answer. He understood: she resisted that line of thought, afraid of where it must lead her. But it was inescapable.

"How did you get the news of my father's and Soerman's death?"

"The papers came from Lloyd's of London. A report on the sinking of the *Thetis* and a list of the passengers and crew lost with it. It was absolutely correct."

"But you never really believed it."

She made a helpless gesture. "I didn't want to think of a dead man when I put you to my breast. A woman who's just given birth to her first child can't think about death. All she knows is that she has given life, and will give life again."

She was so new to him, every word, even her voice. He wanted only to keep listening to that voice. He had to force himself to repeat his question.

"Who actually brought you the news?"

"The Elector cared about nothing but his money. He hoped some of it might still be hidden here somewhere. He kept men on here, searching."

"You're being evasive. Who was it? Who did the actual searching? Who was the person who told you?"

She was silent, staring past him.

"All right," he said, "then I'll tell you. It was my stepfather, wasn't it?"

"What do you mean?" Suddenly she was all resistance.

"I mean he had an interest in withholding the truth from you. And that the first lie forced him to keep on lying and to do away with every letter that came."

"Please," she said sharply, "don't talk like that. Don't forget all he did for me at the time. I was ruined, I had nothing left and would have lost everything except for him. I don't want this to be a barrier between you from now on. It would be better if you'd never heard about it. We can't turn back time like a clock. I'll be very honest with you. Today, when I saw Soerman suddenly standing before me, there was an instant, just one instant, when if I'd acted on my impulse, I'd no longer be here. In that moment, without stopping to think that it's cold at night in a carriage, that I'd need money for places to stay overnight, for food, I'd have been out of here and gone. But the moment passed, and I'm glad I didn't act on that impulse."

"Glad? Is that what you're saying?"

"Yes, that's what I'm saying. I'm saying my place is here. That I've had a good life here all these years. I'm saying I've been happy, maybe in a different way from what I had imagined—but if so, it wasn't his fault."

Robert said nothing. The words wouldn't come—it was all too confusing. He could find no way to express what he felt. "I'll look after Soerman," he said. "How much does Mrs. Retz know?"

"Only that he is a deserter from the fortress. She never knew him in those days. She doesn't even know his name."

"I'll take him across the border."

"Thank you." Suddenly she put her arms around him, not like a mother, but like a young woman. "I'll stay up until you get back."

"No, don't stay up. I have no idea when I'll be back."

She would have liked to hold him back, but all she said was, "Be careful."

Mrs. Retz lived in a little annex at the back of the manager's house. Her front yard was full of rosebushes, not one of them less than a man's height. In summer, when they were all in bloom, all one could see of the annex was the tall chimney with its rounded hood, on which a pair of white doves sometimes perched.

Robert tied his horses to the post at the garden gate. Quietly, he undid the hook and went inside. The air was redolent with the fragrance of roses, even though most of them were still in bud. From the fanlight atop the door, light fell into the garden. He knocked three times on the door. After a glance through the peephole, Mrs. Retz let him in. The table in the dining room was set for a frugal meal of cheese, bread, and butter; there was the aroma of fried bacon. A pair of men's boots stood beside the chimney piece.

Mrs. Retz pointed to the back door. "I've never seen anyone eat so fast and so much," she said.

Robert entered the bedroom. Soerman lay fully dressed on the bed. Robert took the candle from the table and stepped closer. He had expected the man to leap up at the slightest sound, but he was mistaken. Soerman slept like the dead, breathing deeply, looking younger asleep than he had in the semidarkness of the coach that same afternoon. There was a knife stuck in his belt, his fist clutching the handle even in sleep. Here was a man who knew there were bloodhounds not fifty yards away, who had the instincts of a fugitive, and nevertheless could sleep like a child. Robert laid a hand on his shoulder. "Wake up."

Soerman rose up, drawn knife glittering in his half-raised hand.

Then he recognized Robert; laughing, he stuck the knife back in his belt and got to his feet. He took the candle and held it so he could see Robert's face. Then he shook his head wonderingly. "Your father must have been an alchemist after all, of a kind. I've never seen such a likeness anywhere.

This was no time for asking the questions he was full of; all Robert said was, "If you hadn't jumped out of the coach today, you'd have been sleeping in peace a long time ago. You could have broken your neck."

"Cat's know how to jump and fall. You were driving like hell, but the reeds were soft enough, along the way."

"So you didn't jump until we got to the riverbank?"

"I know my way around there." Soerman looked around. "When I lay down, I still had my boots on."

"I'll take you to the border."

Soerman nodded.

Back in the living room, Soerman started to pull his boots back on, but Mrs. Retz suggested a complete change of clothes, because of the bloodhounds: she had a wardrobe full of her son's clothes to select from. While Soerman was changing, Robert made certain there was no one around.

"I need a long, strong rope," he said when he came back inside. As Mrs. Retz fished for the right one in a carton full of cord and rope ends, Soerman reappeared, and for a moment she stared at him as if he were an apparition. He calmly took the piece of cheese from the table. Robert was tying Soerman's old clothing into a tight bundle.

"What are you doing with those?" Soerman asked.

"You'll see in a minute. Come on." He had lost all uneasiness over Soerman. This man would always get away, experienced and cool as he was.

In the yard, Soerman stopped to break off a rosebud and sniff at it. "Have you ever noticed that unhappy women have a special knack for raising flowers?" he said, slipping the rosebud into his buttonhole.

"Is that your specialty—unhappy women?"

"Not exactly, but for a man on the run they can make all the difference."

"Are you on the run a lot?"

Soerman gave a low laugh. "Now that is my true and only specialty, if you like."

The horses lifted their heads as the men approached. "The brown one is yours," Robert said.

After they had mounted up, Robert laid the bundle of Soerman's clothes on the pommel of his saddle and tied the other end of the rope to the saddle horn.

Soerman watched. "I'm beginning to get the idea," he said.

"We have to ride past the kennel where the bloodhounds are kept. They know your scent. There's only one thing to do—distract them with these clothes. Stay here until I have had a chance to open the kennel, and don't move until you see them chasing me. Then ride out of this courtyard and to the left. We'll meet at the great oak—you can't miss it. Wait for me there.

Soerman nodded. "I can see my mistake in jumping out of the coach. You're every inch the man you look to be. The trouble is, I've trusted my first impression too many times only to have it turn out wrong."

The hounds growled, pushing their noses between the bars, as Robert approached the kennels. He rode his mare directly in front of the kennel gate, leaned down to slide the bolt open, then held the bundle of clothing to the opening. The four dogs froze while taking in the scent.

He dropped the bundle of clothes outside the kennel. Instantly, the dogs boiled out of the open gate. He dug the spurs into his horse's flanks and lunged away, dragging the bundle. The four dogs sounded like a whole pack in pursuit; he could hear their eager panting close behind him. Now and then they emitted short, hoarse sounds more like shrieks than barks.

About a hundred yards before he reached the edge of the woods the land began to slope downward. The dogs were still at his horse's heels, foaming at the muzzle, their bared fangs gleaming white. Time to let them have their prey. He drew the knife from his belt and, just before entering the woods, severed the rope holding the bundle.

He turned the horse sharply around and galloped uphill along the edge of the woods. When he was sure the dogs had ceased to pursue him he turned and looked back. The four of them were a single raging knot of activity around the bundle, which seemed to have acquired a weird life of its own, a fifth creature playfully teasing the others.

Freder Soerman emerged from the shadows under the huge oak. "There's only one thing I'd like to know. Why did you risk taking that coach out of the wheelwright's at all? At the time, you couldn't have known who I was."

"You were one man against fifty."

Soerman gazed thoughtfully at him. "You don't merely look like him, you talk like your father, too. You'd really feel at home over there, in the New World. For me, it was too new."

Robert set his horse in motion. "We have a long way to go."

"Not as far as you think. You don't have to take me all the way to the border. The charcoal-maker's kiln in the woods will do. I thought it wiser not to mention this in front of the woman."

"Then it's true what I heard?"

"What's that?"

"That you're a member of Big Hoym's gang?

"These are bad times, and bad times bring out men like Hoym, as a kind of counterweight. Not that I want to defend him, but too many poor farmers can afford only the tariff-free goods Hoym smuggles in."

"And what about the ambush of that Jewish peddler, Veitl Lesser? You were in on that."

"New members of Hoym's gang can't pick and choose their assignments, you know. Tonight is my first chance to prove myself, in fact. Hoym is much choosier than the Elector's recruiters. I'm on the job this very minute, serving as bait. The payroll for the fortress is being transported from the capital to Ramswood tonight. Three talers per man, twenty-four per officer; adds up to a lot of coin in one bag. Hoym's work is made a lot easier if the whole country's off chasing a deserter."

"Are you saying you let yourself be recruited on purpose?"

"So many poor devils are tricked into it. I rather enjoy turning the tables on the recruiters for a change."

Two men rode along silently for a while. From the top of the ridge, they could look down into the long valley. Guard fires flamed in the fields. No one was dousing the lanterns at doors and yard gates tonight.

Ramswood Fortress was a towering silhouette against the night sky, pitch fires smoldering atop its walls, like a wreath of ragged stars burning themselves slowly out. There was a kind of restlessness and tension in the air, like the silence of a man brooding on revolt.

"Over there, in the New World, there are farmers who own whole valleys like this one," Soerman said. "Except the valleys are bigger over there and there aren't any fortresses."

"Why didn't you stay then?"

"I guess I just can't stand good luck. Somehow or other, I feel more at home here, among people who've got nothing but their dreams—dreams that only lead to disappointment, too. Over there it's your own fault if you don't make something of your life. Here, it's different, there's always something or somebody else you can blame it on. . . ."

Imperceptibly, Soerman had moved into the lead. They had left the open country now and were riding along a narrow path in the woods. When the fire of the charcoal pile became visible in the distance, Soerman reined in his horse. "You can go back now."

"You afraid I might see too much of your hideout?"

Soerman laughed. Hands to mouth, he imitated the sound of the screech owl four times in succession. The first response came from the undergrowth nearby, the second from a considerable distance, the third from the top of one of the trees above them. "You see," Soerman said, "we're being watched by a dozen pairs of eyes without knowing it."

"What is it you like so much about this life?"

"It's not a question of what one likes."

"Tell me honestly; why did you leave America?"

"Why not ask me why I didn't stay home in the first place? By this time I could have been a Swedish embassy official with a few ribbons on my lapel—in Stockholm, anyone who speaks more than two languages is automatically knighted."

"And what about running off with my father, then—why?"

"It's really no use asking such questions." They rode on, toward the open kiln. "There's really not much to tell. January 1752 we landed on Staten Island."

"What ship?"

"Certainly not the ship that had our names on its passenger list, according to Lloyd's of London. The Skelnik and Soerman who drowned on the *Thetis,* according to that list, never set foot on board. When you have as much money to lose as we did, you take certain precautions. We sailed on the *Vespucci,* under false names."

How simple it had been for his stepfather, Robert thought. It had all been arranged for him by Robert Skelnik himself; Haynow had merely followed his predecessor's natural lead. To intercept the letters of a man who had struck his own name from the registers of the living was to risk nothing. The time had come for him to know the whole truth, and he listened avidly as Soerman went on.

"Suddenly I had thirty thousand pieces of gold. I can't believe there's another man in the world who'd have dealt with me so fairly. After all, who was I? A little assistant he'd picked up because he could talk to me in his mother tongue. We hadn't agreed beforehand to share the money. I couldn't even take much pleasure in the deal. Somehow I just felt paid off and gotten rid of. I realize that's nonsense, your father just wanted me to be able to make a new life over there."

"And what did he do?"

"He disappeared. Every time he turned up in New York to give his letters to one of the outbound ship captains he looked more of a lone wolf than the last time. Then a whole year went by without a word from him. But one day—by this time I'd moved on to Philadelphia— he drove up in a carriage, elegantly turned out, all in the best of taste. He made me get in with him and took me along. It turned out he'd acquired a piece of land in a lonely region along the Delaware, and built himself a house near the river. The landscape, the river, the way the house was situated, it all reminded me of the region around here. The house, too. It was still being built when I saw it, but the rooms intended for your mother and you were already crammed with the most beautiful things he'd been able to find, everything you could think of, even toys. Maybe I was imagining things, but when I was hiding in your mother's dressing room today, I couldn't help thinking of that house in America. It even smelled the same way. A smell of lavender, or oranges maybe." He paused, then, before Robert could ask, he said, "It was the last time I saw him."

"And you? What happened to you?"

"Nothing, I'm afraid—nothing exciting, anyway. I had those thirty thousand gold pieces, but money's wasted on me. All I do is get rid of it, and that's what I did. But before it was all gone I bought a share in a ship—a smuggler. I enjoyed that, sailing back and forth between Europe and Boston, until one day the English caught up with us. Ship and cargo were confiscated. There was a trial in London, and when it was over, I was cleaned out. They gave me six years, but I managed to escape from Newgate after only seven weeks. There was no money to take me back to America, nor did I especially want to go back. Since then . . ." The horses had kept going of their own accord. Soerman tugged on the reins. "As I said, it's too long a story. And there's nothing further I can tell you about your father. I never saw him again."

"You've told me a good deal. After all, only a few hours ago I thought he was dead."

"I'm sure he'd be glad to know he has a son."

"By this time he probably has other sons."

"Possibly. But I don't think so. I don't believe he ever brought another woman into that house."

They had reached the kiln. There was the smell of resin and tar in the air. In front of the charcoal-maker's shack a man appeared. Again, Robert heard the cry of the screech owl, but he couldn't tell if it came from the man or not. Soerman responded with the same sound. Then the silence spread around them again.

"You'd better turn back now," Soerman said. "There's no need to let them know who brought me here."

Robert hesitated. "Where will I find you?"

"I've already told you everything I know about your father."

"It isn't that."

"You know the Koppin woman, the messenger who takes the mail from Ramswood to Kassel once a week?"

"Yes, she stops at Haynow once a week, too."

"You can trust her with any message for me. She always knows where to find me." Soerman dismounted, and offered the reins to Robert.

"No," Robert said, "keep the horse."

"That makes the second time a Skelnik has given me a horse." Soerman patted the horse on the flanks, the belly, the mane, and stroked its muzzle, as if performing a ritual of ownership. Then he remounted and, with a final wave of his hand, rode away.

Robert watched him fade into the darkened woods. The man in front of the shack had disappeared. There was a crackling and rustling receding through the underbrush, and then silence. Robert stared into the dark, wishing the whole thing might have been a dream, an illusion, something he could forget in the morning. He felt a longing to lose himself in the embrace of a woman. He turned his horse toward Ramswood.

The porter at the Black Bear tavern gave a brief rap on the kitchen window, as always when a visitor arrived for the innkeeper's daughter. There were a half-dozen men who came chiefly to see the daughter of the house, who had such bright eyes and curls the color of hazelnut down the nape of her neck. Not that she yielded to all of them, as malicious gossip had it, but she enjoyed being found attractive. At the signal that one of her admirers was near she stepped in front of the mirror, pinched her cheeks to bring out the roses in them, and tied her apron strings tighter around her slim waist.

Robert gave the reins to the porter, slipped him a coin, and entered the tavern. He waited in the hall for a moment, but when the girl did not appear, he opened the door to the taproom. The little room was dark and filled with smoke. There was only one lamp, over the table near the stove, where the three recruiting officers, Lessberg, Umbach, and Scholl sat. In the window seat, half hidden behind the partition, sat a man alone; before him on the table stood a lighted candle and a plate with the remains of his dinner.

Scholl, catching sight of Robert, stopped shuffling the cards. "Now the luck'll turn. Here's the man who'll win back all that money you boys just cleaned me out of."

Robert tossed his coat over the back of his chair and sat down with the recruiters.

Umbach knocked his pipe out and looked Robert up and down with a crooked smile. "Look at the dandy, will you? Velvet, silk, lace ruffles. Hardly the common fashion around here. Makes a man realize how rusticated he is, by comparison." He reached for the leather tobacco pouch on the table. "I'll take a little more of your tobacco, Lessberg. Wish I were in the tobacco business m'self." He crumbled a pinch of tobacco between thumb and forefinger, and sniffed at it. "Yes sir, travel all over the world, money, beautiful women. Makes a man green with envy."

Lessberg leaned back in his chair. "All we need is a proper little war. That'd put us recruiters in demand again."

Scholl had cut the cards, and was now expertly shuffling them. "War," he said dreamily. "No prince can become great without war. The really great princes never run out of wars, they can't afford to. It's not the castles and the lands that make history, it's the battles, only the battles. Wish I could find another fellow like that big Dutchman, six-feet-seven he was in his socks. Couldn't find pants or boots to fit him. The King of Prussia pays his cabinet ministers three thousand a year. For my Dutchman he paid me nine thousand."

Scholl never passed up a chance to tell that story. It was part of him like his stiff walk, his Austrian accent, and the four rings on his left hand, which were all he had inherited, besides his noble rank, from his father.

Umbach and Lessberg listened with no sign of impatience. An old story was as good as a new one—for days that wouldn't end, and for men whose lives consisted now only of such days.

Umbach filled his pipe again. "To think I have to hand in my annual report in Kassel on December 1. Nothing but expenses. Not one new recruit for the year. There used to be more fellows around than we could take, all hankering for a uniform. Why, I once picked up twenty-five in one day. Not rejects either, but top-quality material."

"Those days will come again."

"Sure, it's not your fault there's no war on," Lessberg said. "In any case, you still have your salary, with or without premiums for recruiting."

"Do you think I'd have become a recruiter if I meant to live on an officer's pay?" Umbach said.

"A war's bound to come along."

"You've been saying that since '63, and this is '75."

"In 1776 we'll have a war."

"In Russia, maybe, and they have enough recruits of their own. They don't need any help from us."

"Umbach, you're the kind that sees only the hole in the doughnut."

The innkeeper's daughter came in and set a tall glass of red wine in front of Robert. She would have spoken, but when she saw the three recruiters' intent eyes upon her, she only smiled. Lessberg shoved his empty glass toward her. "Another of the same." As she picked up the glass, she exchanged a glance with Robert—and hoped she hadn't betrayed herself with a blush.

"Bring the dice," Robert said.

"I don't believe these gentlemen have much left to lose," she said, as she placed the dice on the table.

"Dying to get rid of us, aren't you?" Lessberg took hold of her arm. "Look at those shining eyes of hers."

She smiled coolly. "All the girls from Ramswood to Kassel have shining eyes when Robert Haynow's back in the country."

Robert had piled all the money in his pockets on the table in front of him, making separate stacks of coins of the same value. He took the leather dice cup. "One taler is the stake for each toss of the dice. Everybody takes a dice cup of his own, it's quicker that way. Agreed?"

They nodded, and each man wrapped his hand protectively around his cup, as though holding a living thing. Silence fell in the room; the rattling of the dice became the only sound. Simultaneously, each emptied his dice cup onto the table and leaned forward to study the three dice in front of him. "Nine," Robert said. Lessberg shoved his dice to the center of the table. "Fourteen," he said. Scholl, who had thrown ten, and Umbach, who had a twelve, tossed their dice back into the containers.

Robert paid Lessberg. "Shall we double the stakes?" he said.

"Done," said Lessberg. Scholl and Umbach were too proud to refuse.

The girl brought Lessberg his wine. For a moment she stood beside Robert; he reached out to her as one strokes a cat without looking at it.

Again the rattle of the dice as they were tossed on the table. Robert lost again, and again Lessberg was the winner. The game went on, Robert losing time and again, until he proposed another doubling of the stakes, and when he lost the four-taler throw as well, he said, like a man trying to force his luck: "Eight?" But he lost again. The three officers had ceased to keep track of the figures. They played as though luck was bound to remain on their side; somehow, no matter how low they scored, Robert seemed to score even lower. In half an hour he had lost all his cash. When he had pushed his last gold pieces over to Scholl, he turned to the girl, who was tidying up the barroom for the night. "We need pens and paper."

"You want to go on playing?" Lessberg asked.

"Have you ever known me to quit in the middle of a run of bad luck?"

"If we had any sense, we'd quit," Scholl said. "Wait and see if he doesn't win it all back, and some of ours with it."

"It's only fair to give him another chance."

Umbach grinned. "I believe in the Law of Serial Consistency."

The innkeeper's daughter placed paper, inkpot, and goose quill on the table before Robert. She regretted that vanity had kept her primping too long to catch him outside in the hall, before he'd entered the room.

Robert drew vertical lines down the sheet of paper and wrote a name above each column. The men went back to rattling their dice. Robert kept losing. He did not utter a word; his glass of wine stood untouched on the table. He had forgotten everything except the three "bones" and their black eyes, totally under the spell of a new experience: luck persisted in being against him. He jotted down the figures mechanically, after each toss. He did not register their meaning consciously; all he knew was that he couldn't stop. Umbach had laid his pipe aside, not noticing the sparks that fell out and scorched the wooden table. Lessberg tugged at his tight military collar. Scholl mumbled figures. Even the solitary stranger in the window seat had risen and come over to watch the game.

The girl opened the transom above one of the windows, put away the cutlery, folded napkins. She didn't need to look at the table to know that Robert was losing.

"Five hundred talers," Scholl said huskily. "That should do, I'd say."

"Time to stop. He owes us five hundred. That's more than we'd get for ten new recruits nowadays."

Robert leaned back in his chair. "Would I be worth ten of those to you?"

"How do you mean?"

"I mean exactly what I say."

No one answered, nor did they look at each other. The three recruiters had been sitting at the table since midmorning, eating, drinking, gambling together, in a continuous deep lethargy of boredom. Now, suddenly, they were wide awake. Robert let his eyes go from one to the other. They made him think of children who would like to invoke the devil but lack the nerve to utter his name. "Well, how about it? Are you game? If I win, my debt's canceled. If I lose, I've been recruited by the winner."

The girl came over to Robert and made a move to take the dice cup from his hand. He gently pushed her away, and threw his three dice back into his cup. "What are you waiting for? That's good odds." He didn't know himself what was driving him on like this.

The three officers reached for their dice, keeping their eyes lowered. The rattle of the dice this time seemed louder than before. The door slammed behind the girl. The stranger cleared his throat nervously, and even this sounded unnaturally loud. Scholl was the first to overturn his dice cup; he looked at his throw without waiting for the others. His face darkened as he saw the three ones he had thrown.

"Go on, Umbach," Lessberg said urgently.

"Why me? Why don't you move first?"

"Why not? Here goes, then." Slowly he let the dice slide onto the table. He had an eight. Umbach had five. The officers' faces relaxed.

"I knew it," Scholl said. "With his last throw he'll win it all back." Robert lifted his dice cup. The first die that showed was a five.

"I knew it," Scholl said, looking oddly relieved.

"You've got your man," Robert said to Lessberg.

"How's that?" They all stared at the two ones that had followed the five.

"Eight is more than seven, I take it?" Robert said coolly. "Hand over your service contract."

"You certainly are a cure for boredom." Lessberg's laughter sounded forced.

"Then don't be a spoilsport and let's get me signed up," Robert said.

Lessberg drew a large red wallet from the inside pocket of his coat and extracted a form. He hesitated. "We don't have to take it all so literally, do we?"

"I gave my word." Robert dipped the goose quill into the inkpot and started to fill out the form.

The three officers watched in uncomfortable silence. "Do you have any idea what a catch you've made, Lessberg?" Umbach finally said, with forced gaiety.

"He's not tall enough for the Dragoons."

"Would you have preferred a six-and-a-half foot country yokel to a real baron? The gentry fetch a tidy premium, man."

"Which branch of the service would be the most likely, do you think?"

"I shall join the Hessian Guards, the Elector's own regiment," Robert said. "That or nothing." He passed the signed form to Lessberg.

"On condition you wangle us a war."

"Two Haynows in the same regiment, that's war in any case."

"With the horses and the girls as chief bone of contention, of course." Scholl suddenly burst out laughing. He waved the form in the air and let it flutter to the table. "Look at that. I knew all along he'd trick us. Look at that signature."

Lessberg caught the sheet of paper as it landed. "Did he put down his mark? That's valid. I know many a gentleman of rank who can't do better than that."

"He signed a false name."

"Who told you it was a false name?" There was something in Robert's eyes that could have been mistaken for a smile. "An adopted name may be dropped."

Umbach jumped to his feet. He grabbed the form and stared at the signature. The name signed was Robert Skelnik. He put the paper silently down on the table and took a step toward Robert, wavering just a bit from the wine. "Stand up."

Lessberg and Scholl looked on in uneasy silence, wondering if Umbach was drunk enough to provoke a duel. But the recruiter only laid an arm around Robert's shoulder. "Right you are, brother," he said heavily. "Spit on the Elector's patent of nobility. You were and are a Skelnik. I can't accept an enlistment from you but you're a good man, just the same."

Robert found himself being embraced by one after the other, meeting wine-reddened eyes, breathing alcohol-charged breaths, while all three talked to him at once. There was a certain dream-like implausibility about the whole scene.

"Let's go, boys, let's get all the glasses in the place and smash 'em up," Umbach commanded. "It'll bring 'im luck." Hands and arms loaded with drinking glasses, the three stumbled outdoors, laughing and babbling, much too preoccupied with themselves to notice that Robert had taken the opportunity to slip away.

The stranger was now the only man left in the taproom. He stood near the table where the others had been gambling, looking at the scattered dice, the dice cups, the writing materials, and the document Robert had just signed. As the sound of glasses being smashed on the flagstones began outside, he stood there, smiling to himself. He picked up the signed form, read it over carefully, checked the date, the signature; it was a valid document. Although the mission that had brought him here from the capital had nothing to do with Robert Haynow, or Robert Skelnik, there was nothing Louis Stein found uninteresting, because he had discovered you could never tell what would turn out to be important some day. He folded the document carefully and slipped it into his pocket. Then he picked up the candle from his own table and went upstairs to the room he had reserved for the night. Outside, the drunken voices and sounds of breaking glass began to fade.

In the night, Robert woke and reached for the glass of water that always stood on his bedside table at home. Instead, his hand found the curtain that screened off the bed in the alcove of the girl's room, and he remembered where he was.

He sat up and pushed the curtain aside. The girl beside him was breathing deeply. It seemed a good moment to slip out and ride home, toward his own bed and a few hours of deep sleep before breakfast. But when he moved, two arms made a warm, fragrant noose around his neck and pulled him back again.

The next time he woke the room was filled with tender green light filtering through the leaves outside the window. Birds twittered in the huge walnut tree. The girl watched, her eyes shining, as he dressed. She made no move to stop him this time.

He bent over to stroke the hair from her forehead. "Aren't you supposed to get married soon?"

"In the spring. Then I move to Kassel. My brother's fiancée wants all his sisters out of the house when she moves in—after they marry, you know."

"Is it the owner of the Lion's Inn?"

She nodded.

"His daughters are older than you are.

She laughed. "They're pretty worried about their inheritance, too, I can tell you."

"When you're a widow, I'll come around to console you."

She was still smiling when she stood, dressed now, at the open window, listening to the hoofbeats of his horse as they receded in the distance.

Heron Island

Upon being summoned by the Master of Revenues, the cobbler Johannes Roder, day laborer Justin Stube, and tailor Konrad Haas appeared for questioning this day. They are charged with intention to emigrate to South Carolina. They all confirm that they were incited to emigrate by a pamphlet which has been picked up separately and is included herewith.

This pamphlet or proclamation assures would-be settlers in the New World of a sum of money and a deed to a share of good farmland. Travel expenses to be advanced until settlers have earned the necessary amount to reimburse the company for same. These promises are followed by mouth-watering descriptions of a land where milk and honey flows for all. Point #6, for instance, states explicitly that the soil is extraordinarily fertile. That every bushel of seed yields from fifty to sixty bushels of wheat. That no fertilizer would be required for the first thirty years or so. The whole promotion is quite evidently a most impudent, brazen swindle.

From the protocols of the Hessian Master of the Revenues at Grebenstein, 1753

9

Catherine Sonsfeld had long ago abandoned her marriage bed with its worn silk canopy for the privacy of her own boudoir. And now, when she missed her husband upon awakening, as she did this morning, it was only because she needed a scapegoat on which to take out her bad temper.

When she rang for service these days, it no longer summoned a saucy French maid, of the sort she used to hire and fire by the dozen, only old Gustav and his mute wife, Marie. It was too annoying not to be able to begin the new day with complaints about the service, at least.

Irritably she pulled off her nightcap and felt her forehead to check if it had left marks. There were none, but that didn't help her mood. Even the thought that she'd soon be leaving this castle for good and moving to the capital only made her more aware of how hateful the place was. She did it in self-defense: if she ever stopped hating this house, the dust and general rot that had been consuming pictures, rugs, and furniture would begin to devour her as well.

She threw back the covers with disgust. Though she warmed her bedding every night at the fireplace, by morning it had somehow absorbed the smelly damp from the ancient stone walls. Sitting on the edge of her bed she looked over the large, high-ceilinged room. As a young bride she had brought all the finest things in the castle into this chamber. For those Aubusson rugs from Paris and the brocade draperies from Venice, her husband had sold a rich farmstead. The massive gold rings that held back the drapes at her windows had cost him a forest, the chandelier of Bohemian crystal a well-stocked fishpond. But now, in the uncertain morning light, it was all covered with a pall of neglect and decay.

She put on her morning coat and slippers. On the love seat lay the black silk gown in which she intended to receive the Elector's emissary this morning. On her vanity in front of the mirror stood the new silver-gray wig. Neither the new dress nor the wig had been paid for, but soon she wouldn't have to worry about such things; soon all the dressmakers and coiffeurs and jewelers would be filling her house with their best wares—and they wouldn't dare dun her for payment, either.

She heard a sound outside in the hallway. She opened the door just in time to catch Gustav trying to slip past her room with a basket of firewood.

"Where do you think you're going with that? And kindly stop when I am talking to you!" She watched him turn hesitantly around. "My orders were to heat the little reception room first today."

"There's been a fire laid on in there for an hour." The man always made her think of an old wolf, all skin and bones but with frightening teeth and eyes.

"And what do you call this?" The lady of Sonsfeld pointed to a bit of dried shaving soap on his sleeve. "Didn't I tell you not to take the time to shave your master this morning? An important visitor is due here in an hour and the whole place is still a shambles."

"The courtyard, vestibule, and reception room were put in order last night, Madame."

"How dare you speak to me in that tone. Better watch it, my man. I am fast running out of patience with you. You and your wife are getting too old to find new masters indulgent enough to feed two such lazybones."

With that, she turned her back on him and hurried down the hall to her husband's room. She opened the door without knocking and stopped dead at the sight of the crackling fire and the luxurious breakfast on the table. The warmth, the aroma of coffee and fresh bread—it was enough to make her dizzy with fury.

Count Sonsfeld was turning a spoonful of honey and letting it flow on a thickly buttered croissant. "Do shut the door, my dear," he said without looking up. "You know how temperamental this fireplace can be."

Catherine Sonsfeld drew a deep breath and slammed the door hard enough to make the windows rattle. "Nobody makes a fire for me. Nobody brings my breakfast. I'm sure I'd fare better if I were a maid in this house."

"You're usually still asleep at this hour. You needed only to ring, you know."

"If I'm not to freeze in this place I pretty well have to huddle in bed."

"Won't you breakfast with me?" He pointed to a chair opposite his own.

"You needn't trouble yourself with civilities. To digest bread baked by Marie requires the Sonsfeld ostrich stomach, which unluckily I haven't got."

"Here are some braided breakfast rolls, too."

How she hated him and his unflappable serenity that she knew for the ice-cold selfishness it really was. Nothing ever touched him.

"I honestly think I could die in this house and no one would notice."

He set down his cup and leaned back in his chair. Neithart Sonsfeld's once reddish-blond hair had whitened early, but he was still youthfully slim, and his fair-skinned face, with its aristocratic features, had retained its tautness. No one would have guessed his sixty years. It was too early in the day, he decided, to go into her favorite subject, as to who would die before whom; but he was willing to offer her the little ration of malice she had evidently come for.

"You've always been healthy as a horse," he said. "It was the main reason I married you. As a general in the field one learns to notice such things and value them. I never liked physical weaklings. Look at yourself in the mirror, my dear. No one would guess your forty-three years. You weren't this handsome when we were married."

"I was no beauty. No beauty would have followed you to this crow's nest."

"I know you very well by now. Your bad mood is a simple matter of nutrition. It's always worst when you haven't eaten. Let me ring for Marie to bring your breakfast."

"There's no time for that now. All the work in this place, that used to keep twenty servants busy, has to be done by two old people. You sit here filing your nails while the fruit rots in the orchard because there's no one to gather it up. That's the reason for my bad mood. You take no interest in how much firewood we still have, how long our supply of flour is likely to last, or the coffee for your mocha. You couldn't care less about anything as long as you have your peace and can be shaved twice a day. For whom, I wonder?" She had stepped over to his desk and started to go through his papers.

"Please don't get my papers all mixed up."

"Then why don't you lock yourself in altogether, bolt the doors, if I mustn't look at business papers that concern both of us? Has Heron Island been sold yet? We need the money. I've told you several times. Our supplies are running low. By Christmas all the sugar will be gone, and all the wood."

He slowly removed a cigarillo from a silver case, sniffed at it. "Heron Island is not to be sold," he said casually.

For a split second she was in danger of losing her composure altogether; she wanted to scream at him, turn over the breakfast table—but she caught herself. "Count Sonsfeld is not selling," she mocked. "Count Sonsfeld has never sold anything. His ancestral heritage is sacred to Count Sonsfeld. His farms, his forests, his town houses, have not changed hands. The Count is fooling everyone. He is letting his residence fall apart deliberately, so no one will guess the wealth he is hiding inside. He is doing it all for his only daughter's sake, so that no one will marry her for her fortune, but only for love. Yes indeed, he's fooling everyone, including his wife, who has to mend her own stockings, and the two old servants who haven't been paid their wages for years and years!"

While she spoke, the Count folded his napkin and rose. He wore the smoke-blue vest and silk knee pants that went with his Bordeaux-red dress coat. She stared at him as though she had caught him in some vulgar carnival costume. For so many years she had never seen him wearing anything except his old green dressing gown, that had always been too long and too large, so that it made him look like an old man. Apparently that, too, had been one of his macabre jokes, to show his disdain for her. A costume in which he had been playing an old man for her benefit.

"I don't care whether you sell Heron Island or not. I need five hundred gold pieces by December first."

"Heron Island is as old as our coat of arms. You once took considerable pride in the Sonsfeld coat of arms, the sword and heron feather. I still do. I shall never sell the island."

She decided she had had enough of running her head against this wall of ice and obstinacy. At the door she turned for a final word. "Just in case you've forgotten, I'm expecting a visitor today. He's coming to see me, and me alone. I trust you understand me. I don't wish to be embarrassed by any intrusion from you."

"But, my dear, why do you think I dressed with such care this morning?" he asked with infuriating blandness.

"I will not have you interfere!"

"I have no desire to speak to the man, my love. I merely intend, in all simplicity, to take this Monsieur Stein by the scruff of the neck and throw him out."

That took her by surprise; she wasn't sure whether he was joking or serious. "Stein is the Elector's High Chamberlain, and as such. . . ."

"Stein is a broken-down actor and his real name is something unpronounceable that betrays his unattractive origins."

"He is Lord High Chamberlain and is going to go far. Despite being a commoner, he's already the most important man at Court after Schlieffen, and he's very close to the Elector himself."

"The sort of creatures the Elector likes to surround himself with is his own affair, I suppose."

"Since when do you look down on the middle class? I always thought you were more critical of the aristocracy."

"Where panders and pimps are concerned, it makes little difference whether they are commoners or noblemen."

She walked slowly back to where he stood and looked him up and down. "Your arrogance amazes me, I must say. Of course, everyone knows you saved the King of England's life at the Battle of Culloden Moor, and he still writes to you. I wonder what you find to tell him about on all those pages and pages of expensive stationery you waste on him. Do you boast of the way you've wasted your property, so that you haven't even a dowry to give your only child?"

He gazed at her as though she were a lifeless thing. The days when she had been able to hurt him with her sharp tongue were long gone. That she confused his unshakable calm with resignation and weakness was an advantage rather than the reverse. "Christina bears the name of Sonsfeld. That is dowry enough."

She half turned her head away, assuming what she considered a tragic pose. "The day is coming when you'll pay for the misery you've brought on me and that you're bringing on your daughter."

"If I succeed in preventing you from making my daughter into a whore, I won't fear that day of judgment."

"As I recall, the proud Sonsfeld family's founder was a bastard of the Emperor's."

"My daughter is not going to crawl into a bed still warm from the body of a French coquette."

"You have a dirty mind that makes you see dirt wherever you look." She smiled contemptuously. "We may as well end this discussion right now."

Sonsfeld saw the tensing of her body, the slightly cross-eyed fixity that came into her dark eyes; it reminded him of the young bride to whom he had once made love—more in the spirit of taming a wild mare than anything to do with passion. He rather congratulated himself that that, too, was over now.

For the lady of Sonsfeld an argument with her husband was not finished when she left the field of battle; it merely entered a new phase. She simply began to invent a new version of it, in which she said all the things she had prudently suppressed on the actual scene, including profanity no human ear had ever heard her speak. She conducted these shadow fights with the kind of fervor characteristic of secret vices, preferably in her daughter's bedroom, where she was going now.

Noiselessly she opened the door and whispered Christina's name. Hearing no answer, she stepped inside, closing the door behind her. She stopped at the foot of the bed. Christina was sleeping behind the tulle curtains. Again she promised herself to undo the father's influences on Christina, before it was too late. But soon she was lost in speculations about how to redecorate Christina's rooms in the new house at Kassel; clearly the virginal whites of the pure young schoolgirl's room would no longer do in the new circumstances there. Or would it, on the other hand, be precisely the tone to take? The town house in Kassel still existed only in her imagination, but she was serenely certain her only child would have everything she herself had missed in life: wealth, the glitter of social success, love. The beauty she already had would take care of that.

With eyes half closed, Catherine Sonsfeld considered the sleeping girl through the tulle. White, of course. Christina, with her complexion of a half-opened sea rose, could afford what other women feared. And her hair, that indescribable shade of silvery gold, hair that shone like a summer moon. And those dark eyes, like huge black cherries. Christina's recent metamorphosis from a gangly girl into a blazing beauty had nearly driven her mother out of her mind with joy. Years of anxiety at the prospect of having to marry off an unattractive daughter one inescapable day had now given place to an almost maniacal mother's pride.

Soundlessly she left the bedroom. She was now well prepared to meet Chamberlain Stein. The deal would be made on her terms —she would make certain of that. But when she entered the salon the brutal realities she had to face there dampened her confidence. The wood paneling on the wall facing the mantel was warped. The sofa with the carved gilt frame was hopelessly worn down in the seat. The singed curtain had not been repaired.

The two old servants stood at the door, waiting for her orders.

"We need another sofa," she said wearily.

"When you sit on it, it's not noticeable," the old man said. "I put a wooden crate underneath."

"Fetch the sofa from my room; please be careful with it. And the two armchairs as well. Wait." She pointed to the warped paneling. "Get the large painting of a hunt from the library and hang it over that. And the ruined curtain can be hidden behind the Japanese screen; it's in the smoking room. In front of the screen we'll have the round card table and the two chairs that go with it. Can you remember all that?"

With her finger she tested for dust on the mantelpiece, a marble console, a chair. Like a poor woman, she thought bitterly, with only one luxury to show—cleanliness.

It was simply no use to try hiding the Sonsfelds' poverty. Even if she'd been able to redecorate the room, a man like Stein would never be fooled on that score. He would know the condition of the place before he even entered the front door. The neglected garden alone told the whole story. It was unwise to have invited him here. She should have gone to Kassel for this meeting. Standing at the window she stared at the bright sun outside, struggling against her desperation. Far away, on the road from Ramswood, one of the three that led to Sonsfeld Castle, came a solitary rider.

10

A morning like this, spring in the middle of November, was something new even in the checkered career of Chamberlain Louis Stein. He felt like taking his hat off but he knew what a sudden breeze might do to his courtier's wig.

The air fairly glittered; even the bird cries seemed to sparkle. And if he wasn't hallucinating, there were violets under that bush beside the road. He reined in his horse and dismounted. No mistake—a patch of dark blue violets. He pulled off his gloves, took a knife from his portmanteau, and cut flower after flower with great care, surrounding the little bouquet with a ring of leaves.

In the saddle again, he tried to imagine his hostess's look, at Sonsfeld, when he handed her this fresh bouquet. She would be thanking him in her dreadful, mispronounced French, with an affected smile. Who would have dreamed that one day a Sonsfeld would pass through his hands.

When he arrived at the Court of Kassel six years before, he had been the director of a troupe of actors no longer in actual existence. Except for the prompter and his twin daughters, extraordinarily pretty but so stupid he couldn't trust them with a part that had any lines, they had all disappeared at the last stop before Kassel, taking with them all the money in the till.

The capital city of Hesse was already full of placards announcing the troupe's arrival. The Elector sent a royal dinner from his own table over to the Hotel English Court, with a gracious message to the effect that he would attend their first performance in town, the very next day. Although Louis Stein did not yet have the ghost of an idea what to do about that performance, he unhesitatingly responded with an elegant note of his own, stating that he had prepared a special new production for Kassel, dedicated to his Grace the Elector, whom he most humbly begged to honor its premiere as its only spectator—the most exclusive audience imaginable.

The next thing Louis Stein did was to lie down and have a good sleep. The saving inspiration came to him literally in a dream: a play requiring only three actors, entitled *Casanova in Kassel,* about which a great deal was whispered for years afterward, both true and untrue, and which owed little to the script—there was no time to write one—but all the more to the physical attractions of the twins, dressed for the private command performance in not much more than the indefinite lighting of the stage.

The play was a success—the Elector invited the twins to visit him at the Palace that very night. Next morning he summoned Louis Stein to offer him the position of Court Director of Theater, Opera, and Ballet. There was no need for his Grace to spell out what, precisely, Louis Stein's chief function in that position was to be. Before the Elector had time to get tired of the twins, Stein saw to it that an Italian singing star appeared in Kassel. She succeeded in dominating the Court for a whole winter. Then he engaged a Spanish dancer, and later a French actress of classic tragedy. Three years of such services were rewarded by the Elector's pinning the house order of the Golden Lion on Louis Stein's court dress and dubbing him a Chamberlain.

Stein could have afforded a mansion of his own long ago, but preferred to live unpretentiously in his modest suite at the Palace. His real dream was not a town house, which any affluent commoner could achieve, but the kind of landed property that was the preserve of the aristocracy. And why not? Sonsfeld Castle, for example, would be a masterless fief, sooner or later, there being no male heir, and it would be for the Elector to decide who should be its new master.

When he entered the little salon, he was already feeling like the lord of the manor, and that was how he greeted Catherine Sonsfeld. "My dear—" he stretched out both hands to her, "how enchanting!"

The man has savoir-faire, Catherine thought. No matter what her husband thought about him, he had style. Nevertheless, a certain reserve on her part was called for. "I trust you had a pleasant journey?"

"For a city man like myself, the ride felt positively rejuvenating." He dropped his gloves on the console table beside his hat and handed her the bouquet of violets. "For you, Madame. November violets."

Catherine Sonsfeld held the bouquet up to her nose. "You must be a magician to have kept these flowers so fresh, with the very dew on them, all the way from Kassel."

"At the risk of disappointing you—this bouquet is not from the Elector's hothouses. I picked them for you myself at the side of the road."

"My absolute favorites among flowers, violets," she said with a labored smile.

Stein bowed. They sat down.

"A little refreshment?" she said.

"Gladly."

She rang and Gustav appeared, now dressed, in accordance with her orders, in a wig and dark blue livery. He placed a platter with thinly sliced ham, two kinds of bread, wine, plain tin plates, and horn-handled cutlery on the table.

"I see you are having your midmorning snack already," Stein exclaimed. "I'm so relieved. I was afraid I'd arrive too early."

"You have not yet had your breakfast? What would you like? Tea, coffee?"

"Lots of hot milk and a little coffee, if it's not too much trouble."

Gustav disappeared.

"How is his Grace?" she asked.

Stein spread his hands theatrically. "He is exactly like this day, an autumn sun with all the heat of summer."

Catherine Sonsfeld chose not to collaborate with such levity on that subject. "And how is the hunting season going?"

"I can't remember his ever having been so dedicated to hunting as this season. His falconers have new dress uniforms. New coaches are being built for the entire entourage. At the moment there isn't a craftsman in Kassel who's not working in some way to prepare for the heron hunt."

She listened to him with mixed feelings. It was flattering, of course, that all this splendor was being unleashed for her daughter's sake; on the other hand, she would have preferred the staggering sums of money being wasted on the hunt be expended for quite another, specific purpose. "In your last letter, you hinted at our removal to Kassel," she said.

"My compliments, dear lady, you know how to read between the lines. Yes, indeed, concrete steps have already been taken in the meantime."

"Do tell me about it. Is Du Ry the architect? Actually there's no one else worthy of consideration."

"Madame, I can see you have no conception of his Grace's fieriness, his impatience. The house is all ready. A little jewel of a villa in a little park of its own, on the south side of the Elysian Field. Completely furnished and decorated. There's nothing lacking that would please a young lady. And it has already been through its ordeal by fire, so to speak."

The lady of Sonsfeld leaped to her feet as if she had been stung by a scorpion. "One of his love nests! And that notorious house, in particular! Everyone will know what it means for my daughter to move into it. The gondola bed that all of Kassel was cackling about. That 'lady' had the effrontery to give huge parties, after all. Everyone knows how many mirrors she has in her bathrooms, everyone has seen the table service painted with erotic, risqué scenes. I shall permit nothing of the kind."

"If you are troubled by these minor details, Madame, I can assure you the bed was moved to Paris long ago, the table service that offends you was taken along as a souvenir by the lady, who is a passionate collector of fine porcelains and who regards it as the showpiece of her trousseau. Because the 'lady,' you know, is married now."

"I insist upon my conditions, a new house included."

Stein sighed. "If you do, I can guarantee that it will not be your daughter but someone else who moves into it."

Before she could reply, Gustav arrived with the breakfast.

Marie had provided the French service and the enameled oval tray. Madame nodded graciously at the servant. "Thank you. I shall serve Chamberlain Stein myself."

"One-fourth coffee, three-fourths hot milk, if I may."

As she poured, Stein noticed that the tip of the middle finger of her right hand was covered with tiny needle pricks, from the sewing she had to do. For the first time he felt something like compassion for her.

She did not resume her seat but stood beside the fireplace. "If I have understood you rightly, I have no choice. But only on condition that the house is completely refurnished and redecorated."

"I thought you were an admirer of Du Ry. He did not merely build the house, he designed and selected the wallpapers, the rugs, the draperies, and all the furniture."

"And all of it redolent with the perfume of that woman. My Christina is an innocent young girl, and has a right to live in a style suitable to herself."

"Innocence, Madame," Stein said with a smile, "counts as trump only once. Of course the Elector is particularly charmed for the moment, by your daughter's naïveté. But you and I should realize that this can be a disadvantage for the depth and durability of the alliance. The Elector is a spoiled man."

"It was you yourself who told me he is tired of women with a past, sick of their—sophistication." Catherine Sonsfeld came back to the table and resumed her seat. Her mind was absorbed with matters of greater interest to her than the hours her daughter would be spending alone with the Elector. "What is the monthly budget planned for my daughter? I must insist on matters of this sort being fixed contractually." She spoke nervously, because the conversation was not going as she had intended or imagined it.

"That won't be necessary," Stein said. "As long as your daughter's coachman and footmen wear the Elector's livery, she will enjoy credit all year long, from the baker to the jeweler. The bills can then be passed on to me."

"I prefer the French style of doing these things; so much more elegant. Madame Pompadour paid all her own bills, with the

King's notes. I wouldn't like my daughter to have to account for every detail of her expenditures. Considering her ancestry and rank, after all, my daughter could insist on a fixed allowance, like a member of the reigning house."

Stein set his cup down. "Since you cite the French Court customs—when La Pompadour moved into her rooms at Versailles, neither she nor the King had any idea she would be the uncrowned Queen of France for the next twenty years. I do not think she gained her power over the King by forcing him to assign her a fixed income by contract. I imagine she gave him the impression she loved him more than anyone in the world. I honestly believe this to have been her whole secret. The significant contracts between a man and a woman are not put down on paper. A man like the Elector has possessed many women, but he has rarely been loved. I am with him every day; I know his problem. He is a man who has enjoyed everything in life, who has tried everything. He knows that a man's years are limited. I know his mood, the longing to be young once more, to begin at the beginning, to experience everything again as if for the first time. Your daughter has an extraordinary opportunity here, one no other woman before her has had. You shouldn't run the risk of destroying the Elector's illusions by offering to sell your daughter like a calf. He is dreaming of a miracle. You should give him a chance to experience one. For your daughter's sake."

His words produced the opposite effect from what he intended. Catherine Sonsfeld felt less reassured than ever. She was being cleverly sidetracked by a man who knew how to keep all the aces in his own hand.

"I don't understand your aversion to contracts. Marriages on our social level always involve contracts, and my daughter is entering into a form of marriage, as far as I am concerned. It will be just as well for the Elector to understand that beforehand. I shall give him my daughter only if she is accorded all the rights of a wife. My daughter, for her part, is prepared to be converted to Catholicism." She had never brought the matter up with Christina, but for the moment she was thinking only about gaining ground.

Stein felt as though he were acting in a Molière comedy: life doing its best to justify the satirist's representation of it. The bond between mother and child here seemed to consist of nothing more than the umbilical cord. He felt sure that if he had come to Madame Sonsfeld as an emissary of the Caliph of Baghdad, she would have as confidently proposed converting her child to Islam.

She misinterpreted his silence. "That surprises you, does it? But you see, I do think beyond tomorrow. There might be children, you know."

Stein suppressed a smile. "Oh, yes, the Elector has proven his ability to produce offspring often enough. But don't forget that he detests the sight of pregnant women."

"He has made most generous provisions for each one of his offspring."

"And never again given the child's mother another look." Amusing as he found the conversation, Louis Stein decided to cut it short and make things very clear. "A morganatic marriage such as you envision," he said, "is quite out of the question. I'm afraid you are aiming too high, Madame."

"We will leave that to the future," she said icily.

"And to your daughter," Stein added conciliatingly. "Some women can do anything they want with a man. Perhaps your daughter is that kind of wonder-worker."

Catherine Sonsfeld made no reply. Like all women who had never known a dramatic love in their own lives, she was extremely touchy on the subject, hypersensitive in suspecting allusions to her own failure in this respect. Had her own life been so uneventful, perhaps, because she was not the kind of woman who could do "anything" with a man?

"Another thing," Stein said, "the Elector feels it might be a good thing for everyone concerned to arrange a marriage of convenience—a marriage in name only, that is—for your daughter."

"In name only?" She said it as if she felt insulted. She was sure Stein was lying, that it was his own idea for providing the Elector with a mistress on the easiest terms, and getting the credit for it. "I have nothing to say to that. It would be my daughter's decision."

"Pardon, Madame, but this would be a matter on which the Elector would have to agree with the 'husband.' The marriage would exist only on paper. Your daughter would participate only to the extent of legally bearing the gentleman's name, which would incidentally secure for any offspring the legal status and rank of their 'father.' "

"And whom did you have in mind?" Behind her impassive look her blood was boiling.

"Actually I've not been authorized to mention this. Baron Schlieffen is responsible for the idea. At the time there was an obstacle, in that the chosen candidate was not a member of the nobility."

Catherine Sonsfeld's face became even more inexpressive. "Do go on."

"Well, when Schlieffen decides on doing something, he usually finds the means to do it. So now there is a new barony in Hessia. You know the family I refer to, I'm sure—neighbors of yours, in fact. Baron Schlieffen chose Claus Haynow."

"The Haynows! Never. A member of the House of Sonsfeld will never bear the name of Haynow, not as long as I live." She struggled for self-control. She began to pace the floor in front of the fireplace. "It was never Schlieffen's idea—the scheme bears all the signs of Gottfried Haynow's handiwork. He began by acquiring our property, and now he wants our daughter as well. He wants to give his new rank—which smells of the money with which he bought it—a touch of legitimacy through an alliance with the ancient crest of Sonsfeld. He thinks he can buy anything and everything. He will find himself mistaken."

Stein intently studied his well-manicured fingernails. "I rather expected you to react like this. I hope you will think it over and see the advantage of this choice in particular. Wouldn't it be rather a sweet revenge to have a sizable part of the Haynow property fall into your daughter's hands, Madame? Try to see it from that angle. There's not a family in all of Hessia that can compare with the Haynows in wealth. You and I ought to play with our cards on the table. Not one of the Elector's mistresses left Kassel —if I may put it that way—in a golden coach. A young beauty has to remember that her 'capital' is perishable, and that the day is not far off when she will be glad of a rich husband in her own social class. What's more, your daughter would in this way feel quite independent of the Elector's favors. That, in itself, changes everything."

Catherine Sonsfeld lowered her eyes. Stein was a glib talker, but she was not fooled. All of his glittering arguments added up to only one thing: the Elector intended to spend even less money on Christina than on any of his previous mistresses. For a painful moment she saw what she was doing in a pitilessly clear light: her great plans were no more than a humiliating deal. It was nauseating. And yet she did not have the backbone to send Stein packing.

"I can read your thoughts in your face," he said.

She was too depressed to react with anything but weariness. Not even the idea that he might have actually guessed what she was thinking could rouse her from a numb indifference. "Indeed? And what was I thinking?"

"Something only a mother would think." Stein hesitated, uncertain how far he could go in hypocrisy undetected; but then he plunged. "You were thinking that your daughter would never know how much you've sacrificed for her happiness."

"I never thought a man could understand a thing like that," she said.

Stein got to his feet. He was not quite sure whether she too was being hypocritical or whether he had actually touched her in a sensitive spot. He left it an open question. "May I propose that we put in writing those points on which we agree?"

She nodded. "You may use the desk over there. You'll find paper and pens there."

She walked to the window and looked out on the fields and meadows toward the edge of the woods. All the land, as far as she could see, and more, had once belonged to the Sonsfelds. All had been sold. The only property left to them was Heron Island. Once those last five hundred guilders were gone, she had only a few bits of jewelry. There was no other way, no choice for her at all. She turned back from the window.

Stein had sat down at her desk, goose quill in hand, waiting to set down the terms of their agreement.

"Shall we begin with the furnishings of the house in Kassel?" she said.

11

The contrast between her light blonde hair and her black eyes made Christina Sonsfeld's beauty fascinating and provocative. Such extreme contrasts were evident in her character, too. She was full of contradictions: she was gentle and demanding, dreamy and practical, self-sacrificing and calculating, not each in turn but simultaneously. Stealing down the circular stairs in stocking feet, her riding boots in her hand, she felt both the mischievous exultation of a child about to play a prank and an angry contempt for her parents—ever since she could remember they had forced her into lying and deception.

As a child she had instinctively played each parent against the other to get what she wanted. The game had become too easy; she was tired of it. It was no longer fun to pretend to be asleep under her mother's gaze, as she had this morning, just to escape the usual emotional outburst about her father; it was a bore.

She tiptoed past the salon. She could hear the voices of her mother and the visitor, but she couldn't hear what they were saying. She didn't care; the thing was to get out of the house as fast as she could.

It was a relief to reach the uninhabited wing of the castle. She ran to the door leading to the garden and put her boots down. As she bent over to pull them on, the seams of her hunting jacket threatened to give. In the last six months or so, she had outgrown all her clothes—all but her shoes and her riding pants—which made her proud. She checked the inside pocket of her cashmere cloak, to make sure she had the envelope her father had given her. Then she put on the cloak and stepped outside.

She went down the broad steps leading to the garden. The latest storm had torn away the last of the wooden railing and crumbled several more stones from the steps—a few more heavy rains, and there would be nothing left. Her long shining hair hanging free, she ran along the narrow garden path. Birchwood planks were inlaid every few yards, to keep the soil in place. It was years since the boxwood hedges had been trimmed; spider webs reached for her face as she slipped through what had once been a boxwood arch at the end of the path. The wrought iron gate in the wall hung half open from a broken hinge. A squirrel ran past atop the wall.

When she reached the path leading down to the river, she stopped to think. Her horse would take her down in a few minutes, and she wouldn't have to wait for the ferryman; the river was shallow enough to ford. But to try to get her horse out of the stable was to risk being caught and stopped by her mother. How idiotic to have to go on foot to Ramswood, like a peasant girl, just because her mother mustn't know her errand. But it was worth it. Her father's letter to the magistrate would prevent Heron Island from falling into the possession of the Haynows. She was glad her father had stuck to his guns this time, and that he had a little money her mother knew nothing about. And she was proud that he trusted her with the letter.

She hadn't gone fifty yards before she noticed the ribbon of smoke rising over Heron Island. She stared at it, jealous. Robert was there, on his island, back from Holland, and she was probably the last one for miles to find out about it. Only yesterday she had asked Marie, but Marie had pretended ignorance—afraid of Christina's mother, no doubt. She could understand that; she was just as cowardly where her mother was concerned, no matter how often she resolved to stand up for herself. Some day it would have to happen. Some day her mother would have to understand that she had a will and a life of her own. She ran all the way to the riverbank.

Her mother always called Robert "the savage." Luckily, her mother hadn't the faintest idea how she felt about Robert. It had begun five years ago, during the harvest festival at Haynow House; she was thirteen then. A separate dance pavilion had been set up for the children, and Robert had come over and asked her to dance. Even now, just thinking about it, she blushed all over again. As soon as he had reached out his hand to her, she had become painfully conscious of her faded white dress, with its starched lace inserts. A little girl's dress. And how awkward and ugly she had felt.

She couldn't remember what had happened then—whether they had danced for one second or for an hour. Had her hair really come undone, and had she really given him the two white ribbons from it? All she knew for certain was that his touch had set her aflame. Since then, it was always the same; whenever she saw him, she felt like a pillar of fire.

A lot of time had passed since then. That moment had become enshrined at the core of her being; it was a secret she had shared with no one. Not even with him.

Lost in thought, she forgot herself completely until the ferry crunched to a stop at the landing. She got in, and the ferryman asked where she wanted to go. Then she remembered she was supposed to deliver her father's letter to the magistrate in Ramswood before ten o'clock. She hesitated, looking toward the island. The wind was bending the broad belt of reeds, making it into a solid wall of impenetrable green around the island. Her courage failed her. If Robert had wanted to see her, there were a thousand ways he could have let her know, despite her mother's vigilance. God only knew how long he'd been back and whether he had the slightest interest in seeing her at all. But, she thought, how was he to know how much she longed to see him? The last time they'd seen each other was a year ago, when he'd stopped at Sonsfeld Castle to bring her a dressmaker's manikin—no longer a child's toy, but still, a kind of doll. How could he know she was grown up now?

She heard the oars hitting the water, saw the water parting at the bow, mirroring her face in a thousand fluid splinters. She was gliding, gliding away from herself, letting fate take over.

She looked up at the ferryman. "Row me to the island," she said.

The fire grate in the house on the island had originally been built for Robert Skelnik. Gold was to have been made here, real gold, false gold—in any case, it was being used now to heat water in a copper teapot. Robert was deep in thought, poking at the fire.

The poker in his hand, the fire tongs, the bellows, had all belonged to his father. His father had walked on these reddish flagstones, had sat on the three-legged stool. The shelves that covered the back wall of the laboratory had held his vials of chemical solutions and powders. Robert remembered what the ferryman had said—his father had not put out the fire; there had still been smoke over the island for forty-eight hours after he'd left. His father had disappeared without anyone noticing, not even the ferryman. Robert knew his own departure would be less dramatic, but just as final.

Only yesterday, this crumbling house had meant nothing to him except that it stood for the first great thing in his life: the island. How easy and unproblematic his life had been yesterday. Suddenly, nothing was simple any longer. He had come straight to Heron Island from his night at the Black Bear, because he had made a decision about his life. He saw the island this morning with different eyes—the round, river-polished rocks he had used to mark the easiest crossing, the narrow dike he'd built so his horse wouldn't sink in the swampy edge of the riverbank—it was all part of his youth and of home. He knew he would never see any of it again.

There was nothing more here for him to do. He stood up and went outside. The sun was warm on his shoulders and the back of his neck. From the distance came the cry of a waterfowl. The hum of an insect approached, receded, vanished. Even all this had changed, and he felt as if he'd already left it behind. The past was extinguished; the future was still unknown.

He had heard the sound for some time now; it sounded like a deer thrashing through the underbrush. Something bright rose above the bushes. There was the fluttering of a stone-gray cloak; the dark tip of a boot, shining wet, parted the grass; a few rust-red leaves floated down to settle on shining hair. If it hadn't been for her hair, he wouldn't have recognized her.

"Sorry, I know you don't like to be surprised like this. But when I saw the smoke . . . how long have you been back?"

He did not speak. Hard as he tried, he couldn't connect the girl in front of him with the Christina he'd known before. It was not only the outward transformation. She had been a gawky, awkward little thing, pale, shy, unsure of herself. Now, at an age when other girls discarded shyness along with their childhood, she had acquired a new innocence. She met his searching glance without embarrassment and, what surprised him even more, without coquetry. With amazement he realized he was the one who was stirred and confused. "I'm surprised Ludolf rowed you over here," he said evasively.

"So am I; he can usually find so many reasons for not doing it. But this time he could have said anything he liked. . . ."

"Your mother wouldn't like it if she knew you were alone here with a man, especially a Haynow."

"I had to sneak out of the house. I couldn't even take my horse. I'm supposed to take a letter from my father to the magistrate in Ramswood before ten this morning."

"Is he asking damages because I catch a fish on his side of the island sometimes?" Then he remembered what his stepfather had said the night before, about the final settlement regarding the island. "May I see the letter?" he asked.

She drew it out of her inside pocket without a moment's hesitation. She broke the seal on the envelope and handed him the letter. While he was reading it, she finally had time to look her fill at him. He stood in the shimmering sun, his skin almost as golden as his hair. When he breathed, the fine fabric of his shirt tightened around his shoulders. She felt as if she had made a great discovery. How vague her image of him had been in her daydreams—how lifeless, compared with the breathing reality of his body. She smiled inwardly at what a child she had been; but she was afraid, too, of the mysterious new feelings stirring inside her.

"If you want to be in Ramswood before ten, you haven't much time. Better take my horse."

She barely heard him; all her awareness was on their hands touching as he returned the letter to her. "Are you getting ready for the heron hunt?" she said.

"This time the Elector's falcons will get all the herons," he said. "But they'll be Sonsfeld herons by then, not mine. I had no idea your father had this much fight left in him. You'd better go. If you're late, the island's ours—And remember, my horse is sensitive in the muzzle. Let him have his head."

She looked at him, the letter in her hand. Hadn't he understood what it meant for her to have broken the seal? Didn't he realize what she was ready to do for him, and for herself as well? The chance to do something on her own hook, regardless of what her parents wanted, had come sooner than she'd expected. Her decision was made. What she didn't know was how to tell him.

"Do you have a cup of tea or a bit of bread? I haven't had breakfast."

He turned away to hide a smile. She obviously intended to get to Ramswood too late. Had she overestimated her courage? Was she too afraid of her mother to place herself so unmistakably on her father's side?

He filled the copper pot with water. "Can you put some wood on the fire?" he said. "I was about to leave."

With a feeling that something wonderful was about to happen, Christina had followed him into the laboratory. She bent down to pick up some wood from the box. Then, when she was sure he would see it, she held her father's letter into the blaze until it caught fire and went up in flames. She held the burning letter high in triumph until the flames nearly singed her fingers. Robert watched her, his head slightly tilted, so that his hair fell down over his forehead.

"It was always your island," she said, "and it always will be."

He gave a forced laugh. "I seem to have something that makes women want to give me things," he said. "Though most of the time they start doing that when they suspect they're about to lose me. And that is how they usually do lose me. But it troubles me to see the master of Sonsfeld doesn't seem to know his own daughter too well."

All that reached her was the sound of his voice, not what he was saying. "The island belongs to you," she said. "I had to do this. I owe you so much. I was never able to tell you. . . ." She hesitated. "I'll find a way to explain to father." She turned to him. Why didn't he take her in his arms? Could she make it more obvious that she loved him? Would she have to put it in words?

"If you did that for my sake, it was wrong." He hung the copper pot over the fire in the grate.

"It was wrong?" She sat down on the footstool. "Is that all you have to say? Aren't you glad?"

He looked at her coolly. "If I may give you some advice for the future: a woman with her feelings hurt is the biggest bore there is. It's all right for a woman to tear her hair or break dishes, but a woman who suffers in silence is deadly and nothing else."

"Any more advice?" she asked, in the caustic tone she so hated in her mother.

"If you want to hear it. My father has a piece of jewelry in his safe, a brooch of sapphires and diamonds, from Derenda's in Frankfurt. If you're wise, you'll return it to the Elector; tell him you like only large single stones. Show him your worth, show it right from the start."

It took a while for this to sink in. When it did, she was furious, but then a saving idea took shape in her mind. What if it only meant he was jealous? The thought gave her back a little of her self-confidence.

"Everybody seems to know more than I do," she said. "My mother, my father—and now it seems there's talk even at Haynow. Everybody's hinting at all sorts of things. No one has asked me."

He waited a bit, but then he said it, simply to see her reaction. "I hope you know what the Elector expects of a young woman."

The very same words her father had used this morning; but on Robert's lips they sounded like something very different. In an obscure corner of her mind energies sprang up that she didn't yet know she had. "If I were a man, you'd have been glad I burned my father's letter. You'd have understood, and we'd be friends now. Why is it so much harder between a man and a woman?"

He stared at her in utter surprise; then he took her hand.

It was a gesture she had longed for, but now it only made her angry, and she pulled her hand away. "Why is it like that?" she asked. "Why do you have to hurt me?"

"Have you had your heart broken by a man already, that you can talk like that?"

She looked straight back at him. The truth was on the tip of her tongue. She was not afraid to confess her love for him, but if she did, he would probably react as coldly as before, when she'd burned the letter. "No woman has broken your heart yet," she said, "and no man will break mine. Not after growing up in a home where the conversation constantly turns on money, money that isn't there." She fell silent. Suddenly she realized he had his arm around her shoulder. Was everything all right then? Would he tell her now that he loved her?

"You don't need to justify anything," he said. "I'd probably do exactly the same thing in your place. The problem is this: a woman has only one life, a man has many. Whatever you do now will determine your whole life."

She bent her head. Why was he saying all that? Why didn't he simply say he loved her? "Even you talk like it's all settled. One of the Elector's courtiers is visiting my mother today, and they're talking. My father is talking. How I hate them!" Her own words frightened her, and yet she said it again, "I hate them. They're only thinking of themselves. Father's no better than mother. He despises her, but he made her what she is now." Was she herself any better? Wasn't she living a compromise herself? Her mother had not gone beyond hints, but those hints had been clear enough. And what had she, Christina, done about it? She had said nothing, pretended to understand nothing. Not as a form of protest, but because at bottom she was ready to do anything—even to sell herself—to get away from Sonsfeld Castle, from her parents. She lifted her head. "It's all so ugly—I tried to shut my eyes to it, but that's impossible now. You've got to help me. Please."

The water in the kettle came to a boil. Robert poured the tea.

"Don't you have any relatives you can go to?"

She laughed. "No more relatives, please! I have a gold table service of my own; for eighteen years now my godmother has given me two settings every birthday. You could sell it for me."

"I can lend you money, too, if I know what it's for."

"Don't you know?" She looked at him expectantly, but he didn't say the words, the simple words that would have solved all her problems.

She poured tea into her cup and drank it down. She picked up her cloak from the bench beside the door where she had left it and stepped outside. Nothing had turned out as she had pictured it in her daydreams.

Robert followed her. The sun had risen higher, drying the dew from the grass, filling the air with rich, sweet smells of plants. "I know a country . . ." he said. "You might like it there."

She would have given a great deal to know what he was really thinking. "How much land could I buy for the price of my table service?"

"In America you don't have to buy the land."

"Can I take anything I want there? Fields, pastures, woods, a lake, a mountain? And how would I get horses?"

"There are wild horses, running free."

"I see—the dream land of milk and honey."

"You think I'm joking," he said, "but I'm not."

"Then you're really going to America?" Not until she actually said the words did she realize what it might mean. Did he want her to go with him? Was that why he'd brought it up?

Robert saw the change in her. It was like watching some powerful emotion being born within her, something that would finally make her an adult, that would shape her whole life. She was beautiful. He struggled against his need to touch everything that pleased him; not until he had "seen" something with his hands could he believe it was real.

She stepped up close to him. "When?"

"I don't know yet."

"Will you take me with you?"

Her eyes met his unwaveringly. It was worse than if she had suddenly burst into tears. To escape those eyes, that riveting look, he took her in his arms and kissed her. It was wrong, he knew it, it was crazy, but he couldn't let her go. Other girls grew heavy in his arms when he kissed them, but she grew lighter; then she slipped away from him and ran and disappeared into the shadows under the trees. The branches closed behind her. Again there was the sound as of a deer breaking through the undergrowth. But this time a new sound was added, a dull rumbling. He listened intently; then he began to run. But when he reached the river, the ferry was already halfway to the other bank. Christina stood in the bow, a slim gray-clad figure, her long blonde hair streaming behind her like sunlight. She did not look back, but ahead, toward the road from Kassel. The rumbling sound came from there: a long line of carriages, preceded by runners and outriders, the advance party of the hunting expedition from the palace in Kassel. Everywhere on the baggage vans and carriages gleamed the Elector's red and green coat of arms.

The Courier

Upon receipt of this message sent to you by special courier, you will go immediately to Braunschweig on some pretext or other, and try to find out whether the Duke will let His Majesty have a number of his troops for service in the American colonies.

You may if need be offer the highest price agreed upon earlier, in this case.

If His Highness, the Heir to the Duke, informs you that nothing can be done or expected in Braunschweig, go instantly to Kassel where you are to find ways and means for sounding out the Elector's intentions; here too you must try to achieve the most possible.

Every conceivable best effort must be made in this matter, inasmuch as the King wishes to be assured, one way or another, in the briefest possible time, whether and how soon he can obtain foreign troops for colonial service in America. To this end I am sending two couriers with this message, one of whom you are to send back at the earliest moment you are certain troops are obtainable, without waiting for the formalities to be completed.

Lord Suffolk, Minister for Foreign Affairs to His Majesty, King George III, to Colonel William Faucitt, 14. 11. 1775

12

The relationship between Prime Minister Schlieffen and Baron Haynow couldn't have been called friendship. What bound them together was not spontaneous empathy but the memory of long years in which only their shrewdness had saved them from becoming enemies. Those years of wordless battle had brought them to a point where each knew the other as well as he knew himself. Even so, the distance between them had remained. They had restrained their previous enmity; now they resisted letting their trust sink into a comfortable friendship. Each could rely absolutely on the other, and they both considered that enough. There was no need to demonstrate it, either for themselves nor for others.

When Schlieffen left the Elector at the hunting lodge, he was in no mood for conversation. What he needed was fresh air and a fast horse. The two men rode toward Haynow House at a sharp trot. The night was dark, the sky had clouded over. There was as yet no sign that a cold wintry storm was brewing high above the clouds; only an occasional opening in the overcast revealed the night sky, its icy blue giving lie to the warm evening air.

"To judge by my son's temper, the weather's going to change," Haynow said. "Claus's game leg is hurting him. Unless my wife can pull off a miracle, he won't make it to the Elector's dinner tonight."

"You've spoken to Claus about the marriage?"

"I've only hinted at it. There's no hurry. I'm sure he'll see the advantages."

Schlieffen slowed his horse. "I'd prefer to miss that dinner myself. There's no worse spectacle than an intelligent man sinking to the level of a vegetable. A monument to indolence, that's what he's become. What plans he had when he took the throne fifteen years ago! He had political ideas of the first magnitude, the kind that make history. The League of Small States, as a third power between Austria and Prussia. A fine idea, and he was the man to realize it, too. He had everything it takes: intelligence, enthusiasm, unscrupulousness, ambition, the lust for power. Only one quality was lacking: tenacity. He shies at every hurdle, and doesn't have the patience for subterfuge. Now all he's good for is stuffing himself and his women."

Haynow laughed. "A favorite occupation of crowned heads, not excluding the mightiest, with a colorful tradition behind it."

"You should have been there tonight. It's impossible to reason with him anymore. In five minutes he spent a hundred thousand talers he hasn't got. If my presence hadn't embarrassed him, he'd have made it twice as much. A French ballerina for ten thousand, a whole new ballet company, a glassed-in conservatory with exotic plants and animals for the Sonsfeld girl, an Academy of Arts for Tischbein, the painter. Is this the man whose services I entered fifteen years ago? It's getting to be a monumental bore to plug the holes he keeps making in what we laughingly refer to as our annual budget."

Haynow had seen Schlieffen in such moods before. He didn't take all this too seriously. "I can't imagine a deficit you can't handle," he said.

Schlieffen shook his head. "Be careful, Haynow. Take my advice. Put all your gold and silver coins in a safe place. Our currency is about to be adulterated, like the Prussians'. I don't know who gave him the idea, but it'll be difficult to talk him out of it. 'Thirty-per-cent-talers' is his latest magic formula. He emptied a bag of them on the table, and you should have seen his eyes glitter."

Haynow wondered if Schlieffen were hinting at something, fishing for information, but the tone of anger was too genuine.

"I've worked out a plan for putting our economy and our finances on a sound basis," Schlieffen said, "but he won't hear of it. All he can think about is the shingles that have to come down from the roofs. A decree about fifty farmhouses! All the shingles in Ramswood have to be replaced with tile by the end of December. Under penalty of law. He's taken to behaving like one of those savage chieftains whose leadership rests only on his potency —the more wives and brats, the more power and glory."

"I'm curious about tonight," Haynow said. "I've never seen him do his mating dance before. The Sonsfelds will be there won't they? By the way, your piece of jewelry came. Remind me to give it to you."

"If she were my daughter, he'd never get her, you can count on that. What he needs is someone to say no to him, just once. It might shake him up a little. Everyone's always knuckling under to him, no matter how absurd his carryings-on, and I'm as guilty as the rest. It was inevitable he'd become what he is today. A tree that's never pruned finally bears only bad fruit."

"There'd be a lot to prune, and not only in Hessia-Kassel."

"I know, I know, but it's no good comparing him with the others. When a character like the Count of Anspach shoots a chimney sweep off a roof because his mistress wanted to see the man do a somersault, well, everybody knows the man is feeble-minded. There are always a few cretins who happen to inherit a crown. So much the worse that a man of exceptional abilities like Frederick II of Hessia-Kassel should behave not much better." Schlieffen had clearly worked himself into a state of high prophetic wrath. "You and I may not live to see it, but I tell you the day is coming when the people will rebel against all this and demand their share of the world. Not yet, maybe—there are still too many men like you and me, with too much to lose. But fifty years from now it might be interesting to see what our German princelings and their third-rate imitations of Versailles will look like."

"I'll never make it, but you might, Schlieffen. We'll have a drink on it. I told them to chill the Gondorfer White."

"Are we riding a different way than usual, Haynow? I just noticed. . . ."

"Big Hoym and his gang are making the area unsafe again. We're better off here, on the open road."

"Over there, that village looks new to me."

"You really haven't been here in a long time, Schlieffen. That's Heron Island. The lights are temporary, for the men preparing for the hunt tomorrow. Once we're past that clump of trees ahead, you'll see the bridge, too."

"I wish you hadn't mentioned it. Building a bridge for one day's hunting!"

The road began to climb, giving them a better view of the grassy riverbanks below. At the approach to the bridge, a four-yard-wide strip of turf had been removed and replaced with fine, light-colored gravel. On the other side of the bridge, a bonfire lighted a large cleared area surrounded by tents, pavilions, and brightly colored booths.

"Have they torn up the whole island like this?" Schlieffen asked.

"Wouldn't it be a huge joke if all this fuss drove the herons off the island altogether? What do you think Stein might have up his sleeve to save the day in such an emergency? A ballet of mermaids?"

"Watch your tongue, Haynow. The word 'ballet' is sacrosanct these days. And Stein is a pest, but if I sent him to the devil there'd only be another to take his place. Possibly somebody worse."

The lighted windows of the ferryman's house shimmered through the alder trees. One of the lights began suddenly to move. A man came shouting and waving across the riverbank, carrying a lantern.

"If you want to know what the weather'll be like for the hunt tomorrow, here's the man who can tell you," Haynow said, as the ferryman came up to them. "What's up, Ludolf? Trouble with the workmen?"

"It's your island, sir, not mine. If you don't mind them turning it into a fairground. . . ."

Schlieffen came forward.

"Here's somebody who'd like to know about the weather tomorrow," Haynow said to the ferryman.

"Snow, I expect," said Ludolf without hesitation.

"That'll be rough on the falcons, I'm afraid," Haynow said.

"Will the ground be frosted over?" Schlieffen asked.

"Not enough to matter. It'll be a mild winter this year."

"How do you know?"

"The hedgehogs and the crickets would have dug in deeper, otherwise." Ludolf raised his lantern. "I've got someone in my house who's waiting for you."

Schlieffen and Haynow exchanged a glance. "Waiting for Minister Schlieffen and myself?" Haynow asked.

"For both of you."

13

Count Sonsfeld, leaning against the door of the ferryman's house, took one last drag on his cigar. He drew the smoke deep into his lungs and exhaled slowly. Then he threw the butt to the ground and crushed it with the tip of his boot. While he was smoking he had ceased to notice the strong odor from his uniform; now it grew stronger again. It reminded him, rather pleasantly than otherwise, not of the bunches of herbs hanging in the closets at Sonsfeld Castle to protect the clothes from moths, but of Buckingham Palace. He had last worn his general's uniform the day King George III of England had awarded him the Knight's Garter. It was nearly fifteen years ago, but it felt like yesterday. He didn't feel an hour older. Right after the ceremony he had had a rendezvous with a married woman, a duchess. The things one remembered! She had been neither young nor beautiful, but no other woman had ever made time pass as she had, with her wonderful crazy whims. That day she had suddenly decided she had to know his exact measurements. She had measured him with her lilac-colored silk ribbon, on which she noted the figures in red ink. She gave the whole business the air of a magic rite, and when she finished she announced that his body would always remain as it was that day, that age would not alter it.

As Haynow and Schlieffen approached on their horses, Sonsfeld stepped out of the light coming from the doorway. He was the last man they would be expecting to see here. Not all of their dealings were conducted with the blessing of the Elector's chancellory; not even Haynow's private office would do for certain negotiations. Whatever was going through their minds, they were undoubtedly suffering a certain amount of uneasiness and suspense. The two men had dismounted. Ludolf led them forward with his lantern. Sonsfeld could almost smell their uneasiness. Not even the memory of his English duchess could have made him feel better.

"Ludolf, raise that lantern, so the gentlemen can see they have nothing to fear from this ambush."

"Count Sonsfeld!" the two men exclaimed in open amazement.

Sonsfeld took a step forward. "It was not a simple problem. The distance to your place was too far, not to mention the question of prestige. For you, for the same reason, even half the way to my place would have been too far. Well, I find my solution is acceptable. I think what I have to discuss with you is worth the couple of steps from the road."

Haynow could not shake off his sense of unreality. He had for too long thought of Count Sonsfeld, when he thought of him at all, as an old man who hardly ever got out of his armchair any more, disabled by gout so crippling that, according to rumor, he could no longer even hold up his books, but had to read them piecemeal, page by cutout page. At last he pulled himself together. "If it's about the island," he said, "the deadline for meeting my terms was ten days ago. It's too late now."

"My dear Haynow. That's all past and done with. Let us talk about the future. Since it seems we'll be entering into some kind of loose family relationship—without my approval, I'd like to emphasize—and that we'll be seeing each other from time to time, for example at the hunt dinner tonight, why shouldn't we begin right now? A kind of private rehearsal."

"The contact between our families was broken off by you," Haynow said. "No one has seen you since then."

"Ah well, the sun shines as prettily on Sonsfeld Castle as it does anywhere, you know. Since you were so kind as to relieve me of most of my responsibilities, little by little, including a good deal of annoyance, inconvenience, and the like, I took the occasion to hibernate a bit. Then suddenly I woke up and found I had a marriageable daughter. Not only that, along with my breakfast I'm served a son-in-law and various accompaniments as well. All a man can do is hope the originators of this scheme haven't made an error in their calculations somewhere. Money is subject to calculation, even money one hasn't got; but people? Look out for your sons, Haynow. Claus may do what you want, but your stepson?"

"What about Robert?" Haynow controlled himself with difficulty.

"Whatever kind of a man that gold-maker was, there was one time he made gold all right. When he conceived his son. My daughter seems to think so, anyway. If his brother has to play cuckold for the Elector, Robert may restore the family honor by helping the Elector to some horns of his own. I'm no prophet, but if I know Robert, that's just the kind of thing he'd do. My daughter, anyway, wouldn't make it very difficult for him."

"Is this what you were waiting to tell me?"

Sonsfeld raised a hand, smiling. "My dear fellow! My old tutor taught me that trivia was the only proper subject of conversation in the foyer. Won't you come inside?" And without waiting for an answer he turned and led the way into the cottage, with a young man's confident springy step.

What sort of tomfoolery was this? Was the man senile, wasting their time over some trifle he took to be a matter of state—or was there really something of importance involved? Neither Schlieffen nor Haynow knew the man well enough to guess. For years they had thought of him only as a recluse in a crumbling old castle. Schlieffen had thought he had only the mother to deal with in the Sonsfeld affair; what disturbed him most was the evidence that he had overlooked so serious a factor in it.

Ludolf struck a fresh candle in the brass candlestick on the table and went into the next room, which held by far the greater part of the cast-iron stove that heated both rooms. There was the sound of a damper being opened and the shaking of the coal grate. Sonsfeld pushed the candlestick to one side. "As I say, it seems I've awakened from my hibernation just in time, and I intend to profit from the situation being so zealously arranged for my daughter."

Schlieffen began to breathe again. Sonsfeld's putting his cards on the table like this was both a relief and a disappointment. He had begun to expect something surprising, something unusual. Now it seemed the man only wanted his share of the pimp's fee for selling his daughter. "What do you have in mind, Count?" he said.

"Much as I've been tempted to demand the return of my lands which you, Baron Haynow, have so cleverly managed to incorporate into your own—the fact is, I'm no estates-manager. Fields appeal to me only when an army has erected its tents on them, and oxen only when they are pulling cannon." He stared into the flame of the candle; in his eyes a young cadet's dreams of adventure. "I'm a restless man. At present, I'm out of my element. The most beautiful castle, the most splendid palace—nothing compares with an army camp in the field: fires by night, patrols, plans for battle. In short, what I want is a command as a general."

Schlieffen had his surprise after all. His disdain of a moment ago was transformed into curiosity, as always when he encountered originality in a man. "As long as you don't demand a war from me too, the command is yours."

"I mean an actual active command in the field. As for a war, I won't trouble you about that. I'm in a position to rustle one up for myself." He rose and went to the door through which the ferryman had disappeared. He opened it a crack. "Roworth," he said, "you may come in now."

A young, red-haired officer stepped hesitantly into the room. Sonsfeld took his arm and led him to the table. "This is Lieutenant Roworth, Officer of the English Crown and Confidential Courier on a mission for Lord Suffolk, His Majesty King George III's Minister for Foreign Affairs."

Roworth gave a military bow. Sonsfeld pointed to a chair.

Schlieffen could tell by the way the English officer sat down that he must have spent the last forty-eight hours in the saddle. His mission apparently was not only confidential but urgent as well. And it was Sonsfeld to whom he had been sent! That there was close contact between the Court of St. James and Sonsfeld was not news to Schlieffen. He knew about the lively exchange of letters, if not about their content; maybe that was one sin of omission he was about to pay for now.

Count Sonsfeld pulled his chair closer to the table. "Before Lieutenant Roworth gives you the details, I would like to explain the situation. I assume you're aware of the rebels' activities in America?" Haynow and Schlieffen exchanged a look. "In England the tea riots weren't taken seriously at first. Even when the rebels appointed a certain General Washington their Commander in Chief, no one paid much attention in England. As you so rightly pointed out, my dear Schlieffen, one general doesn't make a war, and certainly does not win a war."

"May we get to the point?" Schlieffen rarely showed impatience so openly. "I'm fully aware of all this." He turned to Haynow. "There hasn't been an opportunity for me to tell you about it. That fellow Washington made good use of his chances as an outsider. He won a few skirmishes, around Lexington, nothing much actually, but by the time the news came, a bit exaggerated, to

London, it was a shock." He smiled. "Tobacco prices will be going up."

Sonsfeld was in no mood to let Schlieffen take over. "The troops are in winter quarters. But a campaign is planned for the summer of '76. Except that troops are lacking. I assume you know about the attempts of the English ambassador in Moscow to acquire troops from Empress Catherine?"

"Yes, I've been informed, in detail," Schlieffen said. "A contingent of twenty thousand men. At seven pounds sterling per man, plus subsidies, half to be paid in advance, the second half at embarkation. The contract should be signed any day now."

Sonsfeld nodded, looking pleased with himself. "Your information service is famous. Nevertheless, there will be no contract with Catherine. The Empress has refused, categorically—a turn of events the English have good reason to keep to themselves. Do you understand now? They've got to have troops, and they hope to get them where they've done business before."

Schlieffen jumped to his feet. The room seemed suddenly too small. He'd heard the rumors buzzing around all the royal courts in Germany and knew that the princelings—Waldeck, Zerbst, Anspach, and the rest—wouldn't hesitate to fill their empty treasuries through the sale of troops. But he hadn't taken it seriously, since negotiations were already in progress in Moscow. If Sonsfeld's information was correct, immense possibilities were opening up. His informants had indeed done shabby work.

"Are you sure?" Schlieffen asked.

Sonsfeld turned to Lieutenant Roworth. "Your turn now. You may speak frankly. This is strictly among ourselves." Roworth tried to begin, but couldn't seem to find the right words. "No need to speak French, Lieutenant; we all understand English here."

Roworth smiled, nodded with relief, and began to unbutton his tunic. Underneath he wore, from the hip to halfway up his chest, some kind of leather armor. "As Count Sonsfeld said, our government wishes to enter into immediate negotiations with the German authorities. Head of our mission and plenipotentiary is Colonel William Faucitt."

Schlieffen lifted a hand. "Will Colonel Faucitt approach the Elector of Hessia-Kassel officially?"

"Empress Catherine's refusal struck us like a lost battle. To avoid a recurrence, Colonel Faucitt is traveling incognito. He will act officially only when he has firm assurances that he will get his troops. This is why I was ordered to make contact with Count Sonsfeld."

This courier was really a godsend, and Schlieffen decided it was time to become diplomatic. It would be up to him how much this deal would be worth. In the monotone that had worn down many a negotiator he said, "Your Colonel Faucitt—could he be the same man who was on the personal staff of your Crown Prince during the Seven Years' War?"

"Yes, sir. He was chosen for this undertaking because he knows Germany and has personal friends at many of the courts."

Schlieffen nodded. That was another stroke of luck. Faucitt was the most untypical English officer he had ever met: a worker ant, tireless, industrious, conscientious, selfless. A man of many virtues, each one sufficient to undermine his position in the kind of negotiations involved. His worst flaw was his unshakable conviction that every man who was friendly to him was as honest and unselfish as he himself was. This man would be putty in his hands. "I'm glad King George put the matter into such good hands," he said.

Sonsfeld leaned across the table and said, in German, "You don't have to pretend indifference in front of me, Schlieffen. I'm perfectly aware of how much this news means to you. And you, Haynow—I beg your pardon, Baron Haynow—I'm sure you see the possibilities for contracts to supply the new troops—food, supplies, wheat, leather goods, uniforms, arms and ammunition. If I remember right, the end of the Seven Years' War left you sitting on a mountain of hardtack and cloth for uniforms. If you still have the stuff, it could be worth its weight in gold now."

Haynow laughed aloud. "The King of England has a fine advocate in you, Sonsfeld. Or is it a budding family feeling that has so sharpened your eye for my advantage?"

"How large a force will you need?" Schlieffen interjected.

"No upper limit has been set," Roworth said.

But Schlieffen, to Sonsfeld's growing annoyance, refused to show the slightest enthusiasm. "As regards the number of troops our Elector can put at his Majesty's disposal, I cannot at the moment make any promises. I do hope Count Sonsfeld has not aroused expectations we may be in no position to fulfill. What England requires is extremely unusual, and I understand the Empress Catherine's reluctance only too well. To transport troops across an ocean, to a foreign continent, where they will be out of contact with their homeland, is unprecedented. To keep replacing losses in troop strength over such distances is difficult. These are just a few of the practical problems, not to mention the Elector's unpredictable temperament. I shall have to approach him very cautiously about this."

The word *hypocrite* lay on Sonsfeld's tongue, but he forced himself to swallow it. This was no time to make an enemy of Schlieffen. Far better to learn from him.

Schlieffen perceived Sonsfeld's inner struggle and warmed to the man. Inborn slyness repelled him, but he respected a man's ability to use his intelligence. He turned to Lieutenant Roworth. "When may we expect Colonel Faucitt?"

"The Colonel left Stade on November 24th, some time after I left. He should be in Braunschweig by now."

"You're negotiating with Braunschweig?" Schlieffen said abruptly. "That makes my work a bit harder. The Elector will not be pleased to hear he's not the first to be approached."

"Those talks are being held in absolute secrecy," Roworth hastened to say.

"Which other German courts are involved in this?"

"At the moment, none that I know of."

"Better inform Faucitt he would do well to cancel any dealings with others."

"In that case, may I tell him that Kassel is prepared to negotiate?"

Schlieffen turned to Sonsfeld. "I assume Lieutenant Roworth is your personal guest?"

Sonsfeld nodded.

"I shall inform you within forty-eight hours whether the Elector is prepared to negotiate with Colonel Faucitt."

The men rose from their chairs. Sonsfeld called to Ludolf to get the horses ready. Haynow was the first to leave the cottage. Sonsfeld and Schlieffen stopped on the threshold. "Forty-eight hours is a long time," Sonsfeld said.

"You are free to approach the Elector personally," Schlieffen said coolly. "As long as you let me know. You had better decide whether we're to be allies or rivals in this matter."

Sonsfeld measured Schlieffen with the glance of an old man who is really only testing the flaws of another to see if they remind him of his own. "It's a good thing I'm nearly twenty years older than you," he said quietly, "but as it is you have an ally in me."

Schlieffen regretted his brusqueness. Actually he envied Sonsfeld. This man possessed the freedom he himself had lost. Nothing about him was disguised. Sonsfeld was straight as the two furrows on his high forehead. "I'll see you at dinner then," he said amicably.

As different as Haynow and Schlieffen were in temperament, they were both taciturn men. They rode the distance from the ferryman's house to the Haynow estate in complete silence, each busy with his own thoughts.

Schlieffen considered the troop situation in Hessia. Five thousand men were immediately available. Another seven thousand could be drummed together in another two months, if he scoured the prisons and the poorhouses, netted every vagrant on the roads, mobilized his recruiters to send swarms of press gangs combing the country. In Moscow the English had offered seven pounds sterling per man. They would have to do better than that for him. The English needed troops, and they were in a hurry. That gave him considerable leverage.

Schlieffen had been studying earlier contracts involving the sale of troops. In the last few months, since it had come to skirmishing in America, they had become part of his reading matter. He was thoroughly prepared, even to having calculated in which currency he should demand payment. Probably it would be a good idea to have the money paid into a London or Amsterdam bank, so it would be out of reach of the Elector and could bring in interest. Though, on second thought, placing the actual cash out of reach would never stop the Elector from scattering money to the four winds.

The night sky became for Schlieffen a huge slate, on which an invisible hand wrote glowing sums. Sixty crowns per man, including officers; there had to be a way to get the English to funnel the money through his hands. He would demand double the usual subsidy for the duration of the war. With 12,000 men at 37½ crowns per head, that made 450,000 crowns—772,600 talers per year, plus interest. The English would accept his terms. They had no choice. Besides, they didn't expect the war to last. There, he would have to depend on his own nose and luck. If the war lasted only a year, then it would be a mistake to demand double the subsidy in wartime, with no continuance in peace time. But if the war dragged on, he would make a profit of sixty thousand pound sterling per year; in ten years, four million talers.

A cool ecstasy seized him. He could already see it in front of him, his masterpiece, the ultimate contract; he could feel the paper, chosen by himself, he could feel the pen in his hand, ready for the signature. The farmers in his Pomeranian homeland had a legend that on certain nights of the new moon a whole crop could ripen at once. This was his night, and the crop that he saw ripening was gold.

14

Anna Haynow had given her servants the evening off. She would be alone and unobserved. Once more she glanced around the room, but there was nothing there to keep her, nothing to help her do what she would have to do. Her new dress for the dinner at the hunting lodge was draped on her dressmaker's dummy. In the dim, flickering light from the candlestick she held in her hand, the brownish-pink silk shimmered like red gold. On the table lay her gloves—one of twenty pairs she had bought from the Austrian glover Balthasar Ploetz—her fan, her open jewel case, all laid out in readiness by her maid this afternoon, like a fashion display.

Anna closed the door behind her and hurried along the hallway, one hand shielding the candle flame. She stopped on the top stair, listening to the grandfather clock striking down in the vestibule, amazed to find it was nine o'clock already. Time, lately, had ceased to be an orderly succession of hours and days, and had become an uninterrupted stream that dissolved the walls between yesterday and today, making past, present, and future seem equally far away. She gathered up her dress in her left hand and descended the stairs.

The door to the counting room was not locked. On the table lay business papers in readiness for the coming day; there were three freshly filled inkwells and the large, flat penholder full of quills. She took the key out of her pocket and opened the door to her husband's private office. Here, too, everything was prepared for the next day, the fireplace was newly swept, fresh logs laid, a supply of beech logs was piled in the brass woodbox.

She put the candle on the desk and knelt to light the fire. The kindling of pine needles under the logs caught fire quickly; the flames crackled and flared. She sat here often these days, almost every evening when her husband was out. It was a good place to think things through, to make her peace with the ghosts that had come into the house with Freder Soerman. They were with her tonight, too.

She knew where the key to the cabinet was kept; the fireproof chest that was built into the cabinet had twenty-four drawers. In the third from the left in the bottom row she found the letters, three separate bundles tied with string. She pulled out the drawer and carried it to the fire without touching the letters. Then she moved the stool close to the fire and sat down with the drawer on the floor beside her. She sat staring into the fire for a while, losing her sense of time, of where she was. At last she picked up one bundle of letters. The top envelope bore her name, Anna Skelnik. The handwriting could as easily have been that of her son Robert. In the upper left-hand corner, a date, 1752, unmistakably in the hand of Gottfried Haynow.

Anna dropped the first bundle into the fire. She had imagined that it would burst into flame at once, but nothing happened for several seconds. The tight little bundle of yellowed paper lay across a glowing log, but seemed immune to the flames. Slowly the edge of the uppermost envelope began to curl upward. The handwriting faded to a rust-brown, hovered in the glow of the yellow flames: words written to her that had never reached her. There was still time to pull the letters back with the hook at the end of the poker. As if frightened by the thought, she quickly threw the other two bundles into the flames. Again it took a long time for them to catch fire. The bundles remained compact, gradually turning into a gray-red glowing brick. She prodded at them with the poker. Suddenly the string fell away, and what had looked like a glowing coal fell apart into a bouquet of white leaves with rust-red and brown edges, autumn colors. The writing was the veining on those leaves. She watched as the leaves caught fire one by one, moved as with an individual life of their own, dissolved into flying sparks and gray ashes.

There were hoofbeats coming up the drive. It could only be Haynow, bringing Schlieffen. From the driveway they could see the lighted office window; there was still time to blow out the candle, pour sand on the fire until it guttered out, lock up the secret safe. She could find her way back to her room in the dark.

But she remained seated in front of the fire, on the wooden stool, her arms around her knees, gazing into the fire and waiting.

He had stopped at the door, and she let him take his time. In his face, usually so full of energy even when he was asleep, she saw only defenselessness.

His eyes went to the open door of the cabinet, to the drawer on the floor beside her. "How long have you known?" he asked finally.

"Do you remember the young man who ran off with Robert Skelnik?"

"Freder Soerman?"

"When I learned Soerman was alive, I assumed the account of Skelnik's death could not be trusted either."

Why is she sparing me, he wondered. Although he could guess what she would say, he asked her nonetheless. "How did you find out?"

"He was here. Freder Soerman was in this house. He was the deserter who fled from the fortress."

"And you kept it to yourself for three weeks?"

"Three weeks is a long time, but you have managed to keep things to yourself for twenty years. All these years you knew, and lived alone with your knowledge. Day after day you were in this room, day after day you used this cabinet, with all those papers in in it." She looked at him for the first time since he had arrived. "There's just one thing I don't understand: why did you keep these letters at all?"

He made a vague gesture. "Does it matter now?"

She looked into the fire. "At first I wanted you to be the one to burn them."

"Did you read them?"

"No," she said, her voice rising for the first time. "I didn't read them, not now, not after all these years. I burned them the way they were, and I did it not for my sake, but for Robert's. At least this one thing he could be spared from learning."

"Then he knows the rest?"

"Yes."

"Was it you who told him?"

"There was no way to avoid it, or maybe there was, I don't know. Robert took Soerman over the border. I expected him to come to me afterward and tell me about it; there never used to be any secrets between us. This time he didn't come. I have no idea what the two of them talked about. But Robert seems different since then, and it worries me."

Haynow picked up the drawer from the floor, carried it back to the cabinet, and locked it away. He suddenly remembered what Sonsfeld had said: "Money is subject to calculation, even money one hasn't got, but people? . . ." There sat his wife, in front of the fire, on the low wooden stool. He could see the lines of her slim back under the light dress. Copper lights glinted in her hair. He had seen her that way twenty years before, as he had gone over the estate books at the desk in this room, at the old Elector's behest. Then, too, he had felt that her decision was already made, without knowing whether it was for or against him.

He spoke haltingly, he who was never at a loss for words. "I have no excuse, perhaps an explanation, the only one I can offer: I wanted you. The day before our wedding I came dangerously close to giving you the letters. If I had, I'd have lost you then. This fear was always with me. Someday, I said to myself, you'll come home and she'll be gone. Strange, today too, riding home, the old fear suddenly came over me. I have never felt sure of you. It was always the same as in the beginning—all of it, the fear, and the love."

"I haven't asked you to justify yourself."

"What else can I do? The cold facts are that our marriage was conditional upon proof of your husband's death. But by the time we married I had already intercepted half a dozen of his letters and knew that he was alive—our marriage, accordingly, is invalid *de jure* and *de facto*. You are still his wife."

Her back straightened, her head went up, but she did not turn to him. "You are reacting just as I expected," she said.

He would have liked to see her face, but at the same time he was afraid to look.

"You are right," she said. "If you had shown me those letters the day before our wedding, I would have been on my way to him an hour later. You had no other way of keeping me. Even so, you did not besiege me, you did not try to make me forget. You never said a word about the past, about what was behind me, the business about his laboratory, his flight, my decision to follow him to America. There were many things you could have said against him. But you said nothing. You knew that I loved him. I shall never understand that you wanted me for your wife nevertheless. Nor shall I ever understand why you burdened yourself with so much guilt, when there was so little hope for you. You must have understood me better than I did myself. I never thought about any of these things until now. These last three weeks I've thought about nothing else."

What could he do but wait? He still did not know what she had decided to do. He could not imagine her leaving him, and yet he could not imagine how she could stay with him, after this.

She rose to her feet. "It took me three weeks before I could bring myself to burn these letters, and then it wasn't even difficult. It was only paper, and now it's only ashes, and ashes do not outweigh twenty years of life by your side. What the other life would have been like, the one you took from me, I don't know."

He was uncertain whether he understood her words rightly. But he could not bear this uncertainty moment longer. "Are you trying to tell me in this complicated way that you forgive me?"

Seconds ticked by, seconds during which he believed that he had lost her irrevocably. He shut his eyes when she began to speak again.

"Your explanation of how you and I are not man and wife seemed far more complicated to me."

He did not see her face, but he suddenly felt that her eyes were filled with that sad, warm smile that had made him fall in love with her in the first place. She seemed to want to turn to him, but stopped midway, as though she lacked the courage. He went to her, and the rest happened by itself. He put his arms around her shoulders. Words seemed to come of their own accord, without his having to think. "It was November, here in this room. You looked like someone who had suffered a grave illness. I asked you to show me the park, and I saw how everything reminded you of him. I had no illusions; I understood that I had an unconquerable rival, a rival who could no longer do any wrong. Still, you were not the kind of woman who would cling at all costs to the past. I was very sure of that. You have a strong nature, and the strong do not live in their yesterdays. That is what I staked my life on. It was only when Robert was growing up that I fully realized what kind of memories I had working against me."

She had listened to him with bowed head. Now she looked up and nodded. Had she been alone, she wouldn't have been able to hold back the tears. Tears for the man with whom she had known a brief time of immeasurable happiness, and tears for the man at whose side she had lived for more than twenty years.

"I feel like having a bite to eat," she said. "What would you say to a cucumber sandwich and a glass of milk?"

"You remember that?" he said, surprised.

"We were in the park, and when we came back we went to the kitchen. I'm not sure we can find such simple things here today, in Gilbert's domain."

"So much has changed. It's no longer the same kitchen."

"Nor are we the same."

"Does that mean I no longer have a rival?"

"None apart from your sons."

He longed to draw her close, to hold her in his arms, but it would have brought something into this moment that did not belong. It was an important moment in their lives, perhaps the most important, but the rule that lived within them was not warmth, but endurance.

Later, in the kitchen, watching her buttering the bread, slicing the cucumbers, sprinkling salt on them, he suddenly recalled Sonsfeld's remark about Robert. "Do you have any idea whether there's something going on between Robert and Christina Sonsfeld?"

She arranged the open sandwiches on the wooden board. She was glad they had found their way back so easily to everyday things. "The only lasting love affair of his I know of is the one with a Scottish governess at the Court in Kassel. That's been going on for years. Robert has no problems in that area. Women seem to make things easy for him, and he makes things easy for himself, too. I think he has a real talent for painless partings. A girl like Christina Sonsfeld—I believe he'd take care not to become involved. So far anyway. Why do you ask? From what I hear lately, the young lady's ambitions are pointing in quite another direction."

"Shall we say, rather, her mother's ambitions."

"That's the same thing. It was always the mother's will that prevailed at Sonsfeld Castle. I'd be more inclined to suspect some such inclination in Claus. He doesn't tell me these things as openly as Robert does—but if I'm not mistaken, Claus has noticed how the little Sonsfeld girl has suddenly blossomed. As long as he was only a commoner, he'd never have dared to let his thoughts stray in that direction. He would rather have died of his hopeless love; but now he may feel the road is clear."

"When I spoke with him, he never let on in the least," Haynow said thoughtfully. "It's like this: a prerequisite for making the Sonsfeld girl the Elector's official mistress is that she be a married woman, a so-called marriage of convenience. Schlieffen thought it might be the thing for Claus. That's why I asked you about Robert."

"Is that why you were made a baron so suddenly?"

"It could have played a part."

"Then Claus knows about it?"

"I spoke to him about it, confidentially, so to speak. Schlieffen would like the Elector to make the choice himself, which is one of the reasons he had me come to the hunting lodge today. But all that happened was that I spent two long hours in the antechamber, listening to Secretary Voss's grievances. When I think that I myself was one of these Court flunkies once. . . ."

"If Claus agrees to this arrangement, it'll mean a rapid promotion for him, won't it? But in peacetime even that ultimately leads to nothing better than some position at Court. What would you do if you were in Claus's shoes?"

"To be quite honest, my first reaction was to think of it as a kind of insurance on the sums the Elector owes me. As long as I'm merely another creditor, I can be dropped from one day to the next; it's been known to happen, especially as a way of canceling out his debt. The marriage of my son to the ruler's mistress would make such a move on his part very unlikely."

"If Claus is prepared to regard the matter in this light. . . . But, remember, he's a Haynow. When one of your breed takes possession of something, he wants it all. How did he respond when you told him about it?"

"After what you've just told me I'm amazed how calmly he took it. He seemed to be entirely in favor of it. But if he wanted the girl for himself. . . ."

"That makes it complicated, doesn't it?"

"I'll have a talk with Schlieffen. It's still possible, I'm sure, to get out from under. Schlieffen'll find a way." There was a deep furrow between his eyebrows. "Will you try, anyway, to find out if there's something going on between Robert and Christina? Whether it's Robert or Claus—I'd like to avoid trouble if possible."

"Who gave you the idea?"

"I have it from old Sonsfeld himself."

"Oh, is he still alive? Where did you meet him—was he sitting in the Elector's antechamber with you?"

"He's getting a command as a general again."

"At least they're not giving their daughter away. Is that command part of the bargain his wife made?"

"No, I suspect she knows nothing about that yet. We met only an hour ago, on the way back from the hunting lodge. He was lying in wait for us at the ferryman's house by the river—in his general's uniform. Time has left no mark on him. Not a sign of the rumored gout. And he asked Schlieffen outright for his command."

"How does Schlieffen handle that sort of thing, I wonder."

"He's a seasoned military man and, as such, he prefers an open attack to the sly maneuverings at Court. Sonsfeld will get his command, all right." Haynow took the last of the sandwiches. "We ought to do this kind of thing more often."

"It may be our only refuge from the social whirl awaiting us in Kassel." She poured more milk into his glass.

"Are you wearing your new dress tonight?"

"Of course." She smiled that he should be concerned about that now.

He took her hand. "Just a while ago, in my office, when I thought I'd lost you, all I could think of was your room, deserted but for the manikin with your dress on it, a dress no one was ever going to wear."

She gave him only a long, wordless look in reply.

"The carriages will be ready at half past ten," he said. "Suppose I take Claus and Schlieffen in mine, and you take Robert."

"I can't promise I'll find out anything," she said. "Robert will wonder why his mother is suddenly so curious about his private life."

15

Snowflakes sank very slowly through the blue air. Robert stood at his open window, watching the lone heron, barely discernible as it gained altitude. He had discovered it that morning, coming from the river, flying low over the fields and then disappearing in ever widening circles toward the north. Only half an hour ago it was back again, circling, searching. He was sure now that he read the signs right. He took the rifle that lay on his windowsill and went out.

From the courtyard came the nasal voice of Steward Lange. "Shouldn't we hitch up the sleighs?"

"Absolutely not!" Gottfried Haynow called back.

"If it keeps on snowing like this . . ."

"The carriages, please!" Haynow sounded irritated. "We're ready to leave now. We don't want to wait till there's enough snow for the sleighs."

Adrian met Robert midway down the hall, carrying one of the big wicker suitcases. "Which clothes are to be taken to Kassel?"

"I'll leave it to you. You may keep all the things in the small closet for yourself."

Adrian stared at him. "But that's crammed full of things."

Robert went on without answering. A chill wind blew in from the open front door. The hall was crowded with trunks, suitcases, boxes. Mrs. Retz stood atop a ladder tying linen covers around sconces and chandeliers. Steward Lange, dressed in an ankle-length coat with a high stand-up collar, stalked up and down the corridors supervising the servants who were dragging the luggage to the coaches outside. He bowed as Robert came by. "Won't you reconsider riding horseback all the way to Kassel? Winter is here."

"The sun will be out again in a few minutes." Robert stepped outside.

The groom who stood ready beside Robert's horse pulled off the blanket that lay across the animal's back. While folding it up he winked at Robert. "Steward Lange personally put that blanket on him."

"He just likes me, that's all."

A servant came running from the house with Robert's coat. Robert threw it on the saddle in front of him and rode off. He kept looking for the heron through the bare branches of the trees, but he could make nothing out in the heavy, slanting snow. Large flakes were melting on the sorrel's rump. A feeling of exuberance rose up in him as always with the first snow of the year. The white summer. That was what he'd named it when he was three years old, and in that phrase was expressed the pleasure he found in winter, this feeling of being intensely alive that overcame him with the first crackling frost.

Outside the gate he saw a heavily muffled rider galloping toward him—by the way he held himself, it was Claus. They reined to a halt facing each other, the horses capering and snorting. Claus pushed up his three-cornered hat. "Down with a fever yesterday, and out in a driving snowstorm with your jacket open today."

"Yesterday was the hunt. Today it's over."

"I should have known. Your absence was an insult to the Elector. But for you even Mother's capable of lying."

"I'm surprised you missed me. When I come, you're always worried I'll do something to embarrass you."

"Your obsession with that island is embarrasing."

Robert picked up his reins, ready to ride on.

"And where are you going with that gun?" Claus asked.

"After the last hunt I found two wounded birds."

"Are you coming back to Haynow?"

Robert shook his head.

"If you ride all the way to Kassel like that, you'll have the fever tomorrow you pretended to have yesterday."

"And well worth it, if that'll satisfy your passion for the truth. But I won't guarantee it." Robert gave his horse the spurs. After a whole day indoors he craved movement, and his sorrel seemed to feel the same way.

The sky was clearing; a sheaf of rays fanned out through an

opening in the blue-gray clouds. The snow began to let up, then finally stopped altogether. A network of fine white lines lay over Ramswood Fortress and the woods below it. Every chimney, every windowsill, every branch seemed outlined in delicate white lace. A shadow came gliding over the southern slope—the heron. Robert thrust two fingers in his mouth and imitated the heron's throaty whistle of a call.

The bird seemed for a moment to hover motionless in place; then it glided toward him, descended, began to circle slowly as it searched. He kept luring it on down to the river, repeating the call from time to time. He had already recognized it, a strong three-year-old female which had had young twice in the last year. The sorrel followed the well-worn path across the grassy banks to the river. A thin sheet of ice along the flat bank cracked and splintered under its hooves, startling the heron; with a loud beating of wings, it vanished behind a clump of trees.

Robert forded the river. The sorrel shied when it reached the opposite bank. He patted its neck, but he, too, found the island unrecognizable; it looked like a deserted fairgrounds. Behind a band of frost-brown reeds veiled in snow and hoarfrost, the booths and pavilions had a garish, improvised look, like an abandoned stage set, though here the props were genuine and of the best: the pennants were real brocade, the heraldic beasts atop the standards real gold, the garlands wound with real silk ribbons, the tree decorations of painted silver foil. A lemon-yellow awning at one booth flapped in the wind. From its shadow a figure in a blue cape emerged and ran toward him with a happy little cry.

Christina Sonsfeld pushed the hood back from her face. She knew how lovely she looked in blue, especially on a day like this, in the pale soft light that was taking on a pink shimmer now that the sun was hidden behind hazy white clouds.

"I knew you'd come. But why weren't you at the hunt yesterday?"

"A hunt, was it? It looks more like a cheap circus."

"It was a glorious day. You don't know what you missed."

Reluctantly, Robert dismounted. He needed to be alone for what he had to do; and he was determined to get it done. But then he saw how the girl hugged herself against the cold. "Why didn't you put on something that would keep you warm?"

"I've been waiting for over an hour."

He couldn't think of anything to say that wouldn't have hurt her feelings, so he took her hands and warmed them between his own. There was a broken nail on her right hand. "How did you do that?" he said, touching the sharp, ragged edge. "Cooking or sewing?"

"I don't know." Christina looked at him. That morning on the island, when he had kissed her, had changed everything. For years it had been only infatuation, but now it was something very different. Now it was sleepless nights, days spent as if in a trance, a hunger for she did not know what, a thirst for something to extinguish the burning inside. She let herself sink against his chest.

"Aren't you confusing me with someone else?" he said dryly. "I'm the wrong Haynow."

She smiled, sure of herself, sure of her feelings. "I said yes and amen to whatever they said, to keep them from getting suspicious. This way, my mother hasn't a clue, which makes it much easier for us. The wedding's not for another ten days, so we have lots of time. What'll we do? What are your plans? I'd love to see their faces when they find out!"

He couldn't bring himself to hurt her. Her straightforwardness both impressed and disarmed him. He bit his lip. He could see it coming, the day he would marry a woman simply because he hadn't the nerve to tell her he didn't love her.

She sensed something troubling him. She feared his answer, and so she spoke before he could. "Robert, you said something the other day—something I've thought about a lot. You said a woman has only one life. Are you angry with me now for acting on it? Whatever happens now will determine my whole life. But you don't know my mother. She has her mind made up that I'm to be for the Elector—there's no way to talk her out of it. And my father just wants his peace. Neither of them knows me, neither cares about me. You're the only one who can help me."

While she spoke, Robert let go of her hands. She buried them now in the sleeves of her cape, as though aware she was being thrown on her own resources. "I always thought that once I was grown up everything would be simple. I'd marry and be free of my parents. I think I'd have married the first man who asked me."

"That's not so unusual. I know lots of girls who think only of getting married. Then, when the time comes, they get scared, afraid they're marrying the wrong man. If your parents had chosen me instead of Claus, you'd probably have run to him for help."

"Please, Robert, I don't feel like joking."

"What makes you think I'm joking?" He bent over to pluck a blade of grass. "You've known me since you were a child; I'm like a brother to you. It's natural to turn to me for advice, but what you really need is a man who loves you, and I'm not that man."

"Are you saying this because of Claus?" she asked.

I should go now, he thought; it'll only get more complicated. "Christina, I asked you the other day whether a man has ever broken your heart, ever made you go through hell."

"Why do you ask me that?"

"Because I don't think you know what love means."

"Do you have to be miserable to know what love means?"

"If you want to know—yes. To know what love is, you have to know you don't die of it and women especially have to learn that from experience. There are always a few who can't learn, but most women do. A lonely old castle is no place for a young girl. If you'd grown up in a city, it would all have been easier, you'd have been in love a dozen times by now, and you'd know what fun it is to be courted by a lot of admirers."

Christina's features seemed to harden. He was seeing her, Robert thought, the way she would look ten years from now.

"If you had been here yesterday, you'd have seen me courted by a lot of admirers. I was the center of attention, everything revolved around me."

"In Kassel, every day will be like that for you. It's what you were made for. You'll feel as if you were the only girl in the whole world."

She longed to hit back, to crush him with a word, but she

lacked the strength. Since that kiss on the island she'd been so happy, life had become so simple. To keep up pretenses with her mother had become a game, everything was a game, even yesterday's hunt. She had gloried in her secret, in the triumphant feeling of playing each person off against the others, an easy test of her inborn ability to adjust herself to circumstances and to people. An invaluable capability, she had realized during the hunt.

"It's time you rode back," she heard him say. "It wouldn't be good if they were to look for you and find you here."

Suddenly her whole body began to tremble, but not with the cold. "Tell me what to do! You don't have to marry me. But help me, please. I'll go to America with you. I'll do anything. Why do you keep looking at the sky like that?"

Robert pointed toward the clump of alders. "Can you see the heron up there? I've been watching him the whole time." As he spoke, he started to load his gun.

"What are you doing?"

"Watch and see."

"So that's what you're like! I thought you loved this island and the herons. But it's only selfishness. You don't want to share anything. You're no better than the others, you're worse. You're horrible. You've known every heron on the island since the day it was born. . . ."

"The Elector's falcons killed her mate, and now she's looking for him. She won't feed and she won't sleep, she'll just keep circling and circling, searching for him until she drops."

"I see, you can feel pity for an animal."

He began to take aim, then let the weapon sink again. "For this I need to be alone." He turned and walked away, keeping his eye on the heron.

She felt as if rooted to the spot. Once she started to leave, it was all over. As long as she stood here, as long as she could still see him, all was not lost. Robert would suddenly turn around, would come back to her.

He disappeared now into the brush, which was almost as tall as a man. The branches closed behind him, gray-black branches closing on the last shimmer of his golden hair. Then she heard the shot. It pulled her head back as if he had been hit, and she saw the heron. For one long second it hung motionless in the air, silver wings far outspread. Then the tautness melted from its body —lifeless, flopping, the bird sank and fell.

Christina closed her eyes and ran. Somehow she found her horse and forded the river. The whole way back to Sonsfeld Castle she never looked back once.

The Recruiters

The noncommissioned officer must carry a pocket pistol on every expedition, in addition to his sidearms; he must always let the new recruit precede him, never let him follow behind, never let him come too close, and make him understand that the first false step will cost him his life. Lodgings for the night must always be taken where he and other members of his troop are accustomed to stop, so that he can be sure of the innkeeper's being on his side. It is better to spend a little, if necessary, on precautionary measures, than to lose the recruit through negligence. Thus . . . a dog of the right sort can be most helpful. But such a dog must be properly trained, among other things, not to tolerate a stick in the recruit's hand; to bark the moment the recruit stirs or rises from his bed at night; to drive the recruit back into line whenever he, the recruit, steps out of line; to seize the recruit at the first sign of a leap or jump and hold him, never to let go unless ordered to do so by his master; not to let the recruit pick up anything off the ground; and, in short, trained in every skill conducive to the most efficient transport of new recruits. If the recruit shows the least sign of untrustworthiness he must be commanded to cut his braces, cut off his trouser buttons and carry the trousers in his hands.

Instructions to the Royal Prussian Infantry on Garrison Duty, Recruiting Missions, and in the field. Berlin, 1805

16

Compared with the other women at the Elector's Palace in Kassel, she looked like a child of nature—dark-haired and freckled, her brown eyes sprinkled with points of amber light. She refused to hide her hair under a wig or her freckles under thick layers of powder. Nor was there anything else about the Scottish governess Ruth Connors to indicate that she had any ambitions beyond teaching the English language to the Elector's bastard offspring.

She walked along the outside gallery in the morning sun coming through the tall windows. The marble statues in the park were boarded up, the great central fountain covered, as were the rose beds. It was January here, but in some countries it was already summer. The earth was so big, and how little of it she'd seen so far. In the little country school her father ran in Leadshill—a one-room school with only three benches in it—there had been maps printed on the walls. Every spring, after she was old enough, she helped her father freshen the colors on them. As other girls dream of marriage and children, Ruth had dreamed of some day seeing with her own eyes all the countries and oceans she drew in colored chalks on the white walls.

To leave Leadshill—that she had managed. But what had it gained her? London had been first, then Spa, and now the Court of Kassel. In a way, it was progress downhill.

Her eye lit on a breakfast tray on a side table. A pink napkin was spread over the breadbasket, but she could see the outline of Robert's favorite croissants underneath, and she could smell them. She could take them to him, but it was still too risky, it was still too far to her room—the chance of encountering somebody was too great.

When she arrived safely at the door that led from the gallery to the dark hallways of the servants' quarters, she regretted not having taken the croissants. The door swung closed behind her; the air smelled stale in the dim light. A serving cart was piled high with remnants of breakfast, but she passed it by with a look of revulsion. Any food returned from the Elector's chambers had undoubtedly been pawed and slobbered over by his dogs. She would find a way even today to get hot coffee, milk, bread, butter, and honey.

She put the school books and notebooks she was carrying on a shelf behind a curtain. The top shelf held the props for her collar and cuffs. She carefully withdrew the needle that held her lace cuff, part of a set Robert had brought her from Holland. It was more valuable than the slate-gray dress she wore.

She could hear the dumbwaiter coming up from the kitchen and smelled onions and thyme. After a while, there came the sound of steps on the circular staircase—Betty had kept her word again, even though the extra service was hard on her; she was no longer young and not in the best of health. The cold and damp were extremely bad for her. Only the other day an asthma attack had nearly caused her to faint. Ruth ran to meet her and took the food tray.

"Careful," the woman said, breathing hard. "I'm a little late, but it was worth the waiting." She wiped her brow with a corner of her apron. "The traveling knife grinder didn't show up, and I was able to get the breakfast that'd been ordered for him. None of the delivery people have showed up. Everybody's avoiding Kassel these days, even if it means not collecting on their unpaid bills. The press gangs have scared them off. The recruiters are snatching everybody they can get their hands on to supply those troops to the English."

Ruth Connors checked the tray. There was hot coffee, a pitcher of milk, croissants, brioches, almond toast, butter, cheese, ham. "Thanks, Betty. Thanks a lot."

"Better try to save some of the ham, cheese, and the black bread. I may not be this lucky next time."

"I'm afraid there won't be much left. I'd forgotten what quantities a man can eat."

Betty smoothed her apron. "It's been nearly a week, hasn't it? Don't overdo it, now. It's dangerous to risk so much for a man, and it usually doesn't pay. I'm glad to help you all I can, but don't get caught. You've seen what can happen; that poor Burchard girl is locked up in an asylum now. When it comes to the lives of his subjects, our Elector is a very moral man. You'd better go along now."

The stairs up to her attic room were so narrow she had to hold the heavy tray high above the railing. Luckily no one met her on the way. The fresh bed linen on the doormat meant it was Friday. The week had passed like a single day for her.

Friday. There was something she had to do today—she couldn't remember what. Ah yes, it was the day the woman came who brought the messages to Kassel from the country. That was the first thing Robert would ask about. She put the tray down outside the door to her room and hurried downstairs.

Betty hadn't exaggerated. The room where deliveries were accepted was empty except for a few farm women sitting behind their heavy baskets, waiting patiently for the chef's assistant. He was haggling over prices with the egg woman.

Ruth recognized the messenger woman from Robert's description—a skinny little creature despite her three petticoats and padded bodice. Her basket, filled with bunches of lavender, stood on a low stool beside her. Ruth pretended to search for lavender in the basket. "Do you have only green and yellow today?"

"What color did you want?"

"I ordered blue ones," Ruth said; it was the password Robert had made her memorize.

Life came into the old woman's eyes. "I've never yet forgotten an order," she said, rummaging in the folds of her voluminous skirt.

They had breakfast in bed, by simply setting across it an old page's bench that was as long as the bed was wide. The two of them sat buried in a mountain of covers, though Ruth kept pushing the featherbedding to one side; his greeting had made her quite warm.

Robert raised the steaming coffee cup to his lips. "Your kitchens seem to be adjusting themselves to my tastes. I've never had such good, strong coffee." He handed the cup to Ruth for a sip. There was another cup for her, but they enjoyed drinking from the same cup and eating from the same plate. "I could get to like this life," Robert said. "How long have I been here now?"

"That sounds almost like a declaration of love."

"Maybe it is. I haven't left this bed in . . . what is it, a whole week? If anybody had ever told me I'd be spending a whole week in a woman's bed. . . ."

"Don't forget the cold," she interrupted, "and my father's books. The way you buried your nose in his travel descriptions made me jealous."

He kissed her lightly on her bare shoulder and readjusted the shawl she had draped around her against the cold. "It must have been quite a decision for your father—sending his precious manuscripts across the Channel. And you say there's another batch coming?"

"Everything he could scrape together about the American West and South. I was expecting it from Hamburg today. I never expected him to part with his writings either; you're the first person in the world to lay eyes on them. My mother was always hoping some printer would persuade him to publish them."

"I'm going to have them published. At Richmond and Barker's, in Philadelphia. Yes, my love, thanks to your father I really know my way around over there. Between New York and Philadelphia I won't need to ask anybody for directions."

"When I think that he never left Leadshill, himself. In fact he hardly ever left the house except to walk to the post office, in case a packet of books had arrived for him. He stuffed our tiny house full of books. I think his geographical library is the largest private collection in all Scotland; he put every penny into it. Then he wrote his travel descriptions at night at the kitchen table, with my mother by his side, knitting. He said he needed to hear the gentle clicking of her knitting needles; they helped him concentrate his mind." She leaned back among the huge, goose-down pillows. "I owe everything to his imagination. Other little girls play with dolls; I played Robinson Crusoe. In the evenings, when his pupils were gone, the schoolroom belonged to me. My father's desk was my hut. Sometimes I fell asleep under it. If I'd been a boy, I'd certainly have gone to sea."

"You should have married a sea captain."

"Nonsense, he'd have had to be a pirate to interest me, and pirates rarely come looking for a bride in a little mining village like Leadshill. It was a pure miracle that Lady Menton strayed in our direction, and she only did it because she was looking for a present for Lord Menton and she heard of my father's map collection. Lady Menton would have paid any price, but my father wouldn't sell a single one of his maps. That really impressed her no end. So, in order not to have come such a long way for nothing, she took me back with her. She was a real bluestocking of a lady. She and her friends planned a new era the way an architect draws blueprints for a house, a new era in which women would be as free as men to develop their gifts, free to attend schools and universities, to study for the professions, and free to live the way they pleased. She was delighted to hear I was interested in seeing Germany. She got me the job in Kassel. I'm tempted to think she envied me a tiny bit when she packed me off for the Channel boat."

"Does she know you have to live in this cold garret?"

"Nobody's forcing me to stay. I could have left after a few weeks."

"But then I came along. That's the cage you women always walk into. What good is your having brains if. . . ."

She placed a hand on his lips. "Nobody forced me into that, either."

He looked at her and came close to telling her he loved her. Her words always seemed to mean more than they said. When he had first met her, he attributed this magical feeling to her foreign accent and the great care with which she chose her words—but the magic remained though her German had lost much of its foreign flavor.

He picked up the two bags of blue lavender off the tray. "So she came today. This must be Friday then. You can depend on the old Koppin woman's calendar." He felt the rough linen of the bags. One of them he put aside, then he loosened the string on the other. He drew a slip of paper out of it and handed it to Ruth. "Go on, read it to me."

"I thought it was a secret."

"Between you and me?"

Hesitantly she unfolded the paper. She had always known he would leave her one day. Every day, every hour she had tried to be prepared for it; but, now that it was happening, it seemed sudden, unexpected. In a low voice she read the message: "This afternoon at five, at Manz's house in Altenbauna." It was signed: *Freder Soerman.*

Robert took the note from her and held the paper into the candle flame.

"What kind of a man is this Freder Soerman?" she asked. "I still can't believe you want to give up everything, your heron island, your family. How is your mother going to take this?"

He wanted her to go on talking. He felt the kind of uneasy curiosity that moves a man to look into the mirror after arising from a sickbed. "If it only had been a mood," he said finally, "it would have vanished in these few days with you. But it's final. I already feel like I'm on board ship."

She drew the shawl closer around her shoulders. "I must admit, it baffles me. I've always thought of you as the kind of person whose life moves forward in a straight line, not zigzag, not broken off here and starting new there, but a life—a life like a ship that stays firmly on course."

"It's not something I expected, either. Or wanted. I don't deliberately complicate things the way my brother Claus does. He needs thunder and lightning to make him feel right. All I need right now is a dependable west wind to take me straight to America."

"And what about me? What's my part in this? Don't worry, I'm not about to complain. But I like to understand people, you more than anyone. Is it only the island, is it something to do with your real father? Or is there something else involved—an unhappy love?"

"Surely you don't really think I came to you to have my broken heart mended? You'd have known it and sent me away."

She brushed the hair back from her forehead. "You make me out to be better than I am. Where you're involved, I can even give up my pride. Only I still don't like to deceive myself—too proud for that, I like to think. When I was very young, it was always all or nothing for me. I made myself very unhappy that way. Now I take life as it comes. I accept what it can give me, even if it's only a part of the whole."

He gave her a searching look. Was it resignation or wisdom she was expressing? Neither of these was something he'd expect from her.

"The men I would have married were out of my reach," she went on, "and the men who wanted me, I didn't want. I was about to become a full-fledged eccentric when your curiosity intervened. Think how much poorer I'd be today if I had sent you away out of pride."

A silence fell. They were feeling very close, so close they shied away from even looking at each other.

"Tell me, does your decision have something to do with the rebellion in America?"

"What makes you say that?"

"All of last week I was working in the Confidential Secretary's office. Contracts between King George III and the Elector of Hessia-Kassel for troops to fight the American rebels."

"The poor devils. Luckily, I can pay my own passage."

"You have your passage booked already?"

"Within the next three weeks there are two ships departing from Rotterdam." His eye wandered to the packed wicker baskets beneath the window. How had she known, he wondered, that he was leaving her? Or could she be hoping he would take her along?

If she was really waiting for him to say the magic word, she gave no sign of it. Why not ask her, if it would make her happy? It wouldn't cost him anything to say it.

"Would you like to come with me?" he said.

She looked up at him; her eyes, with the amber points of light in them, were grave. "You shouldn't say what you don't really mean."

"What if I meant it?"

"At the moment, I might. It'd be too easy to say yes. I'm twenty-eight, and I know miracles aren't likely to happen to me any more. But we women can't give up waiting for miracles to happen." The hint of a smile brightened her face. "Every time I wished for something too much I never got it. When I leave it to chance, my luck is much better."

"Is that your answer?"

She nodded and drew him close. "I'll ask just one thing more of you," she said. "Don't write to me. Don't, under any circumstance, ever write to me."

17

The village of Altenbauna lay in an oppressive atmosphere of loneliness and quiet. The houses seemed to cower beneath their red-tiled roofs. Loaves of bread had been laid out to cool on a bench beside the bakery; starched linen, frozen by the cold wind, hung on a line. Even these signs of life—smoke rising from the chimneys, the sounds of a sawmill—only made the village seem more deserted.

Robert came across deep ruts in the road from the wheels of a carriage. They had been obscured by hoof marks here and there, but both horse and carriage tracks led straight to the house of the gendarme, Willibald Manz, where he was to meet Soerman. Reins tight in his hands, he rode into the yard. He had an uneasy feeling he was being watched, but he couldn't see anybody.

He dismounted with some hesitation. Nothing was stirring anywhere. Somewhere a hinge creaked. He turned and saw Soerman in the shadows at the front door of the house.

They shook hands without a word. His eyes are light gray, Robert thought, and realized he was seeing Soerman in daylight for the first time. He looked hard at that face; so far, it had been nothing but a white blur with two fearless eyes. But even now, with Soerman in front of him, it remained an impenetrable face, a surface that offered no hold, gave nothing away. It was the face of a man who had had no time to be young, an unfinished, contradictory face still clouded with unresolved childhood dreams.

The sawmill had been silent for sometime; now it started up again.

"The last person who looked at me this long and this hard was my father," Soerman said.

"It's good to see you again," Robert said. "Have you become the gendarme's adjutant?"

"Let's put your horse in the stable first." Soerman took the stallion's reins and led him away.

Robert was surprised to see so many horses in Manz's stalls. "Looks like two dozen, at least," he said. "Not the kind of tired nags the gendarmes ride either. I take it you're not alone. Damned if this doesn't look like the Big Hoym gang. Where are they?"

"I've recited that line to you once already: they're where they can see everybody and nobody can see them."

"Did it get too cold for you in the forest?"

"Let's say too hot."

"So you're setting up winter quarters here, on the main road to Kassel, where the press gangs come by every day? Are you a full-fledged member of the gang now?"

Soerman had tied the animal to the post and tossed him some oats. "I could have made quite a career of it with Hoym; I could have made quite a career of it anywhere. If only I could take something seriously enough to stick with it."

"You evidently took my message seriously enough," Robert said.

"I was surprised to hear from you. Hadn't expected ever to see you again. What is it then? Nobody sends that kind of message by the old woman without a good reason."

Robert found it hard to begin. "It's not easy to explain. I've come to a decision. You remember the talk we had in the forest, about my father and all that? That's what it's about. I want to leave here, I want to go to America. And I was wondering if there's really anything to hold you here."

"Is it your father, or is it the war?"

"To begin with, it's me." Robert said. "You know your way around over there, you could help me find my father. Will you come with me? Actually, I had a feeling you'd just as soon take the first boat back, if you could."

They stepped outside the stable.

"Well, what do you say?" Robert said.

Soerman latched the stable door, picked a straw off his sleeve. "I'm willing," he said finally, "if it doesn't have to be this minute. There's a little detail I have to take care of first. Besides, it's a good idea to start that kind of trip with a full wallet."

"And you plan to fill it here in Altenbauna?"

"Not exactly. We're only waiting for dark; then we ride to Kassel. You know the Latour factory just outside of town—they make military braid, uniform accessories? They're looking for workmen to fulfill an army contract for silver braid for ten thousand uniforms. Do you realize how much silver you need for that kind of an order? I couldn't believe it, but they've got it right there, in pretty, handy bars of solid silver. It occurred to us we could think of better uses for it. . . ."

Robert burst out laughing.

Soerman interrupted himself. "I thought it was funny at first, too," he said, "but the information checks out. They've got so much silver that . . ."

"I know, I know," Robert said, restraining his laughter. "Your information's correct, all right. But you don't seem to know who you're stealing silver from."

"What do you mean? Are we supposed to worry about the widow Latour? . . ."

"You'll be stealing it from my stepfather, Baron Haynow. A few weeks ago he bought the factory from the widow Latour lock, stock, and barrel, for practically nothing—coincidentally, just twenty-four hours before the Elector, meaning Minister Schlieffen, awarded him the contract for the ten thousand uniforms. Do you see?"

Soerman would have liked to see the joke, but couldn't.

"Your stepfather has more than his share of guardian angels. Damn! I knew something was bound to foul it up. And I already had visions of the money. Come on . . . you better tell Hoym yourself. That's . . ."

Soerman stopped, checked by Robert's hand on his arm. Behind the monotonous sounds from the sawmill they could hear something else—hoofbeats, rolling wheels, and the unmistakable beat of the press gang's drums.

The circular saw kept eating its way into the log, splinters and sawdust arcing away on both sides. Weibrecht, the sawmill owner, was dragging another log into place with his son when the foreman came running from the log pile.

"The press gang," he shouted and ran to stop the waterwheel that powered the saw.

"Leave it," Weibrecht shouted. "We'll keep right on working."

Weibrecht's wife appeared at the door of the house, wearing a white apron, her hands still sticky with the dough she'd been kneading. Anxiously, she waved the son toward the house.

"No," Weibrecht said, squaring his shoulders. "He's not going to hide."

The woman ran out and took her son by the arm. "Don't provoke the recruiters! Come, Vitus, come into the house!"

"He stays here. I have an official document from the town council: they can't take him, too."

"A lot of them have had official documents and got taken anyway. The brewer of Kirchditmold had one, and they tore it up right in front of his eyes, that's how much good it did him. I won't let them take Vitus, I'd rather send him out of the country. I should never have let them take his brothers."

The foreman spoke up. "Your wife's right. Why tempt them? You know how they are. If they've had a bad day, your document won't make a bit of difference."

"The boy stays here. And you, woman, go back in the house."

The woman hesitated. "Only yesterday you put another lock on the cellar door." But her resistance was broken. Slowly, head down, she went back inside.

The boy waited until his mother disappeared into the house. Then he said, "Thank you, Father."

The old man nodded. The log was cut through and the saw was turning in empty air, but they were too distracted to notice it. The press gang had reached the village square; father and son stared at the wagon carrying the new recruits. The two women on the wagon had been given a blanket; the men sat in the cold, some in their shirt-sleeves, their suspenders cut and hanging down—cutting the suspenders was a favorite method of preventing escape while new recruits were being transported to barracks. On a platform behind the coachman stood the drummer and beside him a soldier with his rifle cocked. Another armed soldier was stationed at the back of the wagon.

"The horses get blankets, but not the men," Weibrecht muttered. "It's enough to make you sick. I've had enough of it. Your mother's right. Tonight I'm sending you over the border to my cousin in Munden; he'll be glad to get a good carpenter. And your mother and I'll be able to sleep nights without worrying about you."

Looking at the wagon, young Weibrecht saw several that he knew—from market days and local dances. "There're over twenty of them," he said, "and only four guards. They'd never get me onto that wagon, not alive anyway."

"They've got Roeder's only son."

The cavalcade turned off the road and rolled toward the sawmill. The two foremost riders came riding ahead, horse and man outfitted as though for a parade—white-plumed helmets, royal-blue coats with brass buttons, the horses in silver-trimmed harness.

"It's Lessberg." Weibrecht went red in the face. "The bastard! That's why they've got so many today." He turned to the foreman. "He got your brother-in-law. Don't let him see it in your face. Just water their horses and keep quiet."

Lessberg and Scholl pulled up and dismounted with a flourish. They had covered a lot of ground that day, as always when Lessberg was in charge. He missed nothing, not the tiniest village, not the most isolated farmstead. He had the nose and the persistence of a trained hunting dog. Scholl preferred to ply his trade at a tavern table; in times like these it sometimes took only a glass of wine and a threat to make a man betray his brother just to save his own skin.

Grinning broadly, Lessberg walked over to the sawmill owner. "Your sons are doing fine," he said. "They look splendid in uniform. They must be the best marksmen in the whole company. They'll make their fortune, you'll see. In a year they'll be coming home in officers' uniforms. You'll be sorry you didn't let your youngest go along."

Weibrecht felt as though his circular saw was cutting through his heart.

The foreman had taken the reins of the recruiters' horses and was leading them toward the millstream. Lessberg looked up. "What's going on there? Is the fellow going to poison our horses with that swill? Take them to the well, man! Your well's supposed to have the best drinking water for miles around, Weibrecht. And those are the two best horses for miles around. Any objections?"

"Yes, as a matter of fact. There's a water shortage this year. The well is for people, not for horses."

"Not for horses, he says! What do you say, Scholl, are we going to put up with that?"

"Ah, come on, Lessberg," Scholl said. "Let's get going. It's been a long day."

Lessberg was not to be mollified. "So your water is only for people, is it? You'd better drink it up then. Let's see you drink a pailful, enough for a horse. Shall we say five quarts? Get a pail there. Let him guzzle the water he says is too good for our horses."

Silence fell in the courtyard, except for the sound of the saw, still turning in empty air.

"Move!" Lessberg shouted at the foreman. "Bring on that pail! And fill it to the brim." He sliced the air with his riding crop.

The foreman, head down, brought a pailful from the well. Scholl tried to intervene, but Lessberg pushed him aside.

"They say there's room for a whole brook in every miller. Let's see what you can do, Weibrecht. If there's just one drop left in that pail, we take your youngest son. I mean it, Weibrecht. Drink it all, or the boy comes with us."

Weibrecht bent to pick up the pail, his eyes steadily on Lessberg, so evenly that not a ripple showed on the surface of the water. With the full pail at his mouth, he stood rigid, frozen. Then, without warning, he took one step forward and threw the water in Lessberg's face. "Get out of my yard!" In his hand he had the curved knife he used to peel the logs. "Get out! You shouldn't have said that about my son. There's room for lots of water in a miller, is there?—Well, I'm full up to here!" He saw Lessberg's pale face, the drops of water glistening in the trimmed moustache. He was boiling with rage and humiliation; a man could be stepped on and degraded for only so long, could stand still for it only so long. . . .

The guard on the wagon saw only the flash of the knife in Weibrecht's upraised hand; he threw his rifle to his shoulder and fired.

All eyes were on Weibrecht. He stood there like a tree, legs braced apart. The hand with the knife sank, and then he fell, without a sound, weightless. The knife was still in his hand, clenched, even in death.

Suddenly the sawmill yard was a turmoil; men seemed to sprout from the ground. From every woodpile, from every stable, haystack, and barn, Big Hoym's men poured out of hiding, followed by half the men in the village. There was no hate and no fear in their faces, only blind determination. The villagers had no weapons, and they needed none. A roaring tidal wave, they swarmed across the yard, a dark, irresistible flood of bodies. Lessberg was seized, tramped to the ground; someone jerked him to his feet again.

"Get a rope!" somebody yelled. "Get a rope!"

Until then, everything had happened so fast, Lessberg hadn't fully grasped it. But when he heard that shout, passing from man to man, his blood froze; he knew that it would cease only when the act was done.

By the time Robert and Soerman reached the scene, it was all over. They had hoped to prevent the worst, but it was too late. The first evening shadows were falling into the yard, advancing tremulous edges across the bright sawdust. The sawmiller lay face down on the ground. Lessberg hung from the crane used for lifting logs, the end of the rope dangling down his back.

The villagers huddled together around the body, mute and motionless, only beginning to realize what they'd done. The press gang, too, stood in shocked silence. Not one of them had tried to help Lessberg, and now they were afraid to move. Scholl stood beside the wagon, his horse's reins in his hand. There was nothing to keep the recruits from jumping down and escaping, but they were as stunned as their guards. Scholl caught sight of Robert.

The Austrian stared at him, didn't seem to recognize him. His face was gray, his eyes wide with shock. Slowly, painfully, he struggled for words. "You. Haynow? What're you doing here?"

Robert had the impression Scholl was talking not to him, but to himself.

Scholl suddenly came back to life. He swung up into the saddle, spurred his horse up beside the wagon team, and slashed at their flanks with his riding crop. The team jerked forward; the wagon began to roll. No one tried to stop them, to rescue the recruits; the recruits themselves were still too stunned to do anything but cling to the sideboards of the wagon as it rattled out of the yard. Within seconds the press gang was gone.

Slowly, the circle around the hanged man loosened, opened. The villagers seemed to fear him even more now that he was dead; carefully they avoided the long shadow cast by the body. The foreman and Weibrecht's son lifted up the miller's body and carried it into the house. The yard emptied; now only Hoym's men remained.

Robert saw a tall man coming from the direction of the gendarme's house, hands on his silver-ornamented belt, his coat unbuttoned. Hatless, his head seemed too small for his thick neck and broad shoulders. From the way the man carried himself, Robert knew it must be Hoym himself.

Hoym walked in a wide circle around the blood on the sawdust, never once glancing up at the hanged man. "Stop that saw!" he commanded.

One of his men ran to the millstream and dropped the gate into place that halted the waterwheel. The shrill whir of the saw slowed to a stop. All eyes were on Hoym, as if just his presence would put things right again.

"Don't expect me to congratulate you," he said coldly. "If there's one thing I despise it's this kind of hotheaded lunacy. If you were going to hang him, you should have hanged every man jack of them. As it is now, the militia'll be here inside two hours. My advice is to get out of here as fast as you can." He raised a hand to silence a man who was about to say something. "I can't do a thing for you now. Get out. You haven't got much time."

"What about our plan, our money? You promised us. . . ."

Hoym's eye moved over the faces of his men until he found the one who'd spoken. "I still make the rules here. You do as I say, that's the first rule. This is no time to start challenging it. You killed the man, now you'll have to save yourselves. We'd be crazy to try to pull off that job now. These villagers haven't realized just what they've done yet, but they do know what they can expect. You should know at least as much. Unless you want to join him up there. Take the horses, they're yours. And don't stay together. Every man for himself—that's the safest. And good luck."

He stood with the left hand on the hilt of his sword, watching his men disperse. Then he waved Soerman and Robert to join him and turned back toward the gendarme's house.

In the gendarme's stableyard, Hoym's men were mounting up. Each rode off alone, like strangers whose horses had been coincidentally stabled together. One of them brought Hoym's horse out; he waited till the big man had set his hat on his head, then he handed him the reins. When the last man had ridden away, Hoym mounted his own horse.

"And I always thought I'd made something better than a band of brigands out of them," he said. He turned to Soerman. "I'd advise you to do likewise. And you probably ought to tie up the gendarme, smash up his front door a little. That might help him. He doesn't really deserve the gallows."

Willibald Manz hadn't waited for anyone to help him. He had smashed his living room with his own hands, and had done it thoroughly. One window was completely demolished, another was twisted out of its casing. The drawers had been pulled out of the chest and their contents strewed all over the room, with muddy footprints over some of them. He had given himself a bleeding cut across the forehead with an old razor and now he sat in the midst of the debris while Robert and Soerman tied him up.

"Tighter, damn it!" he growled. "That's better. And now the legs."

Soerman tossed Robert the end of another piece of rope. "Aren't you going to be cold? These broken windows . . ."

"The more miserable I look when they find me, the better. Before you leave, shoot out a few more windows." He pointed at one of the open drawers. "There's some stuff in there you can gag me with. You do it," he said to Soerman. "You seem to have the knack. And then just send the dog in to me. But leave the doors open."

After they finished tying and gagging him, Robert and Soerman went out to get their horses.

"Do you think they'll fall for it?" Robert asked.

"For his sake I certainly hope so."

Robert stroked his sorrel's muzzle. Soerman noticed an odd little smile on his face. "What are you thinking?"

"I was thinking that now we have to leave the country. Both of us. Scholl recognized me. You know what they'll do to anybody that was even faintly connected with this hanging."

"Well, I was planning to leave the country anyway. We were going to pull one last job and split up. The press gangs are making things too hot."

"Why not come to America with me then?"

Soerman had finished tightening the cinch. His face rose behind the horse like a polished stone emerging from a river. Robert asked himself whether this man had really never taken anything seriously enough, as he claimed, or whether it was only that he had understood too early what a paltry thing life was. "Well, what do you say?" he asked.

"It's not me I'm thinking about. I don't know how to explain it. Don't forget who you are and who I am. You're one of those born with a cowl—that's what they call it, in my country, when a man's a born winner. But me—a while ago, at the sawmill, when I saw the recruiter hanging from that crane, it occurred to me that the way my life's been going it's bound to end just like that. I'd rather you didn't hang beside me."

By the time they stepped outside the stable, leading their horses, darkness had fallen. The sky had clouded over and seemed not much higher than a ceiling.

"It smells like snow," Robert said.

"Just as it did when your father left Heron Island."

"A good omen, don't you think?"

Without another word, it was settled between them. They mounted up. "Better not ride through the village," Soerman said. "The beekeeper's garden'll take us close to the woods." He gave his horse the spurs and jumped it over the low railing.

The grass muffled their hoofbeats. The village was only a silhouette of red tile roofs; no sound came from it. As they approached the woods, the garden ended in uncultivated ground, where the parallel rows of apple, pear, and plum trees ended and brush took over. A crow sailed through the air. Deer looked up from browsing under the great walnut tree. The first snowflakes of the night blew through the branches.

18

Every evening at six Colonel Rall took a bottle of red Burgundy from his private stock. Usually he drank it alone; he never invited officers to join him in his hour of relaxation before dinner. If he felt like conversation, he was likely to choose a veteran campaigner like Sergeant Luib.

Rall placed a full glass of wine before the sergeant. The men toasted each other silently. Luib's lumpy face made a little grimace of appreciation. "That's my kind of medicine, all right. I wonder whether they'll have a drop of good stuff for us in the colonies."

"Have you finished the regimental lists?"

Luib handed Rall a bound ledger. "If Minister Schlieffen didn't have such a good head for figures, it'd be a lot easier. He'd have caught my corrections in ink. I made up a whole new ledger, with doctored figures. That way, in case he checks, it'll look like the regiment's been up to full strength all along."

Rall tossed the ledger onto the table. "Let me have a look at those undoctored lists. They can't be all that bad."

Sergeant Luib untied an old folder, chose a few pages from it, and gave them to Rall.

Rall sat down and ran his eyes over the lists; something arrested his gaze. "Fifty men! This regiment is a bottomless arrel."

"Last year we had two hundred men below par."

"So now I have to pay those recruiters a fortune. How c n you get anywhere at all this way? And when I'm bled white to ay for recruiting them, these scum go and cripple themselves and waste my money."

"I understand the one that shot himself in the foot has a brother or a cousin or something back home."

"The premium's yours if you get him, Luib. We'll go get the healthy one and hang the crippled one. Have to keep the system in order."

"Better not delay the execution then. If he gets gangrene he'll be done for. I didn't like his looks yesterday—not a drop of blood left in his veins, it looked like."

Rall leaned back in his chair. "It's easy to draw up contracts. Their lordships collect their money and then it's up to us to round up the men for Minister Schlieffen. If only they hadn't let it be known we were going all the way to America to fight. These country bumpkins are terrified of having to cross an ocean—maybe never to come back. Even Russian service, service against the Turks, is preferable to them. To have to cross that Atlantic ocean is too much."

"Once we have them out of the country and aboard ship, the wind'll turn. The appetite comes with the eating. Supposed to be a rich country, this America. I keep dreaming of golden, ripe tobacco fields as far as you can see."

"Oho, so you've got America on your mind?"

"I'm thinking about the English money they're paying us. This is my last chance to save something for my old age."

"That may be all right for you. For me—I expect only to lose by it." Rall was a restless man. He stood up, filled both their glasses, then walked up and down with his glass in his hand. "Look at it this way, Luib. This is the way it looks to me: losses, nothing but losses. I certainly don't look forward to this war. According to the old regimental list, my regiment held seven hundred men. Of these, two hundred existed only on paper—but we collected their pay. Those men were glad to stay home, and I was glad to get their pay. All the commanders do the same thing, and some of them have tricks up their sleeves you never heard of."

Rall had reached the opposite wall and turned around. "And now, from one day to the next, I'm supposed not only to bring my regiment up to full strength but to double it. Do you know what that means, Luib? Hessia has three hundred thousand inhabitants, more than half of whom are women. Of the remaining number you have to deduct the men who are too old and the children. That leaves less than fifty thousand men. You've got to have at least two men per farm, one man per workshop, and then there's the nobility, the clergy, the students. How Schlieffen imagines he can get more than twelve thousand soldiers out of what's left, I just don't know. But he wants it, and he'll do it, because he makes money on every single man recruited. But for your Colonel Rall it doesn't pay. Until now I had a regiment of five hundred men to worry about, and I cashed in on seven hundred. They even ruined my take on the uniforms."

"I thought I saw the cloth merchant here yesterday?"

"Oh yes, it's a wonder they'll still allow me to choose what cloth I want for the uniforms. The news is that Haynow is the new contractor for uniforms, at a fixed price, period, no haggling. So I ordered the most expensive cloth there is, and I hope the court keeps him waiting for his money like he was the least of the licensed Jews who supply the court. He's supplying the forage, too. And braid for the uniforms. It's Haynow, Haynow, Haynow, wherever you turn. Let me tell you, Luib, it's a tradesman's world these days. We officers are just here to be fleeced by them. Yesterday there was a new memo from the minister's office. All officers to learn to give commands and orders in English. That's how far we've come."

"I'd give something to see the treaty Schlieffen signed with the English. They're known for their sharp dealings, sir."

"Yes, but Schlieffen's wide awake. You needn't worry, he knows how to deal with the English, and the Elector is sure to get his cut." Rall laughed. "Only one silver lining: now that his Grace has the money for his little pleasure chalets, he won't have the men to build them."

"Will the English pay us direct?"

"We'll see."

"You mean, it'll be the same as before—the Elector'll skim off half our pay."

"Come to think of it, the fellow was right to shoot off his foot. We're the crazy ones, to sell our skins so cheap."

There was a knock on the door. Sergeant Luib opened the door to a man carrying a large package. There was snow on the man's hat.

"What is it?"

"Vohdin's my name, at your service, sir. Silversmith Vohdin. The officers of this garrison ordered a large silver cup from me, for the marriage of Major Haynow. To be delivered today, sir."

"Let's have a look at the thing." Rall pointed to the table. "Here, unpack it. What's it weigh?"

"Two pounds thirteen ounces, sir." He unpacked the bowl with tender care. It had a broad rim in which the officers' names were engraved.

"How many men in your workshop?" Rall asked casually, without deigning to look at the bowl.

Vohdin straightened up. "This will be the last piece made in my shop for a long time, sir. Tomorrow, my most experienced craftsman has to join up. I can't keep it up alone. A jeweler can do his work by himself, sir; a silversmith needs at least one other man, preferably a third."

"What will you be doing in that case? Have you served yet?"

"I served in Prince Carl's regiment, sir, the whole Seven Years' War."

"What do you think of Rall's regiment, then?"

"I've signed up already, sir, with the Linsing grenadiers."

Rall lost interest.

Sergeant Luib accompanied the man outside. When he came back, he looked the bowl over appreciatively.

"That Claus Haynow knows how to look out for himself. He's got his father's gold in one pocket, and the Elector in the other. You can get to be a major in a hurry that way." Luib pointed at the center of the silver bowl. "There, his coat of arms isn't quite right. I miss a pair of horns in it."

"Watch your tongue, Luib! That family has a long arm, and the Countess Sonsfeld is no little actress, you know. You've got to give those Haynows credit, they use their heads, especially with figures. I wouldn't mind such a pair of horns myself. It's better than having to drag a wife on your back all your life." He pulled out his pocket watch. "I'm off to dinner. Lock everything up, especially the papers. They concern no one but you and me." He fumbled in his coin pocket, fished up a silver coin, pressed it in Luib's hand, and turned to go.

The door burst open. Scholl, the recruiter, almost fell into the room, forgetting to salute, his eyes wide and feverish. One fastening of his uniform coat was torn off, his collar open. On his dark hair there was a crust of frozen snow, but sweat was pouring down his face.

"You're steaming like a horse ridden too far too fast," Rall said. "What happened, did you meet up with the devil?"

Scholl stared at Rall with a sense of relief. A good man to see at a time like this, a tower of strength.

"Speak up, man," Rall said. "What the hell happened to you?"

Scholl took a step toward Rall, reached out to him as if for support. "They strung up Lessberg," he whispered, out of breath. "In Altenbauna. We only stopped there to water the horses. I still don't know how I managed to get away. I just started to ride and kept on riding. I don't know why I'm not hanging there next to Lessberg. They strung him up . . . It happened so fast . . . I really don't know how I got away . . . I can see him hanging there . . ."

"Calm yourself," Rall said. "Sit down. Take a drink. Then tell me what happened, one step at a time."

19

Friends had persuaded him to stay at the casino for a game of billiards, which is how it happened that Claus Haynow had remained at the fortress this afternoon; though impatient to be off, and a little distracted, he had managed to win a round of games.

This didn't surprise him; he was having a lucky streak and getting used to winning. The new title of nobility, his majoralty, the impending marriage with Christina Sonsfeld—life was finally treating him as he'd always felt it should. When the orderly came to the casino to request his presence in the Commandant's office he was sure it would be for something pleasant, a fresh opportunity to distinguish himself.

He was in too good a mood to register any warning signs, even after Scholl started his story of Lessberg's murder—until Robert's name came into it. Then he understood. He was unprepared for it. Blindly trying to impress Rall with his own impartiality, he began to ask searching questions, like a prosecutor before the bar. Scholl, who basically hadn't much to report, found himself beleaguered, forced to find answers. Before long, the story had grown, especially Robert's part in the whole thing. Claus was still dissatisfied, however; finally he declared with an air of impartiality that he would set about getting a clarification.

Now, however—having left Rall's office and finding himself alone in the dark corridor outside—he had no idea what to do next.

He could hear the men downstairs leaving the mess hall noisily after supper, a free evening in front of them. Footsteps came up the stairs. He couldn't tell whether it was the solid tread of the common soldier or the metallic rattle of spurs that denoted an officer; he only knew he didn't want to encounter anybody. He pressed his tricorne low on his forehead, muffled himself up in his uniform winter coat, and got out of the building somehow.

By the snowflakes that blew into his face he knew he had left the fortress. Lanterns flamed in the courtyard, whirling islands of light in the blue dusk.

A figure separated from the shadows near the stables and he recognized his orderly, leading his black horse toward him. Much as he loved to ride, the idea of being seen on horseback—now, when he longed to hide—made him shrink into himself. He looked around and saw the cart the recruiters had been using. The horses had been taken to the stables, and the shaft slanted to the ground. Two men were lifting down the great drum. Was it his imagination, or had they turned their backs when they saw him?

The orderly had brought his horse and made ready to hold the stirrup. Claus shook his head. "This is no riding weather," he said. "I'll take a carriage."

The beautiful black Arab turned its head and butted his shoulder. His horse's familiar touch, which would normally have soothed him, this time had the opposite effect; a savage grief shot through him, awakening an old forgotten pain, a pain so fierce he had expected to die—that time he fell off his horse, that early morning he'd been practicing on the hurdles he'd set up himself, so that he could become a better rider than Robert. The fall, the shock, the pain that wouldn't end . . . and above him, the horse's head with its bushy mane between its ears and the moist, steaming nostrils . . . the dragging reins that he tried to take hold of and found he couldn't lift his hand. Lying there immobile, numb with pain and the terrifying thought that he would never walk again.

He felt like running away, but he knew there were eyes watching him. Somehow he made his way to the carriages for hire that stood waiting outside the gate. Snow was blowing into his face, his eyes, creating the illusion of a shimmering mirror between him and the world; for a moment it was as though he were looking at things through the wrong end of a telescope. Everything, the gate, the carriages, looked tiny and far away, out of reach—like tomorrow morning, when his wedding with Countess Christina Sonsfeld was to take place. Blindly he opened the carriage door, took refuge inside. "Take me into town, the shortest route."

"Pardon, your Excellency, they started razing the fortress walls at the old harbor."

"Get going, man."

"I only meant, if your Excellency, the Baron, is in a hurry, a horse would be much faster, because of the detour I have to take."

"If you'd started off when I told you we'd have been halfway there by now." Claus pulled the side curtains shut. The thin fabric, partly frozen to the windowpanes, gray-green and soiled, tore off in his hand. The carpet at his feet showed red wine stains, the upholstery gave off an odor of decayed sea grass. It was one of those carriages the officers of the garrison used for their hurried amorous adventures.

"I find it more exciting in a carriage than in a bed," Scholl invariably said when the talk turned to women. Claus closed his eyes, determined to shut out that voice. But it was hard to get rid of, the Austrian rhythm of it, low-pitched yet obtrusive. It was in the same voice, the same rhythm, that Scholl had reported the Altenbauna incident. "And who do I see but Baron Robert Haynow." In the end the one thing everybody would remember would be the fact that a Haynow had been present when the mob hanged Lessberg.

Where was Scholl now? Probably in the officers' mess, with at least a dozen men hanging on his words. How many more times would he tell his story today? By curfew every man in the fortress would have heard it; by morning, everyone in town.

Claus was suddenly thrown forward; the coach had jerked to stop. A collection of elegant carriages, belonging to the Elector's entourage, barred the road leading along the Fulda River into town. The horses were covered with blankets; the coachmen and footmen stood beside them, bundled up as best they could, watching the skaters on the river.

The river was the shortest way home, so Claus paid off the coachman and started climbing down the embankment. When he stepped on the ice, his spurs rang. It seemed unnaturally loud and conspicuous; he wished he could go back and take the other road, the one over the fortress wall, but that would take him past the whole line of court carriages. The skaters were sufficiently preoccupied with themselves, but the coachmen and footmen guarding the carriages had nothing better to do than stare.

Along the embankment, tall poles held torches of pinewood. The blue twilight was beginning to turn violet, but the daylight was still brighter than the yellow flares of the torches. The ice glittered like silver. The snow had let up; only isolated flakes still floated gently downward. Musicians in the little inlet that held rowboats in the summertime were playing for the skaters. A small group of ladies stood apart, watching.

Several skaters came across the ice toward him; he recognized the young women who had formed Christina's circle ever since she had moved to town—Christina's own little court, in effect. He was relieved not to see Christina among them; she was the last person he wanted to talk to at this moment. He tried to evade the skaters, but they surrounded him, a crowd of plumed hats, muffs, blowing shawls, the fragrance of perfume. Tiny gloved hands would not let him go.

The women were all talking at once, trying to pull him out onto the ice. Suddenly a long crack shot through the ice beneath their feet. They screamed and fled back toward the others. Behind them, a dark network of fine cracks stretched across the ice, where the skates had roughed the surface into a white powder.

Relieved, Claus went on, carefully setting one foot down after the other. The musicians had stopped, the skaters were leaving. Women were fluttering up the embankment carrying their skates. Footmen helped them up and to their carriages. Only one lone figure remained circling on the ice. Her fur collar cupped her neck like a chalice. Blonde hair curled and waved around the edges of her white fur cap.

It was Christina. She hadn't seen him. Oblivious to the voices calling her from the riverbank, she skated to the sound of unheard music.

Anna Haynow finished reciting the sentences she was memorizing in English, under Ruth Connor's tutelage, for the great ball in honor of the English Colonel Faucitt. She hadn't had to look at the text once. Even so, she was not altogether pleased with herself. "It sounds better when you say it. Please repeat it for me once more, word for word."

"It was very good. Really. Only the *th* still gives you a little trouble. All my pupils start off with a present from me, a little pocket mirror." Ruth Connors stepped over to the vanity, picked up a silver-backed hand mirror and handed it to the Baroness. "Now, look into the mirror, stick the tip of your tongue between your teeth, and say it: *th.*"

Anna shook her head ruefully. "But it feels awful, lisping deliberately like this. The Colonel speaks such excellent German. Why don't you admit it, I'll simply be making a fool of myself."

"If Colonel Faucitt were a Frenchman, I'd agree with you. But the English love to hear their own language abroad. We're dreadfully sentimental, I'm afraid. Why don't I change the last sentence so there's no *th* in it?"

"Oh, I thought we were all done."

"Just seven words more. 'How do you like our Hessian soldiers?' "

Anna gave Ruth Connors a surprised glance. "If you weren't an Englishwoman, I would swear there was disapproval in your voice when you said that."

"I'm a Scotswoman. We consider ourselves entitled to disapprove of anything the English King does. Here's your next text to be memorized, on this slip. The pronunciation is in parentheses throughout."

"How stupid of me to have kept all this for the last possible moment." Anna smiled—a warm smile which admitted her invitation had been something of an ambush. "I've been wanting to ask you here for a long time," she said, "but something always came up."

Ruth played with the lace cuff on her sleeve. "I suspected you hadn't brought me here from the Palace for the sake of a few English sentences. Both of your sons speak excellent English, after all. It's on account of Robert, isn't it?"

The two women looked into each other's eyes. Suddenly they had changed roles. Ruth Connors had said the words that Anna Haynow had lacked the courage to come out with.

Anna twisted her broad gold wedding band on her finger, as she always did when at a loss for words. "I assure you," she said finally, "I do not ask my sons questions about their private lives. Nor do I spy on them. And now that I've met you—I mean, I can understand that Robert. . . ." She was at a loss for the right way to put it. "It's usually better when a mother doesn't know the women with whom her son may be having an adventure." She bit her lips; the words sounded coarse to her ears, but there was no retreat for her now. "I was always interested in you, because I believe Robert owes you a great deal. Isn't it true he spent the past eight days with you?"

Ruth hesitated—not because she was unsure of what to say, but to emphasize the trump card she had up her sleeve. "That's true. He was studying day and night—books about America."

Anna stepped over to the sewing table, pushed the plate of sweets about aimlessly. To avoid the subject now would have seemed petty.

"Then he's told you his plans?"

"More or less." Ruth Connors smiled her gentle, resigned smile. "He always comes to me when he needs to clarify something in his mind." She looked up at Anna. "I don't know if that's a compliment for a woman—sometimes it seems to me it is, and sometimes not."

Anna had not known this young woman for as much as an hour, and yet she felt completely at home with her. She could understand why Robert had been drawn back to her again and again despite his restless nature.

"He's going then," she said softly, not as a question, but as a conclusion. "I must have done something wrong, or he wouldn't be going. And yet I always believed I wasn't like other mothers."

There was a silence. After a while, Anna raised her head and gave Ruth a deeply probing glance. She hesitated before she spoke, but at last she came out with it. "You'll be losing him too when he leaves." She took Ruth's hand in her own. "I really would like to study English with you seriously. In future I expect the English language papers will interest me more than the German. I shall personally ask the Elector's permission; I promise you it won't mean trouble for you."

"English is easy enough to learn," Ruth said. "As soon as you can read a little, you can learn it virtually by yourself. Shall we go through your sentences again?"

But before Anna could reply, the door flew open. Gottfried Haynow stood on the threshold. "I've been looking for you everywhere," he said. "I've got to talk to you." It was only then that he realized his wife was not alone.

"This is Miss Connors," Anna said. "I've just taken an English lesson with her."

"The Scotswoman at the palace?" Haynow said, as though Ruth Connors were not present.

"It's going to be a gesture of hospitality toward Colonel Faucitt."

Haynow seemed upset. "The Scotswoman," he repeated absently. "Didn't you say just recently that Robert was having an affair with the woman?"

Ruth Connors took her coat. "It's time for me to go," she said.

"Miss Connors, I don't know what I can say to apologize for my husband. . . ."

Ruth nodded and made for the door, but Haynow barred her way. "Just a minute. When was the last time you saw Robert?"

"Gottfried! I don't understand you. What do you think you're doing? Robert's a grown man. Miss Connors owes no one an accounting."

For a moment it seemed as though Haynow might speak to his wife as rudely as he had to the visitor, but he was preoccupied with something more important. "Was Robert with you today, Miss Connors?"

"Yes, he was with me. And now, if you'll kindly step out of my way."

Haynow's face brightened noticeably. "I'm afraid I've been rude," he said, more in mockery than in apology. "You look like a reasonable woman. You could do me a great service if you wouldn't leave just yet. I'm sorry I can't explain, but that's how it is." He turned to his wife. "Will you ask her to stay?"

Anna lifted up her hands in puzzlement. "I honestly know as little as you do about all this, Miss Connors. Will you stay, nevertheless, as a favor to me?"

Anna was still too shocked by her husband's conduct to ask any questions. She didn't even try to guess his reasons. Surely it was some trifle having to do with the ball tonight. Her diagnosis seemed confirmed when he led her to the crooked passage behind the dining room. Ten years ago, they had installed two large dumbwaiters here, never thinking until it was finished that utility tables would be needed, so that it was an overcrowded place even when a family dinner was involved. As a result, whenever they had a large number of guests, this corner was the scene of veritable catastrophes—usually set off by the head of the house himself. Ordinarily indifferent to household affairs, he became transformed on such days into a perfectionist who made a fuss over a simple thing like a wineglass too near a plate.

Regardless of what it turned out to be, she decided to agree with him; it was the best way to calm him down.

He glanced tensely around, then went to the door leading to the musicians' dais. "Here we can be undisturbed. Watch those steps." She gathered her long skirt up and followed him up the dais.

The curtain separating the dais from the dining room was drawn; some light came from the oval window in the wood-paneled semicircular wall that closed off the little stage. The chairs and music stands for the musicians had been pushed back to the wall. And there stood Claus, in his coat, his tricorne in his hand. Anna stopped on the next-to-the-last step and looked at Claus; his face was strikingly pale, and she felt as if an icicle were piercing her heart. She made it up the last step only by holding fast to the silken cord that served as a railing. This obviously did not concern the kind of little domestic upheaval that was the usual accompaniment of a big party. Something terrible must have happened; worse than that, whatever it was, it had come to roost here, in her own house, in this brownish twilight where Claus stood facing her.

"What's wrong?" she said. "Tell me what's wrong."

"Claus, it's all right," she heard her husband say. "It's all cleared up. We have a witness who'll testify Robert couldn't have been there when it happened. His love affairs have finally paid off. There'll be nothing to worry about."

"I have my doubts about that," Claus said. "The word of a woman against . . ."

Anna stepped between the two men. "Will someone please let me in on what you're talking about?"

Outside in the passage there were steps; someone was whistling a tune.

"Isn't there a corner in this whole house where one can hold a private conversation?" Haynow fumed. He pulled aside the curtains to the dining room and helped Anna back down the steps.

When he sat down behind the desk in his office at last, Anna was reminded of a ship dropping anchor. They had made their way through the house as if in flight. But when she looked at Claus, who had stopped inside the door, she knew that her sense of having reached a safe harbor was illusory. She put her hands on the back of the chair in front of her and waited. Soon she would know—and suddenly she wished she could postpone the moment of knowledge.

"At Altenbauna this afternoon a recruiting officer was hanged by a mob." Gottfried was looking straight at her. "I believe you've met him. Major Lessberg. He used to be a steady client of the Black Bear tavern in Ramswood, if that means anything." He noticed that Claus was becoming restless. "Why don't *you* go on with the story, Claus?"

"I don't believe mother's interested in these trivial details."

Anna lifted a hand. "Please don't start this kind of argument."

Gottfried Haynow drew his silver penknife from its leather case and ran the edge over his thumb. "It happened in Justus Weibrecht's sawmill. The press gang had a wagon jammed with recruits. How many had they caught?"

"Father, what difference does that make?"

"What's happened to Robert, please?" Anna said. "I thought this was about him."

This time Claus spoke up. "Robert was at the sawmill when the whole thing happened. Don't interrupt me, please. Lessberg wasn't alone—Captain Scholl was with him. He saw Robert, with a deserter they've been looking for, the man who escaped from Ramswood Fortress, a certain Soerman. Even if nothing had happened to Lessberg, just that Robert was seen in the company of that deserter would be enough to hang him."

Anna sat down, but she sat very straight. "Who told you this story?" she said calmly.

"It's making the rounds at the fortress by now. I was playing billiards at the casino there when Rall sent for me. Scholl had gone straight to him with the story. Rall felt—I think it's very decent of him—that I should be the second person told."

Anna looked down. "So all the sawmill people were there, and probably some of the villagers saw it as well?"

"The whole village," Claus affirmed. "And Hoym's gang was involved too. . . ."

She nodded. "Considering how many people were standing around gaping, how can Scholl state that the deserter was in Robert's company particularly?"

Claus sensed the reproach in her question. "The fact is that an officer was hanged by a rebellious mob. Everyone present is considered guilty of the crime insofar as they did not come to the victim's aid," he said vehemently.

Anna looked briefly up at him. "The press gangs are armed, aren't they? Why wasn't Lessberg rescued by his own men?"

"It all happened so fast . . ."

"But this fellow Scholl had time to notice, among so many strange faces, the presence of a deserter, and to link this deserter with Robert. Scholl is obviously trying to gloss over his own failure in the case, don't you see? He's prepared to lie himself blue in the face for that."

Claus stared at his mother, dumbfounded by her coolheadedness—he had never seen her so self-possessed in such an emergency—but even more stunned by the clarity of her thinking. This was how he should have thought, how he should have spoken, in the presence of Commandant Rall. He had failed his brother disgracefully. "Lessberg is dead. That, in any case, is a fact. Another fact is that Rall sent a punitive expedition to Altenbauna. By this time the whole village may be in flames. Tomorrow Lessberg's body will be laid out for all to see at St. Martin's Chapel, and the whole town will hear about it."

"And many will say he only got what he deserved."

"Don't let anyone hear you say that, Mother!"

"I will not keep silent, even if you do. Robert has nothing whatever to do with that whole business, I tell you, and you should have said so when Scholl served up his fairytale."

"My God, don't you understand? Nothing I could have said would have helped! A recruiting officer was executed by a mob, and a member of the Haynow family was present when it happened!"

"Anyone could accidentally get mixed up in a thing of this

kind, just by happening by at the wrong time. Even you. But Robert, in your place, wouldn't stand here worrying about what people will say. He'd try to find ways to help you."

Claus grew deathly pale. "Of course, I should have known. How could I forget that in your eyes he's always the better man. No matter what he does you find a way of defending him. You were always on his side. From the beginning, always. You might be my *step*mother, for all I know, from the way you act. You never worried about me. When I fell off that horse—I've never forgotten this—you called a stranger in to nurse me. When I came down with scarlet fever, your only fear was that Robert might catch it from me. Whenever *he* had a touch of fever, though, you never left his bedside for a moment. With you, it was always Robert, Robert, Robert."

Gottfried Haynow sat through all this at his desk, his face an impenetrable mask, the silver penknife in his hand. The dispute between mother and son disturbed him more deeply than the problem over which it had arisen. The problem itself was something he felt he could handle; something could be arranged, he was sure of that. The other thing frightened him. Suddenly he was looking at two strangers; the family he had always regarded as an indestructible unit was falling apart before his eyes.

"Are you finished?" he asked, as though he had just witnessed a slight difference of opinion about something of no consequence. "We really must think about what's to be done. We can rely on the Scotswoman's testimony, at any rate." He turned to his wife. "Do you think Miss Connors will stick to her story under oath?"

"Is that your witness?" Claus gave a bitter laugh. "Women who would swear Robert was with them come by the dozen, even the court will know that. Besides, she's a foreigner, she can't even be made to testify under oath. Her testimony against Scholl's—that only strengthens the evidence against Robert. There's only one way: Robert has to disappear. He has to leave the country. We'll have trouble enough even if he goes, but at least he'll be safe."

Anna struggled to control herself. Her husband's expression begged for silence, but she couldn't suppress the thing she had to say. "To help him escape is as good as admitting his guilt."

"Mother, please! You're right, but there's no other way. Hoym's gang has scattered to the four winds. The village is burnt to the ground. Lessberg will be buried two days from now—and after that, there'll be a trial. And for that trial they'll fasten on Robert, because they'll have no one else to put in the dock. He's bound to be their scapegoat. And he won't be the only one. Even if he is a Skelnik, legally he bears the name of Haynow. Whatever he's done, the family will be tarred with the same brush. Or do you suppose my marriage is still likely to take place? Do you think I can ever set foot in the fortress again, after this, as an officer of the Elector's? They would tear the uniform off my body. That's our situation. We're done for. He's got to go. If there's anything left to save, it can be done only by his escape."

Haynow rested his chin on his fist. "I wish I could believe Claus is saying all this purely out of fear. Unfortunately, much of what he says is true. There are too many people who've been waiting for the merest hint of a weakness in our armor, for an opening of any kind—and I'm afraid this is their opportunity."

"What makes you so sure Robert hasn't taken himself off already?" Anna rose from her chair and walked to the window. Her palms on the glass, she looked out into the night. When she turned around, she said with assurance, "I really think you're worrying needlessly."

"In a case like this they close the borders," Haynow said. "On orders of the highest authority—Schlieffen, that would be. Normally, he would issue the order immediately, instantly, but he may wait until tomorrow morning. That would give us time enough."

"You forget the Elector keeps up with the police reports before anything else," Claus said. "He's likely to receive this particular news before Schlieffen and issue the command himself, immediately."

"He's more likely to give it to Schlieffen. He won't concern himself with the exact moment it issues from Schlieffen's office."

"Aren't you putting your trust in Schlieffen rather too unconditionally?" Anna asked. "I'd rather you didn't draw him into it at all. And may I remind you both that we are giving a ball tonight, and a wedding tomorrow? We have to behave as if nothing had happened. If we succeed, then by tomorrow morning Kassel will regard Scholl's stories as the nothing they are."

Haynow studied his wife with a mixture of admiration and anxiety—there was something a little strange, uncanny, in her incomparable poise under the circumstances.

"Are you saying we're to do nothing?" Claus said. "And what if Robert hasn't fled at all, what if he appears at the ball tonight?"

"The ball will proceed as planned," Anna said firmly. "And I suggest you both turn your attention to getting dressed for it. Our guests are supposed to arrive in an hour, and don't forget, Claus, you promised to pick the Sonsfelds up yourself."

Claus stood facing her, his face ashen, still in his coat. She longed to take his head in her hands and kiss him on the forehead, but it would only have been an expression of pity, and she was afraid he might sense as much. He looked once more at his father, then turned and walked out of the office; they listened to his receding steps.

Baron Haynow slipped his silver penknife back into its case and put it down beside the sealing wax, his baronial seal, and the letters destined to go out with tomorrow morning's post, each one sealed in three places. The gleaming red wax with the coat of arms imbedded in it hurt his eyes. He felt unbearably tired, unable to stand up, to check the preparations for the evening's entertainment, make conversation with his guests as if nothing had happened. A man of usually inexhaustible energy, tonight he would have preferred just to turn out the lamps and sit in the dark, alone. But he pushed back his chair and rose. "You're right," he said to his wife. "It's time to get dressed."

The Mercenaries

Four regiments are already aboard ship, the Grenadiers to embark tomorrow, the Rifle Battalions await the next transport. . . .

All . . . are exceptionally fine-looking regiments, completely uniformed and armed and ready for service anywhere in the world. There are slight differences only in the height of the men, the first rank being perhaps half an inch to an inch taller than the rest, but there is not a man under five feet eight inches, and each section is uniform in height. While the men in the middle are a little less tall, all are young, healthy, and good-looking men. Only seven out of the whole number have deserted, one died, three are sick. . . .

The Rall Regiment is the worst of all those I have seen, in physical size as well as strength of the men. It has been a peacetime regiment on garrison duty, and rather hastily drummed together to fill out its ranks for overseas duty. But the energetic and excellent Colonel will quickly whip them into shape.

Colonel William Faucitt to Lord Suffolk,
Foreign Minister of King George III.
25 March, 2 April, and 12 April 1776

20

Robert and Soerman had hidden out until dark on a hill that was part of the Elector's former mulberry plantation, high above the city and the Fulda River valley, on the southwestern border of

Oberneustadt. The snow illuminated the night, and from where Robert was sitting he could see every chimney pot and attic window in Kassel. Even tonight men were working on the fortress walls at the foot of the palace. Others were chopping ice in the park and placing it in buckets.

Freder Soerman emerged from the mulberry trees, where they had tethered their horses, walking with a springy step and humming a tune. "I guess we'd better get moving," he said. "But I still don't like this. The whole country's probably on the lookout for men on horseback."

"I've been thinking about that, too." Robert said. "We'd be better off trying it in a carriage."

"That might be a little difficult, getting a carriage."

"I'll get one from home. I think it would be very appropriate for me to leave in my own coach. It's one of the best in Kassel."

"That's quite a detour, all the way to Haynow House."

"I'm not talking about Haynow House. All our carriages are in Kassel, because of the wedding tomorrow."

They exchanged a look—two men for whom the most important part of this was that they were risking it together. Each measured his own coolness against the other man's, sensed in the other the same restlessness that made a conventional bourgeois life impossible.

"Logical thinking will solve any problem," Robert said. "That's what the director of my Latin school always said."

Soerman nodded. "Come on, we'd better go."

They mounted their horses and moved off. At the edge of the plantation, the highest point on the ridge, Robert stopped his horse for a last look at the city below. "See that pointed church tower down there, and right behind it the gable with the round window? My first girl. A little seamstress."

"Couldn't you have had half a dozen ladies' maids at home?"

"I left those to my brother—Look at that." Robert pointed to the fortress walls on the other side of the river, where men were at work in the red light of torches. "Those aren't ordinary workmen, they're soldiers. Before they're shipped to America, they have to raze those walls for the Elector. They're kept at it in three shifts, day and night. Slave labor, called in the regimental records "outdoor maneuvers." All they get for it is an extra meat ration for the week. And there to the left, a little further on, those well-lit windows, balconies with turrets, two weather vanes. That's our town house. Look at the way the smoke curls from the chimney. That's from Gilbert's kitchen—I can smell the pheasants and squabs all the way over here."

"Homesick already?"

"Just plotting ways and means to improve our rations for the trip. To leave Kassel without tasting just one more of Gilbert's truffled pastries . . ."

"Look there. What was that? Sheet lightning?" Soerman pointed eastward. The brightness returned, but this time it stayed against the dark sky.

"That must be Altenbauna," Robert said tonelessly.

Slowly the firelight spread and colored the horizon a deep red. Robert kept staring at it.

At last Soerman thought he understood why Robert wanted to go to America. These farmers whose homes were burning, and whom no one could help; the soldiers doing slave labor on the Elector's walls; no doubt there were plenty of other reasons for Robert to leave the country. The news that his father was alive in America had only triggered something that had been a long time in preparation. Adventurousness was part of it, of course, but only superficially. Basically, Robert was not like Soerman; he was not a ship without an anchor; he had his own inner center of gravity that held him steady as a rock. In that respect, too, he was like his father. A man like Hoym, a real thief, genuinely belonged to this old, corrupt, feudal world where a successful man was one who best learned how to take from others. The Skelniks took their share only as a legitimate heir takes possession of his heritage, and then they had to leave the Old World behind, repelled by its morbidity, its moribund state. They had to get all the way away, even to crossing the ocean.

"Let's ride," Soerman said. "I've had enough."

Robert came back from his reverie and picked up the reins again. He took the lead, skillfully leading his horse down the precipitous path. They rode past the back of the opera house. An open window gave them a view of the interior where the costumes were stored. On a coat hanger hung the fluffy tutu of a ballet dancer.

They could only move at a walk in the slippery snow. For Soerman it was too slow. He was uneasy, and he didn't like it. He tried to hide it, but that only made it worse.

They heard a coach coming down the street behind them, turning in from a side street. Two lanterns shed a dim light from the coachman's box. The coachman cracked his whip to make them clear the way; they were blocking the middle of the road. For a second it looked almost as if the coach would run them down, but then the coachman reined to a stop. "Isn't the road wide enough to let me pass?"

A man stuck his head out of the coach window. "What's going on? What are we stopping for?"

Robert rode up to the side of the coach. He couldn't have said why he hadn't followed his first impulse, which was to avoid the encounter altogether. When he recognized Claus, he knew he'd made a mistake, because Claus stared at him as if he were a ghost. His mouth opened as if to shout, but then he ordered the coachman to drive on. To Robert's surprise the coach turned into the little square at the end of the street and stopped under the great twin acacia. Claus stepped out of the coach. The coachman clambered down from his driver's seat, listened to Claus's orders, and ran off into the dark.

Soerman's horse capered nervously in place.

"It's all right," Robert said without looking at him. "It seems we don't have to fetch our carriage, it's being brought to us."

"You mean you told somebody where we were?" Soerman said incredulously.

"Wait and see. Stick by my side. It's my stepbrother."

He stopped, because Claus had come over to them and grasped the snaffle of Robert's horse.

Claus was almost incoherent with anger. "You've got to get away from here. . . . If you're seen . . . Get down off your horses —or no, better still, ride them over to the carriage." As he talked, he kept pulling Robert's horse in the direction he wanted them to go. When they reached the carriage, he pulled Robert off his horse, meeting no resistance. There seemed to be nothing for Robert to say. Claus, too, was at a loss for words. He stared at Soerman with a mixture of disgust and impotent rage. "I have to speak to you alone," he said to Robert.

Robert nodded to Soerman. "Get our baggage into the coach. Take your time, and don't leave anything behind."

Robert's calm made Claus lose his last shred of self-control. He seized Robert by his coat lapels as if to shake him. "You're bringing disaster on us all! How can you be so low, getting mixed up with the Hoym gang? How can you dare come into town—after all that's happened? You're probably proud of it, proud of what you've done! . . ." He was choking on his hatred, his overwhelming fear.

Robert gently loosened the spasmodic grip of Claus's fingers. "So you know about it. Does Mother know, too? And Father? Believe me, I had nothing to do with it."

"The whole town knows." Claus moved his head as though trying to slip out of a noose. "You should never have come into town." His eye moved to Soerman, who was carrying the saddlebags into the coach. "And with him, of all people."

For a moment Robert felt tempted to tell Claus the secret of Soerman's identity, tell him what Soerman's information, brought to Haynow, had meant to him personally, but he thought better of it. He put his hand on Claus's shoulder. "Go on home. If you're not at the party, it'll look suspicious. We'll get away, don't worry."

"Where do you intend to go?"

"Toward Hannover, up the Weser River toward Bremerlehe." He sensed Claus's hesitation, his inner struggle. There was no way he could help, since he didn't know himself which he preferred: for Claus to leave and forget they'd met, or for Claus to help him escape.

"I'll take you to the border in the carriage," Claus said.

"Two men will attract less attention than three."

"You think so? And what about the patrols, the spies everywhere looking for men on the run? What'll you do if they stop you? What can you say to the guards at the city gates?" He ripped open his coat. "When they see this uniform they won't dare search the carriage. They won't even ask any questions. This time you need me. I'm the only one who can get you safely to the border. Or don't you trust me?"

"I just don't want to drag you into it, that's all."

"I'm in it deep enough already!" Claus moved closer to Robert and, with a slight inclination of his head toward Soerman, said in a low voice, "What about him? Do you insist on traveling with him?"

"Absolutely. It's both of us or neither."

Claus bowed his head without a word. He felt numb. All he knew was that there was no retreat.

Soerman approached them. "Everything's stowed away inside. What do we do with the horses?"

"We take them along. Tie them to the back of the coach."

Robert and Soerman exchanged a glance; it was all that was necessary. Ever since they had met in the courtyard of the gendarme at Altenbauna they'd known they were in this together, for better or for worse.

Claus caught the look that passed between them. He sensed instinctively that this stranger was closer to his brother than he was, that this stranger, in fact, was to Robert what he had always wanted to be—a man Robert considered his equal. His eyes tried to pierce through Soerman's impassive mask of a face, but the man was impossible to read. "Tell him to get inside the coach," he said grimly.

Soerman vanished into the coach.

The two brothers tied up the horses in silence.

"Are you sure you want to do this?" Robert said. "You can still back out."

"Don't imagine I'm doing it for you," Claus said. "I'm thinking of myself and our parents. I want to make sure you two are out of the city, sure that I'll never have to see you again. I hope you realize you can never come back. Never. Get in, and shut the curtains. And no matter what happens, don't budge out of the carriage until I give you the signal."

Claus climbed up to the driver's seat.

Robert hesitated for a moment at the carriage door, as though a voice were warning him, urging him to use this one last moment to remount his horse instead. But when he heard Claus removing the brakeshoes, he knocked the snow off his boots and got in. The coach instantly jerked forward. In the darkness he heard Soerman's breathing. "What's worrying you?" he said.

"A comfortable prison. I feel locked in. The horses are running, but I'm not holding the reins."

Robert sensed that Soerman had leaned back among the cushions.

"How do you and your brother get along?" Soerman asked.

Robert did not answer at once. Then he said, "I'd do the same for him."

"He always wanted to be like you, right? I know all about that, except it was the other way around in my case. I wanted to be anything at all as long as I wasn't like my father. This sort of thing rarely has a happy end."

"Claus wears the uniform of a Major in the Hessian Rifle Corps. Even if he weakens no patrol would dare seach his vehicle. We're in luck." He stretched out his legs. "Sit back and enjoy yourself. Just this once let somebody else do the driving. Wake me up when we get to the border." He switched to the other side and lay down comfortably.

Soerman handed him a cushion.

"Thanks." Robert adjusted the cushion under his head, and in the ensuing silence, his breathing slowly changed into the rhythm of a man in a drowse. Just before he fell asleep he murmured, "In Gimte there's an innkeeper who makes a jugged hare you wouldn't believe."

Gimte, Soerman knew, was a little settlement on the other side of the Weser River, the other side of the border.

Ever since the levy of troops had begun for the regiments sold to England, Kassel had become a huge military barracks, and the city gates were guarded by soldiers instead of militiamen, as if it were wartime. The Leipzig Gate was currently the responsibility of the First Regiment of Hessian Rifles, Claus's own regiment; a lucky circumstance, he thought, but the closer he came to the guard post the more he began to wonder if it wouldn't have been wiser to choose another exit from the city. They'd probably already heard what had happened in Altenbauna—or had they? The last relief had come at four that afternoon, quite some time before Scholl's return. The next relief was due about eleven.

A tall chimney with a tin hood jutted up from the low roof of the guardhouse. Icicles hung down from its edges. The whole thing looked like a bearded, menacing giant standing guard at the gate. Sentries stepped forward as he approached. Claus stopped the coach, and called out the password. The sentries saluted.

"Be quick about it," he said. "I'm in a hurry."

They ran and opened the gates, then stood back against the walls, saluting again. Claus looked down at his hands as if they didn't belong to him; he watched them holding the reins, moving slightly to guide the horses through. He heard the rattlings of the wheels. Ahead, outside the gate, he saw coach tracks, still fresh—but the post coach to Karlshafen had left early that afternoon. The tracks were unusually broad and could have been made by a private carriage—or else, a patrol wagon?

No, he thought, they must have sent all the patrols to Altenbauna. Everything'll be all right. Robert's always had luck on his side. Why should it be any different this time? The relief patrol would not arrive till eleven. The men who came to relieve the guards at the Leipzig Gate at eleven would know all about the Altenbauna story. I'll have to go back before then. I've got three hours to make it. I won't need that long.

He knew he was doing the right thing, that there was nothing else he could do—and yet he was in misery. It rose inside him like groundwater rising inside a flooded cellar. It wasn't fear. He could manage that. It was the irrepressible knowledge that he had become an accomplice. What if a patrol comes along? What if they see me? If they open the carriage door—then I'll hang, too.

He stared at his hands. Why did he keep driving? He looked at the fields on either side. The earth was brighter than the sky. The snow made a smooth blanket on the ground and looked like a fine lacy veil over the fields sown with winter crops. The carriage tracks kept running on before him. It was another half hour to the border. I'll make it, he told himself firmly.

What if something happens to the carriage?

The carriage is brand new.

Suppose one of the horses slips?

We have extra horses.

I'll turn back in Speele. They can ride that last bit to the border. Right, I'll turn back at Speele. I'll have done my share then.

The lanterns swung from side to side, creating ghostly shadows in the snow, like running dogs beside the moving coach. The land was flat. How far was their light visible? How far could the rattling of the carriage be heard?

Searching the fields, his eyes seemed to detect fixed shapes beginning to move, shadows growing out of the furrows, trees changing place. And then he saw the fire reflecting in the sky. Altenbauna. They've set fire to it; they've burned it down. They're already on the way back, carrying the corpse of Lessberg. They'll be entering the city by the Leipzig Gate. Our ball—what will Christina think about my failure to pick her up? Everyone noticing I'm not there. Nobody believing Father's lies about it.

I must go back, this instant.

I can't go back, I can't.

He drove on, unable to come to a decision, flooded with contradictory voices, torn apart inside. I've got to get Robert out, across the border. If I keep on, he'll be saved, and I'll hang instead of him. Lights appeared in the distance. The village of Speele. But he didn't stop, he drove past it, whipped the horses harder. His coat had come open and fluttered behind him, but he didn't notice the cold, didn't even shift the reins from one hand to the other. He drove on, trying not to think, not to question what he was doing, just to keep going.

The road dipped downward. The Weser Valley. Lights. Torches. Down there the tiny ferry lay covered with snow, floating like a bit of paper on the dark, slow-moving river.

Beside the guardhouse at the border stood a cart. Claus remembered seeing that cart once before today, when he'd left the fortress. Two men had been lifting the huge recruiting drum down from it.

The torches along the river bank started to move. The door of the guardhouse opened, and a beam of light fell across the ground. A troop of soldiers came running across the yard. His horses seemed to have stopped of their own accord.

Men carrying guns; the glint of light reflecting from the barrels. Their faces were unrecognizable in the dark, but he recognized Scholl's voice.

"Is that you, Major Haynow?" Then Scholl said to his men, who had been about to surround the coach. "It's all right, stand aside." He stepped over to the box. "Are you expecting a visitor from the Hannover area?"

Claus gripped the reins and began buttoning his coat.

"You have extra horses?" Scholl said. "Are you traveling that much further?"

Claus stared around him. Caught in a circle of light, caught in a circle of weapons. And yet—if he said a single word, the guards would go back inside their shelter and back to the riverbank. It was so simple. One word, one word of command, was all that was needed—but the journey had worn him out. He would betray Robert not because it was what he wanted, but because he lacked the energy to offer further resistance.

"Are you alone? Or do you have guests inside the carriage?" Scholl's voice, his hand stretched out, ready to open the carriage door.

"They're inside," Claus heard himself saying. "Robert and the deserter. I'm surrendering them to you."

21

He was no one's enemy, no one's friend—that was what they said in Kassel about Minister Schlieffen. It was said most of all by people who considered themselves either his enemies or his friends but who were unsure which category Schlieffen assigned them to. He was not the kind of man who made it easy to know such things about him, since he showed no malice as an enemy, and no affection as a friend. Nothing seemed to come from his heart; whatever he did was done with his head.

Schlieffen was content to leave people uncertain about his feelings but it wounded him to feel that what he had to offer, which he considered rather valuable, went unrecognized. Compared with the Elector, who did everything on impulse, whose mood was the law all were subjected to, Schlieffen was the advocate of reason and justice, yet he found himself unrecognized and unappreciated.

To be no one's friend and no one's foe—only Schlieffen knew how hard it was sometimes. He had always known the day would come when he would be able to serve justice only by sacrificing his reputation as an impartial arbitrator. That day had now come. There was just one brief respite left. This morning was the funeral of the youngest member of the Star League, an order of Freemasons founded by the Elector of Hessia, at the Lodge House. Maybe a saving idea would come to him there; it had happened at Lodge meetings before.

The session was taking place in the Hall of the Past. The walls were hung with blue silk. Wax tapers burned in the candelabra that were placed in each corner of the hall. In the center stood the sarcophagus on a raised platform. Four falconers, each holding a falcon on a fist raised in the direction of the sarcophagus, stood the deathwatch. Schlieffen sought a firm point on the floor to fix his eyes on, to help him concentrate: a black circle in the mosaic. But as hard as he tried, it wouldn't work. How could it with Gottfried Haynow only a few rows away?

Schlieffen would have denied publicly what he could no longer deny to himself: the impossible had happened, even the Lodge had become a scene of public judgment against the Haynow family, a judgment demonstrated by the whole city. The original cause no longer mattered, it had receded from everyone's consciousness. As in the case of an earthquake, nobody stopped to ask what had caused it; everybody tried to save himself. No occasion was passed up to demonstrate to oneself and others that one had never had anything to do with the Haynow family.

Haynow was the last to have entered the hall. Schlieffen had watched as not a single man present dared to offer Haynow even the hint of a greeting—this toward a man who had done nothing blameworthy before the laws of the world or the laws of the Lodge. Considering that the Lodge was a self-proclaimed fortress of justice, of fraternity, of absolute loyalty . . .

Schlieffen was filled with indignation and shame, more against himself than the others. Had he behaved better? Almost a month had passed since Robert and the deserter had been taken. Since then not a day had passed that he hadn't expected Haynow to turn to him for help. But he had done nothing of the kind. He hadn't even tried to approach him in secret.

There he sat now, in his traditional seat, surrounded by noticeably empty chairs. He sat there with an air of calm and introspection as though he were the only man here doing justice to the occasion; the only one who had truly left the world outside and opened within himself the door to that other world, to which this occasion was meant to be a bridge.

Invisible choirs filled the large hall with song. The music seemed to be coming from the cupola in the center of the ceiling. The service was being held for the son of the Chief Falconer Wittung, who had drowned after breaking through the ice while skating on the pond.

Schlieffen tried to concentrate, his head lowered and his hands covering his temples, but his eyes kept wandering off to Haynow's profile. The man looked solid, rather robust in fact, and yet there was great sensitivity in his profile, great vulnerability. To soothe his own conscience Schlieffen had been telling himself in the last few weeks that Haynow was a man of tough fiber, resistant enough to survive even the terrible blows he had suffered lately. At this moment he was plagued with doubts. He kept remembering how often he felt misjudged by others. The more he studied the lines of Haynow's face, the more he saw in them not strength, but despair.

Did Haynow know that there was to be a secret session at the palace at ten o'clock, when the death sentence against Robert would be submitted to the Elector for his signature? Schlieffen's eye wandered to the Elector's face. He was holding his head up and slightly back, just as he did when listening to a favorite cadenza at the opera. His devoutness was nothing but sentimentality and a pose. After these sessions at the Lodge he would continue for the rest of the day to exhibit an exalted expression, transfigured, a man who understood all and forgave all—a true Serene Highness.

At last the antiphonal music came to an end in an ethereal diminuendo up in the cupola. One of the falcon's became restless, so that for seconds there was only the sound of those huge beating wings in the hall. The Elector rose, stepped to the sarcophagus; the others followed. Each man laid his hand on the silver-ornamented coffin.

Schlieffen was tempted to steal away, hurry to the Palace, and check the agenda for the meeting to make certain there was nothing that would change the Elector's mood before they reached the Haynow case. He was impatient for the ceremony to come to an end, even though he was not entirely sure whether he had decided to help Haynow or whether he was simply being influenced by the mood of the place and the occasion, a mood that would dissipate as soon as he had left here.

Schlieffen's aide, Jacob Hanslin, was alone in his office, as always when he was expecting Schlieffen for a final look at the agenda for a council meeting. As usual he had spread out those papers he assumed would be of special interest to Schlieffen on the desk near the window. When Schlieffen entered, Hanslin lay down his pen.

"I'd expected you earlier, sir."

Schlieffen went to his desk. The top document on it was the one that was uppermost in his mind. "You wrote this death sentence yourself?"

"I had to make sure there wouldn't be half a dozen copies of it in town tomorrow morning."

"That only means one of the court recorders will be selling them off instead."

"The trial records are in my hands. It wasn't exactly cheap, getting them there. I could have appealed to precedent, but that would have taken too much time. So I paid for them."

Schlieffen looked up with pleased surprise and smiled. "Indeed—and was it worth it? Did you find anything that would help their case?"

"Nothing. Statements tending to exonerate the two defendants were not put on record. But there was one thing I did find." Hanslin handed Schlieffen a document.

"A recruitment form?"

"Look at it closely. This is the piece of paper they built their entire case on—premeditated murder."

Schlieffen laid the sheet of paper on the desk and smoothed it with his hand. "Recruited for the First Hessian Rifles, etcetera, etcetera, that's the printed text, followed by the entry, handwritten: 'Baron Robert Haynow, 24 years of age, 6 foot 2 in height, Ramswood, 2 November 1775.' Then the signatures, Lessberg, and next to that—" Schlieffen glanced sharply at Hanslin— "He signed it '*Robert Skelnik*'? "

"The judges considered this further proof of premeditation—first premeditated fraud, then premeditated murder."

Schlieffen shook his head. "This is the first time I've heard of this document."

"The same with me. Reported to have been found in Major Lessberg's papers. Sometime in the course of the trial it suddenly turned up on the judge's desk. Nobody knows who put it there."

Hanslin stood up, went to the door, and looked out into the hallway. When he came back Schlieffen looked at him expectantly.

"You arouse my curiosity. What else did you dig up that you'd prefer to tell me in a language no one besides ourselves understands?"

Hanslin pointed to the recruitment form. "It has to do with that. Last night, right after I found the paper among the other trial records, I rode to Ramswood. Not that I was too hopeful of finding anyone who'd remember that evening at the Black Bear. But I was in luck. November second was the day Soerman deserted from the fortress, and the innkeeper's daughter remembered that day very well. Robert Haynow was throwing dice with the recruiters, he lost, and it's true: he ended up staking himself, and Lessberg won. Haynow insisted on filling out the recruitment form, even though nobody wanted to take him at his word. Nor did the innkeeper's daughter recall seeing Lessberg pick up the signed form from the table. In short, the barroom was empty that whole evening, because everybody with the exception of the three who were gambling there was on guard duty somewhere or other, but—" Hanslin looked at Schlieffen for emphasis— "there was one other guest who'd arrived that evening and was staying the night at the inn. That man witnessed the whole incident. The innkeeper's daughter gave me a complete description of him."

Schlieffen made a gesture with his hand. "On the morning of November third, Chamberlain Stein paid a visit to Sonsfeld Castle."

The two men exchanged a long, eloquent look. Hanslin picked up the form and placed it back with the file. "He's likely to testify that he's never seen this document before. And there's no way of proving the contrary. I can't see through this thing. What advantage can he derive from the execution of Haynow's son?"

"There's a great deal in this story I can't understand either," Schlieffen said. "Disasters of this kind have a logic of their own. I may, of course, have underestimated that fellow Stein, but I still think he's only a little cog in this storm machine that's been set in motion. The son—he's only a pretext; the whole thing is aimed at Gottfried Haynow, at his destruction, no less."

Schlieffen stared at the window. He suddenly felt very old. Ordinarily he was pleased at his ability to keep his emotions in check, but this time he could almost believe his self-restraint had turned into too much of a good thing—emotional paralysis. "When was the last time the Elector signed a death sentence?" he asked.

"I sent for the records of the last five years."

"All I'm interested in is the year '75."

"In May a girl who killed her newborn baby; in June a woman who poisoned a relative; in October an arsonist. The others had to do with banditry on the open road and encouraging desertion from the armed forces. Since November all death sentences against men have been commuted to imprisonment at the fortress. Some of these men have been pardoned and inducted into the army since."

"How many commuted death sentences?"

"Nineteen. Three pardons, three executions. I've been thinking that we could drag out the Haynow case until the Elector's journey to Italy. He plans to leave as soon as the troops have been shipped out."

Hanslin was waiting for an answer; instead, Schlieffen was giving him a sudden broad smile that took Hanslin so completely by surprise he couldn't decide what it meant. It was ironic, but it was also very warm.

"And here I'd been thinking that wisdom was merely a product of old age," Schlieffen said.

Hanslin found the statement as mysterious as the smile, but he gathered from the tone in which it was made that there was a further and deeper bond of mutual confidence between them, though he would have been glad to know how he had managed to earn it.

The great council chamber was all that was left of Frederick II of Hessia's political aspirations. Proportioned on the model of the reception hall of the Palazzo Medici in Florence, all marble walls and rows of columns, it indicated a claim to empire that had never been fulfilled, and never would be fulfilled.

Schlieffen called it the mausoleum, but his sense of humor could not save him from the depression that overcame him every time he set foot in the place.

On this occasion the Elector and Stein had preceded him. He saw them standing in a window recess, chatting, a footman beside them holding a tray of wineglasses. For weeks Chamberlain Stein had been enjoying the prerogative of keeping His Grace company at breakfast. It made Schlieffen uneasy. In the course of these hectic weeks he had lost sight of Stein, and the wily man had made good use of his opportunities. To judge from his new self-assurance, he had moved from petty schemes for his own immediate advantage to conducting intrigue in the grand manner. But as

Schlieffen entered with Hanslin, he saw at first glance that the Elector's mood of godlike benevolence had carried over unimpaired from the funeral rites at the Masonic Lodge. A quick look at the footmen told him that the conversation between the ruler and his panderer must have been tripping along in the Elysian fields of easy sex. . . .

"Have some of this good port!" the Elector called out jovially as he let himself drop into a chair. He was surrounded by footmen who seemed ready to catch their lord and master if the delicate French chair should disintegrate beneath him. His Grace pointed to the pile of documents at Schlieffen's place and raised an eyebrow. "You spoke of a few minor details on our agenda."

"Your Grace promised to give me an hour."

The Elector looked at his pocket watch on the table. "Seven and a half minutes of your hour are gone. If Chamberlain Stein hadn't stayed to amuse me, the session would already be over. You and your stacks of papers!"

"I recall Your Grace's saying, one time, that this council chamber transmutes everything into the stuff of power."

The ruler's eyes dwelled on the marble walls around him; he was not meditating on the essence of power but savoring the knowledge that at last he had money again, enough to cover more of his palace walls with shining Carrara marble.

"To get back to the English contracts for a moment." His Grace was gazing intently at his fingernails, but what he contemplated was marble—blue, green, red marble, gleaming loggias, rows of Greek columns. "In the future I would like the following procedure in the case of our foreign correspondence: after we have conferred about it together, a first draft, a translation to be given to me, the original letter to be dispatched only when I have passed on it in translation. Kindly say nothing about the time this will take. We managed it, after all, at the start of our negotiations with England."

"At the time we had Miss Connors doing the translation."

"Are you telling me there's no one else in Kassel who can read English? It seems to me we import these English governesses only to fatten them up and give them a chance to make a good marriage in Kassel. In future we shall hire only women over fifty as governesses. But to get back to our subject. I ate my way through your English pudding and picked out a few raisins. . . ."

Schlieffen leaned back in his chair. The session could not have started off on a better tack as far as he was concerned. As long as His Grace was concentrating on England, he was seeing the world with the eyes of a man who had witnessed a miracle, and that transfigured everything for him. His niggling tone was only a way to mask and preserve his delight.

"That fellow Faucitt," the Elector went on, "behaved in his audiences with me as though we were the only court with which England is drawing up contracts. What about the others one hears about?"

"Has Your Grace looked at a map of America recently? Merely to guard the harbors on the East Coast requires three times the number of troops we can deliver. The important thing to remember is that George III is paying three times as much for a Hessian as for a Braunschweig man."

"I'm amazed to find a fellow impresario in Minister Schlieffen," Stein said.

"I'm glad you reminded me, my dear Schlieffen: those Braunschweig contracts. The English promise to pay thirty crowns for every Braunschweiger soldier killed. I have found nothing on that point in our contracts. Is a dead Hessian worth less?"

"I deliberately left the point uncontested, sire. Let the Braunschweigers have their dead. No other country but Hessia-Kassel is receiving a double subsidy from the English; no other country is being paid for its officers, and paid in gold at that. A Hessian costs the King three times as much, actually, as any other mercenary. So much for the practical side. But these contracts have another aspect. At every point in the contract I was mindful of the fact that these agreements will still be functional when you and I are no more."

Schlieffen observed with satisfaction that the Elector's face took on a new glow. The sentimental devotions at the funeral rites, the splendid breakfast that followed, the port consumed in quantity, the awareness that he now had, beneath this throne as it were, an ever-gushing fountain of money—and now, to top all this, the incense of immortality. The Elector was bound to be in the best possible frame of mind. Now was the time to bring up the Haynow matter as quickly and smoothly as possible.

The Elector placed his hand on Schlieffen's arm. "You give me an idea. I want a historian to go along to America with our troops."

"A marvelous idea!" Stein said enthusiastically. "But it must be a man able to express sublime thoughts in a great style."

"Are you thinking of yourself?" Schlieffen couldn't resist this opening for his malice. Stein seemed dumbfounded by the idea, and Schlieffen couldn't resist firing a second arrow after the first. "Surely Chamberlain Stein is not among the class of Your Grace's subjects who are not permitted to travel abroad?"

The Elector measured Stein with an amused eye. "I don't think he is a tall enough specimen for the Guards. But who knows? If we should find ourselves embarrassed at the time replacements are in order, why not? Monsieur Stein, you mustn't argue. You've cost me so much money already, it would only be fair for me to recoup a little of it by the sale of your person some day."

Hanslin felt the time had come to begin collecting his signatures. Without waiting for Schlieffen's signal, he drew a paper from his case and passed it over for signing. "The decree for closing the borders, Your Grace."

A page handed the ruler a pen, and someone else heated the sealing wax over a candle. The Elector personally pressed his seal on the red lacquer. "This will keep them inside the country," he said. "But what about our foreign recruitments? I shall expect a final plan for those at the next session. We must begin to concern ourselves with further supplies of soldiers. There's not much left to be got from this country, so we must look around elsewhere, and kindly don't talk to me of your conscience, Schlieffen. Just think of the King of Prussia. His faked gold and his stolen mercenaries have made him great. What else have you got there, Hanslin?"

"The draft for the sermons to be given in the churches, Your Grace."

"Let me see." The Elector glanced over the text. "Who wrote this?"

"Pastor Moralt, sire."

"I thought so. You Protestants are neither fish nor fowl. Too stingy with the fuel for feeding your hellfires. Oh no, this won't do. The Jesuits are much better at it. I want this rewritten by Father Erlafried, he has the knack to put the fear of God into them. That reminds me . . ." He lowered his voice, making the footmen take a discreet step backward from the table. "Father Erlafried can hear the grass grow, as you know, and he just brought me a little leaflet; '*To Help All Womenfolk to Know in the Most Natural Manner Their Fruitful and Their Unfruitful Periods*' is its title. This penny sheet is being hawked about for a high price, too. Imagine, gentlemen, if this kind of thing really gets around—if our wenches only got the children they wanted!"

"Does anyone know where this flyer comes from?" Schlieffen asked.

"That will be for you to find out. Look into the print shops, tighten customs procedures at the borders, search everybody, forbid the popular gazettes to mention this concoction. I want the birth rate in Hessia to go up! Hanslin, will you note this down for procedures during my Italian journey: birth statistics to be sent to me in Italy once a month. Schlieffen, what do you think about the state offering a premium for each baby born?"

Schlieffen had to control his impatience. "Your Grace, I find the mortality figures more significant than the birth statistics. It's not our women but our doctors who are at fault."

"Thank you, I'd rather not have any mortality figures served me with my breakfast. Neither here nor in Italy. Do whatever you want with the doctors, but leave me out of it.—Now, are we finished?"

"One more signature, Your Grace." Schlieffen tried to sound as bored with the matter as the Elector. "The sentence against Robrt Haynow and that deserter."

The Elector placed a hand over his eyes in a theatrical gesture of extreme fatigue. "My dear Schlieffen, I put myself entirely in your hands. Tell me what you want me to do and I shall do it."

"When you began your reign, Your Grace, your motto was the unity of law and justice."

"You're being evasive, Schlieffen. Tell me, what would you do in my place?"

Schlieffen couldn't put his finger on what it was that sounded a warning note in his mind. Partly fearing that his answer might be too studied, partly irritated by Stein's watchful eye, he said cautiously, "The two condemned men would be in a bad way if the matter depended on me, sire; you once called me your severest critic, remember. It's quite true, my tendency is to be harsher in my judgment of people than they deserve. But you, Your Grace, are possessed of the magnanimity it takes to be lenient at the right time."

The Elector sat with eyes half-lowered, which gave him an expression of low cunning; his right hand rested on the trial records Hanslin had spread out before him. "From time to time a higher justice seems to intervene," he said at last. "You remember that business of the alchemist, the gold-maker Robert Skelnik. Twenty-four years ago he gravely injured our country. My father was merciful at the time; he refrained from holding the criminal's wife responsible. The property she had inherited from her parents and her uncle was not confiscated, as it might have been. I am not inclined to criticize my father's decision at the time, but doesn't it seem as though a higher court has reopened the case, so that justice might at last be done? This young man is only the instrument of a higher judgment. The gold his father took with him was never restored. The man was never caught. But the son never got past the Hannoverian border guards."

Schlieffen felt as if he were listening to His Grace's father confessor. What exactly was he trying to say? "Are you thinking of letting Baron Haynow pay a commensurate sum in restitution, on behalf of his adopted son, sire?"

"I am thinking somewhat beyond that kind of thing. Such a model case calls for a model verdict. Any sort of fine would make the whole thing ridiculous. No, I mean to make an example of the case." He paused. "My decision is to confiscate the Haynow property—movables and immovables, lands, houses, goods, warehouses. We can't touch the cash; they've banked it abroad. But we can deal with that, too, by decreeing that Baron Haynow must pay the sum of five hundred thousand taler if he wishes to leave the country as a free man."

Schlieffen was speechless for a moment. "Sire, you are destroying a man who has given us invaluable service."

"The execution is to be carried out as scheduled," the Elector continued, unmoved, "to take place tomorrow morning at six. The confiscation will be in force from that moment on. Until then, not a word must leak out about it. As regards Claus Haynow's demotion, I've considered and rejected it. After all, we owe the capture of the two fugitives to him. Tell me, Schlieffen, would you really have given a milder verdict?"

Schlieffen lowered his eyes. "I would not have been able to take such responsibility upon myself."

"You're saying a great many different things in one. You can't deceive me, Schlieffen. Must I say it? Your character is much too noble to comprehend a phenomenon like the elder Haynow. Otherwise you'd have grown rich with him. I know what it means to have a Minister whose official miserliness is not the other side of a selfish personal greed. For a long time I have been wanting to find a commensurate reward for your selflessness; I have it now. I want you to consider the Haynow estate as your property, henceforth. It is not only my wish, it is an order.

Schlieffen pushed back his chair and stood up. He had put on a suit of gray silk for the funeral that morning; its simple, almost military cut, the absence of any ornament, even the orders and decorations commonly worn by a courtier gave his slim figure a dignified, noble appearance that made him stand out among the others in their courtly glitter. He was aware of it, and it gave him the strength he needed.. "Once before in my life I have refused an order that was given to my advantage. I must do it once more. Your Grace, I must ask you to release me from your service."

The two men locked eyes. The Elector felt anger rising inside him, as always when Schlieffen assumed that cold, piercing look. Nobody dared look at him in this fashion—nobody except this impoverished nobleman from Pomerania who had risen to the top in his service. He was the only man among those who served the Court of Hessia who was not a lackey. And the Elector both hated and loved him for it.

"Not so fast, Schlieffen. You were wrong to refuse an order from the King of Prussia, but the King of Prussia did an even greater wrong in letting you go. I shall forget my order to you, and I shall even forget your disobedience."

Schlieffen gave a slight nod. "With your permission, your Grace, I shall withdraw. The hour is nearly up."

"But Schlieffen, Schlieffen! I don't understand you at all. Usually, you are by far the better head for figures of the two of us; the realist, always scolding me for not thinking enough about our economy and all that. And now that I've found something I can do to fatten up our accounts, you're displeased with me. Think of it, you can cross off our debts to this parasite with one stroke of your pen. You know better than I do how enormous those debts are. And I won't even mention the salutary shock this will be for half a dozen would-be Haynows. You will see, Schlieffen, how quiet our creditors are going to be for some time to come. And there's another item we can take off the debit side of our ledger: Baroness Sonsfeld will not cost the state exchequer one penny."

"How is that, Your Grace?" Schlieffen asked reluctantly.

"Quite simply, by giving the Haynow estate, which you have just declined, to Christina Sonsfeld, with all its income from the tenant farmers, etcetera. Have you made a note of this, Hanslin?" The Elector turned to Schlieffen: "How do you like that?"

Schlieffen could not avoid responding to the Elector's smile with one of his own; but despite the Elector's effort to bridge the differences between himself and the man he respected more than any other and understood less than any other, Schlieffen's forced smile only emphasized the gap between them.

Everything had turned out in a way he could not have forseen, Schlieffen thought. There was nothing to be done about it now. There would be time enough later to brood about the reasons for it. What could not be postponed was some way to get Chamberlain Stein out his hair. Schlieffen saw clearly that Stein had his fingers in this pie, and was counting on a reward for his services. Well, Schlieffen would see to it at once.

"I must say, with unfeigned admiration, your Grace has thought of everything," he said. "Only one detail is missing in this work of art, though I am certain Your Grace has thought of that, too. There is the question of the young Countess's marriage, since Claus Haynow is no longer eligible. May I offer a suggestion?"

"Do, Schlieffen. I can already see you as the model husband of Kassel."

"I couldn't risk refusing an order of yours twice within the hour, sire, so I suggest Chamberlain Stein. It seems to me he is the very man for this extremely delicate position."

"This is how I like you, Schlieffen!" The Elector glanced at his watch. "We have two minutes left. That should be quite enough for transforming Chamberlain Stein into a Count Sonsfeld. Have you made a note of it, Hanslin?" The Elector rubbed his hands, not without malice in his smile.

"How kind of you, sire," Stein murmured. At last he had reached the fulfillment of his boldest dreams, but he was more frightened than pleased. Not even the knowledge that this news would hit the Sonsfeld family like a bolt of lightning enabled him to savor his triumph.

"You look terrified," the Elector remarked. "I must admit, two minutes is not a generous allowance for making such an adjustment." He was no longer smiling. "Nevertheless, in two minutes men can rise very high or fall very low, as you have just observed. Don't ever forget it. Perhaps in that idea we can find a fine motto for your new coat of arms."

22

Soerman held the tallow candle near Robert's face. Robert blinked and turned his face to the wall.

"You sleep by night, you sleep by day." Soerman sat down on the edge of the cot. "Move over a bit. Don't you hear the rain?

This endless drumming on the roof drives me mad. How on earth can you sleep through it?"

"I've always been a sound sleeper." He was still half asleep but slowly coming out of it.

Soerman stared into the candle flame. "Why do you think they took our leg-irons off today? Preparation for our last meal?"

"If I had ideas like those, I suppose I couldn't fall asleep, either. Forget it. Anyway, if you're right about what comes after, you've got plenty of sleep to look forward to."

Soerman stood up and set the candle down on the table in the center of the cell. On the table lay a deck of cards and two folded napkins.

Robert lay on his cot, facing the wall. There was nothing to talk about. Talking had long ago become only a way of avoiding the ominous quiet.

"Do you really believe there's life after death?" Soerman said.

Robert sat up, folded his legs against his chest and put his arms around his knees. "If you insist. Listen carefully: the first principle of the Creation is the Law of Conservation. Nothing is lost. Therefore I shall live on."

Soerman shook his head. "Another principle of nature is that a man with twelve bullets in his body lies down and never gets up again. And depend upon it, those soldiers are good shots. So you can count on your twelve bullets." He picked up the cards and started to shuffle them. "I always knew I wouldn't die peacefully in bed. At least it won't be the gallows. Anyway, death—if that were all, I wouldn't lost any sleep over it."

"Then get some sleep."

For a while there was only the sound of the cards being shuffled. "I was a good prophet, though, wasn't I?" Soerman said. "I told you I'd bring you bad luck. It all began when you met me."

"If you want to ease your conscience, you'd better call a priest."

"You can't fool me, so why keep trying? You've been thinking, too. If there is such a thing as a Last Judgment then what's likely to count most against me is that I didn't get you out of this.

If this were the usual kind of prison, it'd be child's play. But this well-guarded fortress . . ."

The vesper bells began to ring all through the town. Whenever Soerman started to talk, Robert found himself getting impatient at the futility of it; and yet, when Soerman wasn't talking, he found himself waiting for him to say something, anything. He had lost track of the time since the trial; neither of them had thought of keeping a record of the passing days. Hours and days that could be counted had ceased to exist by now, time had ceased to flow, had become instead a solid, frozen mass, an oppressive weight, a burden that grew heavier as they recognized its inescapability.

Robert was reminded of the wheelwright's place at the moment he had seen Soerman there for the first time. Surrounded by forty armed men hunting for him, Soerman had sat in the coach like a traveler coolly, if somewhat impatiently, waiting to be on his way. Now he was much the same. He was nervous, he waited, but no differently from the way an impatient traveler might be waiting to move on.

He tried to imagine Soerman laid out flat, his face bloodless, but he couldn't. He laid his head on his knees, closed his eyes, held his breath. But the more he tried to feel his way toward that dark gate, the more intensely he felt that he was alive, that his heart was beating, his chest rising and falling as he breathed.

The bells became more muted, until one after another fell silent, their last echoes drowned out now by the drumming of the rain overhead. If he kept his eyes closed and kept counting the steps of the sentries walking back and forth outside their cell door, he would soon be fast asleep again.

"Someone's coming," Soerman said.

As usual it seemed to take them forever to open all the bolts and locks, until there could be no doubt that they were indeed headed for this particular cell. The cell door opened, and Captain Glaser came into view. Behind him was a priest in a black cassock. Two guards covered the door.

Robert avoided looking at Soerman. "Now?" he said.

"Tomorrow morning at six," the captain said.

"All I want for breakfast is coffee—very strong, very hot. And a barber. Can you arrange it?"

"And you?" Captain Glaser asked Soerman.

"The same—minus the barber."

The officer drew a slip of paper from the wide cuff of his coat and handed it to the priest. "Will you take care of this, too?" he said. "It's in your department." Unable to restrain his distaste for the kind of duty he'd been saddled with, Glaser started to leave the cell.

"Take the priest with you," Robert said. "We didn't ask for him."

"I have my orders. He's to spend the night with you whether you like it or not."

Alone with the two prisoners, the priest looked around in embarrassment. Then he remembered the piece of paper in his hand, and took it to the tallow candle on the table to read. After a quick glance he made a move to hide it.

"Let me see." Robert reached for the paper. "Why, it looks like a bill." Suddenly he laughed. "It really does belong in his department, too."

"What is it?"

"A bill for twelve taler and seventy pence, for two pine coffins. And four taler for the gravedigger." Robert tossed the paper onto the table. "I'm surprised they forgot the bullets and powder for the firing squad. Unless that's charged to the pastoral care of our souls—which is free, am I right, Father? Who sent you? Nobody asked for you to come."

The priest opened his black cloak, dripping with rain. He looked around the cell, and his eye lit on the playing cards. "Could you use a third hand?" he asked.

"If you promise to confine your conversation to your bids. Can you afford our penny ante stakes?"

"In my student days I often ate on my luck at cards."

Robert nodded at Soerman. "We can take a chance on him, I think."

The two hosts cleared the table, fetched the hamper with provisions, and found a third stool for their guest.

"What's your name?" Robert said.

"Wittaler."

"New in Kassel?"

"How long since you went to church?" the priest said.

Robert exchanged a glance with Soerman. "Let him be the first to deal, since he was the last to arrive."

At five in the morning the three men were still at their game. The food hamper was empty, the last of the wine was gone. Their bill for coffins and gravediggers was totally covered with score charts.

Father Wittaler shoved twenty pennies over to Robert. "I always thought I couldn't lose at cards. What have you got that I haven't?"

"Your trouble is, you need *good* cards to win."

From somewhere beyond the cell door came the sound of voices, the rattling of keys, growing louder and coming closer.

Soerman leaned back in his chair. "Just when I'm starting to feel ripe for bed!"

Robert shoved the mounds of coins he had collected during the night across the table to Father Wittaler. "Here, take it all. Pay for the coffins and the gravediggers and keep the rest. No—" he said firmly, when Wittaler tried to speak. "I've nothing more to say: no request, no message. Except—yes, I do want to ask something: don't come out with us."

"I paid no attention to the trial or the talk about it," the priest said. "I never do; it only complicates things. But after this night in your company I know you two are innocent."

Robert looked him up and down for a moment, then burst out laughing. "So that's why you lost at cards. Let it be a lesson to you—next time concentrate on the game, or you'll be losing money at every execution."

"The fact that you can laugh only proves to me. . . ."

With a dull rumbling the heavy iron bolts were drawn.

Robert held out his hand to the priest. "Let's make an end of it. Go home and get some sleep."

The priest put on his cloak and stood rummaging in his pockets, his head down. "Here's something I nearly forgot. . . ." He dug into his pocket and held out a gold medallion to Robert. "I was asked to give you this."

"Don't touch it!" Soerman suddenly stood between Robert and the priest. "Don't touch it! Do as I tell you!"

"Superstitious?" Robert had never seen Soerman so excited.

"Don't, I'm warning you. To receive a talisman at a time like this, especially through an intermediary, is bad luck, believe me."

Robert smiled. "How can a man about to be executed have any more bad luck?" He held out his hand. "Who sent this?"

"Count Sonsfeld's daughter . . ." The priest hesitated.

"I see." Without a glance at it, Robert slid the medallion into his pocket.

Behind them the iron door opened. The priest murmured something and hurried out. Four guards were stationed at the door; an orderly brought hot water and poured it steaming into the two basins; another brought coffee, mugs, milk, bread, sugar, all of which he set on the table. The barber unpacked his tools.

Captain Glaser had stationed himself with his back to the tiny, barred window, his arms folded on his chest, watching silently. The courtyard behind him seemed to be coming alive with the sound of hooves and wheels.

"You look as if you hadn't got much sleep last night," Robert said.

The captain's bloodshot eyes narrowed to slits. "You make me sick with that stiff upper lip of yours. So what if I didn't sleep? I wanted to be up when the pardon came through. I wanted to be the first to hear about it, and to be the one who told you. Damn it, man, don't tell me you weren't waiting for the same thing! You're still waiting for it, I tell you, and you'll still be waiting for it when. . . . Ah, the hell with it, you get on my nerves, that's all." He came away from the window. "I'll say good-bye now. The firing squad will be a group from the Rall regiment." He shook hands with Soerman, then with Robert. He seemed to have something more to say, but turned abruptly and walked out.

A squadron of mounted riflemen were lined up outside the prison. The rain had stopped, but the green cover on the wagon was shining wet. Robert and Soerman, escorted by two armed guards, climbed on the wagon. The coffins were already inside, pushed against the spars. Robert sat down on the coffin to the left; Soerman remained standing. There was no sound apart from the stamping of the horses being moved into place. Robert expected the drummers to give the signal for departure, but they did not move their sticks. Without a word of command, the procession got under way.

Robert paid no attention to where they were going, nor to his thoughts and feelings. All that had ceased to be of concern to him; only memory linked it to a cluster of habits now grown irrelevant. He was displeased when Soerman sat down beside him and started to talk. "They've kept it quiet. There's not a soul on the streets. What could they be afraid of?"

Robert laid a hand on Soerman's arm. Soerman understood, and lowered his head. After a while he put his hand on Robert's; for the rest of the journey not another word was spoken.

The meadow was surrounded by poplars, their branches bare except for a few yellowed leaves at the tips. The mounted squadron had formed a semicircle; the twelve men of the firing squad had dismounted and formed a straight line between the two ends of the semicircle.

Robert and Soerman were led past the line, as one man after the other spoke the ritual words asking forgiveness for what they were about to do. Robert suddenly stopped in front of one of the marksmen. "The powder pan is open on your weapon," he said "How are you going to shoot me without your priming?"

The commanding officer, Major Wessels, gave the drummers a signal. Three times the muffled roll of drums sounded over the meadow. The law officer stepped forward and read the sentence. Then Major Wessels asked, "Is there anything you wish to say, Robert Haynow?"

"Nothing."

"And you, Freder Soerman?"

"Nothing."

Gray clouds scudded overhead. Except for bits of snow at the roots of the slender poplars, the rain had washed the brown winter meadow bare. At its edge stood the pine coffins.

Major Wessels paced off the distance between the marksmen

and the condemned men. The regulations called for six paces; he took long steps. A swift dazzle of light broke through the gray twilight over the meadow; a sudden outpouring of sun through a break in the moving clouds casting a brief ghostly light over the scene.

Once more the drums beat their muffled tattoo. Robert made no resistance when they tied on the blindfold. Through the drums, his sharpened senses were aware of the marksmen readying their weapons.

Then he seemed to spend an eternity waiting, wondering whether the sound or the impact of the shots would be the quicker, the first to reach him. For a second he had the crazy idea the bullets would ricochet off his body as if it were armored. But none of his expectations or fancies materialized.

The air was suddenly full of strange outcries. Someone touched his arm, a sensation that struck him like a bullet. The blindfold was ripped from his eyes; the light dazzled him as if he were seeing it for the first time; he was surrounded by faces, eyes. Then he was sitting on the wagon again, on the pine coffin, Soerman beside him. Trees slid past, cottages, the Fulda River came into view—all shadows he could no longer invest with meaning. When they crossed the bridge over the Fulda, he took the medallion out of his pocket and tossed it into the river.

23

To deal with his mail was an effort Commandant Rall made as seldom as possible; actually, he did it only when his desk had become too cluttered to leave enough space for a wine bottle. Since most letters, he believed, answered themselves if you could just let them lie long enough, the task was quickly done once he addressed himself to it. There was no need to trouble Adjutant Wardein or Sergeant Luib; all he needed was a good blaze in the fireplace and gallons of tea, generously cut with rum, on such rainy days as this twentieth of February. After a cursory glance at the correspondent's name and a rather more careful check to make sure none of his own titles had been omitted in the salutation, he tossed letter after letter into the fire.

When the last of the letters had gone up in smoke, he leaned contentedly back in his chair. His feet rested on the raised hearth of the marble fireplace, in two deep depressions he had worn into it with his spurs. The wooden armrests of his desk chair also showed evidence of his tenancy; he loved to carve them up with his sharp-edged letter opener. This particular morning he was carving wavy lines that curved deeply back and inward, high-cresting waves in a storm at sea. To an uninitiated observer he might have seemed the most peaceable soul in the world, without a spark of temper, the kind of man who would never raise his voice. But Sergeant Luib read this pose of mindless relaxation only as an accurate indication of just how much rum his commandant had imbibed thus far.

Luib was always out of breath because he kept his paunch strictly corseted; the hissing sounds he emitted with every word since he'd had two front teeth extracted rather emphasized this shortness of breath. "They're here," he puffed.

Rall nodded.

"I sent them to the quartermaster for their uniforms."

Rall weighed the letter opener in his hand. "The old Elector would never have been so lax. If a man had forfeited his life, he had to die. What's the point of long-drawn-out trials if you're going to pardon everybody in the end? It's no skin off my nose, but wait until these troops are gone. This town will be robbed blind. What's to prevent it? Where's the risk in it, if felons are rewarded by being made soldiers? How was it? Was there any rioting when they got back?"

"Nobody was there but the guards, sir. In this kind of weather . . ."

Rall shivered despite the fire. "Seconds before the execution, already blindfolded—call that a pardon? Something fishy about it. I'd say it was the priest's idea, whispered into the Elector's ear. When it comes to torturing a man, those Catholics have an inexhaustible imagination. How did those two fellows behave?"

Luib shrugged. "Very cocky, I'd say. But why not? They must have been treated like guests of honor in the guardhouse, judging by the shine on their boots alone. But all I came to ask, sir, was whether you want those two quartered in tent eighteen?

"And why not?" Rall dropped his feet off the raised hearth, with a clank of spurs on sheet brass.

"If I may say so, any other tent would be preferable."

"Tent eighteen never shows up on our disciplinary lists."

"That's just it, sir. The men in tent eighteen are a real problem. All the others I can understand. The other fellows stick together, they take care of each other. They'd share their last piece of bread. But tent eighteen has never even had one meal together. It's every man for himself, careful not to move a finger for one another. They never even hammered together a common table. They don't need one. They don't talk, they don't play cards. It's far too quiet in there, sir."

Rall was in no mood to ponder complicated psychological problems. "To change the subject," he said, "have the dogs arrived?"

"Yesterday afternoon. A hundred and fifty of them."

"I requested three hundred!"

"They could barely squeeze the hundred and fifty into the kennels."

"When I say three hundred, I mean three hundred! How do you think I'll get my troops aboard ship? Without dogs they'll desert en masse at the last minute, and they'll take their guards along. The scum are more terrified of dogs than they are of being shot. I need all three hundred. Why do you think the men are gorging themselves? Every one of them's planning to escape and is stuffing himself so as to last longer on the run."

"The second batch of dogs was supposed to be delivered this morning."

Rall stood up. He picked up an oak branch and laid it on the fire; he still hadn't been able to get all the chill out of his bones. "I want the dogs right here in the barracks. Tell them to clear the nearest coach house for the dogs." He stood close to the fire, warming his hands. "I wish we were aboard already. Garrison life is a disease. Gray hair, cold feet. The only place for a man is active combat. You're to call me, Luib, when the dogs arrive. I intend to give the men a demonstration of the kind of security guard to expect on the way."

"Then you do want the two pardoned men quartered in tent eighteen? I can't put my finger on it, but something's making me uneasy."

"Is Willibald Manz in eighteen?"

"As you ordered, sir. Although, to be frank, I don't understand you in that respect, either. That business in Altenbauna smells. Between Manz and Niklas there's not much to choose. That tent is full of odd fish."

Rall laughed. "You leave Niklas alone; it took a lot of maneuvering to grab him away from the Linsing Grenadiers. A man who robs the collection boxes in churches is on my list for promotion. That's the kind of man we'll need in America if we don't want to starve to death. Niklas is a man who can find rabbits in the desert. But what about Manz? Has he got his new papers? I haven't seen them yet."

"We could easily cut six years off his age. You'd never recognize the man with his hair dyed. Why, we could put him in the first rank."

"He's a miserable shot, though." Rall burst out laughing. "If the English knew what kind of soldiers they've bought! Is there a single trained soldier in eighteen?"

"Captain Kunkel of the Silesian cavalry. His commission is in order. Another disappointment to me, though. I thought I could count on him to make that mob in eighteen into a unit of some kind. But he acts just like the rest of them; thinks only of himself. Out nights, mostly. Women, night after night. Thin as a green bean, but the strength of two men in him. Yesterday he took that redheaded canteen woman pickaback and ran her twice around the women's tent. He wasn't even winded at the end, and the woman weighs two hundred pounds."

Rall had been pacing the room to warm his feet; he came to a stop in front of Luib. "All right, then, out with it—what's eating you about tent eighteen?"

"Well, sir, I don't know your reasons, but tent eighteen is full of old friends of the two pardoned men. There's the Austrian glover, Balthasar Ploetz, there's Louis from the Haynow wheelwright's, and the day laborer from Ramswood, Klemm—the man, you recall, who always cut the hazel switches for you? Not to mention the Weibrecht boy, the only defense witness at their trial. If that doesn't trouble you, of course . . ."

"On the contrary, having them all together like that is good for my peace of mind. Don't you understand I've got them all under control this way—that I always know everything they're up to?"

"Then you've got an informer in tent eighteen?"

Rall give the old soldier a benevolent look. "Sometimes I honestly believe you think with that paunch of yours; it's the only way to explain the low speed at which you do it. Well then, is your mind at rest? Good."

"If I—"

Rall said firmly, "So it's tent eighteen for those two. Is that settled now? Embarkation is two days from now."

The rain puddle under the tear in the tent had been growing bigger for the last day or two. Every man in tent eighteen had been watching it grow, but none lifted a finger to do anything about it. Sergeant Luib had sent them some material to mend the torn side with, but it lay untouched on an old drum. Nor had anyone bestirred himself to do the next best thing and dig a ditch to drain the miniature lake in their tent off into the nearby canal. If Sergeant Luib had not intervened to make the men move closer together, Ploetz, Weibrecht, and Manz would have had to lie in the puddle all one night. But even these three had shown no gratitude whatsoever; they seemed as dull and indifferent as the others.

This morning, with life stirring everywhere else, tent eighteen was still quiet. From his spot near the entrance, Balthasar Ploetz peered through a slit out into the courtyard. Half a dozen men were preparing breakfast in front of the neighboring tent. Two were bringing wood and kindling, one was peeling potatoes, another man was scraping soot off some bacon rind. When the fire was well started, they hung a kettle over it. Other men gathered around waiting for the great copper basin to be filled with warm water so that the morning wash could begin. Ploetz could remember a time when he would have found the noisy camaraderie out there irresistible; now he found it repulsive. When the bacon began to sizzle in the frying pan, he had to turn away.

The smell of the cooking next door began to remind the men in tent eighteen of their empty stomachs. But not one of them made a move to cook breakfast. Each one rummaged among his belongings for whatever rations he had hidden away—a piece of bread, an apple, a chunk of sausage. Each of them ate with his back turned to his neighbor.

Suddenly a loud voice just outside the tent called, "Atten-hut!" The entrance flap was lifted from the outside and a gust of wind blew in. Instantly the men scattered. Sergeant Luib's mud-covered boots appeared, crowned by a big paunch balanced on his legs like a fragile object of great value.

"Make room for two new men!" Luib shouted, filling the tent with his voice. "Don't you people ever let any fresh air in here?" He turned to the two men behind him. "Come on, I'll introduce you."

In the last weeks Robert had forgotten what it was like to be among people. He almost wished he were back in his cell at the guardhouse. His new uniform over his arm, he stayed near the entrance to the tent, waiting to have a space assigned to himself and Soerman. He watched silently as two straw-filled sacks were dragged in, in lieu of mattresses, and sawdust was scattered on the wet flooring.

Sergeant Luib supervised the proceedings. He had expected trouble from those people over his putting two new men into their overcrowded tent, and he was surprised at how readily they accepted it. He wished he had a reason to stay, to see what developed. But a look at the men told him they were only waiting to be left to themselves. He looked once more around the tent; he felt like giving them some advice, but decided not to—he didn't want to appear too friendly.

Louis held the tent flap open so Luib could go out. He waited until the sergeant's steps were no longer audible; then he went over to Robert, slowly, as if to prolong the moment. Gingerly he stretched out his hand and touched Robert with his fingertips. "It's you," he said, "It's really you. You remember me, don't you? Louis, from the wheelwright's? Remember the white rabbits you got me, and the coach with the newborn kittens? I knew it, I told them all along those bullets would never hit you." He lowered his voice, almost whispered. "Did you save the bullets?"

None of the others laughed; they were in no mood for laughter. They had heard of Robert's trial and conviction. And no one was surprised when Robert reached into his coat pocket, brought out a handful of bullets, and poured them into Louis's cupped hands.

Carefully, the boy carried them through the tent, holding them out for each man to see. Each of them looked at the bullets as if they were some kind of magic talisman, but nobody said anything; nobody asked any questions or expressed any doubts that might break the spell hovering in the tent.

Niklas was no less impressed than the others, though he knew the business with the bullets was a kind of carnival trick, a very effective one. If he didn't want this new man to outshine him, he'd have to get him on his side. He took out a deck of cards, and, looking at Robert, let it fan out in his hands. "I've heard some fantastic things about you," he said. He looked from Robert to Soerman. "How about a game?" He started to shuffle the cards. The deck was brand-new and made a sound like a flock of sparrows exploding out of the underbrush.

Everybody was waiting for Robert's reaction. He said nothing.

Niklas kept on shuffling his cards. The others watched—anything was better than the paralyzing silence they were used to here.

Finally Ploetz got up his nerve and went over to Robert. "Remember me? On the road to Kassel you took my horse, unhitched it right off my wagon." He lowered his voice. "The riverboats are ready on the Fulda. I have reliable information that we're going tomorrow or the next day."

While Ploetz was speaking, the others had formed a semicircle behind him. "We'll do anything you say," young Vitus Weibrecht whispered pleadingly. "We trust you. Only tell us what to do." The men moved even closer, all eyes gazing expectantly at Robert.

"Forget it!" Niklas jeered. "*He* doesn't trust *you*. After that kind of an experience no man is the same."

"We have to give him time," Weibrecht said.

Ploetz grasped Robert's hand. "You've got to help me. I won't go to America. I won't, I'd rather jump in the river. I've got to get home. If I don't get home, my wife'll lose the liquor concession, and we still owe money on it. You've got to help me!" He couldn't understand Robert's lack of response. "You know everybody in Kassel. You could send for that doctor that used to come out to your estate all the time. If he testified I'm sick, that I'm not fit to be a soldier . . ."

Captain Kunkel extricated himself from the circle of men. "Do what you like," he said, "but leave me out of it." He walked toward the open tent flap. "I'm coming with you," Willibald Manz said. The others let him through; they were silent, still looking expectantly at Robert.

"You don't have to leave," Robert said. "I can't do anything." These were the first words he had spoken since the blindfold had been ripped from his eyes. Not a single word had passed his lips on the ride from the place of execution to the encampment, nor in the storage room where he was handed his uniform, nor on the way to the tent with Sergeant Luib.

He took in the sound of his own voice. It sounded the same as before. He had used words the same as before. Among the men who had been surrounding him, and who were beginning to move back into the semidarkness of the tent, there were faces he remembered from before. They had talked to him, asked him for something, but he had no answer for them. He could no longer see their faces, but he could feel their disappointment. He went over to the bedding that had been put down for him and lay down on it, his arms under his head. In a few minutes he was fast asleep.

Faced with the choice of taking off his hat and exposing his badly powdered wig or else bending over too low for his dignity, the officer of the day, Thurn, chose to enter the tent the second way, a decision his gallbladder instantly punished him for.

"Robert Skelnik!" he called out angrily. The tent was too dark to distinguish anything but shadowy movements. "Robert Skelnik is to report to me."

Robert felt someone touching his arm. He sat up. "Button your coat," somone whispered. He did so, ran a hand through his hair, and stood up. "Your hat," the voice whispered. He picked up his hat and made his way through the narrow passage between the straw mattresses toward the front of the tent.

"Damn it, man, why don't you report at once, the way you're supposed to?" Thurn glared at Robert, and for the second time felt a spasm of pain in the region of the gallbladder. He turned to go, miscalculated how low he had to duck under the tent flap, and lost his hat. Robert caught the hat before it hit the ground. Thurn accepted it more with irritation than gratitude. "A private's place is to the officer's left," he snapped, "at a distance of half a pace."

They walked past the other tents, past the canteen booths, and finally, leaving the encampment behind, crossed a muddy riding track to the exercise yard. The yard was covered with black ashes. An officer stood there, his back to them. The broad stripes of silver braid on his collar and on the huge upturned cuffs of his coat looked like solid bands of light under the gray sky.

Thurn stopped, as did Robert, half a step behind him. "Robert Skelnik, as ordered, sir."

The officer didn't move. He stood very straight, very slim; the green cloth of his uniform flawlessly smooth, as though nothing must betray that there was a living body inside. Then he turned around.

His face was extremely pale. The skin, damp from the moist air, had the sheen of polished stone; there was life only in the dark eyes. Robert could feel those eyes trying to tell him something, but the message couldn't reach him. That last night in the cell was still with him; he was still back in that long second in front of the firing squad, still blindfolded, still waiting for the impact from those twelve rifles. He could not accept this sudden gift of life; there was no room in him for it; he was still filled with the expectation of death. Death was here too, in this pale face with the dark eyes. The signs of death he had been unable to imagine in Soerman's face he could see clearly in the face he was looking at now. Everything he had just passed through seemed etched in his brother's features, as if Claus had lived these last hours in his place.

Claus signaled the officer to move away. The man stopped at a few paces' distance, his hand on his pistol.

"Do you want him to hear?" Robert asked. "Do we need a witness?"

A deep vertical furrow appeared on Claus's forehead. "Commandant's strict orders. Every officer speaking to a private must have his orderly officer with him."

"Is there so much to be afraid of? In an army of volunteers? Surely they're all volunteers—like myself." The face before him remained cold and bloodless as before. "Well, then, what is it? Something in the line of duty? Or is this a private conversation?"

"You haven't changed," Claus said. "Don't you realize how close you came to dying?"

"Were you there?" Robert said. "Somewhere in the background? Are you disappointed now because they didn't finish the job?"

"You probably never believed your death sentence was real."

"Probably."

"It was real, though, I assure you. And just one more second and the pardon would have come too late. Nobody at the guardhouse or in the firing squad had any intimation of it beforehand."

Robert could hear that Claus's voice was barely under control; he watched the blue vein throbbing on his brother's right temple.

"Can't we change the subject? What good is all this, Claus? Let's forget what happened. What happened at the border seems a long time ago. I don't hold it against you, I even understand you, in a way. It was insane of me to get you mixed up in it. Forget it, and . . ." He stepped toward Claus but stopped when he saw Thurn drawing his pistol.

Claus had moved back a step. His voice was toneless. "I don't intend to say another word about it. That you voluntarily resumed the name of Skelnik makes it easier. I'll be brief. You and

Soerman have been assigned to my battalion. That won't be to your advantage, nor was it intended to be. I plan to keep an eye on you and Soerman. I don't intend to suffer a second time because of you, is that clear? The next time it could cost me my rank—so there'll be no next time. Remember: you've been warned. Don't even think about deserting. And don't put your hopes on America. I'm never going to leave your side. Whatever you do, wherever you are, I'll be there, always, everywhere. If you try it anyway, if you give me cause to kill you, I'll do it. This is to let you know, to make sure you know how it'll be. So don't forget it, and don't ever forget who I am. I'm Major Haynow. You're Robert Skelnik. The rest of them can keep on thinking of you as my brother—but that's precisely what you have ceased to be, as far as I'm concerned."

Robert kept his eyes down. Like this morning when they blindfolded him for the execution, it was a matter of waiting until the words had stopped, so that he could begin to understand them. What was Claus trying to tell him? The rules of the game, not so much for themselves as for the benefit of the onlookers?

"Have I made myself understood? Do we understand each other?" Claus's voice was still toneless but more relaxed now. "In any case, I'm warning you: I'm not going to let you destroy my life."

Robert looked up and held out his hand. Had he really expected Claus to take it? He knew there was no point in asking, but he had to. "Why do you hate me?"

Claus said nothing. His silence was his answer; with this silence, he sealed his hatred, buried it like a seed in the earth between Robert and himself, earth that was covered with a layer of black ashes. He signaled to the orderly officer. "Take him back."

24

She watched her hand reach for the bell cord, as one watches a child to see if it will remember in time to refrain from doing the forbidden thing. Not until her fingers had touched the green-and-gold brocade did she drop her hand. It was still her house; the grace period set by the Elector had not yet run out. She could have called all the servants in, given orders to light the fire, to bring food. She was still the mistress of this house, but standing amidst the half-packed trunks and wicker baskets Anna Haynow asked herself if she wouldn't do better to leave these things, too, behind. All the evening gowns, a fortune in silk, brocade, and lace; not one gown among them had she worn more than once, and some not even once. But what good would they be to her in the future? On the other hand, the two dozen housedresses would be useful. She took four from the top of the heap and laid them into a wooden valise. She sensed, by a slight tremor of the floor, that someone had entered the room behind her. It was Mrs. Retz, in her coat, with a black-and-green shawl wound around her head and neck like a hood.

"You've done your own packing," the housekeeper said reproachfully.

Anna picked up a box of gloves off a chair. "Sit down, you've been on your feet constantly since early this morning."

Mrs. Retz opened her coat. "I was kept longer than expected on that errand." She rubbed her hands together. "No one made a fire for you either." She undid her shawl as though she suddenly found it hard to breathe. "The monsters. They were never so well paid or well cared for as with you, but now they've all forgotten. They don't even have the decency to preserve appearances. You wouldn't believe the trouble I had getting two of the girls to clean out the linen closets."

"The linen is part of the confiscated goods. I told you—I made a point of telling you."

"And let the Sonsfeld maids cut up that lovely damask when they take out your monograms? Sorry, I guess I didn't hear you. The linens are all at the Stockholm Inn already." She had taken the shawl off and was folding it in her lap. "I'm disappointed in your personal maid, too. When I paid her off, I gave her clear instructions to help you with the packing before she left."

"Since I don't know when I'll be unpacking these things, if ever, it's better if I know exactly where each thing is."

"You were always much too kind, and this is the thanks you get, of course. Only one man has behaved as one would have hoped; Gilbert packed every last egg, every ounce of flour, in two laundry baskets full of provisions for you. I sent them over to the Inn along with the linens. For the next several weeks you'll be well taken care of. They'll be keeping the wine and the fresh food for you in a little cupboard at the back of the fruit cellar. A cool, dry spot that I picked out myself." Mrs. Retz stopped when she saw the smile in Anna's eyes. For weeks that face had been frozen, those huge dark eyes had looked dead; and now—could she really be smiling again?

Anna had grown thin in the weeks since Robert's arrest. Her cheekbones were more prominent, but oddly it only made her look even younger. The loose fit of her dress gave her figure a new, fragile attractiveness.

"I'm sure you've eaten nothing all day," Mrs. Retz said. "I'll go get you something."

"Please don't." Anna put her hand on the woman's arm, as if to assure herself that someone like this still existed. No matter what happened, Mrs. Retz would never drop her hands in her lap and waste time on idle lamentations; she would always think about the next meal, about putting fresh sheets on the bed, about whatever needed doing. Anna was thankful this woman was still by her side.

"How about that baked ham you like so much?" Mrs. Retz coaxed.

"No, really—I need you to help me with this, now that you're here. Otherwise these boxes and trunks will never get filled. They've left me so little to take, but I'm tempted to leave all that behind, too. Do you remember how often I've said I'd be happy to give up everything if I could help Robert by doing so? And Robert lives . . ."

They looked at each other in silence. Ever since the morning the Elector's confiscation order had arrived, the two women had avoided looking at each other, or talking of anything but immediate practical necessities: paying off the servants, moving the few pieces of furniture the Elector had permitted them to keep, packing the clothes. There had been times when Mrs. Retz felt she would burst if she could not speak out, but in each instance Anna's elusive eyes had silenced her again. Everyone in the house had gone about their work without talking, without looking at one another. The days had passed without anyone ordering the midday meal, the afternoon tea. No deliveries had come to the door; no carriage had stopped.

"May I take a tray to Baron Haynow in his office?"

"Baron Haynow has gone out. He'll meet us at the Inn." Again the shimmer of a smile passed over Anna's face. "The Elector overlooked one thing: he didn't ask us to return the patent of nobility. But my husband didn't overlook it; he gave it to the chamberlain, in the original sealed envelope, to take it back." She was silent for a moment, thinking. Then: "A family that holds together has no need to fear the future." The tone of her voice betrayed just the faintest tremor of doubt about those words, even as she spoke them. She drew a deep breath. "Come," she said. "Let's get this packing done now."

Mrs. Retz took off her coat and pushed back her sleeves. "If you'll give me the tissue paper . . ."

"Do you really think I should bother to take all these court dresses along? I'll never wear any of them again."

"Since the death of her husband, the Countess Nienkarn has kept her household going by selling her court dresses," Mrs. Retz said severely. "Baron Haynow can tell you how much this lace alone is worth; it can be detached and sold separately. More tissue paper, please. Unless these clothes are stuffed properly the fabric will break at the folds after a time."

In half an hour, the two women had finished packing. Mrs. Retz was going through the rooms. She stopped in front of two pastels of Robert and Claus hanging in a window nook. "Aren't you taking these?"

"The confiscation order says everything must be left as it is, except for those few pieces of furniture expressly mentioned."

"Then kindly look away while I take them for myself. Don't

you know what it'll be like here, once the door shuts behind you?"

"Why, nothing will happen. The Sonsfelds aren't monsters. Nothing will change for the servants." She hesitated, then looked at Mrs. Retz. "To avoid misunderstanding: I would not consider it disloyalty, if you'd like to stay here with the Sonsfelds. . . ." It was hard to say this. "They're sure to ask you, and they'll certainly make you a good offer."

"My trunks are already at my cousin's."

"Do you have the prospect of another position then?"

"Since an hour ago."

"Would you tell me about it?"

"It was quite unexpected. Not that I couldn't have found something here in town, but I'd intended to leave Kassel anyway. The idea came to me when I went to the Miller Gate at the barracks earlier, to give the message to Claus. I asked for an interview with Commandant Rall. Beginning tomorrow I'm in charge of his regimental infirmary."

"You? With Rall? I always thought you were horrified by uniforms?"

"Inside the uniforms are a lot of poor devils."

The women exchanged a look.

"But you didn't want to stay in Kassel—does this mean you're going with the troops?"

Mrs. Retz nodded. She took a step toward a chair and leaned on the chairback. "I am going with them. To America." The loud, gruff voice she had deplored all her life sounded unusually light. "I'll look out for your sons. I'll write to you as often as I can." She turned away, then stopped at the door. "I know what it's like to wait and hope and get no news. . . ." She kept her eyes down, her hand on the door handle. "I'll tell them you're ready."

Anna Haynow only nodded. She couldn't trust herself to speak and keep both her own and Mrs. Retz's emotions under control. When she could no longer hear the woman's steps, she left the room.

It was the time of day they had always gone through the house together, lighting the candles and winding the clocks.

Apart from her own steps, there was not a sound to be heard.

The house had never seemed so silent as this, even when, during the last several weeks, unable to sleep, she had walked at night to the library for a book. Like the servants, the house itself was drawing away from her. All of her things—pictures, clocks, cabinets—seemed to be standing back with their eyes down.

On the stairs she felt suddenly dizzy, as though the ground were yielding under her feet, as though the whole house were wavering—and there was nothing left in this house to give her any support. It took all the strength she could muster to descend the last few steps without falling. A beam of light fell diagonally across the hallway. A figure stepped forward out of the dusk. It was Lange. The steward lifted his lamp higher when he recognized her. "Are you leaving already, Madame?" He was no longer wearing the simple dark attire he had considered beneath his dignity since his first day of service with the Haynows, but a flowered brocade coat over silk knee breeches, and a many-tiered white wig with a pigtail.

"Yes, Lange." There was no point in telling him how glad she was at the ease with which he had adjusted to the new situation; he wouldn't have understood. "Send for the carriage. At the side entrance."

She moved quickly out of the circle of light made by his lamp; for a moment, it gave the house its old accustomed look.

It was an enormous effort to climb back to her room, up the side stairs. The room looked bare, alien. She closed the small valise she would carry with her. Then she threw on her coat and shawl and reached for the bell cord.

The two candelabra at the head of the main staircase burned brightly. All the servants had lined up in the hall, wearing their best, looking subdued.

Anna Haynow set down the small valise, smoothed back a wisp of hair from her forehead. She hadn't planned to make a formal farewell speech, and couldn't think of what to say; she was relieved when Gilbert, the cook, stepped forward. He was dressed for travel, like herself. He bowed silently. The other servants moved backward.

He held out a little package to her, tied up in silk cord. "You always said I ought to write my recipes down, Madame. There was no time to have these bound for you."

She took the offering. "Thank you, Gilbert . . ." She was too moved to continue. Then she asked, "Are you going back to Strasbourg?"

"I don't know yet. I was informed that my application for a post at the palace would be welcomed, but I wouldn't think of it. If you wish, Madame, I'd be glad to continue in your service—no reflection on the cuisine at the Stockholm, but . . ." he stopped, listening. The other servants, who had been standing quietly in the background, turned toward the entrance. Wheels could be heard coming rapidly closer. Gilbert looked out the narrow window beside the entrance. "In a hurry to move in, aren't they?" he said contemptuously.

For a moment Anna was tempted to avoid the encounter entirely. All she had to do was to pick up her little valise and slip out through the side entrance. The wheels had come to a stop outside. There was still time to escape, while they drew down the carriage steps, the footmen arranged themselves, the lady descended and straightened her skirts—she had been through this often enough, she knew how much time it took. None of her servants would have noticed her disappearance, with the possible exception of Gilbert; they were all staring expectantly at the front door, waiting for it to open. It was not the people that prevented her from slipping away—it was her sense of the house, as though the house had its eyes on her and would not tolerate Anna Haynow stealing away like a thief. She picked up her valise and walked toward the front door. She stopped on the top step and awaited Catherine Sonsfeld.

In a dress cut too low for the time of year and for her age, a fur cloak loosely thrown over her shoulders, and a little black dog in her arms, Catherine, Countess Sonsfeld, mounted the steps to the Haynow town house. She had not expected to find the former owners still there, but when she saw the grave, pale woman standing at the top of the stairs, she didn't mind; on the contrary, it added a certain spice to her triumphal hour. In this mood she spoke to Anna as effusively as if they were the best of friends. "I do hope I haven't arrived at an inconvenient moment. I know I'm a bit early. It's maddening, I assure you, to have a maid who can't be relied upon to know the time of day." Although she didn't have a hand free, what with holding her furs with one and the dog with the other, she gave the impression she was about to embrace Anna.

Anna gracefully waved Countess Sonsfeld inside. "Go right in. Everything is ready. The servants are expecting you."

Countess Sonsfeld glanced possessively into the foyer. "To be quite honest with you, I had hoped to find you still here. You know the pitfalls of the house better than anyone. If I ask you very nicely, would you take me around it?"

"Monsieur Lange will be delighted to do it, and he knows the house more intimately than I do."

Catherine Sonsfeld moved a step closer. "Incidentally, if there should be something you're particularly attached to . . . We women should be more magnanimous among ourselves. Life would be unbearable if women stopped mediating and smoothing out the differences, don't you think?"

"I always regarded our town house as only a sort of hotel."

Catherine regarded the other woman with narrowed eyes. She didn't at all care for the way this encounter was turning out. This woman had no right to use so free a tone; it was not at all becoming to someone who had just lost everything. The only thing about her that was appropriate was the simple coat she was wearing for her journey. But even this somehow only emphasized the woman's self-assurance. Not only that, there was also—it was the most irritating aspect of all—her astonishing youthfulness.

Steward Lange arrived with two footmen carrying luggage. He bowed deeply to Countess Sonsfeld. A coach came around from the side entrance, looking more elegant than the Countess's own.

"Oh, were you permitted to keep the carriage and horses?" She stopped herself, not out of embarrassment but out of indignation at the Elector's laxity. "My son-in-law has the inventory," she said. "If there should be any irregularity—you can be reached at the Stockholm Inn, can you not?"

A third and a fourth trunk were being carried out of the house. Again Lange passed by; again he bowed to the Countess. He was not at all pleased that the new mistress had caught him in the midst of his last services to his former employers. He kept trying to catch her eye, to plead mutely for her patience, but her attention was riveted on the Haynow luggage, piece after piece of which was being paraded before her as it was brought outside. To her, the confiscation of the Haynow property had suggested an image of the Haynow couple, with a single bundle, alone, on a dark street. She had to restrain herself from ordering the trunks opened. "I thought your luggage had already been taken to the Stockholm along with the furniture."

Anna did not reply. She picked up her valise. The two women's eyes met for one last time. Catherine Sonsfeld tried to think of some final grace note, something to say that would do justice to this turning point in their lives. But there was something in Anna's eyes that silenced her. It was not hatred, pride, despair—it was the tiny gleam of a smile.

House Steward Lange made his third low obeisance to Catherine Sonsfeld. "If you please, Madame."

She followed him into the house. The double doors were held wide open behind her. In addition to the two candelabra at the main staircase, sconces were now lit all the way down the hall. The servants had lined up in a semicircle beside the staircase; the men bowed, the women sank down in deep curtsies, looking for seconds like a garden bed of puffed-out skirts and frilled lace caps.

Anna Haynow took it all in at a glance, without grief, without regret, as one casts a glance, in passing, inside a strange house.

With her light step she hurried down the outside stairs toward her carriage. The old coachman, in the family for years, knew her destination, but she called out, "To the Stockholm," as if directing a stranger hired for the occasion. Her sense of estrangement from everything her life had been made no exceptions. She saw the houses, the streets, the squares, everything they passed on the way, as if for the first time, and forgot it all before it could leave an impression. She looked out the window with indifferent curiosity, like a traveler moving through a city where he will be stopping only because it is too late at night to continue onward. The house she had left behind was forgotten, Kassel was forgotten, her own self was forgotten.

Ever since the owner of the Stockholm, Borromaeus Guffler, encouraged by ten years' tax exemption, had transformed his inn into the local grand hotel, he considered himself too important a man to greet his guests in person. These days he put in an appearance only when the hotel porter gave him the signal, by knocking on his office door, that it would be advisable to do so.

The mirror in his office had informed Guffler who the new arrival was. He reluctantly buttoned his coat. He would rather have had enemy soldiers billeted on him than have to take in the Haynows. He had considered making them an attractive offer for their furnishings, and had even reserved a large traveling coach, in case they could be induced to move on at once. He would have done anything to avoid putting them up. What if they took it into their heads to dine openly at his table d'hôte? But perhaps there was no need to fear that, considering the two huge baskets of provisions sent over by Mrs. Retz. To think that the old witch had dragooned him into giving her special storage space in his cellar! In any case, he'd have preferred to face Gottfried Haynow himself at the moment. In this kind of situation women were apt to have damned little pride and a will of iron.

He shut the kitchen account book that was always on his desk and walked hurriedly out of his office, like a man who had been interrupted in the midst of extremely pressing business.

"No need to disturb yourself," Anna Haynow said, "if you'll just be so kind as to give me my keys."

Guffler hadn't counted on this. He didn't know whether to feel relieved or frustrated. "The keys . . ." he said with an air of confusion. "I'm afraid the rooms aren't ready. . . ."

"Not ready, indeed! Give me the keys and send someone up at once."

The porter disappeared at a sign from Guffler, who was left alone with Anna. The hall was decorated more like a winter garden than a hotel lobby. Two stoves were kept going all day and night, and in the hothouse that resulted, the plants and shrubs flourished in their porcelain pots. The tables and chairs were hardly visible behind the leaves and flowers.

Guffler leaned an elbow on the reception desk, then removed it and stood erect again; the gesture seemed too friendly. "I had thought it was only a question of putting the furniture up somewhere for a while. I had no idea you intended to stay for any length of time. We'll have the rooms heated at once, of course."

Anna's look, a mixture of indifference and impatience, did not change. She reached inside her coat and laid a well-stuffed purse on the desk. "I shall expect dinner served in forty-minutes. For four persons." She handed him a slip of paper. "Here is my menu. If any changes are necessary, I should like to be consulted beforehand."

Guffler nodded, his eyes arrested by the purse. The fine goatskin revealed the outline of large gold coins. Guests who paid as well as this could be ticked off on the fingers of one hand; Kassel was not the kind of city that held rich travelers for more than a few days at a time. The number of foreigners passing through did increase from year to year, but for most German travelers the Stockholm had become too luxurious and expensive. And he remembered that all the officers who had been eating at his table d'hôte every night would be leaving town day after tomorrow. He picked up the purse, weighing it in his hand, determined not to return a penny of it. He straightened up and tilted his head back with an air of lassitude, a gesture—recently picked up from the English colonel, Faucitt—which he found most aristocratic. "They've taken away half my personnel. Actually, I'm barely able to continue operations at all. Give me an hour, Madame, please."

Anna Haynow took the key, and turned to go. As she ascended the stairs to the first floor, a bell rang shrilly through the house.

The platters on which the food was being kept warm had been changed twice. The two waiters stood beside the serving cart in ritual posture, left hand on their backs, right forearm draped with a serving napkin and bent across the chest, eyes straight ahead and expressionless, as if they were fast asleep on their feet. Anna could endure their presence no longer. "Take the food back to the kitchen," she said. "I'll ring if I want anything."

It took a while for the two figures to thaw. They bowed silently. One waiter opened the door, the other rolled the serving cart out, and then they were gone.

Anna breathed easier, no longer hemmed in by the smell, the silence, the thoughts of strangers. She sat with her hands in her lap, forgetting herself and those for whom she was waiting. A table set for dinner, where no one ate; a bed made for the night, where no one slept; a door that no one entered; a clock that no one heeded. Now and then, if she moved, her dress made a sound like the rustling of autumn leaves—it was all that was left of her. Nothing else.

So she sat, released from her thinking, released from her feelings, gradually forgetting as well that she was waiting. She saw the brass door handle move, in the light of the candles, and Claus came in. Blindly, she looked at him. She waited until he had shut the door, then she said, "Where are the others?"

His spurs clinked a little; an odor of damp leather had entered the room with him. He stopped on the other side of the table, hidden behind the lights of the candelabrum.

"Come here to me," she said. "Sit down with me. I've been waiting a long time."

His face was nearly as white as his severe periwig with its regulation pigtail. He stood stiffly before her, his hat in the crook of his arm.

Was it the flickering of the candles, or was he really avoiding her eyes? "It wouldn't be the first time you two have kept me waiting, but your father never has before. The two of us have often sat at table, waiting dinner for you and Robert. Did you get my message?" Her voice seemed to come from far away. "What is it? Why don't you speak? Did they refuse Robert permission to leave the barracks? Has he been pardoned, or not? Are we still a family—or not?"

Claus laid his hat on a chair and rested both hands on the chair's back. His eyes remained fixed on the candle flames in the middle of the table. "Mother, I have bad news. I don't know how to tell you." Her shoulders straightened; she raised her head. It seemed to Claus as though a veil had suddenly been lifted from her face.

"Look at me," she said. "Look at me and you'll know there can't be much left that can hurt me, after all that's happened. We've lost everything we had; I am sitting here in a hotel room with a few belongings and a few pieces of luggage, and that's all. There's little left that can still be taken from me."

It would have been easier for Claus if he had found her in despair. As it was, he felt paralyzed by her poise, her ability to keep above it all, because this was indeed all she had left, and the most precious of all. Once he spoke, this too would be gone.

"Well?" she said. "I am waiting."

"Two of the Elector's grooms exercise his horses every day in the park. Toward five o'clock—twilight was setting in and they were on their way back—they heard a shot. That's how they found him. By chance, that is; otherwise, he probably wouldn't have been found until tomorrow morning. He was lying on the grass border of the artificial pond. His gun was beside him."

"What are you talking about? What's happened to Robert?"

"Not Robert. Father. He shot himself, with his double-barreled hunting rifle. They called a doctor right away."

She had taken in only the sound of his words, not the sense. It was as though a tidal wave of fluid fire, were coming to overwhelm her. She made no effort to resist. She would have liked to be totally extinguished, never have to think, never have to act again. She stood up but remained where she was, between her chair and the table, uncertain that her legs would hold her up. "He was always so strong, stronger than any of us." She looked at Claus, eyes questioning, yearning for an answer. Why should his strength have deserted him now? Because he had lost all his property? It couldn't be that; he'd have overcome that. It had to be something else. What was it he had lost so irretrievably?

For a while, neither said anything. Then she asked, "Where is he?"

"The doctor could do nothing for him."

She cut him off. "He's dead—I know. Your father never did anything by halves or on impulse. Hand me my coat."

"They took him to the barracks. They didn't know what else to do with him."

"There was no room for him in Kassel while he lived," she said vehemently. "But there will be room for him now that he's dead. I shall see to that. The Lodge can exclude the living, not the dead."

"Isn't all that's happened bad enough? Why do you want to make more trouble?"

Anna turned brusquely away from him. She took a few steps toward the window. There she stood, looking out.

When he had entered the room, he had still felt strong enough to give his mother some support. But he was not equal to the anguish that spoke so eloquently out of her quiet self-control. By turning her back to him she had in effect ordered him to be quiet, but he could bear it no longer. His head was whirling with thoughts, images. . . . The corpse he had been called to identify. The gaping wound, the smashed skull, the white bandage around the head soaking up blood, browned and encrusted at the edges. The face was uninjured, the skin waxen, the bluish eyelids closed —and Robert. Again and again Robert injected himself into the scene. The scene between them this morning out in the exercise yard.

"None of this would have happened except for Robert's behaving like a madman, getting mixed up with that Hoym gang. You wouldn't be sitting here like this, Father would be alive, everything would have remained as it always was." His words came tumbling out uncontrollably. "But he'll pay for it, I'll make him pay for it! It's all his doing."

Anna turned sharply around. "Be quiet! Not another word! We will forget what you just said."

"You can't prevent me from saying it."

"Yes, I can," she said. "I can. I can, be still."

"I will not be silenced. You're going to listen to me! I hate him. Do you hear me, I hate him! I hate him as much as you love him. He'll pay for everything. He's the one who's hurt all of us!"

'You don't know what you're saying." Her voice sounded more restrained now.

"I have kept silence too long, far too long. That night, that night at the Weser crossing, if I'd only had the courage . . . I shouldn't have turned him in, I should have shot him myself!"

Anna gazed at her son, examining his face, without a suggestion of reproach. "Then you betrayed him intentionally? I always believed it was only a moment of sudden fear."

"Say it, why not? Go ahead, say it, so I can hate him even more. Yes, it was fear, nothing but cowardice. I lost my head, I didn't know what I was doing. Yes, I was afraid. To kill him—that would have taken courage. Is it that you don't *want* to understand me, or can you really not understand?" He came close to her, seized her shoulders. "If Robert had been executed this morning, wouldn't you have blamed me? Wouldn't you hate me for it?"

She moved back a step. Her hands slipped to her sides.

"You're both my sons, one no less than the other."

He stared at her. "He was more your son than I was. He was always closer to you. You loved only him."

Her head sank. "This is terrible," she whispered. "This is the worst thing of all. And I wanted to believe there was nothing left for me to lose."

He felt tempted to take her in his arms, but waited instead, stubbornly, for her to come to him. Her eyes were down, under her long lashes. He felt anger rising in him again, irresistibly. Something was compelling him to hurt her. He needed to revenge himself, on her as well. "I can see it in you now. You think of no one but him, no one but Robert. Father and I—we were never anything but strangers to you."

He stopped. Her cheeks were wet with tears. He saw it and asked himself: has it finally happened, what I've longed for ever since I can remember? Have I finally won her away from Robert, does she belong to me alone now? He put his arms around her, but even now, embracing her, he could feel only the distance between them.

"When a family is struck down as we have been struck down," she said slowly, "everyone is to blame, or no one."

He was still holding her in his arms, still hopeful.

"I don't know how you can live with such thoughts," she went on. "I'm powerless to defend Robert, because I know that by doing so I'd only make everything worse. I'm powerless to make you bury your hatred—nothing lasts like hatred, it lasts all the way to the end. You make me feel afraid."

Quickly and inescapably, as love and hate can shoot between two people, a wall grew between them, a wall made of spoken and unspoken words. Claus felt as though an occult force were moving his mother away from him, as though the room were expanding, her form fading—a silhouette now, paling to nothingness.

"Where will I find your father?" Her voice, too, seemed to come from very far away.

"I shall see to it," he said.

"Where is he?"

"At the barracks. I'll take care of everything. It'd be too much for you."

She went into the next room. When she returned, she was wearing her coat, holding a black veil in her hand. She gave him one more look; her eyes were unbearably naked; he could see nothing there he might have expected—neither hatred nor contempt, nothing but an unquenchable grief. She lifted the veil with both hands and let it fall over her head and face. He heard the rustling sound of her dress, the click of the door handle. Then she was gone.

25

During the twelve days of her journey, Anna Haynow had left the coach only when horses or coaches were being changed at the way stations, or for a night's rest in whatever hostelry offered itself along the road at sundown. By this time she was well acquainted with every sound made by wheels or carriage springs, so that she did not need to look out to know whether they were passing over cobblestones, sand, hard clay, or the planks of a wooden bridge. Alone in her hired coach, undistracted by talk or by the landscape behind drawn curtains, she was wholly at the mercy of these sounds. For the first few days they had tormented her until she became numb to them, and finally they helped to drive away her thoughts by taking their place.

But this time there was a new sound; she had been noticing it for quite a while now. The horses were slowing up, and finally the coach came to a full stop. She pushed the curtain aside and lowered the window—and couldn't believe what she saw: the wheels stood in water up to their hubs. If it had not been for the houses to left and right, they might have been stuck in a riverbed.

The coachman had put on the brakes; he leaned down from his box seat. "I'm afraid we'll have to turn back."

"Impossible," Anna said unhesitatingly. "Why do you think I'm paying you double? You said yourself we haven't a moment to lose if we're to make it to the ship in time. You also advised me to go by road instead of by riverboat. Drive on at once!"

The coachman, a young man whose sailcloth coat and gray-green weatherproof cape made him look more like a sailor than the driver of a coach, shook his head. "There was no way I could have foreseen this river's flooding its banks for a second time. It hasn't rained for days. It must be a rising tide driving the river water back."

"Whatever it is," she interrupted, "we have to keep moving. I've got to get to the ship in time."

The coachman dragged at the collar of his cape. "If we turn around now, we may lose less time than we would continuing on this way." He waited for her consent, but her face told him she would sooner get out and walk. Women who traveled alone in special coaches were apt to be full of surprises. They might climb in as nuns and emerge at the next stop in men's clothing, or emerge from the hostelry where they had stopped for a meal with a child in their arms. . . . This one here, too, seemed to be some kind of special case. "If you won't let me turn back," he said, "there's only one thing to do. You climb up here on the box seat with me, and I'll drive you to the river pier. There you can take a boat to the harbor."

"Couldn't you have said that at once? Help me up."

The coachman climbed down. He had to move slowly to avoid getting his boots full of water. After he had helped her up to the box seat, he put a rough blanket over her lap.

"Your shawl has come untied," he said solicitously. "Better make it fast." He misinterpreted her stubborn silence. "Honestly, I was sure we'd be able to get through, or I'd never have taken you on."

She nodded, and he picked up the reins and urged the horses on again. From time to time he gave her a sideways look. Wrapped in her cloak, she sat erect, eyes forward, her face grave and pale. He couldn't guess her age. She had been very light when he carried her up to the box seat, like a young girl. Her skin was smooth and delicate. When she smiled, she must be lovely. But he was unable to imagine those eyes and that mouth smiling.

A boat came sliding out of a half-submerged entrance to a house. A woman sat in it, holding an infant bundled up in a pillow. A man was poling the boat forward. A ladder leaned against the upper-story window of another house. On the public square, men in hip boots were building catwalks, planks on top of trestles, along the house fronts. Water was gurgling into cellar windows; debris of all kinds—fruit, wood, toys—was bobbing along on the water's surface.

"It happens every year," the coachman said. "These folks are used to it, but twice in a row like this, that's rare. You should have seen what it was like last week. Just when the Hessians were marching through, too. The whole army marching in water up to its knees. You can get a flood like this within an hour, without warning."

Anna kept her eyes straight ahead. She didn't dare ask questions. A whole week ago? Could that mean she would miss the ship after all? Could the ships have left Bremerlehe already?

Later, sitting in the boat with her few belongings, being rowed to where the ships were anchored, she didn't dare ask the boatman this question. What if it were true, if she had missed her ship?—There was no going back, and there would be other ships.

From the moment her black veil had dropped over her face, she had lived and acted as though in a trance. She had forced the Lodge to give her husband the burial rites to which he was entitled; with that, her energies were exhausted. The days that followed might as well not have happened for all she remembered of them. A woman in an armchair, staring at the cold ashes in the fireplace; a woman wandering aimlessly through the park. One morning she had found herself standing in front of the narrow house where Mrs. Retz's cousin lived, without knowing how she got there, but Mrs. Retz was gone; she had left Kassel with the Hessian soldiers.

Mrs. Retz, gone with the troops? Everyone had known it except her. No one had told her, not even Claus when he had come to say good-bye. Robert and Claus—she had forgotten her sons over her dead husband. She belonged where they were. She had hurried back to the hotel then, and when she took off her black veil it felt like an awakening. She had emptied the huge traveling trunks on the floor, sorted out the things to be sold. She kept only enough to fit into a suitcase and traveling bag.

The boat, which had been moving steadily, now began to dip and roll. The river had widened. Long waves came rolling in.

The only sounds were those made by the water and the boat.

The boatman rested his oars for a moment and let the boat drift with the current. A sea gull shot past overhead, flashing in a cloudy sky so bright the colors seemed washed out and objects insubstantial. The water was only a play of reflections. The light not only entered her eyes, it flooded through her skin, seemed to stream inside her with her breath and erase the shadows of the past. She felt as light as the drifting boat, light as the gull letting itself be carried out to sea by the breeze.

A seawall rose on the horizon, the masts of ships, the rooftops of houses—shimmering like a mirage. As the man turned the boat toward the pier, the wavering light slowly solidified into reality—the wharves, the mass of ships, so densely together they looked like a dike, made not to sail on the waves but to protect the land against them.

The boatman helped her up. "We were caught in a countercurrent, or we'd have been here sooner."

She looked at him and nodded, as though his words held a very special meaning for her. She took her suitcase and the traveling bag.

The narrow steps up to the quay were wet and slippery, but she climbed with a light, sure step, as though led by an invisible hand. The weight of her luggage in her hands told her she was not dreaming, that she had begun to rejoin reality. Suddenly a roaring shout soared up, like a sheaf of flashing arrows flying out to sea above her. The same words shouted over and over: "*Long live the King!*" She kept on climbing, leaving behind the sound of waves crashing against the seawall, moving toward the voices. She stopped at the top of the stairs—the instinctive hesitation of someone returning from the no man's land of solitude, taking the first step back into the land of the living.

Slowly her eyes felt their way along the cobblestones. When she lifted them up, she saw a wall of shiny black boots with yellow puttees. The men stood motionless in their blue uniforms, row upon row, light dancing on their silver braid. She could not distinguish individuals here; these were not men, not soldiers, these were life-size marionettes in blue. All the mouths opened at once. Invisible strings snapped the arms upward, the hats were raised, replaced; the arms fell back.

The square on which the regiment was formed faced on the quay wall. Behind the regiment the narrow houses—the medieval gable roofs, the chimneys, windows, and even the people crowding those windows—looked like stage scenery painted on a backdrop, to frame the mustering and swearing-in of the Hessian mercenaries.

Now the first row of men took one step forward. A group of English officers passed along in front of it, counting, examining, inspecting. She recognized one of those officers; he was the one for whose sake she had memorized a few sentences in English, to welcome him to her party in his honor, in Kassel.

Suddenly she found herself swept along by a crowd of spectators, toward the houses where a larger crowd had gathered behind the troops filling the square. Transient peddlers had set up their booths here. Colorful pennants fluttered in the breeze; fresh herrings lay roasting on charcoal fires; a man with a basket full of fresh bakery goods cried his wares. One stall offered copperplate engravings, miniatures of German cities. There was even a goldsmith selling memorial watches and medallions, on which the date and place were engraved: 20 March 1776, Bremerlehe.

"A penny for a seat." A poorly dressed woman was offering Anna a stool to sit on. When Anna looked at her, she blushed. Her stall consisted of a huge green umbrella, under which she had a pile of baskets for sale. The woman noticed Anna's leather suitcase and started to say something, but a roll of the drums drowned her voice. The blue-clad rows of men made a turn to the right and marched across the square to the ship. A wooden gangplank was lowered to the quay and made fast at both ends.

Two by two the Hessians marched up the gangplank, the hard bright rhythm of boots on cobblestones followed by the deeper reverberant sounds of boots on yielding wooden planks. Row upon row they flowed into the ship. At the top of the gangplank the blue figures seemed to hang in the sky, then to lurch down, like cutouts knocked off in a shooting gallery. They were swallowed into the belly of the ship.

The gangplank was cleared, but only for a moment. Gulls dropped from the sky, dived, and scattered, as the women, laden with bundles and baskets, stormed the pier. The cries of those in front were drowned by those shoving from the rear. Hair and shawls flying, skirts billowing, they fought their way up the gangplank until they, too, seemed to be sucked down into the ship.

In the filigree of tall masts, broken before only by small bits of canvas here and there, huge white sails unrolled now. Their white reflections hurt Anna's eyes; she looked back to the deserted square. Only the English officers remained there, chatting, smoking, occasional officers strolling from group to group, their stride measured, calm, self-assured. Their red coats seemed very bright. The scene reminded her of the horse auction in Ramswood; this was the way it was when business was done, when the horses had been led away and the dealers stood around discussing their purchases.

One officer separated from his group, walked along the quay and picked up a crushed tricorn with his saber point, his white teeth flashing under his red moustache.

Laughter sounded across the square.

"I don't know how you feel," the basket woman said, "but it makes my blood boil just to look at those Redcoats. Here, have a cup of hot tea, it'll do you good. Careful, the handle on that cup is broken."

Anna took the large cup in both hands; for the first time, holding the hot porcelain, she realized how icy cold her fingers were. She drank slowly. The tea was strong and sweet.

"Good, isn't it?" the woman said. "My husband has a tinful with him. I smuggled it into his baggage. The stories you hear about the food and conditions on those ships make your hair stand on end. They're jammed in there twelve men to a cabin."

"How do you know?"

"They've been packing the men in for three days now. As soon as a ship is full, it moves out and drops anchor in the harbor. The penalties are awful, but a few men have already jumped overboard anyway."

"Do you know which regiments these are?" She was looking at

the ship's stern, where the British flag was going up—red, white, and blue.

Commands were barked out on deck. A tremor ran through the ship when the ropes were cast off. The yardarm of the mainsail swung around, the huge white canvas billowed out, and the ship slowly drew away from the quay. Anna was filled with impatience. What was she waiting for? Why didn't she do something? She was about to pick up her bags when she was jostled by a sudden surge of the crowd and found herself trapped in the middle of it. Fear of being crushed gave her the strength to fight her way through the restless mob, until she found herself face to face with the guards. Bayonets drawn, they were keeping spectators back from the open square. She could hear distant music coming closer—a military march. They came out of a side street, out into the square in parade formation, the drum major, the drummers, the fifes. The drums were booming like explosive charges detonated to clear the narrow streets for the marching columns behind them. The spectators fell silent.

Anna looked at the faces beside her. A few old men, the rest women, women of every age. Their faces looked grave, full of helpless protest. All individuality seemed extinguished. Faces with the light gone out of them, all alike, a handful of seeds from the same harvest, flung into life by the same hand, condemned by that hand to the same fate, the fate of women: to be left behind, to accept the inevitable, to have no way of protest but silence.

She drew her cloak tighter around her. The columns of soldiers marched past, wave after wave of them. Reflected in their passing, as in moving water, she kept seeing the face of Gottfried Haynow as she had last seen him in his coffin, even in death showing his typical look of impatience; impatience for the awakening. For the first time she began to understand, as nearly as she could, what he had done; it was perhaps nothing more than a last passionate protest against the inevitable. On and on went the marching tread of the soldiers across the square, to the endless beat of the drums. Behind them came a swarm of women pouring out of the side street, scattering among the other spectators.

The ritual of mustering the troops and swearing them in began again, but there was a difference: this regiment was dressed, not in blue, but the green of the Rall regiment.

Someone touched her arm. She paid no attention, her eyes fixed on the soldiers in green. She stood on tiptoe, trying to discover among those pale blurs under cocked hats the faces of her two sons.

"It really is you!" said a voice beside her. "What are you doing here, how on earth did you get here?"

Reluctantly, Anna turned. She saw a tall woman in a hooded cloak, a strand of gray hair blowing in the wind from under the hood, a green shawl wrapped around the figure as if by the wind, a leather pouch slung over one shoulder.

"This is the Rall regiment, isn't it?" Anna asked.

"Don't you recognize me? Have I changed so much? Or do you miss the smell of starched linen and lavender? It's me, your old Retz."

"Are my sons with this regiment?" Anna said, still numb, unable to respond.

"You've come all this way to see them one more time? You won't recognize them at this distance, but they're here, both your sons, and they're in good health. I'm surprised we haven't run into each other before. Are you staying at the Lion, too? After the terrible boat trip on the Weser I simply had to have a few nights more of sleeping in a bed like a human being."

"I've only just arrived."

Mrs. Retz noticed Anna's traveling bags for the first time. Their eyes met and held each other briefly, without questions, without anxiety, only in confirmation that the old trust between them was still there, fully restored. "Let me take the valise," Mrs. Retz said. "I'll find a spot for you where you can at least see your sons when they go on board. And if we don't manage to catch their eye, I'll tell them you were here to see them off, that you made this long journey just to see them once more. If you have any messages . . ."

Anna interrupted: "Tell me—do the British check on the women who follow the men on board?"

"What? You don't mean to say you. . . ." Mrs. Retz gave her a horrified look. "I beg you not to think of such a thing. You don't really intend to come, too."

"Are you afraid I'll be seasick?"

"You can't imagine what it'll be like!"

"No different from what it will be like for my sons."

"But you're a lady. You should have come with us on the river transport—the crowding, the cold, the miserable food, the men cursing, the humiliation. Take a good look at the kind of women going with them. These women are used to this kind of life. And it'll be much worse at sea. I beg you, try to remember who you are."

"And you?" Anna said. "Who are you, and why are you here? Just tell me that."

Mrs. Retz waved the comparison aside. "I'm not old enough to sit in a rocking chair knitting socks all the time and devoting my days to a canary. I'm still not too old to bind up wounds and wash the sick."

"And I'm not too old to help you."

Mrs. Retz didn't have time to argue the point, nor was she any longer inclined to do so. Five hundred men were swearing the oath of loyalty to King George III, their voices roaring waves that broke against an abrupt wall of silence, then a single thin voice reciting another phrase, then the returning surge of the wave again. Five hundred men waved their tricornes in the air. One of those arms was Claus's; one of those hats was Robert's; one of those white powdered wigs, with the dark ribbon at the back, was Soerman's.

"Long live the King!" The shout rang across the square and the harbor. Anna knew that one of those men was remaining silent. She could see him in her mind's eye, standing there with the rest, his mouth open, but mute—Robert would never swear loyalty to a foreign country, to a foreign king.

Soon those green ranks would break up, form into columns, march up the gangplanks. When the last man was aboard, the women would follow, a wild, noisy swarm, and she would be one of them, pushing forward, shoving others out of the way, exactly like the rest.

Gusts of wind came from the open sea, cutting at her eyes. She breathed the salt air. As if hypnotized she stared through the shimmering forests of bayonets toward the bare masts of the ships at the pier, a dazzling thicket behind which the future lay hidden.

BOOK TWO

The Master of Redford

I . . . do acknowledge the United States of America, to be free, Independent, and Sovereign States, and declare that the people thereof owe no allegiance or obedience to George the Third, King of Great Britain, and I renounce, refute, and adjure my allegiance and obedience to him, and I do SWEAR that I will to the utmost of my power, support, maintain, and defend the said United States, against the said King George the Third, his heirs, and their successors and his and their abettors and adherents, and will serve the said United States in the office of . . . with fidelity, according to the best of my skill and understanding. So help me God.

—Oath of the Officers of the Continental Army

26

Three hours by horse from Trenton, on the other side of the Delaware River, stood the main house of Redford, crowning an estate that covered eleven square miles of land. Only twenty-three years before, this vast expanse of fields and grazing lands, houses and well-tended paths, had been an impenetrable wilderness. When the name "Redford" came up in the talk of the elder generation, it still echoed with the fear they felt for what had been an Indian stronghold.

For a long time after the last Indian had gone, the land had remained masterless, haunted by dark legends and guarded by mysterious red markings on the trees, left by the Indians, that had given the region its name: Redford, the no-man's-land that no one dared to make his own—until one day late in the year a stranger came riding from the north who knew nothing about the past. He was riding south, following the river, and he saw that all the roads ended here, and he liked that. With satisfaction, he breathed the air, cool from the river and thick with the pungent smell of the woods. He crossed the river, entered the wilderness, and came finally to a clearing. There he saw what was left of a shelter and an iron grate lying atop three large stones. He made a fire, roasted two quail, and when night fell he bedded down under a huge pine that had a strange rust-red mark burned into its bark. Lying there, hands supporting his head, wrapped in the silence of the woods, he knew he had found the piece of land he had been looking for.

The iron grate and the three field stones on which he had cooked his first meal on that land became part of the manor house in time, built into the fireplace in the hall, where the master of the house always lit the fire himself. The huge pine tree with the Indian mark, under which he had slept that first night, was still there, too. Visible from far off, it was a towering signpost to travelers in search of Redford; to the people who lived there, it was all but sacred.

It was not only that those years when the pine bloomed, swarms of bees humming in its branches, were always years of especially rich harvest; the cook of Redford Manor, an Indian half-breed with the Irish name McGill, could foretell the weather from it. She did it by rubbing a fresh shoot, which had come from the topmost point of the tree, between her brown fingers. If the sap stayed green, it would be a rainy year; if the sap turned quickly red, it would be a dry year. That McGill never cooked fish or game without adding to the pot the chopped insides of a cone, or a decoction made by boiling a handful of pine needles, was her secret, unknown not only to her employer but even to the second cook. Guests who pursued her to the kitchen in quest of her recipes received evasive answers as a rule; Redford trout, quail, and hares, she said, were just of better quality than they were elsewhere. In fact, this judgment held good in the marketplaces of the region for all Redford products, so that for a long time now, cartloads of wheat, potatoes, corn, hams, cheese, and fruit, had been going not only downriver to Philadelphia, as the lumber used to go, but also upriver to Easton and Phillipsburg.

The main house was a long building, the ground floor of red brick, the second built of massive wooden beams which were painted white each year along with the broad veranda that enclosed the house to the west and south. The stables, barns, and utility buildings lay at some distance, separated from the main house by an orchard surrounded by raspberry bushes.

The fall weather was so mild this year that the deep blue flowers kept opening until late November. A truly astonishing year. In the earliest morning hours the pale white light of the sun came filtering through mists that floated higher than the fog but lower than the clouds. But toward noon the sky opened up and a golden warmth poured out over the land.

The two horseback riders who left Redford shortly after midday still wore summer cottons and summer hats of the finest Panama, though the man's hat was dark brown and the girl's straw-colored. They did not take the bridle path leading from Redford down to the Delaware but the shortcut across the fields. The sun shone in a cloudless sky. A light rain during the night had washed the dust off the sprouting winter grain; the earth was green as far as the eye could see, all the way to the blue woods that sheltered Redford on the north and west.

The horses slowed to a trot as they approached the enormous pine with its red Indian markings. The man tightened the band of his hat. "Am I riding too fast for you?" he asked the girl. He was only trying to start a conversation, to express the contentment he felt at having her beside him—something he was never able to do except in a roundabout way—but she misunderstood his meaning, as nearly always. She gave him a look from under the brim of her hat, and kicked her horse into a run. At first he was tempted to accept the challenge; then he decided she was already competitive enough, without any encouragement from him. When he saw she'd reached the riverbank, he even slowed up a little, as if to give her time to catch her breath.

The Delaware made an east-west elbow turn at this point. The river flowed sluggishly, seeming in some places to stand still, though the smooth surface of the water was broken by occasional eddies and rapids. The owner of Redford gazed thoughtfully at the river—it had become part of his life. Then he rode over to the girl. "I can remember only one year this river didn't freeze over during winter—and that was twenty years ago. To think you weren't even born then. A year ago today it was frozen solid. Right here is where it usually begins to ice over."

The girl energetically pushed back her broadbrimmed hat, so that it hung down her back by its neck strap; her free-flowing hair, redder than it was brown, caught the sun. "One down for you! Finally there's something I know better than you. You're only three days off but you're wrong about when the river froze over last year."

Again the man refused to take up her challenge. "Do you keep a diary?" he asked peaceably.

"Wrong again. I don't have to write that kind of thing down. It was exactly November twenty-fifth when the river froze over last year. I remember because it was the day Abigail had her sixth baby, and Jan Kellog caught the last ferry to bring her medicine from Princeton. One of these days I'll have just as many things to remember as you do."

"Is that what you want? I'm not sure I'd want you to get that wish, Mary." Usually he had no trace of an accent, but when he was moved, as he was now, there was a suggestion of foreignness.

The girl hesitated, gave him a quick glance. "Do you think Abigail meant to have this baby in November again? . . ."

"There's probably a simpler explanation. The men usually get their furloughs from the army in March. . . ." He broke off. "Since when are you interested in that kind of thing?"

"You forget I'm going on nineteen. Lots of girls are married at my age." She usually had a great deal more to say in defense of her maturity, but this time she was distracted by the ferry coming across the river. She shielded her eyes against the sun. "Look. Doctor Banks took the little ferry this time. He's never done that before."

"I'll have to take you to Philadelphia next time I go. I always thought you had good long-distance vision, at least. That's the big ferry."

"Spectacles on my nose—you'd like that!" She laughed. "I suppose you want me to become a spinster."

The man slid from the saddle and examined his horse's bridle. "Who's driving all the young men away from Redford, me or you? I wouldn't have minded your getting engaged to John. John was serious about you. And it'd have made it easier for him to go off to the army."

"What's that got to do with it? John's fighting because he believes in the war." She looked older than her years; she always did when she was on the defensive—and she often was, or thought she had to be. Neither in character nor appearance did she show the immaturity of so many girls her age.

"I thought John was sure to win you the day he brought the Declaration of Independence all the way from Philadelphia just so you'd be one of the first to know about it. Nothing else he could have done would have said how much you meant to him. Young as he is, John's a good judge of human nature. And once the war's over you'll see what a good lawyer he'll make."

"I don't love him, and I told him so. I admire him, but love is something else. Why are you starting that again? Can't you wait to be rid of me?"

The man pressed his lips together. He walked over to help her out of the saddle. For a moment she was in his arms, laughing, before he gently set her on her feet. Clearly Mary was no longer the little girl who had come to Redford six years ago.

She had just turned twelve when he took her into his home. Her father had been his friend, Pastor Haverill from Boston, son of an English immigrant and one of the most militant preachers for American independence, for a revolt of the colonies against the Crown. From his pulpit he preached more fiercely against George III than against the Antichrist himself. It had happened on March 5, 1770, a day that had entered history as the Boston Massacre. That early in March there was still snow on the ground. Later, no one could say exactly how it all began; whether it was started by the soldiers guarding the town hall, or by the men who had come out of the church with Pastor Haverill; whether it was a boy's snowball that triggered the fight, or a shot fired by a soldier made nervous by the gathering crowd. Haverill, who had spent his life preaching against tyranny and for freedom, was one of the first to fall.

Skelnik had been there when they buried Haverill beside his wife, who had died giving birth to Mary. He had himself declared the orphan's guardian and took her back with him to Redford.

Mary at twelve was a tomboy, given to wearing boots and riding breeches and loose woolen shirts rather than dresses, more often outdoors on horseback than indoors. She wore her chestnut hair in a severe pageboy cut. Though she was quiet, not given to talking much, she brought something to Redford that had been missing: youth. Suddenly, he'd had a young creature with him at dinner and before the fireplace in the evening and beside him on horseback when he rode. On her sixteenth birthday he had had to tell her, with a heavy heart, that she would have to leave Redford and move to Madame Soderstrom's in Philadelphia, to learn all the things a young lady was expected to know. Mary had nodded without a word, but he had seen tears in her dark eyes for the first time since he'd known her. He had taken her in his arms then, to comfort her—and realized for the first time that she was no longer a child; and that he hadn't yet accepted his solitude as final.

It had only been a moment, a moment that changed nothing and that no one ever heard about. He was proud of his self-control. Nevertheless he hadn't insisted on her going to Philadelphia; he gave in and agreed to teach her himself. It gave him a secret delight to see how she cared about her lessons, how eager she was to learn. He knew it was selfish, but he was glad she hadn't found some young man to fall in love with yet. That reminded him of John Compson. "Forgive me for starting on that subject again, but hasn't it ever occurred to you that John's one of the richest young men between New York and Philadelphia? An only son, who'll inherit all the Compson property? Think of it, with Redford added on some day. At my age, a man has to think of things like that."

She laughed. "What's happened to your sense of reality? You forget John's father's a fanatic royalist. When John joined the rebel army, he not only disinherited him, he told him never to come back. And as for your age, you never miss an opportunity to bring that up—you're positively vain about it."

Skelnik was silent, looking downriver, watching the ferry come nearer. The horses grazed freely.

"Besides," she said. "John's much too young for me."

"Too young?"

"Yes, too young." She avoided looking at him; it was easier to go on talking this way. "When I fall in love, it'll have to be a man like you, a man who's experienced life. Young men know as little about life as I do—sometimes even less. I like a man to be like a ship that's crossed the ocean at least once, through every kind of weather. When I was a child in Boston I used to go down to the harbor a lot. You can tell a ship that's been through it; even when it's old, stripped of sails and everything, it's far more beautiful than those neat little coastal craft that never get out of sight of land. I'm not afraid of experienced men, I am afraid of inexperienced men."

There were only two passengers on the ferry. One of them, dressed like a farmer, held the leads of the two horses on board; the other, wearing a bright plaid coat, sat on a side bench, uneasily watching as the ferry docked. Noah Banks was profoundly suspicious of anything that moved, a character trait that made life for the Trenton doctor an endless series of conflicts. Patients who were capable of coming to him he regarded as intruders; those who had to request that he come to them, thus forcing him to leave his own house, annoyed him. He'd been in an irritable mood, his usual mixture of ill humor and misanthropy, ever since the Redford messenger had fetched him away from his dinner table. He hadn't been able to vent his spleen on the messenger—Jan Kellog was so thick-skinned insults bounced right off him—and his irritability had been festering all the way from Trenton; it had about reached the bursting point by the time he saw Skelnik waiting on the riverbank for him.

The ferry was tied up. Jan Kellog led the horses ashore. Banty-legged, his boots worn, the doctor stalked past the ferryman without a word. Morosely he handed his satchel to Kellog and climbed on his horse.

"Thanks for coming," Skelnik said. Both he and Mary had remounted.

Noah Banks carefully straightened out his reins; only when that was done did he condescend to look up. His manner showed how very put-upon he felt. "I'm damned if I know why I let myself be talked into this, Skelnik. You know my practice lies on the other side of the Delaware, and it's too large as it is."

"Abigail Hancock needs a doctor. Our own doctor's off with the army."

"You had me dragged here for a lying-in? What happens when you need a doctor yourself? With a woman in labor, an hour more or less makes no difference. But a heart that's failed you once will do it again."

"The doctors in Philadelphia are very pleased with me."

"Are they, now? It's not what I've been hearing. The fact that you look healthy doesn't impress *me* anyway. I know all about it. Doctor Wyngard in Philadelphia even ordered you to stop riding a horse. You stopped going to him instead. I hear you're taking the stuff that Indian cook of yours mixes up. I'm warning you: in a couple of years she'll have you poisoned inside and out. Wait and see. Go ahead and poison your innards, but don't come to me when it's too late to do anything about it."

"Shall we change the subject and get going?"

"All right. But this is the last time you lure me across the Delaware. The idea—sending the only doctor for miles around off to the army! That's politics for you. You're the one who ran off to Philadelphia and swore allegiance to the new Constitution—not me. Rebellion against the Crown, fiddlesticks. No good'll come of it. This whole war is sheer goddamned madness. And what for, I ask you? Why fight at all? All you have to do is look at our population rate. Take your Abigail Hancock—a baby every year. Some day the British'll have to leave simply because we'll outnumber them. There's no better way to win our rights."

Mary had turned her horse at the doctor's last words and rode off. Noah Banks looked after her with disapproval. "Poor child.

So you've planted your revolutionary ideas in her head, too."

"If anybody planted ideas in her head, it was the British soldiers who shot her father."

Doctor Banks shrugged. "There's always somebody determined to die a martyr for a cause."

Mary galloped ahead. Skelnik watched her widening her lead; she seemed to fly, weightless, melting into the flickering haze ahead. The sun had passed its zenith; the air had turned a deeper blue. To Skelnik, Mary's diminishing figure seemed to emphasize the vastness of the land. His land. He had cut down his first tree on a day like this. He could remember vividly everything about it: each blow of the ax, the smell of the wood and the freshly peeled bark; the plow in his hands when he cut the first furrow after the land was cleared; the first seeds he laid into the earth. His earth. His land, created with his hands, more than that—with his heart, wherein lay the roots of his longing: to find a piece of earth, untouched by man, fresh from the first day of Creation, and to live there, not according to the laws of a king but according to the laws of nature.

That his heart was tired, what else did that mean if not that his longing had been appeased? The fact that he might die any minute didn't frighten him in the least. The sickness in his chest was not his enemy; he had learned to live with it, just as he had learned to live with those two rooms in his house that he hadn't set foot in in twenty years, though he still carried the keys to them everywhere he went.

Mary had disappeared into a hollow. Trees came into view, and behind their crowns, the line of a gabled roof. Smoke was curling up from the chimney. They passed a horse paddock with yearlings inside. The doctor's mare, recognizing the place where she had come from, strained toward the gate.

"Is this all that's left of them?" Noah Banks' tone indicated he'd seen his darkest predictions verified, not without a certain satisfaction. "All those horses gone to the army, like your doctor? How are you going to work your fields without men and horses?"

"It'll be good for the fields to lie fallow for a year."

"A year? Do you really believe that? And what if the war comes this way? Have you spent twenty years building up all this just to see it devoured by an army of Redcoats?"

Skelnik reined his horse over toward the doctor's. "You once told me your father couldn't even write his name. But he had the courage to get on a ship and cross an ocean to a new continent. Which is why, today, you're not the chattel of a Scottish landlord, but a doctor in Trenton. My father served a Polish prince. When my father got married, the prince ordered the bride to his bed on her wedding night, and she obeyed." Skelnik made a sweeping gesture at the surrounding land. "Here there aren't any princes and there aren't any serfs. Here, every man is free—and shall remain free, which is what we're fighting for."

"A few greedy tea merchants don't want to pay their taxes, and a few power-hungry lawyers and preachers are making a war out of it. Give them no men, no arms, no horses, and you'll have peace tomorrow."

"It isn't a question of a few tons of tea. For forty years now the King of England's been trying to strip us of one right after another."

"What are we arguing about? You talk like I'm a royalist. All I want is peace. Your goddamned war means men losing arms and legs, and me not able to do a thing about it. It means men without the use of their eyes, men—have you ever seen a man with his belly slit by a bayonet? The King of England's a long way off. Let him make his laws; what business is it of ours? The day's coming when no crowned George will mean a thing to any of us."

Mary, who had been waiting for the men at the Hancock gate, caught the doctor's last words. She could not resist the opportunity. "Did I hear you right, Doctor? An England without a king? Doctor Banks, you're a rebel!"

Noah Banks raised his eyebrows, and a totally benevolent smile lit up his face. As a veteran of three marriages with three quick-witted women, he took a connoisseur's pleasure in feminine malice. "There came a day when there was no Pharaoh in Egypt, and no Caesar in Rome, too."

Mary laughed. "If we were royalists, Doctor Banks would

make the fieriest spokesman for the rebels. He's happiest when he has someone to contradict."

They rode into the Hancocks' yard together. A swarm of children came yelling out of a barn, led by a boy holding a huge kite with a long fluttering tail; Abigail's children, three boys and two girls, were easily recognizable by their coppery hair.

The yard sprang into noisy life. The dog, a black shepherd, rushed barking from his kennel. David, the stableboy, whose left foot was heavily bandaged and soled only with a piece of leather tied to his foot with string, came limping toward the riders. The old woman who had been working at her loom on the veranda got up and chased the children around behind the house.

The three riders dismounted, and Noah Banks stalked toward the house. Unbelieving at first, then horrified, he looked at the fruit wine fermenting in the big-bellied bottles on the veranda railing. "This is the last straw. Have the Hancocks nothing better than this old woman's wine to drink? Had to deliver all your corn whiskey to the army, too, I suppose. Why, Abigail's corn whiskey was the only thing that would have reconciled me to making the trip over here."

Mary took the doctor's arm and led him over to the loom. A broad piece of coarse wool fell to the floor. She picked it up and rubbed it between her fingers. "Look at this," she said with pride. "Every homestead has one or two of these weaver's looms now. This is where our army's winter coats are coming from. We're sewing them at Redford, too."

The doctor made a face. "I'd wait with the cutting," he grumbled. "This war'll be over before the first frost is on the pumpkins." Before Mary could reply he turned around to enter the house.

Mary held him back. "I'd like to help," she said. "I want to learn how to do it. Just in case you really can't make it across the Delaware some day when we need you." She had expected a protest, but there was none.

"I've seen young doctors keel over the first time they helped at a birthing," Banks said. "But come along if you want to."

The doctor and Mary disappeared into the house; Skelnik hesitated, then decided to wait outside. The children's voices had receded behind the house; the old woman had gone back to her loom. The silence was broken only by the rhythmic sound of the shuttle, by a bee humming around the bottles on the railing. The windows of the house were open, but there was no breeze to stir the light-blue curtains. A broom stood beside the door; the light-colored sand of the yard showed traces of a recent sweeping. The peace that followed the harvesting season on a farm enveloped everything.

Jan Kellog had unsaddled the horses and was rubbing their backs dry. Five years ago he had brought a consignment of horses down to Redford from the north and had stayed on. Apart from his name, and that he was a trained blacksmith, Skelnik knew nothing about him. No one asked a man about his past in this country or, if he did ask, minded not getting an answer. In the five years Kellog had worked on Redford, Skelnik couldn't recall the man starting a conversation once. He walked over and said, "Anything new in Trenton?"

Kellog stuck out his underlip, gave the horse another two strokes, and then managed a one-word answer. "Rumors."

"Good or bad?"

"If that's the way you put it, bad." That, as far as Kellog was concerned, concluded the conversation. He began rubbing the next horse dry.

"Any news of the army? It's been days since we've had word. Not a messenger, nothing. It's like the earth had swallowed our people up. It's not necessarily a bad sign; it's an old, proven tactic of the general's—keep the English mystified about where our army is. The English are said to have gathered twenty thousand men between Boston and New York. They still think they can end the war within the year."

"Rumors," Kellog said angrily. "Lies and rumors. Making up lies, that's where they're hard to beat. The whole of Trenton's a miserable nest of royalists."

David Woodrock, the stableboy, was limping over to the horses with two pails of fresh water, drawn at the well. Skelnik felt a sudden urge for that cold clear water; he bent over one of the pails, scooped a little out, dunked his face in—once, twice—till his skin tingled with the icy cold. Sucking in air, he straightened up again, shaking the water from his hands. "What's new here, David, anything going on?"

"I didn't want to mention it while Doc was out here," the young man said in a low voice. He stood with his bandaged left foot slightly to one side, keeping his weight on the right leg. The youngest of the help on the Hancock place, he had not yet had to shave. That he was no longer with the army he owed to a splinter from an English shell he'd caught in his foot at the Battle of White Plains. Part of it was still in his flesh, and the wound kept festering. "Last night we had unannounced visitors again. Two men; they slept in the feed barn."

"Anything stolen?"

"The usual, two of the men's work clothes."

"You mean two men from our army?"

David nodded. "Two deserters. Remember the last time: three men, stayed overnight, stole some clothing, and were gone the next morning? And a few days later we got the news of our defeat at Chatterton's Hill."

"Are you sure?"

"Want to see the uniforms they left in the hay? I found them myself, uniforms, caps, and muskets; they were from the Virginia militia. The rats ran away." He looked earnestly at Skelnik. "You told me, last time, that this was a deliberate move on the general's part. That he was making a strategic retreat, now, because it was too risky to force a decisive battle yet. But how are we going to win a war if our troops just keep on retreating? How long can we keep it up? The deserters are a sign—" He stopped and spit out a plum pit he had been sucking on.

Skelnik wasn't afraid to tackle such questions head-on, but he found himself wishing he didn't have to this time. "We have no choice, for the time being," he said. "To force a showdown with the English just now—why, we'd be doing them a big favor, the biggest. We're not strong enough yet; we have to retreat. You're right enough, David, to say it makes us look bad. But that's just it, that's the way to lure the English away from the coast, where their strongest positions are, deeper into the country, our country, where our chances are better. They win, sure, and they'll win again, but in the end, even if they win one battle after the other, we'll be winning the war."

David had listened attentively, feeling honored every time Skelnik spoke with him so seriously. "God knows there's not a man here who doesn't hope you're right," he said emphatically. "When I found those uniforms, I thought, those reprobates—I could have cried, I was so mad. But then I looked closer, and those uniforms were more like rags. And I started thinking what it must be like for a man to have to swallow one defeat after another. I started wishing for something to happen that'd give us back our courage."

"We'll get it back," Skelnik said. He looked across the yard at the house—an image of peace that was stronger than his doubts.

When Mary had entered the kitchen, she'd thought the steamy heat was going to choke her, but she was shivering now. The kettle of boiling water had been moved aside on the hearth so that the heat of the fire hit her directly in the face. She kept her arms pressed to her body, crawling, as it were, inside herself in an effort to keep down the trembling of her knees. Through the open door she could see the bed where the woman lay in labor. For a few minutes now it had been quiet; the only sound was the rustling of Doctor Banks's newspaper. If it hadn't been for the doctor, she would have been tempted to run out of the house. But she had volunteered, so she would have to go through with it.

The woman on the bed gave a low moan and tossed her head from side to side. Flaming red hair framed her pale face.

Then, suddenly, she spoke, in a menacing low voice Mary had never heard before. "I'll set the dogs on him, I'll shoot him down, this is the last time he blows up my belly. Year after year. . ."

Noah Banks seemed oblivious to it. He dropped his paper and said in a disgruntled voice, "Hardly anything left in the paper a man can read. Nothing but recipes for making tea out of acorns and appeals to send clothing and shoes to the troops."

Abigail's mutterings gave way to hysterical sobbing. Mary

pressed her palms against her ears and shut her eyes. It couldn't be her Abigail lying there—a woman she had never seen other than with a baby in her arms; a woman always wearing a simple blouse easily unbuttoned, always ready to nurse her youngest, always cheerful and high-spirited.

Mary hadn't noticed Robert Skelnik entering the room. Bending to get in under the lintel—the doors of the cottage hadn't been designed for a man of his height—he took off his hat. "How are you coming along?"

Mary tried to smile back at him, thinking how astonishingly young he looked.

Abigail, between sobs, was now gasping out nothing but swearwords, in that terrible, unfamiliar voice. Mary whispered to Skelnik, "It's been like this the whole time. And I always thought she was happy, and so proud of her children." She was talking only to distract his attention from the awful things Abigail was saying; she was ashamed for Abigail.

With a groan, Banks got up from his rocking chair. "Put the kettle on, young lady." Skelnik followed the doctor to the woman's bedside.

Mary went to the hearth and hung the kettle on the open fire, which she stoked and fed more firewood. Reluctantly she followed the others to the lying-in room.

Skelnik stood beside the bed. He dipped a towel into a basin of cold water, laid the compress on the woman's forehead and cheeks, moistened it again, and cooled her hands and arms with it. Suddenly her head, tangled hair sticky with sweat, burrowed deeper into the pillow. Her body reared upward—but not a sound came from her mouth. Skelnik held Abigail's hands in his own until the pains passed. He put a fresh pillow under her head.

Banks eyed Skelnik's activities with malicious humor. "Would you like to tell me why you brought me over at all? I warn you, if you demote me to serving as your assistant, I'll double my fee."

Abigail lay exhausted on her back, her eyes open, staring at Skelnik. When the next seizure came, her hands tightened convulsively on the bedclothes. Skelnik put a hand on her shoulder and bent over her. Mary saw something blinking in his hand—a gold piece. Abigail hesitated for a second, then she opened her mouth; Skelnik slipped the coin between her teeth. The woman's face relaxed; she even managed a faint smile.

Mary, looking on, felt as if she was making a discovery, something disturbing and confusing, and tinged with jealousy. Skelnik was doing it all so easily, so naturally; she couldn't help wondering if he hadn't stood some other time at the bedside of a woman giving birth—to a child of his. After all, what did she know about this man, who was as close and as distant to her as a father? The only past he spoke of had to do with Redford, as if his life had had its beginning in his encounter with the marked pine tree. Where had he gotten the money for all the hired men, for the horses that had filled his stables from the day they were built? He was not one of the thousands of immigrants who had started life in this country with nothing but their bare hands. He must have brought money with him, a great deal of money. She remembered the gold coins he always had on him and sometimes gave away as a kind of talisman. Coins from another world.

"Your turn, doctor," she heard him say; she felt his arm on her shoulder, drawing her away, and her questions were forgotten.

The sunlight outside, the fresh air, the cold well water into which she dipped her arms to the elbows, all slowly brought her out of the dizziness that had come over her as she left the house.

She stretched out her wet hands and watched the water drip to the ground. It was quiet in the yard. The old woman had stopped her work at the loom; two girls in their early teens were whispering to her excitedly, apparently curious about what was going on inside.

Skelnik smiled. "No need to be upset by what you just saw, you know. Or what you heard. It's been like that from the beginning of time. If you reminded her later of the things she said just now, she'd deny it, and very indignantly."

Mary poked in the sand with the tip of her shoe, not looking at him. "The way she calmed down when you came in—I asked myself why you never married. Or shouldn't I ask you a thing like that?" She dared lift up her eyes to him only after she had gotten this out. To her disappointment, he was smiling.

"You know how old I am. I'm thirty-five years older than you."

"Do you think I haven't noticed the way women look at you?"

Abruptly, he burst out laughing. "Then you've noticed more than I have." A strand of hair fell over his forehead; the silver in it enhanced its silky sheen.

Mary felt encouraged in her probing. "I can certainly understand your not being taken with the women around here. But you never talk about your trips to Philadelphia and what goes on there. But I see the clothes you pack when you go to town."

He came close and framed her face in his hands, tilting it up. "The ideas inside this little head—I never realized! Haven't I asked you every time whether you'd like to come along?"

"You only want to buy me a pair of specs."

He was still holding her head in his hands; it was a familiar gesture, the way he said good night to her every evening, with a fatherly kiss on her forehead, trying to make her feel loved and safe. It was exactly the same as always. And yet it was one of those moments that came more often, these days, when for the duration of a heartbeat he wished he were young instead of old and wise. He was glad when Doctor Banks came out of the house and Kellog led the horses toward them. Skelnik tightened the cinch straps and swung into the saddle.

The old woman came running across the yard, holding a bottle up toward the doctor. "With thanks from Abigail."

"I drink only corn whiskey," Banks said gruffly.

"Of course, Doctor, we know that. Here's corn whiskey, the best, made by Abigail herself. She wouldn't let me give it to you till after the baby was born. You see, Doctor, we know you very well here, even though you're a Trenton man."

"All right, then, if you insist—guess you'd just as soon I fell off my horse and broke my neck. . . ."

The old woman giggled as she put the bottle into the doctor's saddlebag. "Why, sure, one royalist more or less don't matter so much."

When Banks sat astride his horse, he pulled out his watch. "You wasted my whole afternoon, Skelnik," he grumbled. "For no good reason at all. That woman could have had her baby without any help from me."

"I know," Skelnik said seriously. "Abigail never needs a doctor."

"I really don't understand what you thought you were doing."

"Don't you, really? Think of the impression you make, Doc, riding through the country with your satchel. The people see you coming the way you always did, wanting your corn whiskey, demanding to be paid in hard coin—don't you see, when Doctor Banks crosses the Delaware on the ferry as usual, it's like peacetime and nothing so much to worry about."

He leaned toward the doctor and Mary saw the glint of the gold coin he pressed into the doctor's hand.

The sun was sinking when they came within sight of the Delaware. The sky had a greenish tinge, and a white, almost transparent moon had risen on the eastern horizon.

They had come the whole way in silence, riding slowly, taking their time.

A flock of birds streaked smoothly across the sky, as delicate and insubstantial as the moon. Noah Banks was the first to speak. "Wild geese, this time of year. I can't remember them ever flying south this late."

They were close enough to the river to hear the rush of the water. Jan Kellog, who rode ahead, reined in his mare. The sun's last rays were reflected from the surface of the river. Kellog shielded his eyes to see across it.

"This light's blinding," Banks said. "What is it, Kellog?"

"The ferry. It's gone. It's on its way over to the other side."

Skelnik spurred up beside Kellog's horse, and Kellog pointed to where a troop of riders, tiny in the distance, was milling around on the opposite shore. Skelnik had the feeling that all would be well as long as he did not budge, but that as soon as he moved, something terrible would happen. A gust of wind from the river fluttered the horses' manes and tugged at the wide brim of his hat.

"What is it?" Mary said. "What's wrong?"

Without taking his eyes off the opposite shore, Skelnik rode his horse down to the landing stage, followed by the others. The ferry was in the middle of the river. In the uncertain light, it took him a while before he could be sure it was moving off toward the troop of horsemen waiting on the other side.

"Uniforms," Kellog said. "You can see their weapons flashing. Looks like a dozen or so: blue coats, white breeches."

"Could be our own New Jersey militia," Skelnik said.

Banks stood up in his stirrups, peering across. "I wouldn't be too sure," he said. "What if it's the English? Would that surprise you? One of these days, there they'll be. And once they've reached the Delaware, the river wouldn't stop them if it was twice as wide at it is."

"Blue coats, white breeches," Kellog mused aloud. "The doctor could be right. One of them's holding a pennant, but I can't tell the colors from here."

"My guess is, they're our own men. Couriers on the way to the Congress in Philadelphia maybe. They might be bringing the latest news." Skelnik dismounted and Mary followed suit.

They stood side by side, staring across the river in the deepening twilight. The air was still; there was only the rustle of river, the horses munching at clumps of grass. In the waning light the landscape had a special beauty, tinged with melancholy.

They saw the ferry touching the other shore. Two horses were led aboard, followed by two men; the others stayed on the bank. As soon as the ferry pushed off, a signal sounded, and the rest of the troop galloped up the slope. They formed into a single file and rode off eastward, one behind the other, led by the man with the pennant, like so many toy soldiers.

"You were right," Mary said. "They're militia. I can see their colors plainly now. But why are the others going back?"

"Two are enough to deliver a message," Skelnik said.

"Seems it takes too much courage these days for two militiamen to ride through New Jersey alone," Banks said. "They need a whole company. That's what we've come to in this country. But I promise you, they can bring their wounded to me by the thousands, they can lay them right at my doorstep, and I won't lift a finger for this war."

Skelnik raised a hand to silence Mary; he could guess what she was about to reply to that.

The shadows were lengthening at their feet. As the light faded, the still glittering river lost some of its width, seemed to withdraw to the opposite shore. For a moment the ferry was half in the light, half in the shadow, itself a soundlessly gliding shadow. Then suddenly it was swallowed up in the shadow this side of the river; there was only the sound made by the rudder, the creaking of its overhead hawsers.

Kellog stood ready at the mooring post. For the last fifty yards, where there was barely a current, the ferryman stood at the bow holding the rope ready to toss to Kellog.

Noah Banks buttoned his plaid coat up to the neck, put up his collar, and picked up his satchel.

"Thanks for coming," Skelnik said. "And in case we don't see you again, Merry Christmas."

Noah Banks twinkled at him. "You believe in that, don't you?"

"Believe in what?"

"Fate. Christmas will be Christmas. You give away your horses, sure that you'll get others. You haven't kept enough men to get the harvest in, but you're sure there'll be another harvest. In Connecticut the English burned down scores of houses, and the Hessians slaughtered all the cattle, but Redford will be Redford forever. Do you realize, my friend, how entirely you have become an American, one of these goddamned, optimistic Americans?"

"Oh, is that what I am?"

"Yes, sir, that's what you are, and so I'll wish you a Merry Christmas in the devil's name, and if you feel like it, come on over to Trenton and let's finish that chess game. The pieces are just the way we left them, and I warn you I'm ahead, so if you want to save your game. . . ." He broke off.

The front ramp of the ferry, let down like a drawbridge, had crunched ashore. Kellog was tying the hawsers to the mooring posts. The ferryman brought two horses ashore and handed their reins to Kellog. One of the yellow saddle blankets had dark stains on it. The officer who had followed the horses off the ferry wore the uniform of the Pennsylvania militia. On the upturned brim of his hat was the insignia of General Washington's Guards. He was a stocky, broad-shouldered young man; his uniform fitted him like a glove, but at the moment it seemed to drag at his shoulders like a dead weight. It was spattered with dried mud, and his boots were stained from heavy riding.

Skelnik rummaged in his memory, sure he had seen the man before somewhere. He tried to imagine him in civilian clothes, but that didn't help. But when the man took off his hat, he knew him. "Lieutenant Blyth! How good to see you. How's General Washington?—Is something the matter?" he interrupted himself.

Andrew Blyth hastily smoothed his wig. "We've just spent ten hours straight in the saddle, sir. I can't remember when I last took off my uniform."

Skelnik turned to Mary. "You remember Lieutenant Blyth of General Washington's Guards, don't you?"

Mary held out her hand to Blyth. "I do hope you can stay a while, Lieutenant. And I hope you bring good news."

Blyth's face was extremely pale, and for a moment the stolid figure seemed about to collapse. Looking steadily down at Mary's outstretched hand, he said in a low voice, "You'll have to be strong. These are bad times for all of us. We must be strong."

Mary stared at him, then cast an uncertain glance at Skelnik. Noah Banks pushed through between them and ran toward the ferry. They heard his boots on the loose planks, then his shout: "My satchel—Kellog, bring me my satchel. Hurry!"

Andrew Blyth blocked Mary's way. "No, don't go down there." Then he realized it was useless to stop her. "It's John," he said. "John Compson. And he won't need a doctor any more."

"Let her go," Skelnik said. He made no attempt to stop her; he watched as she went, very slowly, down the bank to the ferry.

The body lay on the floorboards of the ferry. The doctor was kneeling beside it; he had pulled off the blanket. Jan Kellog came running with the doctor's satchel, but Banks waved him back. The doctor got to his feet and shook his head.

"There's nothing to be done. He's lost every drop of blood, looks like." He turned to Andrew Blyth. "It must have just now happened, during the crossing."

Lieutenant Blyth nodded without looking at the corpse. "He

was still alive when we brought him on the ferry. I thought till the last minute we might save him yet."

"You transported him like this, with his wound untreated?" Banks said indignantly.

"He insisted on it—he wouldn't listen to reason. He rode the whole way, from Fort Washington to the Delaware."

"You must have passed a dozen doctors on the way."

"He wouldn't hear of stopping. He had to go straight to Redford—to her. . . ."

All eyes turned to Mary. But she saw no one. A sudden gust of wind rocked the boat; the water splashed against its sides. The dead man rolled with the boat. Skelnik and Kellog exchanged a glance and bent over to pick up the body.

"Are you taking him to Redford?" Noah Banks semed to be the only one present capable of speech. "His father won't like that. Better have Kellog help me take the boy to his father in Trenton. God knows I don't want to. I'm a doctor, not a gravedigger. But I'll do it; I don't know why, but I'll do it."

Skelnik shook his head. "You heard it; he wanted to get home to Redford."

Banks picked up his satchel. "All right, then, take him with you. He's only the first of the dead to come across the river; he won't be the last." He was talking himself into a real anger. "Pretty soon your graveyard won't be big enough to hold them all. Go on, take him; tie him on his horse and take him to Philadelphia. Take him through the streets, let the people see him, let the Congress see him. Let them see what independence did for John Compson."

Skelnik and Kellog carried the body down the ferry ramp. The left arm was dangling. Mary took the cold hand and held it until the men had brought the body ashore and could lay it down again.

One of the ferrymen untied the hawsers. The water gurgled as the ferry slowly drifted into the river; then the current took hold of it. From the shack at the landing stage Jan Kellog brought a length of green canvas and spread it on the ground near the body.

Mary, who had been keeping her eyes glued to the dead face as if waiting for it to breathe again, talk to her again, finally turned away when the men placed the body gently on the canvas. She walked slowly to her horse and picked up the trailing reins. She slipped them over the horse's head, grasped the pommel, and swung into the saddle. Each move seemed infinitely hard to do, as though a great weight were pulling against her.

The river glistened in the slate-gray twilight. The ferry was pulling away; Noah Banks was silhouetted in the bow, slowly, receding. The wind buffeted the bushes and whispered in the air. Mary looked across the river. There, on the other shore now hidden in the thickening gray dusk, she had seen that troop of riders, horses capering restlessly, the gleam of metal on weapons, the fluttering pennant. Until today, the Delaware had kept the war away, on the other shore. Now the dead young man had brought the war home.

27

The moon that had risen so pale and disembodied that afternoon now gleamed brilliantly above the trees. It was one of those nights with a deep blue sky, stars so close it seemed you could reach up and pluck them, and that glassy feel in the air hinting at chill and frost to come. The desk at which Mary sat stood directly under the window. It was the only piece of furniture she had brought to Redford from Boston after her father's death. On the polished yew-wood top, where her father had composed his sermons, lay the box in which she kept John Compson's letters.

Considering that they had known each other only six months in all, there was a sizable number of letters—though they were not love letters. She couldn't recall the word "love" ever coming up in her talks with John, and his letters could just as easily have been addressed to a friend of his own sex. She couldn't remember the first time she met him. It must have been sometime in May. Her memories began with the fifth of July, the day John Compson had ridden to Redford with the Declaration of Independence, just printed in Philadelphia, so that she would be one of the first to read that momentous document of America's final repudiation of English rule.

His first letter to her was a note of thanks for the new flag of red-and-white stripes made on Redford. She herself had removed the Union Jack and replaced it with the thirteen stars on a blue field. Afterward he regularly reported on what was happening in Congress. She had been very proud that, on some details, she was better and earlier informed than anyone on Redford, Skelnik included. But now that she read the letters again, she could see that all this had been merely a pretext to write to her, to be in touch. Now that she thought about how rarely she had answered him, she felt guilty and sad.

He had loved her. It was there, in every word of his letters. There was her name, Mary, over and over again; and while he tossed off his communiqués in a light casual scrawl, each letter of her name was drawn with loving care. His last letter was dated just three weeks back, November second, and had been written in camp at White Plains. It was only a few lines: "Ever since we had to surrender New York to the British, we've been fighting more with pickaxes and spades than with our weapons. Digging in, throwing up barriers, moving on, is all we do. At Chatterton's Hill we lost 160 men. It was considered impregnable, and we had almost driven the English off when the Hessians under Colonel Rall fought their way up, directly on our flanks. That did it, we had to retreat from the hilltop. That fellow Rall is a terror. Just now the news is that we must abandon camp and cross to the right bank of the Hudson. This will bring me closer to you, but it also means that Washington has to throw himself between the enemy and Philadelphia. Three thousand men are holding Fort Washington on Manhattan Island. It's too late to pull them out of there. . . ." But Mary concentrated less on these details than on her name, lovingly painted in large letters. The moonlight silvered the paper and brought out metallic reflections in the fine lines of ink.

She put the letter down and waited—wishing the tears would come. Why had he loved her? And why hadn't she been able to love him? There was such a thing, then, as unrequited love. The question gripped her and wouldn't let go. It cast everything into doubt; the moment she took a good hard look at something she had always taken for granted, it threatened to dissolve into uncertainties. Even the simple, homely things that surrounded her daily life seemed to have undergone a change. The linen curtains had a silvery sheen tonight, her bare white walls seemed covered with a fine scrollwork, there was a mysterious beauty in everything she looked at. Was it only the moonlight, or was it something else?

She was glad to hear steps outside. Judging by their light, springy rhythm, it had to be McGill. She waited for the energetic knock with which the cook usually announced herself. But this time, when the footsteps ended at the door, McGill hesitantly called her name.

Mary opened the door. "Come in, I'm not busy."

"It's about the geese. Betsy Potter was here today and showed me how it's done. Stuffing them, she calls it." McGill uttered a sound of disgust. "You've got to help me so we won't have to do it here. I don't care if it makes the geese as big and fat as pigs! Betsy makes a kind of flour sausage, twice as thick and twice as long as a finger, that we're supposed to feed them. She pokes it down their throats with the wooden handle of the cooking ladle! You know I'll do anything to help feed the army, I'll find ways to send more food, but don't let them make me do this. . . ." Besides her name, McGill had inherited from her father a light, freckled skin. Otherwise she was pure Indian, with her straight black hair, her prominent features, and her narrow black eyes that seemed not to have to look at things to take them in. "You've been reading his letters?"

Mary nodded.

"Do you want my advice? Burn them. Burn them now, this minute. If you want, I'll do it for you. Fire is better than dust and rot." She spoke in the hesitant but firm tone she always used when the subject was something she believed she knew more about than others. "Did you see the early moon today? I knew a dead man would be coming to us."

"You and your visions. What about when John left? Did you see signs and portents then?"

"What if I had? Could anything have stopped him?"

"Only an hour ago he was still alive, Lieutenant Blyth said. He died on the ferry, in midstream." Mary felt as if she were seeing the dead man for the first time, as if someone were drawing a veil from that image in her mind. That bloodless face, the strand of hair pasted by sweat to the forehead, the beginning of a stubble on those pale cheeks, the lips slightly open as though about to breathe, about to speak.

"He wasn't meant for you." McGill lowered her voice. "The Delaware has always brought good luck to Redford. It's going to bring you happiness. I can't understand today's signs, in fact. The signs tell me the river will bring a dead man, and yet they say it'll bring happiness. It wasn't the ferry, it was the river itself, the water, that brought happiness. I'll have to think about it."

McGill walked to the desk, picked up the letters in their box, and took them to the fireplace.

Mary held her back. "Why couldn't I love him? You remember—the last day he was here and we rode out together to the beehives in the woods? It was a hot day, and we were alone. I'm afraid I was a great disappointment to him."

McGill shook her head. "John Compson was the happiest man the other side of the Delaware. Otherwise he wouldn't have chosen to come here on his last ride."

Mary lowered her eyes. She agreed with McGill, but not quite. There was no justification for unrequited love. "Is it always like that with love?" she asked.

"It's always like that as long as you're still asking questions about it. One day you won't have any more questions, and then it'll be love."

McGill began to toss the letters into the fire.

Mary watched as they went up in flames, turned to ashes. "Here we are, talking about love, and he's dead," she said. It was not a question, only a final way of saying she realized there could be no answers.

They stood for a while together, gazing at the fire; then Mary said, "That Lieutenant Blyth who brought John back—did he bring any news?"

"They're in the library, Mr. Skelnik and the lieutenant, with their heads together. I don't think the news is good. Mr. Skelnik wants us all gathered in the hall, in an hour. He has something to tell us."

Together they left Mary's room. Usually the house was an endless hum of activities this time of day, but tonight everything was quiet. They met no one, even in the foyer.

Mary was beginning to feel a little better. From the first time she had set foot in it, this house had always had a soothing effect on her. Wind, snow, rain, or heat could rage outside, but nothing could faze this house. She felt the thick home-woven carpet underfoot, smelled the wood. Suddenly she stopped in front of a locked door. She had often wondered what was in the two rooms behind that locked door, but she usually walked past it without a glance. For the first time she saw it in a new way. She studied the paneling and the frame—a style of workmanship that must have originated in some other country; there was no carpenter far and wide who could have done such work, and there was in the whole house only one other door like it; the rest were simple oak and plainly made.

"Wait a minute." She took McGill by the arm. "Open this door for me."

"What sort of an idea is that? You know as well as I do your father has the keys to these rooms."

"I also know you dust in there sometimes."

"That's all I do, I dust and I air things, and I always have to get the keys from him."

"Did you know the woman who lived here? Tell me about her. Did she die, did she leave him? I want to know all about her."

"Can you imagine a woman leaving him? Would you leave him? You never took any interest in these rooms before, and no one else in the house does. It was different in the beginning, but that was a long time ago. He even seems to have forgotten her himself. There was a time, they say, when he spent hours in there, whole evenings by himself. Nowadays I have to remind him it's time to air them out."

"Who was she?"

"No one ever lived in these rooms," McGill said firmly.

"There's something you're not telling me. You've got to tell me. I don't care what it is. I can bear it."

"The door will be opened soon. I had a vision of the shutters open, letting the winter sun pour in, and there'll be great joy and great sorrow."

"McGill, please! No more of your oracles." Mary stood as though benumbed, pierced with an anguish quite different from what she had felt at John's death, and yet mysteriously bound up with it. "You really can make a person's flesh creep. I'm going out for some fresh air."

She wanted to be alone, to see no one. She ran down the corridor and took her coat and shawl from the wall hook beside the door to the veranda. The door to the library was open. Inside, Robert Skelnik and Lieutenant Blyth were leaning over a table covered with maps. This morning she would have been delighted to join their discussion. But now her only concern was not to be noticed going out.

She took a deep breath and stepped outside. The garden was flooded with moonlight; a breeze rustled the dried flowers lying on the veranda. She had threaded them together on fine threads; with pine and fir greens and cones they would make Christmas garlands for the house.

She loved to sit on the steps between the pillars covered with the clematis vines. It was the best spot for reading and daydreaming and for making peace with oneself and the world. But this time she went blindly on, past the stables and the herb garden. Finally she found herself at the gate to the little graveyard beyond the gardens, hidden behind bushes and trees, and enclosed by a rough wall of unhewn stones picked up in clearing the fields. It was an enchanted piece of ground, with a different atmosphere, different scents, a different silence from other places.

The wrought iron gate was open. She slipped inside. There were flagstone paths among the graves, but the stones were covered with moss and grasses. The graves were covered with granite slabs, too, but even these had become overgrown with mosses and creepers that made them look ancient.

She had never felt any fear of these graves, because they held no one she had known—men like the woodcutter McRead, killed by a falling tree; Keller, the carpenter who had fallen off the roof; the field worker Callaghan who had died of snakebite; two children drowned in the Delaware; all names which to her spelled the legend of Redford's becoming.

Under a walnut tree at the northern wall there was a stone that bore a name but no date: Robert Skelnik's grave, chosen by him and marked with his nameplate, before she had come to Redford. He had ordered the stone after his first serious heart attack. She never thought about it much. His heart condition was a part of his life before she knew him, something she had never personally encountered, something in the past; but now she remembered things she had passed over at the time. She had never seen him ride a horse very hard, for example; he always seemed to be restraining not so much the horse as himself. Self-restraint was in fact the hallmark of all his activity, as if he were carrying something fragile around in him. Now, looking at his gravestone, she understood at last. The day was coming when he would be lying in that house on a bier, like John Compson. When he thought about the future, this was the point at which his thinking stopped. She felt overwhelmed with a dull despair. She had loved her real father, but he was now very distant; her father had never been to her what Skelnik was: a nearness, a warmth, the feeling that his eyes had seen everything there was to see, that his hands had touched all the treasures of the earth, that his heart had known all of human passion, all a man could feel. Life without him was unthinkable. Everything related to him, everything derived from him; they began each day together, ended it together, he and she.

Fear spread in her like a dark stain. Her eyes seemed unable to avoid that gravestone, that name on it. Could this be the final answer to everything that had been going on inside her, perhaps the only answer? She rebelled against such a thought. She was young; death was still unreal. She would keep death away from Redford, simply by being there. The idea slowly brought back her serenity. Life, which had taken on the look of an unsolvable riddle in the last few hours, began to fill with meaning again.

For a while now she had been hearing something nearby. She looked around and discovered she was not alone. Under a lilac bush at the opposite wall, a man was digging a grave. The sounds she had heard were those of the spade and the clumps of earth falling. Jan Kellog stood up to his hips in the hole he was digging. The heaps of soil around the hole gave off pungent root smells. Kellog kept on digging as though he were alone, moving rhythmically. Whether he happened to be shaping a horseshoe, breaking a horse in, or carpentering in the winter time, he always looked like he was immersed in his favorite occupation. The only exception to this was anything that had to do with the army, the thought of which he hated. She had had a lot of arguments with him about the army, insofar as it was possible to have arguments with so taciturn a man.

"You seem to be in a big hurry," Mary said. "Must this be finished today?"

Kellog wiped his hands on his woolen jacket. "He was in a big hurry to die." He rammed the spade into the earth and leaned on it. "Besides, it's getting colder by the minute. Tomorrow the ground'll be hard as rock." He indicated the sky with his head.

"How can you talk like this—about a man who died for us."

"I talked no different when he was alive. But they won't listen, they have to fight."

"You're doing him a wrong—him, and all the men fighting for our country."

"I wouldn't know about wrong or right, Miss. All I know is, they started something now, that's sure to go on for a long time, and before it's finished, I'll have dug lots of graves."

Mary's thoughts wandered off to the other grave. "When did Mr. Skelnik order his own tombstone?"

"Why do you want to know?"

"I'd like to understand."

"I make the coffins, and I dig the graves, and I do it as well as I can. If there's more than that to it, I don't know about it. The way I figure it, we're here to do what we have to do the best way we can do it. It's the best thing you can say about a man. Skelnik can say it about himself. And that's what I think he meant by it. Only those who're afraid of life are afraid of death."

"And what about me?"

"You're his daughter, you have the same look in your eyes, the look that says you're not afraid, no matter what."

Kellog had raised his head as if to listen, and then Mary heard it, too: a sound like someone drumming on the earth. Kellog set his spade down and jumped out of the grave. Mary peered intently in the direction of the sound; behind the wall, the bushes, the night, it grew louder and closer, a drumbeat of horses' hooves. And now the riders came into view, between the moonlit rows of cedars leading up to the main house.

"Run as fast as you can," she heard Kellog say, "and warn Mr. Skelnik. I'll get the dogs. It's Jacob Compson. Run!"

Robert Skelnik had taken the news calmly; he stood at the top of the front steps now like a man awaiting invited guests. The storm lamps had been hastily lit, and in their light Mary could see neither fear nor anxiety in his face; he looked full of youthful energy, ready to do battle.

Jan Kellog came out of the dark with four black dogs on a leash, followed by several men with muskets. Despite the crowd waiting, the yard was quiet except for the hoofbeats coming up the drive.

"Everybody take it easy now," Skelnik said. "I'm counting on you." He said nothing more, but he had said enough.

The riders came to a halt in front of the steps where Skelnik stood with Mary and Lieutenant Blyth. There were six of them, but only one of the six rode a white horse; in the moonlight even his hair and clothes looked white.

"It's Compson," Mary whispered. She felt Skelnik take her hand; he knew how she felt. John Compson lay on a bier inside the house; his grave was ready in the little graveyard. Funeral candles, an open grave—it wasn't for these that he'd wanted to reach Redford. He'd ridden all the way to Redford because he knew the people here would protect him even in death—him and the cause he'd fought for. This thought finally gave her the comfort she'd been seeking all day. She looked at Skelnik. "I hope you remember who Jacob Compson is. And the way he treated us when the English were still in charge here."

The Redford men had closed in around the Compson riders. Compson's white horse was restless, prancing and snorting, tossing its head.

"It's been a long time since we've seen you this side of the Delaware, Jacob Compson." Skelnik's voice was even, almost gentle. "Why don't you get down and come inside?"

All eyes were on Compson.

"I've got nothing to say to you, Robert Skelnik. You have my son's body. Give it to me, and you'll be rid of me." His voice could be heard all over the yard.

It was a voice Skelnik knew well, a voice that had once dominated the great auctions on the wharves of Philadelphia. For years Compson had been feared by everyone in the region; now he was hated—he and his brothers, Ebenezer in Philadelphia and Samuel in Boston, were the embodiment of everything the rebels were fighting against.

"I'm waiting," Compson said. "Where's John? Where's my son?"

Mary started forward, but Skelnik held her back.

"The last time we saw each other, Compson," he said, "you told me you didn't have a son anymore."

"There wasn't any room in my house for a man in a rebel uniform."

"He's still wearing that uniform," Lieutenant Blyth said. "He'll never take it off now, he'll wear it to his grave."

"Who are you?"

"Andrew Blyth, volunteer from Pennsylvania and lieutenant of cavalry."

"Robert Skelnik," Compson said sharply, "how many sons have you lured away from their fathers, only to send them to their deaths?"

"And who got us into this war?" Skelnik said calmly. "Men like you."

"Do you think I'll let a man like you say that about me? The

Compsons were settled in this country long before adventurers like you infested it. The Compsons—and the King—will still be here long after your kind is gone. Just who do you think you are that you think you can usurp land here and propose to represent this country?"

The men around Jan Kellog were growing restless; the dogs were straining at their leash. Skelnik raised a hand for quiet. He showed no sign of emotion; when he spoke his voice was the same as before.

"Your son rebelled against you long before he rebelled against the King."

"Take care, Skelnik. There are witnesses here. Before long we'll have the instigators of this war up on charges. And I'll make sure your part in it's not forgotten. I know a few things about you you won't want heard. So give me my son before I have to use force."

Mary felt the pressure of Skelnik's hand; his grip was almost painful, but she was glad of it—it let her share what was going on inside him.

"How do you propose to move his body?" he asked.

A murmur went through the crowd, but no one moved. Compson seemed at a loss for an answer.

"My men'll bring him out," Skelnik said. He picked out two of the men at the foot of the steps. "Bring the body out."

Mary took her hand out of his. "You can't do this! He wanted to come to Redford. He rode the whole way just to reach us."

"He expected to live," Skelnik said. He put an arm around her shoulder. "Do you need a grave to remind you of him?"

McGill came out of the house with a lantern, followed by the two men carrying the body. She held the lantern high as they slowly descended the steps and negotiated the distance to the riders. In the light of the lantern, they tied the body across one of the horses. Nobody said anything; it had all come too quickly.

The body was tied fast; McGill lowered the lantern. Silently the riders swung their horses around. Jacob Compson, who hadn't looked once at his son's body, rode to the head of the group, followed by the two riders guiding the horse with the body between them. Without a word, they moved off into the darkness.

Lieutenant Blyth was deathly pale. He turned to Skelnik, started to say something. Suddenly he swayed on his feet, as if the ground had given way under him. He would have fallen, but Skelnik caught him at the last moment. Blyth tried to push Skelnik's arm aside, but he hadn't the strength left. Skelnik saw the feverish glitter in the young officer's eyes, the sweat on his forehead; he took Blyth's wrist between his fingers.

"You have a fever. You belong in bed. McGill will get a room ready for you. How long has it been since you've slept?"

"I don't know, three, four days, maybe. I'm all right now. What I need is a horse."

Skelnik shook his head. "Let Compson go. It was his son he came for."

Through the darkness came the sounds of the Compson party moving out of the yard, the horses slowly picking their way; then they turned into the cedar drive and broke into a trot, a monotonous, receding drumbeat in the night.

28

Robert Skelnik himself might have found it hard to explain why he had built such a large hall in an otherwise simple and practical house. Maybe he had been influenced by his childhood memory of that large game room of the Polish prince his father had served; or maybe he had wanted to preserve under his own roof his first impression of the dim clearing in the wilderness, his first camping ground at Redford. In any case, the huge hall had the air of a structure not made by mere human hands, but *grown,* in the time it takes a forest to grow to its full height.

For years it had consisted only of crudely finished walls, a huge fireplace, a scattering of wolf and bear pelts on the floor, and iron hooks in the walls for the hunting rifles. Skelnik had allowed eleven years for the seasoning of the oak timbers from which he then cut the beams for the ceiling; he waited eleven years before he had the paneling for the walls made from the cedars he had cut for the purpose. Only after the wood paneling was done did he decide on the fabrics for the curtains and hangings, woven to order—unbleached linen that blended perfectly with the paneling. Little by little, a few pieces of furniture had been added: an oaken table that would seat thirty-six guests; high-backed chairs with deerskin pads on the seats; a buffet that held the silver and drinking glasses. These things fitted into the room as though they had always been there.

Cool and shady in every season of the year, the huge room seemed to be more the work of nature than of man. And now that Skelnik put more wood on the fire, a breath of the forest went through the hall.

Mary looked on, glad that they had these few minutes to themselves before the others came in. She sat in one of the armchairs near the fireplace and waited for him to sit down, too.

"Why did you do that?" she asked.

"It was, after all, his son." He stretched his legs toward the fire. "Suppose I had a son who happened to be fighting in a red coat under the British flag because he was in love with a royalist's daughter?"

"Don't say that. John believed in his cause with all his heart."

"I've said nothing against John. I'm only saying there are things that have nothing to do with the war, and love is one of them."

"I still don't understand. Jacob Compson hates you, and he hated his son."

"Yes, he did, and now it's too late for him. That could be why I did it. He had a son, and lost him. The son went his own way, but as long as he was still alive, there was still some hope. Now there's none. All that's left for him is to make his peace with the dead."

"To think you can still defend him."

"I'm only trying to imagine what it would feel like if I had a son and he died before I did. A son—that's a man's future. No man can live without faith in the future, and his future consists of his sons. It's only natural for an old man to take pride in the life of his sons; and it's a terrible thing to see the future die before oneself."

"Why have you no sons?" Mary asked, after a silence.

He gazed into the fire. "I have a daughter," he said. "I have you."

"You don't want to talk about it?" She suddenly felt as if his words had a very different meaning, as if they were speaking of different things.

"About the future? I am talking about it. You're my daughter, and I feel at peace knowing Redford will belong to you some day. Everyone talks of you already as Skelnik's daughter. I don't know who said it first but when I heard it, I was glad. You will always be Skelnik's daughter."

"You believe death makes an end of everything, don't you?"

"I don't know, not for sure, no. But I do think it'll be the way I said. When people see you riding across the fields, and they say, 'See, there's Skelnik's daughter,' then it'll be as if I'm still alive."

"You believe in what you can touch. Is that what your answer means?"

"I've never thought about it. If I think about it—yes, it's true, I suppose, I could get along without my eyes, but not without my hands, not without being able to touch things."

They had both missed the knock on the door. McGill was standing there. "Everyone's waiting for you."

Skelnik stood up. "Then let's not keep them waiting."

It was nothing unusual for Skelnik to call his people together in the great hall. From the seeding of a new kind of corn, the building of a road, the admission of a new tenant farmer, everything of common concern or interest was democratically discussed and decided here. Nevertheless he always felt a certain uneasiness on these occasions. Vague memories rose in his mind of the times his father was summoned to the prince, and how such a summons affected him. The usually cheerful man would look grave, even anxious; he would hurry into his good clothes, while his wife hastily knelt to polish his shoes. Skelnik remembered it all too vividly. The idea that any of his people might feel and conduct themselves so slavishly was profoundly repugnant to him.

But when they came streaming into the hall, he felt reassured.

The men removed their hats, but kept them in their hands. The stableboys came as they worked, in their socks, with their pants rolled up. The milkmaids wore their white kerchiefs and aprons. The cheeks of the kitchen maids were still aglow. Each group brought its own aroma with it, whether it was horses or fresh milk, bread or earth. The older people found chairs, the rest remained standing, but they all seemed relaxed and at home. The last to arrive were Jan Kellog and McGill. The Indian-Irish woman had combed her hair and put on an embroidered belt she had from her Indian mother, to dress up her blue cotton. When everyone seemed present, Kellog shut the door.

Skelnik ran his eyes over the assemblage. "I don't see Jean Daniel," he said.

"I haven't laid eyes on him myself for two days now," Kellog said. "Twenty Leghorns were chewed up by a fox, and Daniel's out after it. You know how he is when he gets worked up about a thing like that."

"And what about your wife, Henry Lee?"

Lee, who was six-feet seven-inches tall, was cheese maker at Redford. "She asked me to apologize for her, sir. They've just started the fires in the smokehouse, and she asked me to say that hams and sausages are more important than a few men arguing about the war. I tried to change her mind, but when it comes to arguments, I'm no match for her."

No one laughed. *War*. The word had slipped out, unintentionally. All eyes turned to Lieutenant Blyth standing beside Robert Skelnik; they had all noticed the map pinned to the wall.

"Then let me come straight to the point," Robert Skelnik began. "Your wife has a case, Lee, though I'd rather she came next time. What we have to discuss concerns the women, too. I admit hams and sausages are important, and they'll get more important as time goes on. But it's just as important to talk about the war, and I hope we can all keep a cool head, as we did outside a while ago. I want to thank you all. I know it wasn't easy to keep your feelings under control. But believe me, it was the best way we could have handled it."

"Is it really best to give in to a man like Jacob Compson?" The question came from one of the stablemen. "Now he probably thinks we're all starting to weaken."

"Try to understand," Skelnik said. "There are times when there's no turning back, once a stand's been taken, and others when one has to see reason. That's exactly what I wanted to talk with you about. You all remember when we pledged ourselves to the Declaration of Independence in July. It was an historic moment: a whole continent proclaiming its right and intention to be free. It was a stirring time for all of us, and a lot of people, not you but others, thought that was all there was to it. They thought the English would just get on their ships and leave America forever. Less than fourteen days later we all stood here again while John Compson told us about the landings near New York, a whole fleet, thirty thousand troops, English and German. I can still hear the way he described it—he said there were so many ships it looked like one enormous cloud bank rolling in off the ocean. I don't know how you felt when you heard that, but it made my blood run cold. John, as you know, died today, trying to reach us."

For a moment, Skelnik couldn't go on. The silence in the room was palpable, and serious. The faces of the listeners around the room were somber and composed, with one exception, that of Andrew Blyth. Skelnik heard the lieutenant's difficult breathing, and when he turned to look at him, he was startled by the fever in the man's eyes.

"I don't need to remind you what's happened since," he went on. "The news hasn't been good. We lost a lot of men at Flatbush, the first time we encountered the German mercenaries, only twenty-four hours after the landings. We lost New York. We were beaten again at White Plains. Only a few hours ago Lieutenant Blyth brought more bad news." He looked at the map on the wall, but he knew he wouldn't need it to explain the situation to his people. Many of them had never been on the other side of the Delaware, but these names and places were branded into their memories. In their hearts, they had participated in the battles, stormed the enemy positions, carried the dead and wounded away, rolled up the flags. He looked out over the room. They were waiting—the men with a touch of impatience, the women with resignation—for the next name, the next place that would burn itself into their memories. He found it easier to go on than he had expected.

"Fort Washington on the Hudson has fallen." He paused, to let them take it in. "Nearly three thousand of our men taken prisoner. Our army has retreated to the woods. That leaves the whole region around New York in enemy hands, including all of New Jersey. They may be right on the other side of the Delaware, any day now."

For a long time no one said a word. Then one of the men spoke up. "And what happens next, if we keep retreating? Where will it end?"

Skelnik couldn't see who the speaker was, nor did he recognize the voice, but it didn't matter; he knew it was what they all were thinking. He ran a hand over his face. "I don't know exactly what the future will bring. I don't know how much longer we'll have to go on retreating. I can't tell you how many more men will die, but I do know how it'll end. We're going to drive them back all the way, yard for yard. We're going to drive them out of the country, off our soil. I can see the day when the last English ship will weigh anchor and sail off over the horizon, forever. That will be a day, a day to remember."

He bowed his head, startled at his own words; he was not a man to wear his heart on his sleeve. He cleared his throat, to find his voice again. "Well, I didn't plan to discuss the future. You've heard how things stand. We've got to be prepared for the general to let New Jersey go and cross the Delaware, to save Philadelphia. That means the enemy'll come in pursuit. In a day or two they'll be facing us across the Delaware. That's the situation. Lieutenant Blyth insists we abandon Redford immediately and go to Philadelphia."

Like everyone else in the hall, Mary had been listening intently to every word Skelnik said. Now she broke in vehemently. "Leave Redford? You can't mean that! Nobody'll go with you!"

Skelnik straightened up and took a deep breath. There was movement in the crowd, even if it was only a shifting of weight from one foot to the other, a gesture to pat a comb into place, smooth out an apron.

"We're here to discuss the issue," Skelnik said. "Anybody who has anything to say should say it now. Then we'll take a vote. As always, one vote here is as good as another."

"I can tell you the result already," Mary said. "And I'm sure I speak for everyone here. No one wants to leave Redford. No one. I don't understand how you could even consider it."

"All I did was repeat to you what Lieutenant Blyth told me. He's just come from the army. He knows more than we do."

"And he knows John Compson died. What did he die for?" Mary had stepped up on the foot-high brick border around the fireplace; when she spoke, she had something of her father's style when he had made incendiary political speeches, in the guise of sermons from the pulpit. "What reason did John Compson have to fight and die? He had given his oath, he had his love of freedom and his faith in freedom, and that was enough. But we have all that and more. We have Redford, we have the land, we have our houses, we have horses, we have women and children. We have winter crops out there dependent on us. We have the best reasons in the world to fight."

A murmur of agreement ran through the crowd. Someone in the back shouted, "I think she's right." Then Henry Lee raised his hand. "I think, well, how shall I put it, are we sure we'll have to fight? Who say they're really coming here, and if they come, who says there'll be a battle? We're not Fort Washington, we're just one farm. What can they do to us? They'll most likely ask us for water and food."

"Oh, so you'd like to feed them, would you?" McGill said. "Next you'll say I ought to treat their wounds, too."

Lieutenant Blyth jumped up, almost knocking over his chair. His face was flushed. "None of you know what you're talking about!" he said. "The English—if it were only the English we had to deal with. But the English have allies, mercenaries, twenty thousand Hessians for instance. Those Hessians are killers, they give no quarter. I've seen them, I've fought them. If the English hadn't held them back they'd have butchered all the prisoners at

Flatbush. At White Plains we had the English almost beaten, before the Hessians came and saved the day for them. Without the Hessians, Fort Washington would never have fallen either. You don't know what they're like, and for your sake I hope you never find out. . . ."

The carpenter Bechtle raised a hand. "You make them out to be devils, but I can tell you this, they're poor devils." He spoke with deliberation, and with a thick accent. "I don't mean to make a speech or anything. I know everybody here's been at Redford longer than I have. I just want to say—I could be one of those Hessians right now. And I can tell you none of them came of their own free will. They were dragooned into the army, and they fight the way they do because they're terrified of their officers."

Blyth had broken out in a cold sweat. "They're like animals. They kill for money, and they do it with pleasure. All they want to do is kill. You can see it in the way they march, in the sound of their drums. Once you hear those drums you never forget it. . . ." He swayed dizzily on his feet, but when one of the men reached out to help him, Blyth rudely pushed him away.

"Just the same," Bechtle said, "I say they're poor devils. Let them come. Let them hear a German word spoken. Give them a good fat beef soup to eat, show them our pastures and our cattle, promise them a bit of land, and I tell you, they'll desert in droves."

"Everyone's talking as if the enemy was already at the gate," the gardener said, chewing on his pipe.

"All I say," Mary said, "is this: we can't let them cross the the river."

There was an eloquent silence. It was as if Mary's simple words had said everything there was to be said. The river. The Delaware. For a moment they all saw its gray-green waters, its banks, the wide bend of the river holding Redford as though in a protective embrace. Then they all started talking at once.

"She's right. We can't let 'em cross the river."

"I'm staying. I won't move an inch."

"Jacob Compson and his kind—they'd like nothing better than us leaving the land to them."

"Let's have a vote. Let those against staying here raise their hands."

Not a hand went up. Not even Lieutenant Blyth's.

"Very well, we vote to stay," Skelnik said. "I therefore propose that we start making preparations immediately. First, I think, we should set up a watch along the Delaware. We have the huts at the ford. We should put up at least two more, and arrange for guard duty around the clock at all of them."

"What about the ferry?" Henry Lee asked. "Shouldn't we stop it altogether?"

Skelnik hesitated. He thought of Doctor Banks and the ferry that brought him over—the ferry meant peacetime. . . . "Agreed," he said. "We stop the ferry. It means gathering in all the boats. No more fishing. We'd better check our supplies. We'll have to make a survey of everything we have on hand. The sale of our products comes to a stop immediately."

"Send a man to Princeton, to the apothecary," McGill said. "Not that we need his ointments; they don't do any good, they just make money for him. But we need lancets, cotton, Turkish rhubarb, and Indian herbs. With those, I'll make you the best medicines in the world."

"As for weapons," the blacksmith said, "we don't need an inventory. I can tell you right now every fowling piece, musket, and pistol we have at Redford."

The men were suddenly talking all at once. Everyone was participating. Everyone had ideas. Skelnik brought the meeting to a close and watched his people filing out of the hall, still talking. He knew he could depend on them; they would still be discussing plans and preparations outside.

When they were gone, only Skelnik, Mary, and Blyth remained in the hall. Skelnik took the map off the wall and rolled it up. Mary touched his arm and pointed to the lieutenant. Blyth was leaning back in the armchair, his tunic unbuttoned, eyes closed, muttering to himself.

"He's feverish," Skelnik said. "Go get McGill."

"Tell me," she said. "you never meant to abandon Redford, did you?"

"No, never."

Blyth was mumbling in his fever.

"I never expected to see a man like Blyth afraid," Mary said. "It's awful."

"He'll sleep. Tomorrow's another day."

How many more such days? Mary wondered. But she didn't say it. Nor did she dare look at Skelnik. She laid her head on his shoulder, and closed her eyes. "Hold me," she said. "Please. Just hold me for a minute."

29

It was the second Sunday in December and all the people of Redford were taking their midday meal together. The only empty place at the table was that of Jean Daniel, but no one noticed apart from McGill. The forester on Redford had always been special; he lived alone in a log cabin in the woods, an outsider the others saw only when he came to deliver game to McGill and to pick up his own supplies. It was as though the forest itself gave the man his special standing.

There were extensive woodlands on Redford, a vast semicircle of forest that rounded it off to the north and west. But when people spoke of "the forest" they meant the dark green, thick growth of wilderness between the main house and the river, virgin forest still going back to Indian times. There was an ancient Indian path through this forest, but it had grown so impassable that most people preferred to ride all the way around the woods on their way to the ford.

There was only one person at Redford who did not fear the woods: McGill. She went in frequently to gather herbs, blossoms, and roots for the medicines she made. The people of Redford were accustomed to seeing her slipping out in the early evening, after work, her willow basket on her arm, and riding off into the wilderness.

But on this particular Sunday, she didn't wait for evening. She left the kitchen immediately after the midday meal, without a basket, and in a great hurry. She was wearing her Sunday dress, and her hair was held up by combs. She had the lightest skin of all the women at Redford, and when she was wearing no hat or kerchief, her blue-black hair was so striking against her dazzling skin that even men who had known her for years were impressed and followed her with their eyes.

She was glad to find no one in the stables. She had put the bridle on earlier, to save time, and now she swung astride her mare and trotted off into the woods. She never felt as warmly sheltered in any house or room as she did among these trees, the more so the denser the trees were together. She loved it most when the forest was so thick that only an occasional ray of light gleamed through the leafy green roof overhead. When the underbrush had grown so dense she had to duck to escape the branches, she dismounted and went on on foot, leading the horse. She was looking for the places she knew Daniel had set his traps, but they were gone.

She had reached a clearing, and it wasn't long before she saw the log cabin off among the trees. She came up on it on the blind side, unnoticed, and led her mare to the little stall. Daniel's horse was there; he couldn't be too far away.

She went around to the front of the cabin. The ground was soft and springy, dense with pine needles. She rarely came here in the daytime, and something was different, strange somehow. There was no smoke curling from the chimney, no smell of cooking food. The traps she hadn't found in the forest were stacked beside the door. Soundlessly she opened the door and stepped inside.

There was no fire in the grate. Daniel's hunting gear and guns hung beside the door, looking abandoned in the cold light of day. His fur cap was there, his coat; his pipe, in its leather pouch, lay in the tin ashtray. The bedding was gone from the bed at the back of the room. The stripped mattress was covered with the blue woolen bedspread she had made herself.

She was glad there was time for her to get used to it all. She heard steps behind her, but she didn't turn; with her eyes closed, she waited until she felt his hands on her shoulders.

"I thought you weren't coming any more," he said. At least his voice was the same.

McGill opened her eyes, turned around, and put her arms around him, as if his presence had driven a ghost away. "I couldn't get away. There's been so much to do. All the outbuildings are being made into sick bays. We have to set up the beds and get the bandages ready." Daniel freed himself from her embrace. "What is it?" she said.

He plucked at his short moustache. "We always used to have time for each other in the winter," he said.

McGill looked past him. On the kitchen table near the hearth she saw two eels, their long, dark bodies still twitching.

"You've been to the river?" she said.

He nodded. "I thought I'd surprise you with something different."

"Haven't you heard? We're not supposed to fish in the river anymore."

He shook his head. "A river full of fish, and we can't fish anymore. The woods full of scouts and patrols, driving the game away. Don't you see what's going on? They're stealing our river, they're stealing the woods. They collected all the boats. One of these days they'll come around collecting all the guns, too, because they need them for the army."

They sat down at the corner table.

"I have to talk to you," Daniel said.

"Do we have to talk?" she said. "Wasn't it the best thing about us—that we didn't always have to talk?"

He looked at her as if it were he who was waiting for an answer. "That's what I always thought, too," he said. "I was close to leaving here, just taking off without a word, without seeing you. I didn't want to go to Redford—and you never came here."

She wasn't upset, not even now, hearing him say it. "I noticed along the way that all your traps were gone," she said.

"I really did think this was a place I could stay on," Daniel said. "I've moved on twice before, since I've been in America. I've been at Redford three years now; I could have stayed for thirty. But the leopard can't change its spots, I guess."

McGill had lowered her eyes. The floor planks gave a little under her feet as Daniel stood up. "I understand how it is," she said.

He stayed where he was. "They'll come here," he said. "The army's on its way. And once they're here, that'll be the end. There'll be no more river and no more woods for us."

"A lot of times I feel like running away too. You know how much the woods and the river mean to me. My people lived here, the river's named for us: the Delaware. This river, this forest—they're like my own father and mother, and they won't be the same after the army comes. But then I think: you can't lose something you really love. It's always up to us whether we're happy or not."

Daniel took a step toward her. He looked down into her dark eyes. They smiled so seldom—but when they did, it was like the sky opening up; it could be the reason, he thought, why he hadn't left Redford sooner. "It's a big country. These aren't the only woods, the only river. It was my own fault I didn't move further inland, that's all. Here, the coast is too close, and wherever you have coastland, you never have peace. This time I intend to go far enough inland. I'll find a river twice as wide as the Delaware, a forest a hundred times the size of this one. Listen, McGill, come with me. This time I'll go far enough."

"Where will you go?" she said. "Show it to me on the map."

Daniel had to smile. "I thought an Indian didn't need a map. Or a compass, either. You've got a horse, I've got a horse. I've got my guns. What more do we need?"

"Here, we've never even needed that," she said and lifted her arms to pull the combs out of her hair.

The shadows had lengthened across the floor. The questions she had forgotten to ask and that came back to her now had also grown in size and complexity—they were harder to answer now. What was she to do? Stay? Go with him? She picked her dress up and slipped it on over her head, sitting on the edge of the bed.

"You never even got the fox," she said, buttoning her dress.

"The foxhole's empty. He must have gone off to find himself

another hunting ground. Even the badgers moved away. Those animals have a fine nose for danger."

She helped him stuff the few things he was taking along into his traveling bag. He took two rifles from their hooks on the wall and handed McGill the smaller one.

She polished its copper mountings with her sleeve. Always when they had hunted together, this had been her gun. "You take it along," she said. "I don't want to have something remind me of you all the time. It'll be bad enough to come back into the woods here, alone, and find your cabin empty."

"It won't be empty for long," he said. He followed her outside, locked the door, and hung the key on a nail under the windowsill. He lifted his head like an animal picking up a scent. "It'll be snowing pretty soon," he said. "Only an hour ago the air was different, like spring. Now there's snow in it."

The bit of sky they could see from the clearing was a delicate gray. There was no sun.

"I guess you're right," she said. "It's going to snow." She gave him a quick glance. "Did you order snow so I'd remember the day better?"

He didn't answer. She helped him saddle his bay and fasten his two leather saddlebags. Then she slipped the guns into their canvas sheaths and tied them together. They led the horses out, and Daniel bolted the stable door. They mounted up and started off, neither of them looking back.

"Which way are you going?" she asked. "Along the Delaware?"

He nodded.

"I'll ride down to the river with you. Just keep riding ahead, and when you don't hear my horse anymore, don't turn around."

Going through the deep green gloom of the woods, Daniel's horse gradually pulled ahead. When they emerged out onto the bank of the Delaware, McGill hesitated—this was where she should stop, at the edge of the trees; there was no sense riding farther; let him go. But the beauty of the river drew her on; she kicked her heels into the horse's ribs and started after him again.

It had been a long time since she'd been to the Delaware, and she'd almost forgotten how beautiful it was. In the background was the deep black of the forest; the sun filtering through the evening haze turned the meadows along the banks a violet blue. The broad surface of the river itself was an icy green.

She couldn't resist; she kicked her horse into a trot and rode up beside Daniel's bay. "Look," she said, "isn't it beautiful? You'll never see this again." It was out before she thought; she wasn't trying to change his mind.

The first snowflakes had begun to fall, looking, in this air, like crystalized flecks of light, faintly blue, and green. She shut her eyes for a second; when she opened them again, and looked across the river, she was stunned. . . .

Sometimes, in dreams, she had seen such images, projections of future events so sharp and powerful they persisted even after she woke. Now, on the opposite bank of the river, dark shadowy figures had appeared in the uncertain light. For a moment she couldn't decide whether it was illusion or reality—she hoped it was neither. But the figures did not dissolve, like a dream; slowly, they took on the hard edges of reality, and she saw horses, uniforms, bayonets, and gun barrels flashing dully in the hazy sun. The opposite bank was jammed with troops as far as she could see. More troops were pouring out of the brush along the river road, flowing in an unbroken stream down onto the bank.

Daniel was standing up in his stirrups, a hand shading his eyes. "Those are our troops," he said. "It's our army." He sank back into the saddle. "*Mon Dieu* . . ." he murmured, in the language he hadn't used for years, since he'd left La Rochelle. "They're crazy. They'll lose more men in the river than they would in a battle."

McGill stared across the river. Several of the figures plunged down the bank, shedding guns and packs as they ran. Several riders followed, the horses slipping on the steep slope; here and there a horse went down, throwing his rider. More troops crowded onto the bank, forcing those in front down toward the water. Endless columns of wagons, carts, and artillery caissons were moving along the top of the riverbank, driving the men on before them.

McGill screamed—men were jumping into the water. They were swept away by the current, heads bobbing, arms thrashing wildly. The icy green water carried them downstream where they were swallowed up in the rapids. McGill knew they were doomed; no amount of struggling would help them in the rapids.

Shots whipped through the silence, warning shots from the sentries on this side of the river; the echoes reverberated through the woods. McGill heard shouts ringing across the water, interspersed with the sharp crack of gunfire. Finally the men on the other shore realized the danger; the wild rout slowed. Riders were moving along the bank trying to restore order.

McGill watched, tears of impotent rage in her eyes. She had an irrational urge to lash at her horse, at anything. She glared at Daniel. "What are you still doing here?" she said. "Go on, get out of here, you said you didn't want to see it. They're taking away the river and the forest, so what are you waiting for? Or maybe you enjoy watching people die?"

The snow was coming down harder. Snowflakes were beginning to stick to Daniel's hair and shoulders.

"We'd better go get the boats," he said, in a voice that was soft and subdued.

Human hands, human will, seemed to have little to do with what went on along the Delaware that night. Boats emerged out of the forest, appearing suddenly in the driving snow, carried by men barely visible in the dark, gliding toward the river as if by some inhuman power. On the opposite bank, the seething chaos of before had been organized into orderly squads—dark walls of human bodies that opened and closed as the boats came and went.

McGill knew she was needed at Redford; there were fires to make, food to prepare. Here she was only in the way, pushed and shoved by the men—but she stayed. She had seen those men leap into the river and drown; now she saw the bloodless faces of the wounded, the first brought across the river; then the others, those who weren't wounded, stumbling ashore in their torn boots, their faces hard, eyes burning with fatigue. They showed no sign of relief on reaching safety; even the energy for that was gone. Eventually the wagons and field pieces and horses were brought over—

and finally, on the near shore, the first tents sprang up, the first campfires.

The snow was falling, slowly and steadily; its white curtain seemed to prolong the light of day, as if, McGill thought, to provide her with light to see it all, as if she had been chosen to stay and witness, until the last man had crossed the Delaware. She still could not rid herself of the feeling that it was all only a private vision of her own; and perhaps it was that which wouldn't let her leave: the mad hope that she might suddenly wake up and find it had all been a nightmare.

30

Mary tried not to hear the voice calling her name and the persistent knocking on her door. She didn't want this short sleep to be over so soon; she clenched her eyes tighter, made herself very heavy. She wanted only to sleep—to hear nothing, to see nothing, to wrap herself wholly in that dark soft cover of oblivion.

"Mary?" The voice grew louder, the knock on the door became an impatient hammering. "It's time!"

She started to throw off the covers and found to her surprise that there were none; she wasn't in bed, but had fallen asleep in a wing chair. In the dim light, the attic seemed strange, out of place. Even after six days she was not used to waking up here instead of in her own room, which she had given up to two army officers.

"Mary? What's the matter with you?" It was Sarah Derwent's voice. "Open the door, will you? I'm bringing you coffee."

Mary stood up, then almost tripped over the blanket which had fallen to the floor. She kicked it aside and went to open the door.

Pretty and looking dewy-fresh, with a ribbon in her curls as if dressed for a ball, Sarah came in and put the tray on the table. The smell of fresh coffee, which usually brought Mary to life in the morning, was nauseating today. Instead of filling her breakfast mug to the brim as usual and drinking the first sip scalding hot even before she sat down, she went back to her chair and huddled in it, shivering a little.

"What's this?" Sarah looked at the unused bed. "You never even went to bed? If you weren't asleep, then why did you let me go on knocking at the door for so long?"

"What time is it?"

Sarah poured coffee into the big mug, added hot milk. "Nearly five. We have to relieve the Saunders girls."

"Five in the afternoon?" Mary pulled up her legs and put her arms around her knees. "Then I must have slept four hours. I only meant to rest in this chair a minute before I undressed for bed. When it's all over, Sarah, I'm going to spend a whole winter the way badgers do; I'll pick out a hollow tree, roll up in it, stop eating and breathing, and sleep for four months."

"You have the funniest ideas." Sarah was busy twisting the spit curls in front of her ears, moistening them, and pasting them to her cheeks. With her snub nose and square forehead, the spit curls seemed a little incongruous, but it might have been the incongruity itself that made her so provocative and attractive to men. When she turned around, she saw Mary's coffee was still untouched. She picked up the mug and held it out. "Remember, those two Saunders girls have a long way home. With all this militia around, their folks'll be worried if they don't get home before dark. They say our own soldiers are dangerous. It makes me so mad! Here we are wearing ourselves to a frazzle, giving them everything we've got, and Lieutenant Blyth can't even get a few men to help us with the sick. Come on, drink your coffee before it gets cold; it'll get you on your feet."

Mary was still huddled in her chair, holding the mug with both hands. She started to drink her coffee. It made her faintly sick, and she was almost glad. She was tired of being strong and brave. What she would have liked to do was send Sarah packing, bolt the door behind her, and sleep and sleep and never have to answer the door again no matter who came knocking on it. But then she remembered the others. Randall, the saddler and cobbler, in whose workshop saddles and army boots were piling up; the lights never went off there anymore, and if McGill didn't bring him his meals, he'd probably never remember to eat. She thought of Jan Kellog, who could hardly keep up with the demand for the coffins he carpentered, the graves he had to dig; of Jonathan Whitcombe in his smithy, hammering away, red-eyed, at horseshoes and replacement parts for the artillery.

"Is my father in?"

"As far as I know he rode to the old tin mine with some other men."

"What for?"

"Believe it or not, he managed to get two wagonloads of sulfur and saltpeter in Philadelphia—two things harder to find than gold and silver. They plan to make gunpowder out of it, at the tin mine."

Mary got up and stretched. "How do the men do it, going for days without sleep?" She went to the attic window and opened it, counting on the cold to wake her up for good.

"Are you trying to catch your death?" Sarah said. "It's gotten so cold out your nose freezes."

But Mary was thinking about the tin mine. She felt hurt that Skelnik hadn't taken her into his confidence; it wasn't the first thing lately she'd had to learn about from somebody else. The air hit her like a steely blow; it seemed to glint with the cold. In the tender blue of early twilight, she could see the rows of pointed tents, and here and there a few early campfires. On that first day when the snow had fallen and covered everything, these same rows of tents looked rather imposing and defiant. But since the snow melted their true condition was only too apparent. The tents of a defeated army, dirt-encrusted, torn, mended only where absolutely necessary; tents full of men thinking not of combat but of flight. Every time she looked down on these tents from her attic window they seemed to have sunk a little deeper into the marshy ground, as if one day they would disappear in it altogether.

She shut the window, but she didn't turn around, afraid her face would betray her thoughts. "I wish it would snow again," she said. "The frost is worse, for those men out there."

The two girls went to the door.

"Why don't you at least get a basin with a charcoal fire put in your room?" Sarah said. "You and McGill are sacrificing your own comfort, while the officers burn so much fuel their stoves actually get red. If they keep it up, they'll send the entire Redford forest up the chimney."

"Since when do you have a poor opinion of our officers? I always thought Sarah Derwent would be the wife of a major in the Continental Army—at the very least—by the time this was over."

"I thought so, too. But since I've got to know them, I'm cured. I don't know what my father would do if they behaved like this in his house."

As they started down the stairs, an officer hurried through the hall and disappeared into the library, which the general was using as study, office, and conference room. At every step he left a wet muddy footprint behind.

Sarah shook her head. "Not even our field workers would come into the house with all that mud on their shoes."

Mary stopped beside the entrance and scrutinized the coats hung on the rack—army coats, blue, brown, gray. Skelnik's green cloak was missing. To see him, listen to him talking, draw on his energy, would have been the one thing that could have helped her pull herself together.

Sarah took her hand. "Come along. We mustn't keep the Saunders girls any longer."

The first moment in the infirmary was always the hardest for Mary, and she always tried to put if off as long as possible by finding something to do in the anteroom. It was bad enough even there, with baskets full of bandages saturated with blood and pus, the pungent smell of medicines, the damp heat from the stove where kettles of water were constantly on the boil, the perennial teakettle included. But when she opened the door to the sickroom itself, with those two long rows of beds on either side, she always reminded herself that she could retreat to the anteroom anytime she wanted to gather her strength again. She clung to this thought even now, as she entered the sickroom behind Sarah. The fetid air made breathing difficult; bodies moved on the flat cots, heads were raised from the pillows, eyes turned toward her.

She was thankful for her white starched cloak; the stiff cloth and the fresh smell of soap when she moved made it a kind of armor. Because she had to force herself even to come in here, she normally took on precisely those chores that cost her the greatest self-control, as if to punish herself for being such a weakling. Today she didn't have the strength to go through with it, so she was all the more grateful to Sarah for taking over so much of the work. Today, she couldn't even bear to look when Sarah opened a bandage to clean a wound and put a new bandage on, or when she patiently slipped a spoon of medicine between a man's lips. She kept her eyes turned away as she handed Sarah the things she needed, glad she didn't have to be in direct contact with the sick. So she went on preparing medicines, setting them out, cooking tea, cutting strips of bandage.

At the far end of the room, separate from the rest, lay the serious cases. Every time she came that far she found a cot empty. She knew about the new graves in the graveyard, but so far she hadn't had to see a man die. Somehow it always happened when she was off duty, but she was haunted by the realization that she was destined to witness a death sooner or later.

The doctor stood beside one of the cots. The tallow candle gave only a dim light, but it sufficed to show the cot, cover thrown back, both legs amputated above the knee. The wounded man was very young, fifteen at the most. The spot of feverish red on his cheekbones only made him look younger. That boyish face seemed oblivious to the hideous wound, the smell of which, a mixture of vinegar and rotten meat, filled the air. He lay quietly except for his left hand, which was feeling along the edge of the bed, and then Mary saw the drum, his drum, on the floor. She picked up a bottle of pain-killing drug, but the doctor shook his head. "Let's save that for those who need it," he said.

A sound came from the boy's lips; it might have been a name.

"But he's in pain," Mary said. "He must be in pain. Is there nothing you can do?"

"What I could do, I've done. Do you want me to saw off another piece, and then another, and still another?"

"How can you talk like this, where he can hear you?"

"He can't hear," the doctor said. "He doesn't know a thing and it'd be best for him if he never knew anything again. Do you think a life without legs is something to look forward to?" He loosely bandaged the stump and covered the body with the blanket again.

Mary shuddered. She put the glass back on the tray, then in a sudden impulse she took the boy's hand in her own. It was glowing hot. *He's going to die,* she thought, *that's why I find it all harder than usual today; he'll be the first one I'll have to see dying.* She was frightened when the boy opened his eyes; his pupils were so dilated it was like looking into two black holes. His lips moved. His words were clear and sensible. "It's in the knee, Doctor. Take the bullet out of my knee. I won't scream, they won't hear a thing. . . ."

Mary gave the doctor a questioning look. "Doesn't he know? . . ."

"Would you like to tell him? Go ahead, do it. He doesn't feel it; what he feels is pain in a leg that isn't there, hasn't been there for hours. Go on, tell him." He turned and walked away.

The boy closed his eyes again, but his lips were still moving. Mary could read the pain in the trembling of his lips, the shaking of his hand, which she was still holding. Slowly he relaxed; only his hand was still restless. His grip was very strong, and it grew tighter when she tried to withdraw her hand. It frightened her, as if he might hold her so fast in dying that she would never be able to loosen his hold on her.

"Better let him go now, Mary, we have lots to do."

It was a relief to hear Sarah's calm voice. Suddenly it was quite simple to let go of the boy's hand. "Do you think he'll die?" Mary asked.

"I think we've done all we could for him," Sarah said.

The back door opened and Robert Skelnik came in. Mary heard his voice, and threw herself into his arms, feeling the chilled surface of his cloak against her cheek. She looked up at him. His face was reddened by his ride in the cold. His fur cap sat low on his forehead. Fatigue had drawn lines around his eyes—and she suddenly realized that her troubles were trifles, not worth mentioning to him.

The evening cold was pressing the smoke from the chimneys to the ground, but Mary, stepping outside with Skelnik, breathed the icy, smoke-saturated air as a treat, grateful to Sarah for saying, "Go ahead, I'll finish up for both of us tonight."

It was quiet in the yard. Light came from the ground-floor windows of the main house; silhouettes moved behind the curtains.

Mary looked down the row of lighted windows.

"I sometimes feel we're only guests in our own house. What is it they do, anyway, with their maps and all these messengers coming and going—and nothing happening?"

Skelnik didn't answer. The dogs came out of the dark and circled around them. The sky was bright with stars, the forest to the eastward was a high black wall.

"Such a strange winter," Mary said. "Do you think it'll snow again?"

"Does it matter so much to you?"

"Maybe only because it'd feel more normal. It's so strange when the snow melts away the same day, every time. Everything's so different this year. For instance, we haven't taken our evening ride together in the longest time."

"Would you like to ride now?"

"If it's not too much for you. You've been to the tin mine; that's a long way off. Does it make sense—your going to so much trouble? Even if you can get enough arms and ammunition—do you believe these men will really fight? In just one week we've had a hundred deserters."

Again he had no answer. A streak of light fell across the yard from the smithy. Its open door shook in the wind. The blacksmith appeared for a moment, then receded again. "Come," Skelnik said. "A ride in the night air will do you good and chase away those gloomy thoughts. Your work in the infirmary is getting you down; the mere sight of those poor devils is enough to do it."

The dogs at their heels, they crossed the yard. The warm smell of horses welcomed them to the stables. Skelnik reached for the lamp hanging beside the door. There was the sudden sound of flintstones being struck, and a quick, blinding flame. Two men stood facing him, Henry Lee and Bechtle, the carpenter, rifles in hand; they were as surprised as he was.

"What is it?" he said. "What are you doing here?"

They lowered their guns. "We're here on lookout," Lee said, "and when we heard steps coming this way. . . ."

"But why are you standing watch in the stables?"

"Because they're stealing us blind, that's why," Lee said angrily. "Everything that isn't nailed down, clothes, provisions, and now it's horses. Last night they stole one of our best mares. Look for yourself."

They walked down the row of stalls. The horses moved restlessly inside. Henry Lee lifted the lamp and lit up an empty stall.

"It's my Nora!" Mary gasped.

"That's right. With the saddle, the new red one from Philadelphia. And they meant to take your bay as well, sir, but he fought so hard he broke down the whole side wall here, so they gave it up. We thought we might catch them at it tonight. The scum! We half-kill ourselves here feeding them and nursing them along, and then they steal our horses and take off." Lee fell silent when he met Skelnik's eyes.

Skelnik had moved on and untied a gray mare. "Saddle this one for Mary," he said.

Lee put his lantern down. For a while there were only the familiar sounds of the stable; an animal pulling a mouthful of hay from the rack, a horse's tail whipping about, the clank of a stirrup, the clatter of hooves on the flagstones when Skelnik and Mary led the horses outside. The table door closed behind them. Skelnik held the stirrup for Mary.

She turned to him abruptly. "I just don't understand it," she said. "The army—when we used to talk about it, before all this happened—it was something great, something we admired and respected. And now—you heard the way the men talk about it. When I bring it up with McGill, she sees red. Sarah used to dream of falling in love with an army officer, and now she won't look at one of them. It's almost as if we had the enemy camping here at Redford." Skelnik was listening, his head down. Mary realized he didn't want to speak until they were out of earshot of the two men in the stable. They mounted their horses and started off down the cedar drive.

When they had left the lights of the main house behind, Skelnik took up the conversation. "It's not so hard to understand. Suppose the man who stole your mare has his home not too far from here, in Delaware, or Virginia, or Pennsylvania. Christmas is not far off. I can imagine what he'd be thinking! 'A horse—and in ten days, I'm home!' He has a wife, maybe children, waiting for him, or maybe parents who don't even know whether he's still alive. I can imagine him lying out there in one of those tents, on the bare ground, thinking about home—and then it happens. I don't approve of it, or justify it. All I say is, I can understand it."

"But you *are* justifying it! If he were with the British army, they'd hang him. What kind of army is this where the men can run away whenever they please? Tell me the truth! What is it about our army?"

"Yes, the British would hang him. The Hessian officers will have a man beaten within an inch of his life if he just opens his mouth to contradict his sergeant. The Polish army will execute a man if he shows up with a bent rifle barrel. But should we deal with our men that way? That's not what we're fighting for. Don't forget who these men are. Only six months ago they were farmers, merchants, lawyers, students, craftsmen. They came to this country so they could be just that, whatever they were, and nothing else. They're volunteers. Voluntarily they closed their shops, cut off their livelihood, broke off their studies—all of their own free will, don't forget. Freedom, their personal freedom in every respect, that's what matters to these men as much as the air they breathe. Obedience to higher authority—that's what they tried to leave behind, forever, because it goes against their grain. It goes against them to trust authorities, the kind of people who give orders. The army, the states, the Congress—each one of our men has done his part to set them up, of his own free will, to safeguard his free will. They're proud of it."

"And yet they run away!" She pointed to the tents. "What can the general do with that kind of an army?"

Skelnik nodded. "It's not easy for him, and I don't say that lightly. You asked me what those messengers are all about, coming and going all the time. I'll tell you. I wouldn't like to be inside the general's skin, for a fact. Everything's against him, and I mean really every last thing. Having to pay his men in paper money that drops in value every day. Never having enough clothing, arms, powder, equipment. A militia to police the army that comes and goes at will, as lawless as the men themselves—volunteers all. Do you know what he can expect at the year's end, if Congress doesn't order a draft of regular troops besides the militia? He's got eight thousand men, all that's left of the Continental Army. Unless a miracle happens, he's likely to have barely three thousand by New Year's."

"You mean that five thousand men. . . ."

"No, it's not that they'd all desert. But on December thirty-first, the militia's six-month enlistment runs out. On that day, five thousand men will leave camp, and the worst part of it is, they'll be going home discouraged. They'll feel beaten, defeated, and they'll spread that sense of defeat wherever they go." His voice sank, as though he were merely thinking aloud. "Something has to be done . . . before that happens."

Where the cedars came to an end, the two horses broke into a trot, in the direction of the giant old pine. To the right of them lay rows of tents in the light of the campfires; at the left rose the dark, silent forest.

They rode on, confidently, despite the darkness, with so many familiar signs to guide them. Finally, when the moist chill in the wind told them they were approaching the Delaware, they turned around and started back.

They were halfway up the cedar drive when they heard a horse coming up behind them at a dead run.

Mary reined her horse to the side of the road. "Anybody riding that fast in the dark is asking to have his neck broken," she said. They had hardly pulled off the road when the horse thundered past, its rider crouched so low that horse and rider seemed to have but one body. "It's Lieutenant Blyth," she said.

"You must have cat's eyes," Skelnik said, "to see that well in the dark."

"My eyes are pretty good," Mary said, "even if you do think I should wear spectacles." The ride had improved her mood; her fatigue and depression were gone. "He's heading for the house."

They followed up the drive, and when they reached the house they saw the rider run up the steps and disappear inside. A man in the uniform of the general's Guards had taken charge of the horse; its hide glistened with sweat and there was froth at its muzzle.

Skelnik and Mary dismounted and went inside. The foyer was empty except for the two sentries at the door to the library. From behind the heavy oaken door came the sound of voices, the rustling of maps.

"I've got to go back to the infirmary," Mary said. "I shouldn't leave Sarah alone there."

"Stay awhile," Skelnik said. "There may still be a fire going in the hall. McGill could bring us something to eat. Why don't we eat together anymore? From now on I'll ask McGill to serve dinner for the two of us in the little room off the kitchen."

He took off her riding coat and led the way into the great hall. In the deep fireplace lay a single glimmering oak log. It was unseasoned wood, sending up a thick smoke.

They sat down in the leather armchairs in front of the fireplace. They didn't ring for McGill; neither made a move to fix the fire. Neither of them said anything. They heard the door opening and a man's steps, spurs clanking on the flagstones, coming nearer.

"Sit down, Blyth," Skelnik said. "Would you like a drink?"

The lieutenant sat down on the hand-carved stool that was usually McGill's favorite seat. Ever since his illness, when he had lain in bed with a high fever for a week, the man had changed. His body had regained its weight soon enough, but his face had kept that sunken look, with sharply jutting cheekbones, and his eyes still had a feverish glitter.

"I guess I'm fated to bring nothing but bad news every time," Blyth said.

"You've seen the general?"

"The news is bad not only for the general. I've just come from Philadelphia. Congress is giving up. Our representatives have removed themselves to Baltimore. To tell the truth, they've fled to Baltimore, and they didn't waste any time about it."

Skelnik leaned over to take up the poker and jabbed at the log. Sparks flew. "Why so? What reason could they have? I hardly think the English have left their cozy winter quarters in New York to sail down the Delaware. Surely the war's over for the year."

Blyth gave Skelnik a fixed stare. But he seemed unable to keep his eyes steady for long. "The Hessians will be in Trenton tomorrow," he said tonelessly.

"Very well, the Hessians will be in Trenton tomorrow," Skelnik said. "And that's enough to scare Congress into leaving Philadelphia, the citadel of freedom? It's hardly news. We've known for some time that the summer campaign left New Jersey in the hands of the English and their mercenaries. They'll plunder New Jersey and strengthen their positions there—we've had enough time to get used to the idea. But they'll only be able to hold New Jersey for the winter. Maybe I don't know enough about it, Lieutenant, but I do know this: they're on the other side of the river, and they are not about to cross it. So don't tell me your news has shaken up the general."

"Lieutenants don't discuss things with their generals. They report to them, that's all. But I can tell you this: tomorrow, the Hessians will be in Trenton. The Hessians, Skelnik. Not the British; they're wintering in Princeton, Brunswick, and Burlington. But they gave Trenton, the spearhead of their forward thrust, to the Hessians. You'll be able to see their blue and green coats across the Delaware tomorrow."

"I'll make a point of riding over to look," Skelnik said.

"He isn't the man to march his troops fifty miles merely to get them into winter quarters. The Delaware won't stop him. He'll take it as a challenge."

"Who are you talking about?"

Andrew Blyth was looking off into space. "Rall, their famous Colonel Rall, of course." It obviously cost him a painful effort to pronounce the name, but as he talked on he kept compulsively repeating it. "I've learned my lesson. First at Flatbush, then Chatterton's Hill where we were winning until Rall appeared with two regiments at the last minute. He didn't have a chance. He had to get his men up those steep slopes without any cover, and they came like they were on parade—the drummers first, then the horns, the fifes—and Rall put Chatterton's Hill in his pocket the way he did with Fort Washington later. That's who I'm talking about, Rall, they call him the Hessian Lion, and our men have felt that lion's paw on their own skins, I can tell you, and when they hear Rall is marching into Trenton. . . ." Blyth broke off—but he wasn't finished. "Rall isn't going to stop this side of the Delaware, I tell you, not a mere thirty miles from Philadelphia. Even if his orders are to take winter quarters in Trenton. Rall always does whatever you least expect. Rall with Philadelphia straight ahead where all he has to do is reach for it!" He fell silent and stood up. Spurs jingling, he walked out without another word, as if he regretted showing how he really thought and felt.

Mary reached for her coat. "When I remember what Andrew Blyth was like before all this happened. There was nothing, ever, he was afraid of."

Skelnik beat the smoking bark off the oak log with the poker, then pushed the log deeper inside the fireplace. Mary waited until he stood up, then she went over to him. She stood on tiptoe, and he kissed her on the forehead.

"Shall I send McGill to you?" she said.

"No, never mind. I think you should go to bed, young lady."

"And what about you?"

"I'll be going along too, in a few minutes."

At the door she turned for another look at him, and she could see that he had been following her with his eyes. Their eyes met briefly, but he didn't call her back.

She crossed the grounds through the thick wet fog outside that tasted of bitter smoke, holding her coat closed over her chest with both hands. The buildings lay in darkness, except for the long, low infirmary building, with its rows of small windows lit up. She saw the door opening, and a broad band of light cut through the fog. Jan Kellog and two other men were carrying a stretcher outside; the door closed behind them. She stopped, struggling with an impulse to run back into the main house, to the man who was sitting there in front of the dying fire. But she forced herself to walk over to the stretcher. The body was covered with a white sheet. She was afraid, but she had to know; she picked up the nearest corner of the sheet. It was the drummer boy. His face was pale and pinched and silent. She covered it again and stepped back. The two men continued on with the stretcher, while Kellog walked behind with the drum; she could hear its faint *thump . . . thump . . . thump* every time it struck against his leg.

The Hessians

I can assure you that the part of America where we are now and through which we have been marching could be rightfully described as a paradise, if only the devil, who is alone to blame, had not sowed the seeds of discord in it. In Brunswick not a house nor a window was left in one piece, all furnishings were thrown on the street, among them the finest white linens, and all kinds of tin and copper vessels. The beds were cut up and all the feathers emptied out. Our people slaughtered more than two hundred pigs and left them to rot where they lay.

Lacking vehicles, we could take nothing with us, except for some grenadiers who took pocket watches, silver spoons, tea and coffee pots along. Most of the mansions are lordly and built in the Dutch style, and the rooms are ornamented with the finest wallpaper designs. Nothing but luxury, overabundance of goods, and voluptuous living led these people to rise up in rebellion.

Extract from the letter of an anonymous mercenary, dated 4 July 1777, in the archives at Anspach in Germany

31

Trenton had so far been untouched by the war, and so none of the inhabitants had ever heard the drums. They had been told about them, and a few had a friend or acquaintance who had heard them, but that was not the same. Nevertheless, from the first faint distant sound, there was no one who was not convinced

—at any rate, that was the way they would remember it later—that they had recognized the drums of the Hessians long before they saw the troops themselves. It was a clear, sunny day, as usual when there was a wind from the east. And with the wind came the roll of drums over the hilltops to the east of town: a distant muffled rumbling, occasionally fading into silence only to swell ominously up again.

Jacob Eliphas Compson heard it, and immediately ordered his English carriage. Noah Banks heard it in his house near the river, walked into his overcrowded waiting room, and told all the patients to go home, though they'd have gone anyway out of simple curiosity. The streets were already crowded, and there was a kind of unannounced contest going on to tell who would see the Hessians first. While no one in Trenton had anything to fear from the Hessians—they were all faithful to the Crown, and used to seeing the Redcoats—there was no one who wasn't made uneasy by the sound of those drums.

The Hessians were still some distance away, out of sight of the town. The officers rode ahead, followed by the drummers beating out that hypnotic, threatening rhythm. The troops marched four abreast, three regiments, each five hundred strong, and each with ten pieces of artillery. The riflemen wore green coats with red lapels, the grenadiers blue coats and white breeches. For those seeing them for the first time, and from a distance, they were a fascinating sight—endless rows of men marching in perfect unison. Fifteen hundred men simultaneously thrusting a leg out, bringing it down, like clockwork. Fifteen hundred rifles pointing straight up. It was a long column, and the dust raised by the horses, the tramping boots, and the wheels of the supply wagons made it seem even longer than it was.

Closer up, the picture did lose some of its gloss. In the last three days, they had marched fifty miles, each man carrying a fifteen-pound weapon, a heavy field pack, an ammunition case, and a bayonet and a saber at his belt. Their uniforms were dirty and much mended, the colors were faded, the leather cracked and weather-beaten. The boots were no longer uniform; some of the men no longer had boots at all, but wore a kind of makeshift sandal obviously fashioned themselves out of the hide of slaughtered cows.

But it was their faces—those hard, emaciated, unshaven faces—which told that they had been in battle from their first day in America. They had been marching without a break since early morning, and they were ready to drop, but the inexorable beat of the drums drove them on.

At the slightest slackening of the drumbeat, Rall let his horse fall back to where the drummers marched. "Don't you fall asleep on me!" he shouted. "Make those sticks fly! *One,* and *one,* and *one!*" The drumbeat rose up again, picking up Rall's cadence. "That's the way I like it," he shouted. "Do you think I'm not tired too, just because I'm riding this nag? Come on now, let them hear it. Let them know the Hessians are coming."

He galloped back to the front of the column, hatless, coatless, his tunic unbuttoned, a flask filled with rum and water slung from his neck. He took a swallow from it, made a face, spit the tepid brew out. "What a country," he said. "You freeze to death at night, and roast to death in the daytime." But it was obvious that this country and this life were very much to his taste. He was like a new man—freer, more relaxed; his men had won victory after victory, and he was full of reckless confidence, both in himself and his luck.

Sergeant Luib, riding beside him, would have liked to unbutton his tunic too, but didn't dare. "If we don't get to this damned Trenton place pretty soon, those eggs the foragers picked up this morning will hatch out on the road. Call this December? How the hell can a man work up any Christmas spirit in this crazy July weather?"

Rall threw his aide a look full of sympathy. "Better open your collar before you get a stroke. You can button up again just before we reach town. That reminds me: inform the officers they're to sew on their silver braid again. In battle it was different; all that glitter would have made too good a target. But I want all my people looking sharp in Trenton."

Luib had opened his collar and was wiping the sweat off his neck. The air was cool against his skin; a feeling of well-being flooded through him. Life was a good thing when there was a war on.

Rall passed him the flask. "You're losing too much weight; don't overdo it. It won't do me any good if you starve yourself to death. I've still got some use for you. I've still got some use for all of you."

Luib spat out the plum pit he'd been sucking on all day. His expression was self-congratulatory; he was proud of his self-discipline. "Another week and I can have my uniform taken in for the third time. I couldn't have managed that in three years in Kassel. I was afraid we were going to be sent to New York, to those victory celebrations."

"Don't ruin my mood by talking about those English. I see red just thinking about them. We could have had these rebels. . . ." He broke off as Adjutant Wardein reined in beside him.

Wardein saluted. "We've made it, sir. Trenton straight ahead. You can see it from the next hill."

Rall touched the spurs to his horse, and they galloped up the road leaving the troop column behind. The land sloped steeply away, and in the valley below lay Trenton, girdled by the broad river glittering in the sun.

Luib pulled up beside him. "You can't trust these damned maps," he said. "According to the map, Trenton's still an hour's march away."

"We marched at a faster pace," Wardein said.

Rall stood up in his stirrups and examined the terrain—the hills, the river, the town.

"A damned tough place to defend," Wardein said. "These hills are too far from the Delaware to make effective positions for our cannon. The river's no protection at all. We'll have to throw up earthworks, no getting around it. Let's hope there's no sudden frost. We'll have to start on the northwest flank. . . . Hand me the map, Luib."

But Rall, still looking at the valley, waved the map away. "Don't bother me with maps. The maps are all made by the locals, and Luib's right to be suspicious of them. And forget about earthworks. These rebels are just a ragged mob, and poorly armed to boot. They've been on the run ever since New York. They won't risk any serious attack on three regiments of Hessians. If they're mad enough to try it, then let them come; we'll give them a proper reception—with bayonets."

He lowered himself back into the saddle. "So this is the Delaware. The spyglass, Luib." He took the telescope and examined the valley; abruptly he lowered the glass. "But why isn't the damned river frozen over? Wardein, you're the expert, explain it to me." Again he raised his telescope and, frowning, studied the river. "It's wider than I imagined it. Can any of you see anything that might be a ford? I can't see even a ferry. Not a single landing place for a boat. That reminds me—where's that fellow Haynow? What did I send him ahead for? Ah, there—let's hope that's him.

Up the road from Trenton came a horse at a dead run; the rider wore a green uniform and was followed by a small troop of Redcoats, one of whom carried an English pennant.

"Look at him," Luib said. "You've got to admit he can ride, our Major. Compared to him, those English dragoons are only kicking up dust."

"Keep those Redcoats away from me, whatever you do," Rall grumbled. He waited, irritated. He could never quite regard Claus Haynow as one of his men, though he was the best officer in the regiment. Rall had never bothered to conceal this attitude in Kassel, but since they had landed in America he was careful to avoid outright rudeness; he needed every man he had, even if the man's obsessions rubbed him the wrong way.

Claus reined in his horse in front of Rall and took off his tricorne. He smiled one of his rare smiles. "Colonel, you're bringing summer with you. The people of Trenton are already saying we're in command of everything, even the weather."

Rall's features remained hard as stone. "Then it'll be your job to see that winter arrives on time. A real winter, Major, with snow and ice."

The English dragoons had come up, about twenty men; the leader rode up to Rall and saluted.

The veins swelled on Rall's forehead. "What do the English want?"

"Major Merriman and twenty of his dragoons. They were left in Trenton as a kind of rear guard. . . ."

"Get rid of them," Rall said brusquely. "An hour from now I don't want to see an Englishman in Trenton. How you do it is your business."

Claus knew the English didn't understand German, but Rall's tone was probably enough of a message in itself. As usual he hid his embarrassment and his rising anger behind a show of arrogance. "There's nothing to worry about. These dragoons are under your orders."

Rall stuck out his underlip. "Very well. I see they have excellent horses. None of our officers has ever had that kind of horseflesh under them. My first order is that they turn in their horses, tonight. By then I'll think of other ways they can be of service to us."

To everyone's relief, the troop column had caught up with them. Rall wheeled his horse around. Immediately the drums began to beat a faster rhythm. Rall ignored their ravaged faces, the wagons full of wounded, ignored the effort it cost the men to keep up with the new tempo. "Get these legs up off the ground, men! Let's show them!" He tightened his reins and raised a hand. "We'll ride ahead," he called to his staff. "And you, Major Haynow, show us the way to the Delaware."

The closer he came to the river, the brighter was the air. A radiance lay over the water like the trembling summer light on ripe fields of grain, but this light was almost metallic.

Nothing moved on the glossy surface—no wave, no bubble coming up to burst in the air, no shadow of a fish in the depths. There was no landing stage for boats, not a trace of sandy beach, not a sound, not a sign of life.

Slowly Rall rode along the riverbank, his horse still steaming; he had broken away from the rest and had raced through the town to the river in a dead run. Shielding his eyes, he looked across the river, but the light was too strong to make out any details. He heard the others coming up behind him now—dull hoofbeats, the snorting of the horses, the voices of the men. Finally there was silence, and he knew they had arranged themselves in a semicircle behind him. He didn't turn around; he sat in the saddle, uncharacteristically thoughtful, staring across the river. "That's a long way across," he said. "It'd have to be pretty cold to freeze that river hard enough for a crossing. How do the folk in Trenton manage when they want to get over there? There's got to be a ferry, a ford, something." He rode closer to the water's edge and, as though inspired, leaned down to part the branches of a bush. He found himself looking at the sawed-off posts of a landing stage.

"Wardein!" he shouted. "Look at this. Here's where they had a ferry or a landing place for their boats. I want a report from you on what happened to it."

Wardein was about to dismount when there was the sudden blast of a cannon from across the river, followed by a second, and a third. The air seemed to explode. A hail of grapeshot spattered the ground, ripping across the grass beneath the horses. Somebody shouted; a horse reared, whinnying, its rider hurtling through the air. . . .

Rall brought his own horse under control. Most of his staff had already stampeded up the bank; he ignored them. "The spyglass, Luib."

Luib came trotting over to him with a broad grin. "At least those fellows on the other side know what kind of welcome we like."

"Where the devil can they have their wretched cannons positioned? I can't see a thing. This damned river! Polish that lens, will you? No, never mind."

Almost invisible in the general brightness, white puffs of smoke rose above the opposite bank of the river. Neither Rall nor Luib made a move to avoid the second salvo.

The earth shook. Dirt and clumps of grass rose up around them. Again there was the whistling of grapeshot through the grass.

"Back up the bank," Rall shouted. "No sense overdoing it."

In a mad, irregular gallop, a riderless horse was circling the spot where its owner lay, blue and white like a discarded banner of the grenadiers.

"Serves him right," Rall said. "Getting caught in a blind barrage. See who it is, Luib; I'll go after the horse."

He caught the horse in the midst of a third barrage; when the smoke had cleared he led it back to the riverbank. He waited for the next salvo, but none came. With something like a smile, he surveyed the devastated area. A few yards away lay the dead man, face down. Slowly his officers drifted back out of cover and gathered around him, nervously keeping their eyes on the opposite bank.

Luib came to report on his findings. "It's Manz," he said. "His promotion to sergeant didn't do him much good."

Rall was already concentrating on something else. He pointed to a solitary house standing on the flat riverbank. It was made of stone, gray and crude, like the stump of a tower. A Negro was outside, harnessing a horse to a strange, two-wheeled cart with a fringed canvas awning.

"What sort of a house is that?" Rall said. "Do you know anything about it?"

"It's the so-called doctor's house," Claus said.

"What does that mean? Is it inhabited or not?" Again Rall was too impatient to wait for an answer. He spurred his horse toward the house, followed by his officers.

The Negro had finished hitching up the peculiar, two-wheeled vehicle. A man in a plaid coat came out of the house. The Negro hurried to relieve him of a heavy leather bag, and helped him up onto the driver's seat. With its basket-weave back and the colorful awning above it, the driver's seat looked more like a garden swing. An impression of gay irresponsibility hung over the entire structure, the driver's seat suspended behind the two large wheels —the Germans had never seen anything like it.

The Negro had disappeared into the house. When Rall reined in beside the cart, his officers behind him, the man in the driver's seat had just released the brakes. Decisively he picked up his reins, turned to Rall, as if he had no doubt who was the ranking officer here, and addressed him in English.

"What's he saying?" Rall asked.

"He says that, yes, he's a physician, but that he hasn't the least inclination to concern himself with the wounded man." Claus Haynow found a certain satisfaction in translating the doctor's statement.

Rall seemed to find the doctor's position reasonable "I wouldn't think of troubling a doctor for the sake of a *dead* man. Tell him we're not sentimental, and ask his name."

"His name is Dr. Noah Banks, he says, and he's in a hurry."

"Tell him to be patient. I want to know the following: how wide is the river here, how deep? And ask him if it's true the river's supposed to freeze over in December. And above all, I want him to tell me where in the devil's name they keep their boats, or the ferry. . . ."

"Wouldn't it be better . . . ?" Claus swallowed his objection and continued to interpret. "Dr. Banks says we won't find even a broken-down raft for ten miles up and down the river. The rebels took them all to the other side."

Rall let off a round of profanity. "What else?"

"That it's winter, despite the looks of it, and that a doctor is busier in winter than any other time of the year, because the farmers wait until all the field work is done to get sick, and then they have all their saved-up sicknesses at once—" Claus hesitated. "—And that you're wasting your time and his."

They all held their breath at this impertinence, but Rall said calmly, almost benevolently, "Let the doctor pass."

The doctor picked up his reins, clicked his tongue, and the bony horse started off.

Rall followed the little cart with his eyes as it gently bounced along on its way, until it had dwindled to something resembling, not a vehicle, but a parasol borne away by the east wind. Finally he turned to Claus. "I assume, Major, that you've arranged for my quarters in town?"

"The best there is. Everything is ready. Splendid rooms. In the home of a certain Jacob Eliphas Compson. You'll think you're living in London—Hepplewhite furniture, paintings by Gainsborough. Compson is a leading man in Trenton, and a dedicated royalist. If you had entered Trenton as planned, at the head of the troops, Compson would have put his finest carriage at your disposal—he was driving it over to you himself. But since you decided on this ride to the Delaware first. . . . In any case, he's putting the carriage at your disposal for the duration of your stay in Trenton."

"It all sounds as if you should be quartered there," Rall said ironically. He looked thoughtful, then suddenly pointed in the direction of the doctor's house. "I'll set up my quarters right here."

"Here? So close to the river, and so far from the troops? Have you forgotten what the rebels just did to us?"

Rall made a face. "I'm sure those fools wasted the last of their ammunition just to give us a scare. Where could I be better off than with a doctor? Besides, I like the house. I've seen enough of your dedicated royalists." He regarded the river with a look both resentful and possessive. "I want my things brought over here. How are the others being taken care of?"

Claus wondered whether he ought to protest against Rall's decision; he knew none of the other officers would risk it. Finally he said, "I don't know why the English are being so good to us, but this place is a gift of God to our troops. It's a chance to recuperate, to have a real rest, in ideal winter quarters. There are enough featherbeds for the whole regiment, and a lot of the houses are empty. All the rebel sympathizers crossed the Delaware with their army. All those who stayed on are loyal and eager to help us. As for supplies, the countryside's full of. . . ."

"Nothing doing!" Rall interrupted. He dismounted, followed by Luib and Wardein. "My troops will not be quartered in town. All I need is for them to spend the winter in hibernation. What I want is a field camp, one that can be struck at a moment's notice. Mobility, that's what I want."

"The men are exhausted," Claus said vehemently.

"You'll have to leave that to my judgment, Major."

"They'll be overworked as it is, setting up fortifications. There's an enormous amount of work to be done to put the town in a strong defensive position. The natural terrain's not exactly in our favor."

If it had been anyone else, Rall would soon, and brutally, have put him in his place. But he seemed remarkably serene, indulgent, absentminded today. "Please, don't start that again. I don't want to hear another word about fortifications. Let the men drill as usual every day. I mean drill hard, five hours a day; that'll impress the locals like nothing else."

"Shouldn't we at least wait until we get the shoes they've promised us from New York? The men . . ."

"That's enough! Shoes! They could march another thirty miles this way. Even if I have to lead them barefoot through the river myself—" He stopped, as though he had betrayed too much of what he was thinking. "I want all the horses in the area confiscated. Start with the English and the royalists. I need every single nag within a circumference of ten miles." He shook his head. "They call themselves royalists, but they let the rebels steal every boat they have! Send out a patrol. I want to find out what happened to those boats. Next, Haynow, two houses in the center of town to be cleared out and stuffed from cellar to attic with dry hay, or any dry stuff that'll burn readily. Post guards around the houses with live torches, and let it be known those houses will go up in flames at the slightest sign of resistance. . . ."

"The people of Trenton are loyal to the British Crown," Haynow dared to contradict him again. "They've been waiting for us, prepared to help us. No one'll understand. . . ."

"Royalists be damned! I'd rather keep them in fear of us. So do as I said." Rall stalked toward the doctor's house, then stopped and turned around. "Another thing. Find somebody who speaks German. Everybody keeps telling me the place is swarming with Germans." He smiled. "Nothing against you, Major, I assure you. I simply need a fellow who lives here, who knows his way around. Somebody I can talk to without a translator."

"We have a man, one of the jägers, who's supposed to have been here before," Wardein said. "His name's Soerman. He was mixed up in that trial in Kassel. . . ." Wardein cast an embarrassed glance at Claus, but it was too late, the word was out.

"Then get him over here," Rall said shortly and continued on his way to the doctor's house; his stiff-legged walk told how long he had been in the saddle.

32

Although the Trenton marketplace had originally been no more than a widening of the main street, where the forecourt of the post office faced the forecourt of the church, it was the focus of the town's civic pride, and a mayor's popularity depended primarily on what he could think of to enhance its appearance. As a result, the center of the town, which was in other respects merely an overgrown village, had acquired an air of metropolitan elegance. There was a school, the house of the justice of the peace, the offices of an attorney and a notary, a number of artisan's workshops, and a grocery that had not changed since the early days of barter with the Indians.

The square was encircled by acacias shading a paved promenade. Each of the two-storied houses had a well-kept flower garden and a lamppost, the care of which was the house owner's responsibility. The center of this showplace boasted, at the instigation of Jacob Eliphas Compson, who also paid for its erection, a six-sided pavilion in which the band performed on special holidays, such as the King's birthday. At all other times the pavilion belonged to the children, cats, sparrows, and pigeons.

Even an hour after the entry of the troops the square was still full of life and movement. The justice of the peace and his clerk were carrying his files into the schoolhouse; his own house had been chosen for the headquarters staff, sixty men whose first official act was to set up a cannon at the front door. There it stood in a little flower garden, without any conceivable target. Claus Haynow thought it senseless, but impressive. He had ordered a table set up in front of the pavilion, from which vantage point he was organizing the quartering of troops.

Field packs and ammunition cases were piled up under the acacias, alongside rifles stacked in pyramids. The men were squatting beneath the trees, mess kits in their laps. But they weren't to be allowed time even for eating. The orderly officers Claus had appointed were in a hurry; each wanted to be the first to get his company's tents set up. Bugles sounded, calling each unit into formation. At the slightest sign of reluctance, mounted officers drove the men on with threats, jokes, or even with a riding crop.

For Claus, it was still going too slow. The regimental lists lay on the table in front of him, name after name in the big, curlicued script of Sergeant Luib. Many a name was followed by a cross, a date, and a place name, or the laconic note: died of disease. Glancing through the lists of First Company, he saw the name of Klemm, the Ramswood handyman, who had died on the ocean crossing—the first man to die, and no cause of death noted. The name of sawmill-owner Weibrecht's youngest son, Vitus, was followed by the notation: *Flatbush, 27 August,* their first engagement after landing on Long Island. The deaths of Willibald Manz and of two men who had died along the march route had not yet been entered; there hadn't been time for Luib to bring his lists up to date. Claus noted all this only in passing; what interested him was the two names at the end of the fourth page. They had been added late, and stood out from the rest not only because of the lighter ink but because they had been entered by another hand—his own. The names were: Robert Skelnik, Freder Soerman.

"Where's First Company assigned, sir?" Sergeant Luib asked. "It's ready to go."

Claus looked up. The company stood in formation, ready to march. He looked for his brother. Robert had just finished fastening his pack and was picking up his rifle. He moved easily, relaxed, like a man who felt thoroughly at home here. Beside him stood Soerman. They were inseparable in every engagement; afterward they invariably reported back at roll calls unhurt and provocatively self-assured. Claus remembered Rall's order to release Soerman for services as interpreter, but there was no hurry.

"First Company will go to Assunpink Creek," he said to Luib. "That's the tributary that runs into the Delaware south of Trenton."

"We crossed it on the way to the Delaware," Luib said. "The ground there's pretty marshy. Not very suitable for camping."

"I didn't ask for your opinion, Sergeant. First Company will stand guard on the bridge across the Assunpink. Twe ve men at a time, to be relieved every four hours. What are you waiting for? Give them their orders. And where's the list of Second Company?"

At sundown, the warm, summery days of this peculiar December turned, without transition, into piercingly cold nights. The lamps around the market square were lit now, but their light was pale compared to the blazing torches Rall had ordered outside the headquarters.

As Rall had ordered, two houses had been emptied from cellar to attic and filled with hay; the church had received the same treatment, though the field chaplain had protested to Claus.

Claus had moved his base of operations indoors, and was now ensconced in the office of the former justice of the peace. It was heated by two copper basins full of glowing charcoal. Behind his desk chair hung the regimental banner. He had heard the field chaplain's arguments and dismissed him, chosen the watch and assigned places for it, checked through the paymaster's lists. Officers came every hour to relieve him; he sent them away. Not even the beautiful rooms awaiting him in Compson's house, the special supper prepared in accordance with his personal wishes, lured him away, until he had done all there was to be done. Finally he locked up the lists, made a few notes for the coming day, and got up, almost reluctantly, to order his horse brought out. He went outside, crossed to the pavilion in the dark, and waited there, leaning against one of its wooden columns. He could hear the pigeons scratching and fluttering on its roof. The night wind moved the branches of the acacias. The steps of the watch echoed off the walls of the houses that stood curtained and shuttered around the square. There was no sign of life in the houses; the curiosity of the inhabitants had exhausted itself during the day.

Claus found himself suddenly, inexplicably, overcome with images of the past, and with the pain they brought, for the first time since leaving home. He saw the manor house at Haynow, the candelabra at the front door, his mother's lighted window, always the first thing he had looked for when he returned home at night. He remembered how he used to run up the stairs and down the hall to her room—and how, if he heard Robert's voice inside, he would turn away from the door.

Why should he remember it all now, now that it was lost to him forever? That thought was followed by another, seemingly unconnected with the first, but recurrent and familiar enough though he had never felt it with such agonizing intensity before: never again will I be the one who loses out.

It was a relief when the orderly brought his horse. Behind the orderly came a tall man in a wide cape, his spurs jingling on the flagstones: Captain Kunkel. When Rall had attached the Silesian to his personal staff, the Hessian officers claimed it was because of Kunkel's extraordinary ability to hold his drink, and even though Kunkel had long since proved he was as impressive under fire as he was with women and the bottle, he hadn't been able to shake the general opinion that he'd gained his spot because he was Rall's favorite drinking companion.

"You weren't fooling," Kunkel said, his voice rough from rum and tobacco. "This looks like a good place to spend the winter. There's another point in Trenton's favor you never mentoned to our colonel—the kind of women they grow here. Not bad. The postmaster has a couple of daughters. . . . I'll tell you, I never saw anything like them back home, and that's saying a lot. Our Silesian girls . . ." Kunkel fell silent; he wasn't too drunk to remember that Claus Haynow was his superior officer and could be a little touchy with people who tried to get too familiar. "There's a billiard table at the postmaster's," he said. "How about a game?"

"We'll see." Claus swung into the saddle, fastened his cloak at the throat. "Maybe after I've made my rounds and checked the sentries."

"Do you mean the sentries in general, or one post in particular? The one guarding the bridge over the Assunpink, for instance. Oh, look, somebody has to tell you; everybody's talking about it. Behind your back, of course."

"Talking about what?"

Captain Kunkel was not the kind of man to start something he wouldn't finish. "If you really want to know—why don't you leave your brother alone? What is it about the man that bothers you so much?"

"Who says I'm bothered?"

"You persecute him. You don't miss a chance to give him the dirty end of the stick. The trouble is, it works out like a kind of left-handed compliment. Now don't get angry, but sometimes you act like your battalion consists only of one man. Do you still think he's going to desert? God knows he's had plenty of chances. And if he did, do you really think it'd reflect on you? I can't believe that. Come on, let's play some billiards instead. We've got a few Redcoats there, miserable players but awfully easygoing with their pay, good English coin. Come on. I'll let you have one of the postmaster's daughters if it helps."

For a moment Claus felt tempted. A cozy public room with a crackling fire in the grate, wine, laughing girls. But then he said, "Go ahead. I may look in later on." Abruptly he turned his horse and rode off.

The Assunpink was a narrow stream flowing into the Delaware, irregularly and without a fixed riverbed. The so-called bridge across it consisted of loose planks without a railing, just wide enough for two sentries to walk on it side by side. Their steps rang loudly through the silence.

The bivouac of First Company lay on the bank near the town—flat, marshy ground where only a few crippled apple trees had taken root. A few shriveled apples still hung in their branches.

Any other staff officer would have been welcomed to the camp, but not Major Haynow. The men knew it wasn't concern for them that brought him but surveillance. They feared him more than they did Rall; the colonel was ruthless in battle, but he knew when to be indulgent. Claus Haynow had no such spark of generosity in him; he overlooked nothing. He heard everything, saw everything, and punished everything. Even at night, sometimes, when everyone else was asleep, he would suddenly show up, restless, domineering, inescapable. When they saw him coming, quiet warning signals went from tent to tent.

At a distance, the misleading light of the campfires had given him the impression the tents were all set up. Closer by, he could see only about half of them.

"Where are the rest of the tents?" he shouted at the orderly officer.

"We had trouble finding ground firm enough, sir. So much of this is swampland."

Claus rode closer. Several men were trying to nail together a platform for a tent out of the side planks of a wagon. He couldn't see Robert or Soerman among them. He was about to ask where they were when he remembered what Kunkel had said. "Who gave you permission to demolish a wagon?" he barked at the orderly officer. "Always something extra for First Company, is that it?"

"It was my idea. I thought if the men have to camp here the whole winter. . . ."

"All right, all right." Claus maneuvered his horse closer to the men working on the platform. "I see only older men here. Where are the others?"

The orderly officer looked at his feet. He had expected this, but it took all his courage to go through with it.

"I asked you a question!" Claus said.

"The responsibility is mine."

"What does that mean? Are you giving me riddles to solve?"

"I know we were ordered to set up tents for all the men. But there wasn't enough good ground, and there's an empty house nearby. We drew lots to see who should move in there. I agreed to it; I'm responsible."

The men had stopped their hammering and were listening, heads down, waiting for the inevitable outburst. But nothing of the kind happened.

"I see," Claus said, almost indifferently, "and just by chance the second platoon drew the house. We'll talk about it later. Where's the house?"

The orderly officer pointed in the direction of the apple orchard. "It's a solitary house, a tanner's. I was going to report it to you just as soon. . . ."

Claus gave his horse the spurs and rode directly across the campsite, through the cluster of working men. The wheels of a heavy wagon had dug deep furrows in the soft ground leading toward the tanner's house and in through the broad gate made of unpeeled pine logs crudely nailed together. The gate was silhouetted against the flickering reddish light of the torches in the yard behind it. Claus looked over the fence into the yard. The wagon, belonging to the regiment's food transport service, stood inside, unhitched. The house was two stories high with a workshop attached on the left side. There was light in the windows, and he could hear voices inside. Smoke was rising from the chimney.

He didn't stop to tie up his horse. As he dismounted, he saw a man emerge from the shadows of the apple trees and try to slip in the gate ahead of him. Claus caught him at the gate, seized him by the shoulder, and turned him around.

It was Niklas, the man whose scavenging ability had impressed Rall back in Kassel. He had lost weight; his face was thin, more hollow-cheeked than before. He gave Claus a broad, insolent grin.

"What have you got there?" Claus demanded.

Niklas lifted up two freshly skinned rabbits, still dripping blood. "Careful, Major," he said coolly. "You'll get some of that on your uniform. I just skinned them."

"Go on. Inside." Claus opened the gate and pushed the man into the yard. A lantern on the ground illuminated the well; beside the well a woman was emptying a basketful of laundry into a wooden tub.

Niklas called to her. "We've got a visitor, Mrs. Retz."

Mrs. Retz set down the basket. She picked up the lantern and came toward the gate. The door of the house opened; a woman's voice said, "What is it, Niklas?" Anna Haynow came down the steps and across the yard, one hand holding the hem of her long dark dress off the ground. She walked very erect, and when she saw who the visitor was, her body seemed, if anything, to straighten even more.

She looked at Claus. "Go inside," she said to the other two. "I'll speak with him."

"Niklas stays," Claus said.

"Do as I say," Anna said. "Go inside." She barred Claus's way until the other two had disappeared inside. The restless light of the torches cast flickering shadows across her face. "What do you want?" she said. "What is it this time?"

"Those two rabbits," Claus said. "I could have him hanged for that."

Anna said nothing, but her stiffening posture was eloquent enough. She had long since given up trying to make Claus see reason and agree to a compromise they could both live with.

"You're not taking me seriously," he said. "That's pillage in the field, and the penalty is hanging."

"Of course—I can't take it seriously," she said. "What has the army been living on these last six months? The pittance the English have been supplying? What have you been using to keep your sentry fires going all night? Who tore up all the picket fences in Monmouth last night and burned them up? Colonel Rall ordered that done himself. And you're going to hang Niklas for catching two wild rabbits? You're being ridiculous." These recurrent scenes had cost her much misery once, but with time suffering itself had become an armor. "You can't even prove Niklas stole them."

"A church thief? I'm sure he went out and bought two rabbits."

"When your field surgeon had only enough medicine left for officers, Niklas spent his savings on drugs at the Princeton apothecary's."

"A veritable angel of mercy! He pays the rent for this house as well, no doubt?"

His eyes told him she was still beautiful, even in her unadorned woolen gown; her dark eyes, her light skin, her posture—not even her pallor and slenderness suggested hunger and exhaustion. He felt a perverse longing to hurt her, to see tears in her eyes. Before, when she had come toward him from the house, he had wanted to run and take her in his arms and hold her, warm himself at her warmth, like a child; but in her eyes he could read only coldness and contempt.

"Let's stop this," she said. "It's as hopeless as all the other times. What is it you really want? What have you thought up this time?"

It was not the first time he had heard her say such things to him; words that had given him a kind of perverse satisfaction till now. But this time she said them too calmly, even coldly, with a new air of finality. He saw the gray strands in her dark hair, the lines around her eyes. There were no pearls on her earlobes. When, back in Bremerlehe, he had suddenly found himself face to face with her on board the *Durand,* his first impression was: she's not wearing her pearls anymore. He had never before seen her without her pearls; it was as though they symbolized her fate. Slowly, hesitantly, she had come toward him. It had been the first moment in his life he had had his mother all to himself. He had forgotten Robert, forgotten his jealous torment, all he could think was: she has come to be with me. But she had destroyed it all with her first words. "Robert is waiting," she had said. "Come, let's go to him."

"Mother, please go back into the house," he said now. "Send Robert out to me. I assume all of this was his idea. I want to talk with him."

Suddenly she felt totally drained of energy, incapable of further resistance. "Haven't you done enough?" she asked. "What did he do to you to make you persecute him so relentlessly?"

"Go look in the mirror for your answer," he said. "See what he's done to us. It's all his doing. When will you understand?"

She had turned half away from him, staring into the dark. In a low voice she said, "Don't force me to say things I'd rather not say. You're still my son. I'm still ready to forget that someone exists who handed Robert over to his enemies, and who would have become his murderer if they had executed him."

"Don't ever say that again." Claus's voice was choked. In another second he would have to tear open the tall stiff collar of his uniform if he wanted to go on breathing.

"They all know it," she continued in the same tone. "You take good care not to let them forget it. They know what there is between you. They know why First Company gets the moldy bread, or why it's always chosen for the most dangerous patrols. And don't think Rall doesn't know about it. I went to him myself, and I shall go to him again, if necessary." She turned away. With her left hand she gathered in her skirt and went back into the house.

When she had disappeared inside, Robert appeared in the doorway.

A gust of wind swept the yard and made the torches flare up. There was a smell of pitch and burnt pine. Flakes of soot hovered in the air, gently settling to the ground.

Robert closed the door behind him and stepped into the yard. He wore a white shirt open at the throat and a jerkin over it, but he didn't feel the cold; his senses were concentrated on other things. His eyes took in the entire yard, his brother standing beside the turned-over laundry basket, the washtub, the two torches at the gate, one of which was about to go out. He heard dogs barking in the distance, sounds of a horse roaming over dry grass, a cracking sound in the planks of a shed, the jingling of spurs as Claus started toward him. And then there was another sensation, more intense than any of the others: the hard, smooth metal between trousers and shirt, the sharp point of the knife he could feel with every step he took.

His senses were one thing he was sure of. Time had sharpened them; and having them under control, being able to depend on them, was his life. Everything else—feelings, thoughts, words—had been pushed far into the background.

"You've done it again, haven't you?" Claus said. "Are you satisfied with your quarters, or is there anything else you need? You surely don't think that I'm going to stand for this. You've disobeyed a direct order, and in this case the order came from the colonel himself."

Robert said nothing. He asked himself what exactly he was feeling—it wasn't enmity, it wasn't hatred. Watchfulness, that was it; he was on his guard. Sometime during the past months he had realized with a certain finality that the rift between himself and Claus was irreparable, that, in fact, the embittered conflict between them could end in only one way: one of them must cease to exist. He wondered if Claus felt the same way. He felt as if he had an unfair advantage, as if he should warn Claus of that fact. "You know, I feel like the whole thing's some kind of wager between you and me," he said calmly. "And you surely remember which of us always won."

Claus did not seem to have heard him. "You have women in the house," he said. "It's against orders. Why aren't they where they belong, in the women's camp?"

"Because for the better part of a year they haven't had a roof over their heads. Because they no longer know what it's like to sleep in a bed." He paused, and in that instance it happened; it came over him like a flash, taking him by surprise. "Let's make an end of it now," he said, and he meant it literally. It was bound to happen some day—why not get it over with? He drew his knife from his belt and hefted it in his hand. The red torchlight gleamed on the blade.

Claus bit his lips. "That was a mistake you shouldn't have made," he said. "I don't need to tell you what it means to turn a weapon against an officer."

Robert took a step toward him. "Nobody'll believe you; they'll just think you're trying to get revenge against me again. You have no witness—I have half a dozen." The hand holding the knife pointed to the shed. "Over there—" With the point of the knife he described a semicircle, pointing to the tanner's workshop. "—And over there. That's where my witnesses are."

Claus jerked his head around, stared into the dark.

Robert felt he had to do something. He lifted the knife and threw it at the guttering torch. The torch went out, and the knife embedded itself in the gatepost. Remnants of flaming pitch fell to the ground. Robert went over and trod them out.

Claus had not moved from the spot. He had regained control of himself. "It's a good thing I know now what I'm up against."

"You don't know." Robert turned around. "Come on, everybody, show yourselves!" There was a rumbling, a slatted door opened, and the men came out from the darkness of the shed where they had been hiding. Robert turned back to Claus. "Up until now it's always been you warning me. Now let me return the compliment. One word from me and they'd kill you, without witnesses. All they've been waiting for is a signal, every one of them, for a long time now. You've been persecuting me, but when you do, it hits them too. You sent me into the front lines, but others had to die as a result. These men haven't forgotten that.

Kill me, and they'll kill you, in the next battle, by a "stray" bullet, in bright daylight or at night, in some obscure corner like this; there will be no witnesses. Now *you* have been warned. Don't ever come here alone again."

Claus retreated toward the gate. Then he remembered something. "The colonel wants to see Freder Soerman, immediately." Then he turned and went out the gate, back erect, left leg limping.

No one budged or said a word until the hoofbeats of his horse had been swallowed up in the night. Then Robert walked slowly over to the gatepost and pulled his knife out.

Niklas breathed a sign of relief. "I really thought this was it," he said. "How did you know we were in the shed?"

Robert gave no answer. He stood holding the knife in his hand, his body like a tensed spring. Niklas was right—he had very nearly done it; if only to put an end to the whole thing, the waiting, the silence, the hoping. What had stopped him? Had he done right or wrong? He didn't know.

"What would we have done with him?" Louis asked.

"That's enough," Niklas said. "We have a roof over our heads and roast meat in the oven. Damn, the roast! That idiot Ploetz will let it burn to a cinder!" He turned to Robert. "What about it—do we have to wait for Soerman to come back for supper?"

All eyes turned to Soerman.

"What do you think?" he said. "Do you think he was telling the truth?"

"I guess so." It was hard for Robert to return to the world of commonplace questions and concerns. "You'll find out soon enough in any case."

"What do you suppose Rall would want with me?"

"He wants to promote you," Niklas said, "and we'll celebrate, with a Swedish punch."

Gradually the others relaxed. The house they had moved into so halfheartedly seemed really to belong to them now that they'd been able to defend it so successfully.

"Well, let's get it over with," Soerman said. He started off toward the stable, but Robert stopped him. "Go on foot," he said. "Nobody needs to know we've picked up a few horses."

Robert was beginning to feel relieved, too. When he entered the kitchen, full of warmth and the smell of food, it was as if he had left everything that had happened outside with the cold and the night.

Louis, a tall shoot of a young man in an outgrown uniform that had been too big for him on embarkation, went back to peeling potatoes, dropping the peels into the pail between his legs. Niklas discarded his tunic and shirt and knelt in front of the oven, the iron lids of which glowed red-hot. Balthasar Ploetz was busy preparing the dessert on the big corner table. Spread on a linen cloth lay a thinly rolled dough, which he was tenderly sprinkling with browned bread crumbs and sliced apples. "Where've you been all this time?" he asked. Immersed in the preparation of an apple strudel he had suddenly realized he was alone and had made good use of the opportunity to diminish the rum supply.

Robert took away the bottle.

"You can't do that," Ploetz protested. "Without rum this thing won't have any taste at all. Just let me have one more glass, at least. Today's special."

"Where's my mother?" Robert asked.

"I took her things upstairs, to the room on the second floor. There's a real dining room up there, too. Imagine eating at a real table by candlelight, with a real tablecloth and china and silverware. . . ."

"Let me show you our silverware, Robert," Niklas said, smiling slyly. He pulled up the lid of a corner seat and brought out a handful of silver forks, each with a London stamp. "Silverware for twelve. Sixty-four pieces, weighs about fifty pounds altogether. It only took me fifteen minutes to find it; these people always keep their good stuff in the same places."

"Now listen, Niklas," Robert said, "I want you to put all this back where you found it."

Niklas was undeterred. "I could give you an exact description of the people who lived here. The way people stash away their valuables tells you a lot about their character. First you've got the real shrewd ones who think up the oddest places. . . ."

Robert had stopped listening. He suddenly felt very tired, too tired to convert Niklas into an honest man. The heat and the rich smells in the kitchen were stifling, and he was distracted by the steps he heard overhead, the restless pacing of his mother upstairs.

33

At the women's camp, Anna Haynow had always been the first to unpack her things and arrange an orderly corner for herself. Now, for the first time in ages, she had a room to herself—and couldn't muster the energy to do anything with it. The bag with her belongings stood untouched beside the door, where Balthasar Ploetz had left it.

Dry wood was piled in the fireplace, but she couldn't bring herself to light it. The warmth she needed could not be supplied by a fire; it would take a home, rooms filled with memories, familiar possessions. Even the thought of Robert was no comfort; sons did not take the place of a husband. She had never known before what it was to be really alone, not even during those weeks and months she had waited for a sign from her first husband, Robert Skelnik. The fact that she carried his child, his son, in her womb had comforted her then; and before the full impact of loneliness had hit her, the other man had entered her life. And though he hadn't brought the heat of passion back to her, he had given her the warmth of security.

The light of the candle on the mantelpiece made the room seem bigger than it was. Except for a bed in the alcove, an armchair, a wicker cradle filled with toys, the owners had left nothing in the room when they fled. In the outlines etched into the wallpaper she could tell what the other furniture had been: a wardrobe, a tall secretary, a grandfather clock, a bookcase, two oval pictures. Restlessly pacing the floor, she was only peripherally aware of these things; her thoughts were directed inward. Inside her, too, all was empty and dark; even her memories were becoming shadowy, dissolving into mist, memories of memories—it was what she wanted. No looking back.

Above all, she couldn't allow herself to think of that visit to the apothecary in Princeton, the crate she saw there, with the name MR. SKELNIK hand-printed on it. She banished that image from her mind. It bore the seeds of promise, of hope—she couldn't spare any energy for hope. She had enough to do with trying to forget, trying to forget wishes and fears alike. Lost in thought, she didn't hear the steps coming up the stairs, nor did she answer the knock on her door.

Robert saw her startled look when he came into the room and in that flash of insight when we perceive with our hearts rather than our eyes alone, he understood everything. He went over and put his arms around her. Through her coarse woolen dress he felt her body, the body of a woman still too young not to long for a man. He felt guilty, as intuition told him what it meant for her to be nothing now except the mother of her sons—and how little he could do to make up for it.

He went to the fireplace, opened the ventilator, and lit the fire. The kindling was dry as straw and caught on quickly, crackling and sending up sparks. "You'll be able to rest here," he said. "Once you've had a good sleep, the world will look brand-new again." He pulled her armchair in the fire. "Come, sit down."

She hesitated. "Is he gone?"

He would have liked to see her face, but her head was turned away.

"You shouldn't ever worry about me," he said. "Yes, he's gone, and I have a feeling he'll leave us alone from now on. Come to the fire, Mother. These last few months have been too much for you. But the worst is over now. It's going to be a long winter, and before it's over—" He stopped. What kind of promises could he offer her? He was reminded of his knife, and turned to glance out the window. Luckily, it didn't look out on the courtyard; she couldn't have seen his encounter with Claus. And yet, somehow, he had the feeling she knew everything, that she had stood beside him as he drew the knife, that it was she who had prevented him from doing what could not be undone.

She sat down in front of the fireplace; the fire was taking hold —the crackling had given way to small hissings and whispers and the occasional snap of a brittle twig breaking. For an instant it felt like those evenings at Haynow when he used to come to her room before dinner, and they would sit together staring into the fire without speaking, until somebody brought the tea.

"We're going to fix up this room just the way you want it," he said. "You won't want to leave here."

She smoothed her dress, a gesture he knew so well from childhood on. "We won't do anything of the kind," she said firmly. "We shall touch nothing, change nothing. Leave everything the way it is, please. I want the people who lived here to find everything as it is, as they left it, when they come back." Tears rose to her eyes and threatened to choke off her voice. "I'm afraid, Robert; I'm just afraid. Tell me, why did Claus come this time? It's better if I know. What did he want? Was it only about the house?"

"Rall sent for Soerman, that's all."

She lifted her head. "What for?"

"I don't know. Nothing to worry about, I'm sure. Soerman knows how to handle himself. We'll find out when he gets back. We'd better go downstairs; supper is ready."

"I don't feel like eating. Please, let me stay here."

He shook his head. "Come anyway. You have to try. They've put so much work into it; they've cooked us up a real banquet. You won't believe it when you see it. I'll give you ten minutes—then I'll expect you downstairs."

With Anna Haynow, and Mrs. Retz, there were seven people in the tanner's house, but the dining room could hold twelve if the table was extended full length; and at any rate, they had enough food for twelve, so five men from the camp were invited. The two women had the seats of honor, at the head and foot of the table. There was an empty place for Freder Soerman.

They were all very hungry, but they were awed by the simple fact of eating at a table, and nobody could bring himself to give in to his hunger. They were inhibited by all this comfort, all this food, so there was plenty left when Soerman finally returned.

Nobody asked him anything; there were the five guests to worry about, and besides, no one wanted to disrupt the festive mood. Soerman took his place and ate with slow deliberation. His face gave no hint of what the summons from Rall had been about, and Robert didn't ask He knew Soerman would tell him in his own good time. When the meal was finished, they exchanged a glance and got up, leaving the others to their whiskey.

Anna had been waiting for this; she followed them into the other room. "Come up to my room," she said. "You'll be able to talk in peace there."

They carried two chairs upstairs to her room and threw more wood on the fire. Anna sat in the armchair, Robert and Soerman beside her.

"Rall really did want to see me," Soerman began. "It wasn't an excuse or a trap. The colonel's moved in with the local doctor, by the way. They seemed to like each other. Not that they can speak a word to each other, but they both love French wines and chess. I think Rall had had a little too much of the doctor's Bordeaux when I was there, but you know him, he holds it pretty well."

"What did he want?"

"He needs a man who knows his way around here, and somebody told him about me. I couldn't tell what he was after at first. He wanted to know how cold the average winter gets here, when the Delaware usually freezes over, how long before you can cross it on the ice. He kept coming back to the river, the ferry, the fords—whether you could ford the river here on horseback. Like I said, at first I thought he was just drunk; but he knew exactly what he wanted. Hold on to your chairs—it looks like we're not staying in Trenton very long. I didn't really put it all together until I was on the way back. All those questions can mean only one thing: he wants to cross the river, with the army. Philadelphia's too close; he can't resist it. It must be maddening for him to sit here with the rebel capital only thirty miles away and not an Englishman around to hold him back. Not that the old fox said a word about it; he never once mentioned Philadelphia. But it's clear as day to me what he's got in mind."

Robert got up and went over to the fireplace; he could feel his mother's eyes following him. Every instant of silence, of hesitation, would only make her more suspicious. "Was that all?" he asked Soerman.

"Not quite. The Continental Army crossed the Delaware not

very long ago. And they took every ferry and boat for twenty miles around. Since I know the area, Rall wants me to take a patrol upriver and see if it's true all the boats are gone. In any case, we're to confiscate every boat we find. If he could have found a way to do it, he'd have sent me off tonight."

"This is the chance we've been waiting for," Robert said. "So we were right not to try it sooner." The two men looked at each other, and then at Anna. She was gripping the arms of her chair so tightly her knuckles were white. Robert nodded to Soerman and went over to his mother. "I have to tell you something. I had to keep quiet about till now because. . . ."

Abruptly, she got up and went over to the window. Then she turned. "I know what you're going to tell me. I know you've been planning to desert since the day we landed. Claus knows it, too. Have you waited so long because of me?"

"No, Mother. Our plan depended on getting as close as we could to a certain place in this country. . . ." He stopped, listened to the sounds beyond the door—the laughter at the dinner table. "We couldn't know we'd get so close without having to go it alone."

Anna nodded. "I know that, too."

"You know it? Since when?"

"Since last night, by accident. After we made camp in Princeton, Niklas and I went to the apothecary's for some medicine. Niklas had English money, but we couldn't be sure that would help; you know how hard it is to get the right drugs. The apothecary had a whole wagonload in his back room, an order he hadn't been able to deliver because the man who ordered it lives on the other side of the Delaware. The address was on the crates; and the name was. . . ." She came back to the fireplace. "I still haven't quite taken it in," she said. "I thought I'd faint when I read the name of your father."

There was a long silence. The three of them did not dare look at each other.

"Then you know more than we do," Robert said at last. "We had only a vague hope he might still be here. Soerman saw him last thirteen years ago, and that's a long time. People don't have to stay put in America the way they do back in the old world." He looked at Soerman. "What do you say?"

"I don't know what to say." Soerman shook his head. "It's too good to believe. Too lucky to be real. It scares me."

"How many men did Rall want you to take along?"

"I can take all the men I want. He'll give us horses, too. All he wants is boats."

Anna turned to face them. Her face expressed pure will, a will that would be deterred by nothing. "Then what are you waiting for? Because Soerman's afraid of good luck? Let's go, let's go at once!"

It was all Robert could do not to give in to her. "Not now," he said, "not without thinking about the best way to do it. It'd be stupid to be hanged as a deserter at the last possible moment. We have to plan it."

"There's nothing to plan," she said forecfully. "What only the three of us know now, others are likely to know all too soon. It can't remain a secret. Even Claus may find out. Sooner or later the name Skelnik is sure to come up—we're not ten miles away from his property. Claus will know what to make of that. He's not likely to wait until we've slipped through his fingers—or maybe he will wait, but only so he can catch us in the act. Then you'll both hang. I beg you, let's go tonight."

"We can't just go, Mother. Soerman's authorized to take a patrol. He'll find out what he can, he'll know the best place to cross over. We have the same problem Rall does. To cross the river we need boats, one, at least. As soon as Soerman's back from reconnoitering, we'll decide what to do next. Maybe we can go tomorrow night."

Anna said nothing. She sat down again before the fire. Robert was right, they would have to wait. But reason was not much comfort just now; it couldn't help with her fears, and even less with the confusion of feeling and thought that had overwhelmed her from the moment she had read the name Skelnik on the crate at the apothecary's in Princeton.

34

The house at Queens Street was the biggest and most magnificent in Trenton. Jacob Compson had planned far ahead; he had envisioned the future of Trenton and the future of his family, and he had built for generations to come. His vision so far had justified itself; Trenton had grown rapidly, and his fortune had multiplied. But his house, which his imagination had once filled with sons and daughters, had remained empty except for his son, John.

While John was growing up, Compson had consoled himself with the hope of grandchildren, but that hope had died when he buried his only son. He knew he would spend the rest of his life in an empty house, eating at a table with ten chairs too many, he at one end, his wife at the other, too far apart to talk, but too close not to be a burden to each other, and so day after day he would ask himself in needless self-torment what sense his life made, with no one to carry on his name. And the name Compson counted for a great deal in Trenton. His grandfather had traded the Indians two English racehorses for the land; good land, that he later sold for good money.

What the people of Trenton believed was mourning for his son was in reality only Jacob Compson's dull brooding over himself, his fate, and its meaning; and since there was nothing to distract him from it, it had grown into an obsession. He had lost the other great occupation that once helped fill his life: tea. His tea trade was dead, his warehouses in Boston and Philadelphia were empty, and his ships moved soldiers across the seas. That his capital kept growing was no consolation: he never saw it; it went not through his hands but through those of anonymous notaries in Philadelphia, who lent out his money at usurious rates—even the Congress had taken out a loan from him—and it brought him more profit than he had ever made with tea. That he was making money both off the English, who were using his ships, and off the rebels, whom he hated wholeheartedly, did not disturb his conscience at all. What he found hard to take was the fact that there was actually nothing for him to do. Action was his elixir of life, and when there was none left in his countinghouse, he looked for it at home.

Formerly he had left all that to his wife. But now he poked his nose into the kitchen and into the provisioning of the house—he weighed every egg in his hand, tasted the butter before he bought it, found fault with the fowl and game he was offered, inspected his wine cellar, made up the shopping lists, rearranged the storage of goods. Finally he took inventory of the china in the house and discovered that for the last thirty years he had been eating off an ugly table service while there was an exquisite set gathering dust in a china closet. What had started as an effort to find something to do became a mania. But instead of bringing him forgetfulness, this activity only exacerbated his grief over his pointless life; it remained as empty as his house, which was so rich in everything except life itself.

No wonder, then, that Jacob Compson welcomed the arrival of the Hessians in Trenton. At the first distant sound of their drums he had ordered his carriage, so that he could meet the troops and offer his house to the commander, Colonel Rall. His wife had protested violently; to her, any one of these Hessian soldiers might be the one who had killed their only son.

Betty Compson was not a woman to persist in a disagreement with her husband, but on this occasion she did not give in. They had a bitter quarrel, which she terminated by withdrawing to her room; by the time her husband came back from his excursion, she had locked herself in. Disappointed and irritated by Rall's brusque refusal of his hospitality, Compson was looking for a way to vent his anger, and demanded to see his wife. When she finally stood facing him, as tall as himself, dressed in black taffeta, a dress that happened to accentuate the abundance of bosom and hips—which only reminded him the more poignantly of her lifelong barrenness after their only child was born—Compson lost his temper and poured out every bitter reproach he had stored up throughout their entire marriage. She said nothing in reply, only looked at him, and the only expression in her gray eyes was the melancholy of a person who preferred to let herself be injured rather than injure another. And he fell silent; his outburst had brought him no relief at all, had only led to his further humiliation. "We have a guest," he declared, "who will live in this house. A Hessian major. I want two rooms prepared for him. He will be dining with us tonight for the first time. Understand me: this is not a request, it is an order."

She silently turned her back on him then and went to the window, from which she could see the cemetery where her son was buried.

That evening the two rooms were made ready for the Hessian major, the table was festively set for three persons, but Betty Compson did not come down to dinner; when Compson asked for his wife's whereabouts, he was told she had gone to the cemetery, to visit her son's grave. She did the same thing on the second evening, and there was nothing he could do about it.

This evening, the third since the Hessians had marched into Trenton, Compson again knocked at his wife's door, and again in vain. He turned away in helpless anger and while descending the stairs made up his mind, once more, to divorce her, to start a new life, with a new woman, a woman who would bear him a child year after year. It was a daydream he had indulged in for twenty years now, and for twenty years he had known he would never make this vision come true. In this mood he entered the dining room, found an absurd pretext for berating the maid who was folding the napkins, and was hurrying on to the kitchen to see the cook when he was stopped by someone entering his vestibule. It turned out not to be the Hessian major he expected for dinner but the mayor of Trenton, Thomas Randolph Bratt.

"I hope I'm not inconveniencing you," Bratt said; Compson was all too obviously in a bad mood. Unembarrassed by his silent reception, Bratt walked over to a display of potted plants in the center of the entrance hall. "What a splendid bougainvillea. That's not just your hothouse; that's the green thumb of Mrs. Compson. If my wife as much as looks at a plant it wilts on the spot." Thomas Bratt was a short, tubby little man with a curly gray wig. Arms akimbo he looked straight at Compson, whose expression was one of arrogant indifference.

"My contribution is not due until tomorrow," Compson said, in a tone as though he were speaking to the mayor's petty clerk rather than the mayor himself.

Bratt looked down at his shoes, adorned with huge silver buckles. "Since you mention it: I've made the rounds already. I'll never be able to collect that much by tomorrow. And anyway, I'd never have dreamed our allies would resort to such methods. Like stuffing those two houses with hay and threatening to set the town on fire; that alone was enough to anger the town. Then there was the confiscation of the horses, and now this levy in cash."

"What did you expect, even bigger profits? Your brother the baker is making a fortune every day, and your other brother, the liquor merchant, is making twice as much. The postmaster's cash-box is full every night, too. Let them pay a little."

"Our people didn't expect to be treated like this by our own allies, that's all. Confiscations, penalties, threats . . ."

"In any case," Compson said, "no need to worry about my share of the money levied. You can count on me."

There was a moment's silence. Mayor Bratt folded his hands across his stomach. "Colonel Rall refuses to give us a written receipt for the cash." His pale little eyes darted over the parquet of the hall floor, with only an occasional glance at Compson. "Perhaps he'd make an exception with you. You seem to be in his good books. It might have been better if you were our go-between with him. If only he would give us more time."

"Time enough to let the Delaware freeze over, you mean, so they'll move on without our money? Because they hope to get even more money out of Philadelphia?"

"I don't know about that; perhaps you're better informed." Bratt seemed to have discovered something on the floor that wholly engrossed his attention. "What do you think of the colonel's orders to cut down the trees in the pastures? Would he be intending to make boats out of them?"

"Are you sorry the rebels took all the boats?" Compson said coldly. "You can still follow them, if you like."

"I have always been a faithful servant of the Crown. Everyone here knows it, and I haven't changed. But do we have to have this plundering and repression? Are we to be threatened, in the name of civil order and obedience? Today two more post coaches arrived, full of those New York women. Those women have only come to carry our money away under their skirts. It doesn't help to make the Hessians popular."

Only now did Compson discover the Hessian officer's coat and hat on the hanger beside the entrance. He cast a quick glance into the library, deeply annoyed that no one had told him, and annoyed with himself as well for being so careless. He was tempted for a moment to invite the mayor to dinner, but decided against it; it would mean the whole town discussing his menu next day. "We mustn't forget that this is war," he said in a low voice. "There's always a price to pay. I advise you to collect the levy without delay, and have it in by twelve noon tomorrow." He laid an arm on Bratt's shoulder with all the warmth he could muster when he needed to get rid of someone.

"It's all right, I'm going," Bratt said. "Just one thing: if I can't get the whole amount together—would you lend us the rest, on short-term credit?"

"Sorry. Talk to those men who have the money and refuse to pay their share."

Before the mayor knew what was happening, he found he had been complimented out the door.

They made an odd pair, the American tea merchant and the Hessian officer, dining together in silence, served by two Negroes from bowls and platters loaded with enough food to satisfy half a dozen men.

They came from different worlds, but they seemed to have something in common, nevertheless. Sitting at opposite ends of the long table and raising their glasses to each other with a certain formality, they had a slightly conspiratorial air. In addition, they were both preoccupied with the same subject, each in his own way and for his own reasons: the person of Colonel Rall. Compson had never quite gotten over the fact that Rall had chosen to stay with Doctor Banks in preference to Queens Street. Every detail in the habits of the Hessian commandant interested him, as if he could read in them Trenton's future and his own. He knew that Rall seldom left his quarters except to watch his troops being drilled. He also knew that Rall spent his nights in drinking bouts with his companions. Neither fact was of a kind to allay his fears.

Claus Haynow, too, was obsessed with Rall, and not only because of his daily struggle with the colonel over fortifying Trenton against a rebel attack, with Rall taking back every morning what he had drunkenly agreed to the night before. He was also in doubt whether Rall would be on his side in the matter of Robert. He had done nothing at all about it since he had seen Robert three days ago. He was afraid that his passivity might be regarded as weakness, but he continued to postpone a decision; he was waiting, without knowing for what.

"No, thank you." He covered his wineglass with one hand before the servant in the yellow-and brown-striped, double-breasted velvet waistcoat could refill it. The Negro had moved to his side so soundlessly he was unaware of him until he saw the dark hand with the bottle above his glass. Everything in Compson's house was done smoothly, unobtrusively. He never saw the maid who did his room; he never heard a door slam. It reminded him of the week Robert had spent in prison waiting for his execution. The Haynow town house had been filled then with this dead silence; he had sat alone at dinner with his father, just as he was sitting with Compson now. His mother had stayed away.

He looked up from his plate and met Compson's questioning look. "An excellent dinner," he said. "This is the best time for wild duck. Did you shoot these birds yourself?"

"Alas, no. It's an eternity since I last went out hunting. At your age, though, I used to spend whole days out there."

"How's the hunting for deer here?"

"Nothing special. It's much better on the other side of the Delaware. On this side the ax and the saw have done their work too thoroughly, I'm afraid. Anything new about the colonel? I hear he's ordered information about the Delaware from Princeton—an errand on which he dispatched three officers and fifty men."

"They had to get there all in one day and come back the same night—Colonel Rall feels there's nothing better for man and horse than to keep on the move."

Compson reached for his glass. There was something about this young German that stirred his interest, a vague feeling of empathy that tends to rise more easily between unhappy people than happy ones. "Did your men learn anything about boats?"

"Nothing."

Claus felt particularly irritated about that mission. Soerman had himself chosen the men for the patrol upriver, but neither Robert nor any other man from that group in the tanner's house had gone along; it was as though they were being especially careful not to give him any reason to be suspicious.

"I could suggest a way for Colonel Rall to get his boats," Compson said, after the two men had moved to the smoking room for tea, served on a round ebony table. "I know a number of east coast captains who'd deliver all the boats you want to New Brunswick—though from there, they'd have to be transported overland." Compson studied his guest's face attentively. The major had refused the brandy just as he had his second glass of wine at dinner. How different he was from the common conception of an officer of foreign mercenaries in a foreign country. He had the eyes and mouth of a dreamer—but his dreams appeared to be gloomy ones. "Your silence tells me Colonel Rall would find this solution too slow for his taste."

Claus set down his teacup. "Evidently in a place like Trenton it's not easy to keep a secret. Rall's obsession with boats is pretty recent. You've heard about it from Mayor Bratt?"

Compson gave his guest a quick glance—had he overheard the conversation with Bratt, while waiting in the library? If so, Compson had said nothing it would not have been safe for anyone to hear; nevertheless, he decided to take the bull by the horns. "That wasn't Mayor Bratt's reason for coming to see me. He's having difficulties in collecting Colonel Rall's levy. The citizens of Trenton aren't precisely charmed by the idea. Nor do they like his order to cut down the trees in the pastures."

"That does enable us, secondarily, to post our guns more favorably, you know. From their previous positions we could never have reached the opposite banks of the river."

"What for—shooting holes in the sand? You'll hardly find a man of the Continental Army over there."

"Colonel Rall shares your view there. I'm not so sure."

"Those salvos from the other side that first day of your arrival? That was probably the rear guard losing its head. I would bet those were their last shells and the last of their gunpowder. The Continental Army—that's just a name with no substance behind it. I saw them hightailing it across the Delaware. A horde of ragamuffin bandits, nothing more. Rabble-rousers, hotheads, maniacs." Compson calmed himself. "Your pardon, but I get enraged every time I think of it. I didn't always get so upset about the rebels, even though I am a royalist—not until my son joined them, that is. . . ." Compson bit his lip, but the need to talk about it was stronger than discretion. "My son fell in the battle for Fort Washington, as a rebel. I told you my wife can't dine with us because she is sick. That's not true. She has her meals brought to her room on a tray. You see, every man in the royalist uniform could be the man who shot her son." Compson poured himself a second glass of brandy, and did not stopper the bottle when he put it back on the table. "My son never used to interest himself in politics. No one in our family ever has; we don't chase after will-o'-the-wisps. What started John off on that tack was a dance at that damned Redford place."

"Redford?" Claus said. "Isn't that the Indian forest?"

"Poppycock, old wives' tales. Though the Indians stayed on there longer than they did on our side of the river. The present owner bought his land from them." Again Compson filled his glass, and again Claus refused. Compson kept the glass in his hand after emptying it, and seemed a little bewildered, as if he had lost the thread of his story. "John took to spending more time at Redford than at home," he went on. "He kept it a secret until one day I ran into him accidentally in Philadelphia. The girl and her father were with him; they were coming from a session of Congress. John wasn't the only one ruined by that man. All the young men who went near him caught the disease."

"You mean the girl's father? What sort of man is he?"

But Compson would not be sidetracked. "But for him, John

would be alive today; his wound wasn't necessarily fatal. But he was crazy enough to insist on riding to Redford in his condition. Not home to his parents, but all the way to Redford! Major, you've seen the empty houses all over town. It's that man's work, all of it, I tell you. He talked the men of those families into coming with him to Philadelphia, to those meetings the rebels held there. He got them to come to his house and swear loyalty to their so-called government. And as for the boats you need, I'll wager anything you like you'll find them in his woods somewhere. There are those, even among the people who stayed in Trenton, who admire him for it still. An adventurer who came from nowhere, a Polish rascal to judge by his name, Skelnik. To think that a Compson should have lived to see. . . ."

Compson was too immersed in his own broodings to note the effect the name Skelnik had on his guest. Claus put down his teacup with exaggerated caution, and placed his hands in front of him on the black wood of the table, wondering that they did not tremble.

"What did you say? What name was that?"

"Skelnik. *If* that's his real name. He just arrived one day, with a few wagons, a few people, some weapons, axes, saws, and a plow. Nobody knew where he came from, how long he'd stay."

Claus stared at his hands. His mouth felt dry. He would have liked a glass of brandy, but he held himself in check, tried to keep his voice from betraying too much interest.

"Has he been here long?" He could not bring himself to pronounce the name Skelnik.

"They wanted to elect him to Congress." Compson was following his own train of thought. "But he refused. A man of his driving ambition! There's got to be something in his past he's covering up."

"Do you remember what year it was when he bought Redford?"

"Bought Redford indeed! In those days you could get all the land you wanted from an Indian chief for a silver-mounted hunting rifle. It was all primeval forest, then. But he could have had arable land, then, for less than it cost him to clear the forest. Let's see, when did he get here? . . ." Compson stopped to calculate.

"The late fall of 1753, it was. Strange—that too was a year when the Delaware didn't freeze over."

Benumbed, incapable of thinking clearly, Claus tried to take this in. Compson's voice seemed to come from far away; whatever his words were, they no longer mattered. He had a vision of Robert—Robert with a triumphant smile on his face. Of course. Robert knew all about Redford, on the other side of the Delaware. Robert had merely been waiting all this time to get there.

He stood up abruptly, banging against the table; cups and glasses slid across the polished ebony. He murmured his excuses and left the room.

Compson wondered desperately what he could have said to offend his guest, even as he heard the Hessian officer sending for his horse. Compson was too proud to follow him outside. He went to the window and pushed aside the curtains. The four lampposts beside the stone steps leading up to the front door, four thick candles in each, illuminated the courtyard. There was a clatter of hooves on the cobblestones, and he saw the Hessian major set off into the dark, lashing his horse on with his riding crop.

Claus was not surprised, not even disappointed, to find he had come too late. It confirmed his feeling that his opponent was an equal, that his feud with his brother was no common conflict that could be fought out and forgotten. In the last few days, he had had the feeling it was coming to a head. Robert must have had the same feeling; perhaps he had been making his escape at the very moment the name Skelnik had come up at Compson's. The idea that they were acting mysteriously in concert lifted the struggle above the merely personal, made it a fated thing.

It couldn't have been long since they'd left the house. There was still smoke coming from the chimney, and the tracks of horses in the yard were still fresh. The pine torches were almost out. The front door was unlocked, the felt curtain that separated the entry from the hall held to one side by a leather strap. In the dim light of the oil lamp he saw a pair of old torn army boots discarded on a grate; apparently the men had made new footwear from leather found in the tanner's workshop. He registered every detail without emotion; he was interested only in some clue that might betray which direction they'd gone. The brass metalwork on the dark-stained doors and stair railings shone; the floorboards were redolent of ammoniac and wax; there was a fire in the hearth, a basket of bread on the table, along with plates, and a jug of wine. Had they only gone off on patrol? He lifted the lids of pots on the hearth, smelled a pot roast, beans cooking. Everywhere he looked—the supply room, a little office, a living room, a sewing and laundry room—there were signs of recent occupation. There were playing cards on the table, a half-smoked pipe in a tin ashtry. On a clothes chest stood a plate with apples surrounded with a wreath of evergreen—clearly his mother's touch. He thought he could hear her light step behind him, the rustling of her dress, her voice: *Why are you here again? Can't you leave us in peace?*

When he had first entered the house, he had been so tense it was like walking in a trance. Now, imperceptibly, the tension eased; in its place came an aching torment.

Why was he dawdling over this search? He should already be organizing a troop of riders and dogs and starting in pursuit. He forced himself to climb the stairs to the second floor and look into one room after another. The light of the candle he had taken from the kitchen flickered over bare walls, straw-filled mattresses on the floors. Everywhere there was the smell of freshly scrubbed and waxed floors; everywhere the fireplaces had been laid with fresh firewood, ready to be lighted. Only one room had the remnants of a dying fire, a glowing mound covered with light-gray ashes. An armchair, an alcove, an empty wicker cradle.

He no longer had any doubt that they had gone. But instead of starting off after them he sank into the armchair and sat there with his eyes wide open, overwhelmed with images of the past: a little boy, at home in Haynow Manor, surrounded by warmth, a reddish twilight, a whispering fire on the hearth, waiting for his mother.

The sharp noise of a door slamming downstairs startled him out of his daydreams. Loud steps rang through the house, then came to a stop. He got up and slowly went down the stairs. A babbling singsong came from the kitchen.

The man sat on the wooden bench, his back to the wall, a bottle in his hands. He set it down, wiped his mouth with the back of one hand, blinked at the candlelight. Beaming broadly he held the bottle toward Claus. "Drink up, friend. . . . It's not much as schnapps goes, but it'd be a pity to waste it. Got to drink it up, empty the bottle, I need empty bottles to make more of it, right?" He fetched another bottle from under the bench, pulled the cork out with his teeth, spat it out.

Claus put down the candle. He recognized the Austrian glove merchant, though he couldn't remember his name. "Where are the others?" he asked sharply.

Ploetz put a finger to his lips. "Not so loud, friend. There's not enough of this stuff to go around. Jus' enough for us two. Come on now, siddown and close the door." His tongue was heavy.

Even though Ploetz was very drunk, Claus couldn't find him repulsive. He was more like a sick man, fantasizing, in a fever. Claus almost envied him. When he grabbed the man's shoulder it was himself he wanted to shake out of his trance. "When did they leave?" he shouted.

The bottle fell to the floor, spilling wine across the wood. "Hey, what do you think you're doing?" Ploetz whined.

Claus pulled him to his feet. "Speak up. Where are they? When did they leave?"

Ploetz struggled to free himself. "Hey, who are you? I don't know you. . . ."

Claus dragged the man out of the kitchen, through the hallway, and out into the cold night. Ploetz could barely stay on his feet; he seemed to grow heavier with every step. When they reached the well, Claus let him drop to the ground like a sack of potatoes, filled a pail with water, and poured it over his head. Ploetz shook his head violently and staggered to his feet. "What are you doing, trying to drown me?" He wiped his face with a sleeve. Then he stared at Claus, recognition slowly dawning on his face.

"Major . . ." he stammered. He tried to straighten his clothes. "I beg pardon, Major. . . ."

"Now, pay attention," Claus said. "What's been going on here? When did they leave, and where are they headed? Out with it, man!"

Ploetz swayed on his feet. The shower of cold water had shocked only his body awake; his mind was struggling slowly out of its alcoholic stupor. He stared at Claus, then at the house. "Did you say they're gone?" he said.

"No games now. The house is empty."

Abruptly Ploetz turned and ran into the house. Claus let him go; he made no move to follow. Seconds later, Ploetz came back out. His confusion was clearly genuine. His unsteady walk was no longer just from drunkenness.

"They're gone," he said dully. "They went off and left me. Sure, what could they do with a drunk? I'd have spoiled it for them."

"How long have you known?" Claus demanded. "You had to have known about it. They've been planning it for a long time, haven't they?"

"You can do what you want," Ploetz said. "I made one mistake when I got drunk. I won't make another. You can't make me talk."

"Talking is your one chance. Where are they? How do they plan to get across the river? They *are* planning to cross over to Redford, aren't they?"

"A drunk," Ploetz mumbled. "They couldn't take a drunk. You'll never catch them, never."

But Claus was already swinging into the saddle, kicking his horse into a run, disappearing into the darkness toward the river.

Ploetz began to realize he was alone again. Slowly he crossed the yard. He was longing for a drink, but he stopped in the doorway. On the hooks beside the door, usually overflowing with coats, there was only one dark coat left, with a gun and an ammunition pack hanging beside it. Without thinking, like a man obeying orders, he buckled on the belt, took the weapon, and left the house.

They had even left his horse behind, fully saddled, in the shed.

So they had waited for him after all. They must have put off leaving a long time, waiting for him. If they had waited any longer, the major would have taken them by surprise. The thought sobered him completely. He led the horse outside, swung into the saddle, took the reins. When he rode through the side door in the gate he lowered his head to avoid the low beam above. He found the horses' tracks outside and followed them.

35

The night was clear and cold, with an icy wind blowing along the Delaware. Since Robert hadn't been along on Soerman's patrol, he had to rely on Soerman's description of the fording place, but it was unmistakable. The Continental Army had forded the river here, and the ground was still ploughed up from the horses and wagons. It was littered with empty ammunition packs, broken bayonets, torn shoes, broken wagon wheels–here and there even the cadaver of a horse. The moonlight gave all of these relics a ghostly appearance of life.

Robert had left Louis with the women and the horses and was reconnoitering the riverbank. Soerman and Niklas had gone off to get the boat the Swede had found on one of his patrols and hidden upstream. Robert had imagined the Delaware as the final and easiest part of the flight, almost as a stream that would part to let them through. Now, looking at it, he realized for the first time how powerful and dangerous the river was. The water was very dark; the current didn't look strong, but when he tossed a piece of wood on the water it vanished out of sight almost immediately. The opposite bank was invisible. The only evidence that there was solid land on the other side of the rushing darkness was the ford. He could tell where it was; the river was lighter there–a pale strip stretching diagonally off into the dark, a natural dam of harder bedrock that formed an underwater bridge between the two banks. The water-polished rock was treacherous even for a good rider in broad daylight. In addition, it sloped downward until, on the last third of the way, the water would reach up to the horse's chest. But if it hadn't been for the women, he would have decided to cross on horseback anyway; it was hard to control his impatience.

He selected a flat stone from the bank and sailed it across the water. Skipping, it danced across the surface and disappeared into the dark. He listened. A horse whinnied, then all was silent again, except for the rushing of the river and the sound of the wind. He turned and made his way back up the steep, sandy riverbank. Debris discarded by the rebels lay scattered through the thin grass. He picked up a rebel coat from under a bush; it was damp, but serviceable. He draped it over his shoulders like a cape and went back to where he had left the others.

The two women sat on an old sheep cart, which had lost one of its two wheels; the axle of the other had dug into the earth like an anchor. The wind was more powerful here than down on the river. The horses stood with their backs to it, picking at the few dry wisps of grass.

When she saw him approaching in the wide, pale coat, Anna sprang to her feet—then she realized who it was. "You startled me," she said. "What are you wearing? Isn't Soerman back yet?"

"He won't be long," Robert said. "Come, sit down." He called over to Louis, who was looking after the horses. "Go down to the river," he said, "and see if you can find more coats like this, one for each of us. There's six of us, so we need five more."

Mrs. Retz stood up. "I'll help him. It's better than sitting here waiting."

Robert sat down beside his mother. He took off the coat, spread it on his lap. On the inside panel a name was embroidered in light green, but it was too dark to read it. "Do you know what this means?" he said to his mother. "The women make these coats for their men, then they embroider their names for identification. These people stick together, or there'd be no army. The coat was damp when I found it, but the moisture didn't go through to the inside; it's a very tough wool. It'll keep you warm."

He tried to put it around her shoulders but she shuddered and refused to keep it on. "The idea that the man it belonged to might be dead . . . please, keep it. Why did you pick it up in the first place?"

"If the army hasn't moved on by now, they'll have sentries on the other side. What do you suppose they'll think when they see a boat full of Hessian uniforms coming their way? I don't want something to go wrong at the last minute because of our uniforms." He held the coat in his lap. "Now there's only the river to cross, and we'll be safe."

"I'm afraid," she said, "afraid of the river and of what we'll find on the other side."

It wasn't what she said that alerted him, so much as the disheartened way she said it. "But, Mother, haven't you always told me I was born lucky? And you've been anxious to go every day for the past week. Soerman and Niklas should be back with the boat any minute now. You're not worrying about Ploetz, are you? We can't wait any longer for him. God knows where he is—probably sleeping off a drunk somewhere."

"I'm not thinking of what's past; I'm thinking of the future. We've been imagining all kinds of things, but how do we know they'll come true? Twenty-three years is a long time, a lifetime almost. We're expecting him to welcome us with open arms, but why should he? Twenty-three years—and a man like your father. Do you think he's been a hermit all these years? What do you know about him, what does he know about you? Suddenly a son appears that he didn't even know existed. . . ."

"Why are you talking about me?"

"Yes, why about you? . . ." She drew her woolen shawl tighter around her shoulders. "I'm trying to put myself in his place. The sudden appearance of a son may mean complications enough for him—but me. . . ." She couldn't complete the thought, and yet she was impelled to go on. "When I try to imagine standing in front of his house. . . ." Again she broke off. "I'm afraid I won't have the courage to knock on his door. He waited for me, he wrote me letters—but that was a long time ago, and he never had a word from me. How am I to explain what happened to a man who waited so long? It's too late. We can't turn time back like a clock. Try to understand; I have to point out to you what the possibilities are; it might save both of us a disappointment. According to all I hear, this Redford is a huge estate. No man builds up that kind of thing just for himself. I can imagine what I would feel if I were the lady of Redford, and suddenly there's a strange woman on my doorstep."

Robert had been paying more attention to the night sounds and the river than to his mother's words. There would be time enough to think about all that when they had safely crossed the river. "It's all much simpler than that, Mother," he said. "I'd just like to get rid of this damned uniform. I want to live, to be able to breathe again, to have a life of my own."

"You're a man, you're young, you can begin a new life. But I'm a woman, and everything is harder for a woman, especially one who's no longer young. Men, like cats, have nine lives, but a woman has only one."

For a moment, they sat in silence, waiting and listening. Suddenly the horses stopped grazing, raised their heads, pricked up their ears. Then Anna heard it, too—sounds coming from the direction of the river. She gripped Robert's arm.

"Now you're afraid for your life," he said, "and a second ago you were thinking your life was already over. I meant what I said; I want to live, I care about my life, and one day you'll care about your life again, too. Wherever you happen to be in this country, whatever kind of life it is, it'll matter to you." He picked up his gun.

The sounds came nearer. They might have come from an animal, from the wind stirring the dry thickets. Then something rose above the thickets like the outline of a huge animal: Soerman and Niklas, only their legs visible, carrying something big and heavy on their shoulders.

Robert lowered his gun. "They're bringing the boat," he said.

The boat lay on the riverbank, black inside and out with tar from repeated caulkings. They stood around it, hesitant and silent now after the first excitement over the boat was past.

"It took you a long time to get it here," Robert said; he was suddenly, inexplicably, uneasy.

"Why don't you try dragging something this size for a mile?" Soerman said irritably. "It weighs a ton."

"Is it watertight?"

"What's the matter, the waiting make you nervous? Can you imagine how glad I was to find it at all, with the oars? I had to steal it out of some farmer's shed, you know. It may leak a bit, sure, but it's a boat."

"Please," Anna intervened, "this is no time for bickering."

Robert walked around the boat, examining it intently. "How many do you think it'll hold?"

"Three or four, at most. Any more than that's too risky."

Everybody looked at Robert. He pointed to the coats Louis and Mrs. Retz had collected. "Put them on. It'll be better if we don't look too unfamiliar to those on the other side." He nodded to Soerman. "You take the boat. You, the two women, and Louis; he doesn't weigh much. Niklas and I stay behind." He pulled on his coat, buckled the belt. "Go on, get going."

"Why me?" Soerman said. "Why don't you go with the women?"

"Because you know the river better than I do."

"All right. I'll come back for the two of you as soon as I've got the women across."

"We'll wait here. If the boat can't make it across a second time, we can ride over." He turned to Niklas. "Go get the horses. No, wait a minute. Just bring mine, and get Soerman's for yourself. Drive the others away, so they won't be found here. And now let's get the boat down to the water."

They grabbed hold of the boat and began pushing and pulling it down the bank. The bottom scraped along the sand, and then, gently, the prow slid into the water.

Robert left the rest of the work to the others and turned to his mother, who stood to one side. He took her hands in his. "Do you know," he said, "I have never met a woman who could compare to you. I'm not just saying this, either; I've thought it before. Of all the women I've known, none could hold a candle to you. If my father's the least bit like me, he'll think the same thing." He led her to the boat and helped her in, holding her hand until she had settled herself securely on the seat. Mrs. Retz and Louis followed.

Soerman and Robert exchanged a look.

"Good luck," Robert said. "I'll never forget that we couldn't have made it this far if it hadn't been for you."

"If it hadn't been for me, you might still be back on the Haynow estate."

"Don't start that again. When will you understand it would all have happened without you?"

Soerman hesitated. "Why don't you get in the boat? I think your mother would prefer you went with her."

Robert shook his head. "You'd better go now." He put a hand on Soerman's shoulder. "Take good care of her, that's the most important thing. And I've changed my mind: don't bring the boat back. Take her to Redford. Niklas and I can make it on horseback."

Soerman looked at him suspiciously. "Wait a minute now. What have you got in mind? You're not by any chance thinking you've got unfinished business on this side of the Delaware?"

"You mean Claus?"

"If that's what you've got in mind, it's my business, too. There were two of us in front of that firing squad, remember?"

"Forget it. It never crossed my mind. Go on. And good luck."

Robert stood on the bank, watching the boat move away from shore. He could feel the cold and the damp through the thin soles of the moccasins Ploetz had made for him from leather found in the tannery. The boat slowly disappeared into the darkness. Soon its wake was gone, and even the sounds of the oars faded away, lost in the distance. He turned away.

"What are you doing up there," he shouted to Niklas. "Bring the horses."

"The damned things won't leave!"

In the dark, Robert could hear the hiss of the whip Niklas was using to try to drive off the other horses. Soerman's last question echoed in his mind . . . Claus. But getting across the river was the only thing that mattered now. He looked up at the sky. The night was very peaceful, like certain nights he remembered at Heron Island, when he had spent half the night in a boat, drifting, dreaming, divorced from space and time. From old habit he looked for the constellation of Cassiopeia, but he couldn't find it; this was a different sky, with the constellations in different places.

Finally, Niklas brought the horses, and they mounted up. "Follow me," Robert said, "and let the horse feel its way. Animals have a sixth sense; they know. . . ." His horse reared and whinnied, and in the sudden confusion he realized someone had fired a shot somewhere up the bank. He fought the horse to a standstill. Niklas's horse had bolted; Robert could see him sawing at the reins, until he finally brought it under control. Then there was silence again, and everything was as before, the river rushing past, the stars twinkling overhead.

He searched the riverbank with his eyes, trying to penetrate the darkness. A horse was coming toward them at a dead run; for a second he thought it was one of the horses they were leaving behind, but this one had a rider, a man with a fluttering bandanna around his neck. Another shot was fired; Robert saw the flash of the gun muzzle up in the brush at the top of the bank. The horse was still galloping toward him, but the man begun to sag sideways in the saddle, as if about to dismount; still gripping his rifle, he lurched sideways down the horse's flank, hung suspended for an instant from one stirrup, then fell to the ground and lay still.

Robert swung out of the saddle. A bullet whistled past his ear and slapped the water. He grabbed the man on the ground and dragged him quickly into the shelter of the brush. It was Ploetz; he lay there like Robert had seen him often enough before, looking completely drunk. And as he had done so often before, Robert seized him by the collar and shook him. "What the devil have you done now?"

"He's after you . . ." Ploetz mumbled, his words barely intelligible. ". . . Your brother . . . you've got to get away from here. . . ."

Robert raised his head above the surrounding brush, searching for the spot where he'd seen the muzzle flash, but he couldn't make anything out. Suddenly he saw Niklas break from shelter, and run in a half-crouch toward the sheep cart. He remembered they had left their weapons there, and he realized with a start that he was unarmed. "Back!" he shouted to Niklas. "Get back!" But it was too late. The bullet caught Niklas on the run. His arms flew up, his body arched downward, he stumbled a few steps more, and fell. But Robert was no longer watching; this time he had seen where the shots were coming from—he could see clearly the silhouette of horse and rider.

"For God's sake, go," Ploetz whispered, his voice rough, strange.

"What is it? Are you hit?" Robert suddenly realized the man wasn't drunk.

"Go on," Ploetz said, still gripping his rifle.

"Wait here," Robert said. "I'll get the horses. Don't move."

"Leave me. With two bullets in me I can still shoot, but I can't ride." Blood trickled from the corner of his mouth. "Get going, man. I'll keep him off." He shoved the barrel of his rifle through the fork of a low branch. The heavy gun wavered in his hands, but he managed to steady it. "Start running when I fire."

Robert nodded.

When the shot came, Robert broke from cover, running for the sheep cart. He didn't bother to crouch or take evasive action; he almost felt he would welcome a bullet if it came, but he reached the cart without hearing any more shots fired. The two rifles were leaning against the cart, side by side; he didn't bother looking to see which was his, but took the first one within reach and made sure it was loaded. The figure of the rider had disappeared from the horizon, nothing moved. Gazing across the top of the cart, he searched the terrain along the riverbank, yard for yard. Then, slowly, he started backing toward the river, toward the spot he had left Ploetz. His foot hit something soft. He stopped and bent down. It was Niklas, lying face down. Robert turned him over. He was shocked, in spite of himself, by the wide, staring eyes; he closed the lids with his fingers. Then he continued back to where Ploetz was.

Ploetz was dead, lying under the bush where he had left him. The gun had slipped from his hands. Robert knelt beside him, loosened his bandanna and wiped the blood from his lips. He felt numb, almost lethargic. Still kneeling, he heard his horse approaching slowly, uncertainly, behind him, its loose reins dragging on the sand. It was only when he felt the warm damp muzzle nudging his back that he came to himself.

He stood up, tears of rage in his eyes. "Come on out!" he shouted up the slope. "I know you're there—show yourself!" He waited, listening, but all he could hear was his own echo. In his anger he fired blindly into the dark; again, the receding echo was his only answer. He threw the gun away and stood there, an easy target. Nothing happened. He picked up the dragging reins, mounted his horse, and started toward the river. He had an odd feeling at the back of his neck, as if he were being watched.

The river was black, noisy, stretching into the dark as far as he could see, rippling across the narrow dam of underwater rock which formed the ford. The horse stopped when the water reached its fetlocks, tossed its head, as if waiting for a command. He laid a hand on its neck and kept the reins loose, guiding it only with a gentle pressure from his knees. He kept his eyes on the rocky, underwater path ahead, still feeling as if he were being watched.

He had gone about twenty yards into the river, when he heard the shot and simultaneously felt the shock and pain in his shoulder. The first thing he felt was relief; he had known it would happen, and now it had happened. The horse shied, reared; trying to ignore the pain, he spoke to it softly, maintained the gentle pressure of his knees, until it was calm enough to go on. Then he felt the hind hooves slipping, scrambling, sliding off the rocky bottom; the horse squealed with panic, and went under. Robert felt the cold, the unbelievably powerful pull of the current. He was still in the saddle, still clutching the reins, fighting the horse, the current, the pain.

The River

If we want to be free, we must fight battles;
By God, we must fight battles!

Patrick Henry, Delegate to the Continental Congress from Virginia, in Philadelphia, 5 September 1774

Victory or death

General Washington's slogan to his troops before the March on Trenton, Christmas 1776

36

When she wasn't required in the infirmary, Mary avoided it as much as possible, and so she gave it a wide berth now on her way to the stables. It was a clear, cold morning, too cold for snow, but with a warning of winter in it. From a distance, in the direction of the bivouac area, came the sound of gunfire, whole salvos at regular intervals. It was a familiar sound, now that the Continental Army was drilling at Redford. But it sounded different this morning—hard, abrupt, like branches cracking in the frost of winter.

A troop of militia marched diagonally across the yard, dressed in a motley of mismatched uniforms, dirty and patched. Their faces were red from the cold, but it had obviously failed to invigorate them; they looked tired and resigned. Mary waited impatiently for the column to pass, and then hurried on to the stables, mounted her horse, and rode off in the direction of the river.

She let the horse move at a trot; she was in no hurry. Skelnik had left at dawn for the tin mine, and whenever he was away, she felt uncomfortable in the house. These days, with all the officers coming and going, and the kitchen working from dawn till dark, the house seemed like some kind of officers' mess. She would go visit Jean Daniel; it would be more pleasant in the woods, with Daniel sitting in front of his cabin, silently cleaning his guns. McGill had told her Daniel had planned to leave the day the army had come across the Delaware. Mary could understand that—both his wanting to leave and his reason for staying.

She wondered whether the Delaware had begun to ice over at the edges. She hadn't been to the river since that last ride with Skelnik. Now she took a roundabout way to the cabin in order to see the river again. She passed the ancient pine tree with its Indian sign and knew that soon she'd be able to hear the rushing sound of the water; the river was a world of its own, with different air, different colors.

She breathed in the cold air; in the distance she could see the Delaware shimmering through the trees, a single, thin bright stripe at first. As she came closer the air seemed to grow mistier, the blue of the sky paled; and sailing across it, high and thin, she saw a heron. Above it, she discovered a second heron. She was pleased to see them because the herons seldom left their nests in the thickets of the Assunpink a this time of year. Calm as they looked in flight there was an air of daring about them: they sailed through the blue like silver arrows intent on a distant goal.

On her right she saw a group of riders coming from the river. They wore blue coats, but through the mists the blue seemed to change into greens, violets, even browns. One rider broke away from the troop and came toward her. She hesitated, then spurred her horse on in the opposite direction. She wanted to be alone.

She soon reached the edge of the river. As she had expected, the low bushes along the slope were covered with frost, and the puddles of water near the edge of the riverbank had formed a thin crust of ice. At this point, the Delaware formed a little inlet. Something in the inlet caught her eye. At first all she could make out was a thrashing in the water; she rode closer and was horrified by what she saw. It was a horse, trying to crawl up onto the riverbank. Only its head was out of the water, and it was struggling to free itself from the ooze of the river bottom. But it was obviously crippled; every time it struggled halfway out it fell back again.

She had forgotten the rider following her, but she was relieved to hear his horse coming up behind her.

The man touched a hand to his blue- and white-banded hat. "Sergeant Haughton, Miss. I have orders to warn you not to ride too close to the river. The enemy tried to send a few people across last night."

From the horse in the water came a faint whinny of distress.

"Do something," Mary said. "It must have broken a leg. Shoot it, please."

Sergeant Haughton seemed to notice the horse for the first time. He was an older man with bristly red hair and a graying beard. She looked away, up at the sky, to the herons, as he loaded his weapon. He seemed to be taking a long time, but finally she heard the shot. From the woods behind her came the echo, and she saw the herons suddenly swerve and dive down into the thickets.

She turned and looked back toward the river. The head was submerged now; the horse was only a faint outline beneath the water. Already the current was beginning to bear it away.

"Thank you," she said. "I'm glad you were here to put it out of its misery."

"You'd better get away from the river, Miss. They might try something again, though it isn't too likely in broad daylight."

Mary peered through the sun's rays across the river. Usually the water would be deep green in wintertime, but snow was needed for that. She rode slowly back up the slope, away from the riverbank.

The sergeant saluted. "I have to get back," he said, "Otherwise I'd accompany you." He had slung the rifle back on his shoulder and drew on his wide-cuffed gloves again. "Promise me to stay away from the river. There's a war on, and right now the Delaware is the border."

Mary watched him out of sight, then rode slowly on along the river to the edge of the thicket that went all the way to the river's edge. There were a lot of leafy trees here, the kind that let the warmth of the sun through—an ideal nesting place for the herons.

On one of the blackthorn bushes she saw a shred of pale cloth. She smiled, reminded of her reputation at Redford for finding lost and misplaced things, a knack on which Skelnik was among the most dependent, because he was one of those people who couldn't seem to find what they were looking for even when it was staring them in the face. She leaned down from the saddle and picked the piece of fabric off the blackthorn branch. It was damp; she plucked at it, and its threads came apart. It was the kind of four-ply fabric they wove at Redford to make coats for the Continental Army.

She dismounted, and searched for more of the fabric. She found nothing more, except for a few places where branches had been broken from the bush, recently it seemed. Then she saw the tracks on the ground, not like the tracks made by soldiers' boots. They were only really visible where there was just a sparse growth of grass in the loose sand. There was no doubt that these footprints had come up from the river.

She returned to the blackthorn bush to tie her horse up. Then she made her way deeper into the thicket.

Golden thistles grew in this part of the woods, but the metallic gleam that caught her eye in the shade of these green branches was not a thistle. She wished it were, because she was afraid to step closer and discover that the man lying under the yew tree was dead. He didn't move, and he was wrapped in one of those army coats of which she had cut and sewed so many. He had to be the man whose tracks she had followed up from the riverbank—he had moccasins on his feet. They looked strange under the heavy coat.

Slowly, trembling, she came closer. All the sounds of the woods seemed louder now—the snapping of twigs underfoot, a bird exploding up out of its hiding place, the cry of a blue jay. Very moved, she looked at the man's face. His head was turned slightly to one side; his eyes were closed. A strand of long blond hair had slipped loose from the green ribbon knotted at the nape of his neck.

She knelt down beside him, feeling faintly dizzy. The coat was wrapped tightly around him. She could see no sign of blood, no wound anywhere. She looked at his face again, suddenly afraid he might open his eyes and look at her. For seconds she forgot everything else; for seconds the world shrank to this small piece of earth in the shade of the yew tree.

Suddenly the man moved. His right hand seemed to search for something, his eyelids fluttered; then he subsided again. His mouth quivered, as if in pain, and he seemed to be breathing harder than before. She realized that he was unconscious and must have been wounded. She put her hand on his forehead; it was hot. She lost her hesitation now. She had to find out what was wrong before she could get help for him.

The coat was wet through and hard to unbutton. She finally opened it over his chest—and stopped. The uniform underneath was green with red facings, bleached by sun and rain, the silver braid turned brownish. Slowly, reluctantly, she understood. She stood up, full of regret and disappointment. The man was a Hessian, one of the enemy.

She grew hot with anger. She thought of John and Blyth, of the dying drummer boy in the infirmary, whom she last saw being carried on a stretcher across the yard, with Jan Kellog carrying his drum after him. Here was a Hessian. An enemy. The words of Sergeant Haughton suddenly acquired real meaning for her. So this Hessian had come across the river; she hated him for that and for whatever else he might have done.

Now that she understood clearly how she felt, she was able to get close to him again, to check whether he had any weapons on him. She found none. Then she saw the dark spot high on the left side of his chest. Perhaps the sentries on the riverbank had shot him. But, in that case, why hadn't they pursued him? Unless it happened in the night, and in the dark they hadn't seen him reach the bank? In which case he must have lain here a long time and lost much blood.

She was tempted to let him lie there. It was really all she had to do. She could go back to her horse, ride away, forget she ever saw him. No one ever came into this part of the woods; it belonged wholly to the herons. If the man's body was ever found, the uniform would merely remind people of that winter when the war had come to this part of the country.

She bent over him. He turned his head, tried to lift it. His lips moved, his eyes opened for a split second; then he sank back into his coma. His eyes were green, dark green in the shade of the yew tree.

She had found him, after all, against all probability in this desolate part of the forest; it had to mean something. His life was in her hands. She could not leave him here to die, even if he was an enemy. "I'm going to get help," she said, as if he could hear and understand her.

The water was rushing past, and his hands felt for the reins, closed on emptiness. Around him it was dark and cold, there were voices and steps.

What were the voices doing here? The deep, foreign one reminded him of something, of a cell, the night before the execution, but it couldn't be that. And there was another, a lighter voice—and then again the rushing of the current.

Robert couldn't manage to cross that threshold in his mind. The voices were no help. He tried to open his eyes, but the darkness would not be shaken off. And there was the pain, the pain in his shoulder. When they lifted him up, it ran through his whole body.

Claus. He reared up. Instantly the voices around him grew louder. So he had failed, he hadn't made it across the river. Perhaps he really lay in a cell again, and sentence had already been passed; they were merely trying to keep him alive so they could execute him. Claus. Again he tried to open his eyes. He expected to see Claus, but what he saw was a young girl in a pale woolen dress, with long dark-brown hair hanging down her back.

Someone took him by the shoulders and turned him around so that he lay on his stomach. The deep voice said, in English: "Hold him down like this, with all your strength, and don't let go, even if he screams and thrashes about." Another pair of hands took hold, held him very firmly. The deep voice said, "Now! Hold tight!" and then he felt only the searing pain, as though his whole back were on fire, and he went under.

Jean Daniel straightened up. In his right hand he held his hunting knife, in the other the bullet he had just extracted from the wounded man's shoulder. His dark face, with its thick eyebrows and beard, was beaming. "If it hadn't been for you, I don't think I'd have dared risk it. It's the first time I've used a knife on a living man, instead of a dead animal." He went to the hearth, washed the knife and the bullet in hot water, and laid them down on the table in the corner.

Mary took her hands off the man's shoulders. The green ribbon in his hair had come off during his struggles under the knife; she laid it on the table beside the bullet. "Shouldn't we bandage him?" she said.

"I'll take care of it. Let the wound bleed a little longer. Not that he's got much blood he can afford to lose, but it's better that way." Daniel was tearing a piece of white linen into strips. "I'll only put a temporary bandage on it, because now we need McGill and her herbs."

"Will he live?"

"It's a wonder he's alive as it is. The bullet was deflected by a rib that took the force of it. He's lost a lot of blood these past hours. Besides which, he's wet to the skin, and cold to the bone. He's feverish, and the wound looks ugly. You'd better go and get McGill."

Mary put more wood on the fire, while Daniel bandaged the wound. He turned the unconscious man over on his good shouldeı and stuffed a blanket under the other, to keep the weight off it.

They went back to the table. Daniel picked up the bullet and held it against the light. He looked at it for a long time. Finally Mary said, "What is it about the bullet?"

"Just that it comes from no weapon I've ever come across."

"Not the kind used by our army?"

He put down the bullet, and started stuffing his pipe; then he put the pipe down on the table again, picked up his hunting knife, wiped it dry, slipped it back in his belt. "If you want me to fetch McGill, I'd better get going," he said. "Or would you rather go get her yourself?"

She had seen the look he gave the wounded man's uniform, but he had asked no questions, from the moment they picked him up together, till now. "I suppose you're wondering why I didn't get someone from the army?" she said.

"Why should you?"

"The man is one of our enemies. A Hessian."

"You think he comes from the other side?"

"Before I found him, I saw the horse he forded the river with."

"He could be a deserter. They say a lot of them are only waiting for a chance to escape."

"A deserter? Then why did he disguise himself in one of our army coats?" It was a question to which she didn't really want a good answer. "When you get to Redford," she said, "don't speak to anyone about this except McGill. I'll wait here."

"I'll make it as fast as I can."

"If he wakes, may I give him something to drink?"

"Better not, not before McGill has seen him." He took his fur jacket off the hook. "I'll be back soon."

When she heard him ride off, she had to resist the urge to run after him. The room was suddenly too close. She busied herself with the kettle on the hearth, then stepped outside to escape the man's heavy breathing—it seemed to fill the cabin. She went to the stable and hung the feed bag around her horse's neck. When she became too cold, she went back into the cabin.

She did not look at the corner where he lay in the bed; she tried to behave as if she were alone. A metal mirror hung beside the door. She stopped there and turned it a bit, to see herself better. What she saw was a pale young face with overlarge dark eyes. "There's a devil behind every mirror," her father had told her once. She was only five when Pastor Haverill had said it to her, to counteract vanity perhaps, but he had succeeded in frightening her; she had never forgotten it. She took her two round combs out of her pocket, combed her hair, and put it up. Her dark brown hair seemed more red-toned than usual, but that could be the effect of the metal mirror.

She went to the hearth, turned the wet uniform coat and trousers around to dry the other side, then went back to the table, and sat down. She hoped Jean Daniel had reached Redford by now. There lay his pipe, all ready to smoke but never lit; beside it lay the bullet and the green ribbon. She glanced over to the bed. The man's hair lay loosely spread out on the pillow; she was surprised by how thick it was, but even more by the fact that it retained its golden shimmer even here on the white linen. It probably shines in the dark, she thought. He was moving a little, a hand searching for something on the blanket; then he opened his eyes.

She moved a chair to the bedside. The color of his eyes was changeable. Green in the twilight of the forest, here in the sunlit room they looked mostly blue. His wide-open eyes wandered all over the room but seemed to see nothing, not even her. This unseeing look, and the fact that he was no longer in that uniform, made it easier for her to look at him unafraid. Even when his eyes met hers, she was not so much afraid as startled, as if by a warning signal, just as she had felt before when seeing her own eyes in the mirror.

His eyes rested peacefully on her face. Imperceptibly a change came over his bloodless features; the masklike rigidity softened, as if an idea were being born in his mind, or the search for a word, or even the beginning of a smile. He reached out his hand toward her.

She stiffened in her chair, carefully watching his every move. He braced himself with his hand as though to lift himself up in bed. He said something—strange sounds, words in a foreign language. She pushed her chair back and stood up. Without thinking, she took one of the hunting rifles off the rack and took it back with her to the bed. She was still sitting there, the gun across her knees, when she heard hoofbeats outside and Daniel entered the cabin with McGill at his side.

37

Sergeant Haughton belonged to a contingent of the Maryland militia. Before the war he had been a horse breeder in Frederick, and if there was one thing he detested it was the kind of man who rode a horse too hard. When he saw Lieutenant Blyth come storming into camp, flogging his mount along the narrow passage between the tent rows, he could barely contain his anger.

The campfires in front of the tents sent up bright, translucent flames in the icy air. The bundled-up men squatting around the fires jumped back as the horse thundered past on the frost-hard clay, froth flying from its muzzle, Blyth flailing at it with his crop and shouting, "Make way, make way!" Haughton watched grimly as he brought the horse to a skidding halt, and leaped from the saddle. The horse staggered and, riderless, continued on. Haughton caught the dragging reins, calmed the trembling horse, and turned it over to a sentry.

Lieutenant Blyth waited, visibly impatient, for Haughton's attention. "You're Sergeant Haughton, aren't you? You led that patrol—where's the prisoner?"

Haughton was unimpressed, at the moment, by the lieutenant's rank or his staff officer's insignia. "If I were that horse," he said, "I wouldn't let you get away with that. I'd break your neck the next time out, or I'd get you in the stalls. That horse is bloody from your spurs."

"Sergeant!" Blyth was hot and ripping open his coat.

"Yes, sir!" Haughton presented a sweeping salute that was obviously no apology, and followed the lieutenant into his tent.

Blyth tossed his heavy coat to an orderly. The uniform underneath was brand-new and fitted like a glove. "Where's the Hessian?" he asked.

"In the major's tent, sir. Being questioned."

"Still being questioned after all this time?" Blyth was at the end of his patience. "Why wasn't the general informed sooner?

You Maryland people think you can do it all yourselves, don't you? You don't think it's important to tell the general. Who's interrogating him?"

"Major Young, sir."

"And what have you found out?"

Haughton shrugged. "Nothing. The man won't talk. They can't get a word out of him."

"Two hours, and not a word? I'll make him talk. You were there—what happened? How did you capture him?"

"There's not much to tell, sir. We were patrolling the riverbank from the big pine to the ford. It was a quiet night. I took over the watch at five o'clock. They tried to cross the river just before dawn."

"Your messenger said something about horses."

"There was only one horse. They might have tried horses at first, though I don't think that's likely. It might have been one of the animals they left on the other side. Anyway, the men we saw came in a boat."

"How many?"

"I'm not sure. Some said three, some four, some five. I think there were four."

"You think? But you captured only one?"

Sergeant Haughton lowered his eyes. It was hard to explain now, so many hours later, what had happened at the river. He hadn't wanted it to happen. He felt guilty, even though he had thought he was doing the right thing at the time.

"I led that patrol," he said, "and I take the responsibility for it. When we spotted the boat, I ordered the men to let it come over. I wanted to let them land and capture them all together. There were four of them, five at most, and there were twenty of us; no risk in it at all. We were lying under cover, weapons loaded, and my orders were not to fire until I gave the signal. It just turned out differently, that's all."

"When it really counts, it always turns out differently with us." Something in the sergeant's look stopped Blyth.

"I can't say who started it," Haughton said quietly. "Afterward, it's hard to tell. It was the end of a long night on patrol, everybody's nerves were on edge. Probably something had been building up in those men since they started fighting the Hessians, something that had nothing to do with this particular situation, maybe. All it takes is one finger pressing a trigger, one man losing his nerve, and all hell breaks loose."

"Idiotic," Blyth mumbled.

"The boat sank right away. It must have been full of holes like a sieve."

"Have you found it?"

"Not so far. Two patrols are down there searching for the boat and for the bodies."

"How did you get the prisoner?"

"He drifted ashore. We had to drag him out. Once we had him, he offered no resistance."

The two men stood silent for a moment. From outside the tent came the muffled sounds of the camp—the monotonous tread of the sentries, the hoofbeats of a horse, the rattling of a wagon, a distant bugle call.

"Take me to him," Blyth said.

The staff tent was swarming with officers. A fresh supply of charcoal in a copper basin on a tripod produced more smoke than warmth, but no one paid any attention to that; everyone was looking at the prisoner.

The man sat on a low stool, his arms tied behind his back, a guard on either side of him. Blyth was struck by the contrast between the huddled Hessian and the two guards standing at erect attention; in a way, he was disappointed. The lieutenant had entered the tent without saluting; almost every officer inside ranked higher than himself, but he forced his way through them all, to where the prisoner sat. And for a second time he felt disappointed. He had been prepared to see a man in the hated Hessian uniform. Instead, here was this figure huddled in the dry clothes he'd been given—not Blyth's idea of a Hessian soldier at all. But then he saw the bundle on the wooden crate nearby—the green coat, the flaming red lapels and collar: the colors of the Hessian riflemen that had haunted him ever since his first encounter with them at

Flatbush. He restrained an urge to reach out and touch the bundle. . . .

He had the sudden feeling he was being observed by the prisoner; not only observed but *seen,* all the way into his mind and heart. The man had a thin, bony face, with deep rings under his eyes from lack of sleep. His hair was brown; his age would have been hard to guess. His face offered neither acceptance nor resistance; his expression was withdrawn, revealing nothing. Blyth could understand why they had gotten nothing out of the man, but that was precisely what spurred him on to try.

He turned to the nearest officer. "Sergeant Haughton tells me he won't talk. Any papers on him?"

"Nothing. But that was to be expected. By his uniform he belongs to the Hessian rifle regiment garrisoned in Trenton since the fourteenth of December."

"Rall's riflemen." He had said it so loudly everyone in the tent heard him. The quiet conversation near the entrance stopped. Everybody was looking at him. These men were older than he was, they all outranked him, but he could read the anxiety in their faces, and he felt superior to them all; he hated Rall more than anyone else here, and he knew it. He addressed himself to the prisoner.

"Your silence won't do you any good," he began. "We'll make you talk, one way or another. How many of you were there? Only the four in the boat? Or were there others? What was your mission, what were you supposed to find out?" He spoke in a low voice, intently, like a hypnotist weaving a spell. He discounted the idea that the man might not understand English. He showed no impatience; he was sure he would get an answer.

Major Young did not try to interfere. Before he joined the Continental Army, Young had been a judge in Frederick, Maryland; in the course of his professional life he had seen hopeless cases resolved by a third person—but he didn't believe it would happen here. "It's no use, Lieutenant," he said after a while. "You might as well be talking to a stone."

Blyth turned to him. "Send for an interpreter."

Major Young shook his head. "We're wasting our time. The

man understands every word. Surely you don't think they'd send a spy across the Delaware who couldn't understand English? They made a good choice, for their side. He'll never talk."

Blyth turned to the prisoner again, reluctant to give up. "Listen," he said. "I promise to set you free if you talk. We'll even give you a piece of land. The war's over for you anyway. What's happening in Trenton? What's Rall planning to do?" Had the prisoner moved just then? He looked as though a shiver had gone through his body. "Is Rall planning to cross the Delaware? Before the end of the year? Was that why he sent you over here to reconnoiter?" He kept his eyes on the prisoner's face. Major Young was right, the man understood every word. You could see that, but you couldn't see what he was thinking. "You do know what happens to a spy, don't you?" he said. He paused to let that sink in, but he hadn't expected the effect it had—the prisoner's rigid expression softened; he seemed to relax. This Hessian reacted to the threat of death not with fear but with relief! Blyth clenched his fists. He stepped back from the prisoner and brusquely turned to the semicircle of officers. "What are we waiting for? If he won't talk, let's string him up to the nearest tree."

Major Young came over and motioned to the two guards to take the prisoner away. He waited till they had taken the man out of the tent, then turned to Blyth.

"Lieutenant, I haven't heard a word you said. Understand?"

Blyth flushed. "The man's a spy. He was caught in the act. You know as well as I do, Major, what they did to our prisoners."

"We'll hold a trial," Young said coolly, "in accordance with the law. And then we'll see what verdict we arrive at."

Blyth turned on his heel and walked out. About two hundred yards ahead, receding along the tent row, he saw the two guards and, between them, the prisoner.

Soerman was barely aware of the two soldiers beside him, barely aware that he was walking, breathing, doing things that proved he was alive. Life was over, as far as he was concerned; it had died in him several hours ago, back on the river, when the others had gone down with the boat. Whatever was still keeping him moving, breathing, would soon be dead, too. He was calmer now; of all the words directed at him since they'd dragged him from the water, only the last had registered: "String him up to the nearest tree."

From the first moment he had felt solid ground underfoot again, and realized he was still alive, that he was the only one from the boat still alive, he had had only one desire—to die. It had all happened too fast; in the river he had struggled, had still fought for life, because there was some hope the others might be still alive. And then, afterward, it was too late; he had no weapon, not even a knife. For a while it seemed the men who dragged him out of the water were going to beat him to death, but someone had intervened. Since then he hadn't been alone, unguarded, for a minute.

But that no longer mattered. He walked on, step by step, between his guards, head down. The only question in his mind was —Robert. Could Robert have gotten across the river? Could he be at Redford by now? But even if he was still alive, it made no difference. He would rather be dead than have to face Robert.

The guards stopped. He felt someone put a hand on his arm. All his life he had disliked people touching him; now he welcomed it. A few steps more, then it would be over.

He looked up. He was surrounded by tents, men in uniform, eyes looking at him; there was no tree. Someone pushed him inside a tent. There was a straw-filled sack on the ground, a blanket, nothing else. One of the guards pointed to the sack. He gingerly laid himself down on it. The guard took the leather laces out of his boots, the ribbon that tied his hair in back, the bandanna from the pocket of the coat they had given him. Then he cut the rope that tied his wrists together. The two guards took one last look around, and then left him alone in the tent.

Soerman sat on the straw, his arms around his knees, staring at the narrow slit between the bottom of the tent and the ground. He watched the sentries' boots passing back and forth, and resigned himself to waiting.

38

The place that people around Redford called the tin mine lay in a narrow valley upriver from the estate. Two tunnels had been dug in the earth there, through a layer of dark humus and a layer of gravelly clay. The way the wooden supports in the tunnels had been cut and joined suggested that the place went back to Indian times. At some time in the past the tunnels had partially caved in —some said the Indians had done it to make it useless to whites. Skelnik had dumped there all the rocks and earth collected in clearing the fields and excavating for the buildings at Redford, and over the years the tunnels had largely been filled up.

According to one of the many rumors about Skelnik in his early years at Redford, it wasn't tin in the "mine" but gold and silver; his use of the hollow as a dumping ground was considered a shrewd maneuver to cover his buried treasure. One man, lured by the rumors, had in fact, fallen to his death there one night. While that accident hadn't actually led people to say the place was haunted, they nevertheless tended to give it a wide berth. It was an ideal place, Skelnik had decided, for making gunpowder for the army out of the sulphur and saltpeter he managed, with increasing difficulty, to obtain in Philadelphia. He had restored one of the old tunnel openings, put in new supports, and now had a combined laboratory, workshop, and storage gallery.

A wagon stood now in front of the tunnel opening. Jonathan Whitcombe, the Redford blacksmith, came out of the darkness of the tunnel, carrying a powder keg on his shoulders.

Skelnik, who had spent the morning here working with his men, was supervising the loading operation. "That'll do for this trip," he said. "Better get the next wagon in place and start loading it. What do you think, Whitcombe, how many more loads will we need?"

The blacksmith carefully lifted the powder keg off his shoulders and set it gently inside the wagon. While he slipped wooden wedges under both sides of the keg, he examined the load. "If I take it slow, I could get three more kegs in. Then one more load would do the job."

"I'd rather not risk breaking an axle."

"Have you ever known me to break an axle?"

"No, and I don't want to be around if you do. Easy does it. This powder is supposed to blow up somewhere else." Skelnik waited while Whitcombe hitched the horses to the wagon. "And this time, insist they do their own unloading."

"You can depend on that. We don't plan to do all the work again while the soldiers stand around grinning."

Skelnik sent for his own horse and mounted up. "Remember now, take it easy. And don't forget to close up the shaft when you get the last load out."

He rode off in the direction of the Delaware, and when he reached the open country along the river, he let the horse settle into an easy gallop. The cold was sharp against his face and in his nose. The land here was flat and wide, not much higher than the river; the water seemed about to flood the banks and reclaim the old river bottom.

Halfway back to Redford, he saw a rider coming toward him. Jan Kellog was recognizable at a considerable distance because of the way he sat on his horse; he was a man who felt more at ease on horseback than on foot. Skelnik was proud of men like Kellog and Jonathan Whitcombe, proud of knowing their character, their virtues, their flaws, proud that these men, who had come to Redford by chance, chose to stay and work with him; men who did not give up their independence just because he employed them.

Kellog circled around Skelnik and then came up alongside him. They slowed to a trot.

"Are you exercising the horse or yourself?" Skelnik asked.

"I thought you might need some help at the tin mine. You rode off awful early this morning. I'll never manage to get up before you do, not in a hundred years."

"Anything special going on at Redford?"

"The boots have come in from Doylestown. A hundred pair."

"Have you looked them over?"

"Every pair of them. I warned you not to pay for everything in advance. It always means trouble. I deducted for the ten missing pairs, and the twenty that showed poor workmanship in the last batch. He's going to complain to you about me; just so you know about it. How are things at the tin mine?"

"Two more loads, one of them's all complete now. They'll make it today. What else is going on at Redford?"

Kellog pushed out his underlip. "Something was going on at the river this morning. They say they caught a spy. I didn't pay much attention. Lots of shooting is all I heard myself. You'll find a lot of officers palavering in your house. They sent me to get you. Maybe you can use the chance to convince them to stop ruining the forest. Their men must have chopped down at least twenty more cords of wood. I wouldn't mind if they chopped down the right trees—we've got lots of birches and alders that need cutting. But they just take whatever they find, including new growth. You ought to go out there and see for yourself sometime."

They rode into the yard at Redford and separated with a nod. The first thing Skelnik saw were the horses, dozens of them, ranked side by side at the main entrance. In the vestibule of the big house, caps and hats, with the blue-and-white bands of the militia, were piled on benches and tables. He could hear chairs being pushed back, footsteps; the doors opened, and officers came pouring out into the vestibule.

He stayed in the background, watching. The house quickly emptied. He waited until the last man had ridden off and the front door was closed. He was on his way to his study when the library door opened once more, and Lieutenant Blyth came out. He came toward Skelnik with the same solemn expression the others had worn. "May I speak with you?" he said, with uncharacteristic brevity.

Skelnik preceded him into the study. When he had closed the door behind them, Blyth said, "We've come to a decision."

"What decision?"

"It's to be victory or defeat, life or death."

So much pathos would ordinarily have elicited some ironic response from Skelnik, but the young man was too earnest for that. So he waited to hear the rest.

"I'd almost given up on it," Blyth said, pacing tensely from the door to the window and back again. "There's nothing I can tell you about the condition of the army, inside and out, that you don't know. I don't think any general has ever had an army with so little faith in itself. A lot of them believed the war was already lost. They were ready to go home. I could see us officers left here on our own, an army without soldiers."

Skelnik waited, standing beside the fireplace, knowing there was more to come.

"It's changed now," Blyth continued. "By a word, a simple decision. We're going to attack. We're going to stop running. Our army needs a victory, and it's going to have one before the year is out."

"How? When?"

"The date is not set yet. We'll announce it at the last minute. We have to get ready first. We may choose Christmas; it's a good day for a surprise attack."

"You're going to cross the river by boat?"

"Same way we came. It turned cold today. If it keeps on like this, if we get sub-zero weather, it will take till about the twenty-seventh of December for the river to freeze over. We've got to attack before that date. We have the boats; *he* has to wait for the ice to be thick enough to cross."

"You're talking about the Hessian commandant? You think Rall means to cross the river?"

"We think so. There are all sorts of signs that he can't wait to march on Philadelphia. The Hessians tried to send four spies across this morning. Three of them got away—the men say they drowned, but I won't believe it until I've seen their bodies. We caught the fourth. He won't talk, but the situation's clear enough. Anyway, it helped us to make up our minds. Suddenly even the most undecided were in favor of taking action. The general felt you had a right to be among the first to know. I've got to go now. There's a lot to be done."

After Blyth had gone, Skelnik sat alone in his study—he couldn't have said how long; he usually never needed a clock, but he had lost his sense of time. Was it still morning? Was lunch over already? The fire in the fireplace couldn't have been lit too long ago; the room was easy to heat, but it was still cold. The windows were still misted over. Tea things stood on a tray on the table near the fireplace—left over from the evening before? He emptied an ashtray into the fire. On his desk lay a list of the provisions supplied to the army; he noticed that the daily rations of the men had almost doubled since their first week on Redford, but he couldn't concentrate enough to study the figures. He rang for the maid. "Clear that tea tray away. And bring me some breakfast, and something for Miss Mary, too."

The maid looked at him in surprise. It was unusual for Skelnik not to know everything that was going on in the house. "Miss Mary rode away early this morning. McGill's gone, too, and she has the key to the pantry. It's almost noon, you know."

"Never mind all that. Just bring me some breakfast." Skelnik regretted his rudeness as soon as the girl had gone; it wasn't like him. He went to the window just as McGill and Mary rode into the yard. He waited for her footsteps in the hall, again conscious of how hungry he was. He thought of hot brown tea in white cups, fresh cream, bread straight from the oven, and it made him feel better. Breakfast with Mary would make everything right again.

He turned when he heard footsteps coming to the door, but it was the maid with his breakfast. "Where's Miss Mary?" he asked.

"She went straight to her room, sir."

When the maid had gone, he poured himself a cup of tea, but suddenly he didn't want it anymore. He left the study and went through the house to the wing where McGill's room was. He rapped abruptly on the door, opened it, and saw McGill still in her riding clothes.

"What's the matter with everybody in this house?" he said. "My study's still cold and hasn't been cleaned. Mary's avoiding me. What's going on?"

"Come in," McGill said. "Sit down." She closed the door behind him.

Her room was painted white and had high ceilings like the rest of the rooms in the house, but the handwoven rugs on the walls and the fur pelts on the floor always made it seem darker, and smaller, to him. He took a chair across from her.

She calmly ignored his questions. "I was eleven the first time I saw you," she said. "I remember it vividly. Your hair was down to your shoulders then. It was the first thing I noticed about you, your golden hair. I can't remember much else. Tell me—was there a woman with you?"

"No, I was alone. What are you getting at?"

Her dark eyes scanned his face for a long moment. "Do you know you have a son?"

Startled, he looked at her, unable, for a moment, to speak. "What do you mean?"

"I saw a man today who looks exactly the way I remember you from all those years ago. The same hair, the same face."

"What man? McGill, will you please explain what this is all about?"

"He's a young man, and he looks exactly like you. You'll find him in Jean Daniel's cabin in the woods. He was one of the group who crossed the river last night, a Hessian."

A Hessian—suddenly Skelnik's mind leaped back a quarter of a century into the past, to the princedom of Hessia, the Heron Island, all those unanswered letters, the woman he had tried so hard and so futilely to shut out of his mind, the woman who, the last time he'd seen her, had been carrying his unborn child. If it had been a boy . . . he would be twenty-four years old now. He could feel the beating of his heart, feel the tremors in his stomach. He found it hard to ask McGill the question ringing in his mind.

"Did he say he was my son?"

"I couldn't ask him. He's been wounded, and he was unconscious."

Skelnik felt a sinking inside, a long dormant hope, newly revived, slowly dying again.

"He was wounded in the shoulder," McGill was saying, "and he lost a lot of blood. Jean Daniel cut the bullet out, and I bandaged the wound. He had a fever, but it was going away when I left. He's going to be all right."

Cautiously, not wanting to betray what might still yet be hope, he asked, "How did he come to be in Daniel's cabin?"

"Mary found him."

"Mary found him? Where?"

"In the thickets where the herons nest. She found him just in time; he was unconscious, and he had lost a lost of blood. And it's strange—Daniel says he wasn't shot by our side. The wound wasn't made by the kind of weapons our army uses."

The hope within him was faint, but refused to die. He had to struggle against a rising anger at McGill for bringing it to life, with no real proof to confirm it.

"Why are you so sure he's my son? Just because he looks like me? That proves nothing."

"I can't explain. But I knew he would come. I saw him in a vision the night before they brought John Compson's body. I saw John Compson dead that night, and I saw someone else, too, with your hair and your face. My premonition about John Compson came true the very next day. And now there's this young man who looks like you." She sensed his doubts, his hesitation. "Why don't you ride to the cabin and see for yourself?"

"I saw Mary riding back with you. Why didn't she come to tell me this? Why is she avoiding me?"

"Try to understand her. She is convinced as I am that the man is your son. I don't think she had admitted to herself how great the likeness was until I pointed it out to her—but she found a man in a Hessian uniform, a man on the side that killed her father and John, and I think she might have left him to die in that thicket if it hadn't been for his likeness to you. Mary has had you to herself all these years. If the man is your son, and he is, she'll have to share you with someone else now. Someone who has a greater right to your attention than she does."

He wasn't sure what to think when he left McGill's room. He made his way back to his study and sat down at the desk. He took from his pocket the key to that suite of rooms he had kept unoccupied for so many years. He weighed the key in his hand. Impulsively, he left the study again and went along the hall toward those rooms.

The door was made of carved lindenwood, originally made for the captain's cabin of a dismantled Italian merchant ship, the fixtures and inventory of which had been auctioned off in Philadelphia. Though the carving was simple and austere enough, it seemed extravagant compared to the plain waxed oak doors of Redford. It was an anomaly in this house, as he had often thought in passing it, and as he thought again standing in front of it now.

He put the key in the lock and turned it, with difficulty. The lifeless air of unused rooms met him and for a moment he almost turned back. Tiny beams of light from the closed shutters fell through the semidarkness. He strode across the room, pushed aside the curtains, and opened the windows. Quickly he unfastened the shutters and swung them open, so hard they slammed against the side of the house.

The sunlight was blinding. He went into the other two rooms and there, too, threw open the curtains, the windows, the shutters, letting in light and air. Outside, a flower garden stretched along the windows; the fountain was covered over for the winter; autumn leaves lay on the stone bench.

Was it the blinding sun? Suddenly the world seemed to fall away behind a red veil. He turned away from the window, reaching for support. His legs felt leaden; his head whirled. He felt an intense pain around his heart, an iron vise closing tighter and tighter. Involuntarily, his hand gripped his chest over the heart, as if it could keep the vise from closing.

When the pain receded, and with it the dull fear, he found himself on the sofa. He looked around the room; he couldn't remember getting from the window to the sofa. He wiped his face with his hand; clinging to it was the smell of the essence McGill used on the curtains to discourage moths. As he got to his feet, dust rost from the pale red velvet of the sofa.

He was cold, but he made no move to close the windows. Instead he made sure the hooks were fastened to keep them open. There was a fine network of cracks in the white of the window casing; here and there the paint had begun to crumble away. He caught his hand in the lace curtain; the brittle fabric was as fragile as a spider web. The mirror above the fireplace gave only a blurred gray reflection.

The pain had gone, and now the constriction in the chest gradually receded, too. In its place came a feeling of great weariness; he sank down into the chair in front of the secretary. The gilded lid of the inkstand had turned brown from disuse. The ink had dried solid, the quill pens had turned yellow. He opened the drawer. It was full of browning paper, envelopes, pads that a woman might use to note down her daily tasks, a bound notebook for recipes. He remembered the hours he had spent writing those letters that never brought an answer.

More than twenty years had gone by since then. What were these rooms for, why had he kept them this way? He found it difficult to bring back the past, to remember the original reason. Could he have expected, after all those unanswered letters, that long silence without a sign from her, that she would simply turn up one day, unpack her things, make herself at home while he looked on? Something of that kind must have been his dream. But who could he have expected after twenty years—would he have even known the woman who might have appeared after so long a time? And would she have known the man she found? Twenty-five years. What had he been clinging to? What had he wanted to preserve—the memory of her? It was very possible that he had another, less noble reason: in these rooms he had kept his youth locked away, safe from everything that time was bound to do to the young man he had been.

And now there was this other young man, who looked like him, in Daniel's cabin. He remembered his words to Mary—a man's future is his sons. He felt the pull toward the cabin in the woods, but he was afraid to go; the possibility of disappointment was too great. To stand and look at that youthful face, that younger version of himself, and learn that it was not, after all, his son—he would not be able to bear that.

Then he remembered what Blyth had said about the prisoner—that the man had been in the party that had crossed the river the night before. That man would know; there was no danger in questioning him; it would be only a casual question, asked by a disinterested observer curious to know the name of that young man in the woods.

He got up and replaced the chair where it had stood for twenty-five years. Only when he was halfway down the hall did he realize that he had forgotten and left the key in the door. But he did not go back.

39

While his wounded guest lay asleep, his breathing slow and regular, Jean Daniel had cleaned and polished his favorite musket and stood at the window now, turning it in the sunlight, admiring his work. When he turned back from the window, the man was awake and watching him. McGill had said when she left that the fever would go down quickly, and apparently she knew, as always, what she was talking about. The man's clear eyes did not look like those of a person who had been so close to death only hours before. To Daniel, he was neither friend nor foe, he was simply someone who had needed help. Daniel did not speak to him, but only because he didn't expect to be understood.

The man in bed was leaning on his good elbow, looking at him with an expression that might at any moment become a smile. "What sort of thing do you hunt around here?" he said.

He spoke English. It was better English than his own, Daniel thought, almost accentless. But, judging by his voice, he was still very weak. The question took Daniel by surprise; it was the last question he would have expected.

"There's not much in the way of hunting right now," he said. "The troops are driving all the game away. But in normal times, the hunting's first-rate, for every kind of game."

"I've been watching you. That's a fine musket you've got there. I can tell you know your way around guns."

Daniel pushed a chair over to the bed. "You speak the language very well," he said, "but you shouldn't overdo it. A few hours ago, when we found you, you were nearer dead than alive."

"Was it you who found me?"

"Miss Mary found you. I brought you here."

The man's eyes wandered around the room, as if to touch and

weigh everything he saw; he seemed to be searching for something that would tell him where he was. "Miss Mary," he said. "Long brown hair?—The last thing I remember clearly is when my horse lost its footing in the river." A flicker of uneasiness passed across his face. "Where am I?—Which side of the river, I mean? Who are you?"

"I'm Daniel, this is my cabin. You don't have to worry. Nobody comes here much."

"Is this the other side of the Delaware?"

"If you mean the side where the Continental Army is, the answer's yes."

The man's head fell back on his pillow, more in relief than exhaustion.

"To judge by your uniform, you're a Hessian," Daniel said. "You're with the troops in Trenton?"

Robert looked down at himself as though expecting to see his uniform, but it had been removed. He felt as he had in the woods, when he had sensed the blood draining out of him; only now it was as though his energy were flowing out of him, abandoning him. He could barely keep his eyes open, could barely move his lips. "Redford," he said, "how far?"

"You need to rest."

"Send someone . . . to Redford."

Daniel got up. He straightened the pillow, smoothed the cover over his patient. "They already know about it at Redford," he said. "That's where the women came from."

"The girl?"

"Both. McGill and Skelnik's daughter."

The voice seemed to Robert to come from far away. Even the man's figure seemed to be shadowy, far away. "His daughter?" he said. Then the darkness enveloped him.

The fire had gone down, the room was getting cold. Daniel got rid of the ashes, put on more wood. There was a jar with soup stock on the hearth. He drank a little of it from the ladle. Then he got out a roasting pan, a cutting board, some spices. He had some wild ducks, shot this morning, but they would have to hang and age awhile. But five days ago he had brought home some woodcocks he intended to cook in the manner of the Camargue, with garlic, thyme, bay leaves, a white-wine sauce, and bread. He took his woolen jacket off the hook, and went out to the stable where the woodcocks were hanging. He brought them around to the bench at his cabin door, where he sat down and started to pluck them. He left the door slightly open so that he could hear the man inside, in case he wanted anything.

He had almost finished plucking the last bird when he heard a horse coming up behind the cabin, from the direction of Redford. For a moment there was silence, while the rider dismounted. Then steps came from the direction of the stable. Daniel put down his last woodcock with the rest on the bench beside him and watched Skelnik come around the corner of the cabin.

Skelnik took off his hat. He wore neither gloves nor coat.

"Well, why are you looking at me like that?" Skelnik said. "I know I don't come out here very often."

"First time since I've been here."

Skelnik looked toward the half-opened door of the cabin. It was unfastened, but it didn't move; there was no wind here in the clearing. He swept a few feathers off the bench and sat down next to Daniel. The sun stood almost at its zenith. The planks of the bench, the wooden wall of the house, reflected its warmth.

"How is he?" Skelnik said.

"Sleeping. I talked with him a bit, and it tired him out. But he's over the worst of it now."

"Does he really look so much like me?"

Jean Daniel studied Skelnik's face. Then he nodded.

Skelnik kept his eyes up on the tips of the great firs, watching a buzzard soaring above them. He was still trying to assimilate everything he had learned at the army camp. It had been a totally unexpected shock to see Soerman. Torn between his desire to learn the truth and his fear of disappointment, he had gone to the camp in a state of uneasy anticipation; but to find Soerman there was the kind of surprise for which he had been completely unprepared. It had somehow left him vulnerable to feelings he had thought himself protected against. Nor had he expected the story Soerman told him. He had gone after news of a son, and had come away with news of a wife.

After twenty-five years, it was difficult to grasp. He found it hard to picture her, hard to imagine the twenty-five years of her life that he knew nothing about, hard to fathom that after all that time she had crossed an ocean to find him, that she had been so close, that only last night she had been just across the Delaware. It was unreal to him but he knew that soon it would become real; he could tell by his confusion inside that it would strike him soon, when he least expected it, and he knew it would be painful. He had already buried her once in his mind; now she had come to life again, and he would have to go through it all once more—only this time her death was real.

He stood up and turned toward the door of the cabin. The sun was glistening in the grass, casting deep, cool shadows. "This place is a paradise," he said, "for a man who likes the quiet."

Daniel plucked a fluffy feather from his trouser leg and watched it float to the ground. "Don't you like the quiet?"

"I'm not sure."

It was only five steps from the cabin door to the bed, but for Skelnik they were five difficult steps to take. The stranger, the young man, his son—how was he to fit him into his thinking, his life? Hat in hand, he stood at the bedside, and the fact that the man in bed had his eyes closed did not help. It seemed as inappropriate to sit down as to continue helplessly standing there.

Finally he laid his hat on a chair and sat down on the edge of the bed. *Your son*—McGill had said it first, then Soerman, but it was still only a word, no matter how many times he heard it. Your son? Robert? This was a stranger lying here—until the eyes opened.

Skelnik quickly held out his hand, as if afraid his presence would come as a shock. "My son," he said. It suddenly seemed the most natural thing in the world to say. "My son."

Robert rose up on an elbow. "Then it's true," he said. "It really has come true." He sank back down on the pillow, gazing up at his father. It was very quiet in the room. From a window, a shaft of sun slanted across the floor. "This isn't the way I wanted it to happen," he said. "Everything went like I planned till we got to the Delaware. But then it had to go wrong right at the last minute."

Skelnik didn't take his eyes away from his son's face, but he could find nothing to say. His right hand lay on the blanket; with the left he was opening the buttons of his coat.

"I used to imagine riding up to your door," Robert said. "I had a lot of time to picture everything in my mind. I've lived this moment a hundred times since I found out you were alive. I needed time to assimilate the idea; I guess it was a good thing it took me so long to get here." He smoothed his hair back from his forehead; the skin at the hairline was lighter than the rest of his face. "It must be even harder for you. Yesterday you didn't even know I existed. That's what Mother was so afraid of, last night, on the other side of the river. 'You can't turn time back like a clock,' she said; I can still hear her say it."

Skelnik lowered his head; he couldn't bring himself to say anything. He was grateful when Jean Daniel came in and busied himself at the hearth. He heard the rattling of the grate, the clanking of pots and pans, the sputtering of grease over the fire. Every sound reassured him that this was real; the casual way Daniel went about his business brought his son and himself into the natural day-to-day world of Redford. As quietly as he had come, Daniel left them alone again.

"I was watching him clean his gun," Robert said. "He must be a good hunter."

Skelnik nodded. He would have to speak soon.

"Did she tell you how afraid she was of seeing you again?" Robert said. "I'd never seen her like that before—she was always so competent, so self-assured. That's the way she must have been when she heard you'd gone down on the *Thetis*. But she's probably told you all about it by now."

"There's something I have to tell you," Skelnik said. "I took the long way around to get here, because I needed time too—now I'm not sure I've had enough time." He looked at Robert, examined that face that was so much like his own. McGill was right; he was looking at himself twenty-four years ago. "I could have been here in fifteen minutes. I took an hour. I had to try to adjust myself to everything that's happened, and now I think it'll probably be even harder for you."

"What do you mean?"

"When I saw you just now, I thought, my God, how young he is. You see, you forget a great deal when you get older. You cease to live with all your heart—you lose by it, but you don't get hurt so much anymore either. When I look at you and remember how I was at your age, I know how much this is going to hurt you."

Robert rose up in the bed. "What's happened? Tell me what's happened."

"When you've lived here a while, you'll understand what the Delaware means to us. Right now it's our border, our protection, and for the Continental Army it means security after many long, terrible months of defeat. When they saw that boat coming across the river in the dark they had no way of knowing what it was."

Robert sank back against the pillow, staring at the ceiling. His face was white, as if all the blood had left it.

"It was only one boat," Skelnik went on, "but they were afraid, on the defensive, and they had guns. . . ." He couldn't look at that bloodless face any longer. "They thought it was a boatload of spies. Coming from the other side, it had to be the enemy, Hessians, who are greatly feared. That was justification enough. I must admit, when I first heard about it this morning, I didn't give it much thought. It was only when McGill told me about you that I had an inkling of the truth."

"What about Mother? What's happened to her? I trusted him to keep her safe!"

"Soerman's the only one who survived. They captured him and took him to camp for questioning. They couldn't get a word out of him. When I went to him, before I rode out here—" he stopped to find the right words for this—"he had just twisted his shirt into a rope to try to hang himself."

Robert was still staring at the ceiling. "She never believed she would make it," he said, his voice barely audible. "She came all this way, she suffered through the whole experience . . . but somehow she knew it would all be for nothing. She tried to tell me last night, and I just laughed." Memories rose in his mind, memories he thought he'd put behind him when he'd boarded ship at Bremerlehe—of the wheelwright's place and finding Soerman in that coach, the long shadow of the hanged officer in Altenbauna, that last night in the cell before the execution. He wondered why these were the memories that came to mind. Were they concealing something else, an explanation? What he needed was not an explanation but a target for his despair, for the anger that was slowly growing within his pain. "We were friends," he said, "Soerman and I. The only man I ever considered my friend. I trusted him."

"You shouldn't judge him too quickly," Skelnik said. "It wasn't his fault. And what has happened to him is the worst thing that can happen to a man. Soerman was never an easy man to understand. Most men's lives move in orbit, like the moon; they come up and they go down and around—Soerman lived like a meteor; his life was a continuous falling. If he took hold somewhere he only tore himself away again. He left his home. He left me. There was nothing forcing him to leave. He wanted not just one life, but many. From now on he'll have only one life: that of a man who saved only himself, out of four people. There's nothing worse to have to live with."

"Where is he now?"

"At Redford. They let me take him from the camp. I talked him out of suicide. What he's most afraid of is you—having to face you. I can see him, waiting, dreading it. He'll tell you his story. Don't make it too hard for him."

They could hear the pail being wound up out of the well outside. Daniel came inside, did something at the stove, and left again. The smell of roast meat spread through the cabin.

Robert's head had sunk deep into the pillows. He was looking at the ceiling with no expression in his eyes. "Have they found her?"

"Not so far."

There was another long pause.

"McGill, is that your daughter?"

"I have no daughter, only a son, and only since this morning."

"This man here, Daniel, spoke of your daughter. I forget the name. Long brown hair?"

"You mean Mary."

"That's right, that was her name, Mary."

"The people at Redford call her my daughter. It just simplifies things. Mary's an orphan, the daughter of Boston's most militant preacher; he was killed in a street battle with English troops. Mary was thirteen when it happened; I was named her guardian and brought her to Redford. So you see, this war didn't begin just yesterday. It's been fermenting on this continent for the past forty years. It's another reason why our men are so full of hate, so blind with hate. They were born with it."

"Daniel said it was the girl who found me. In a thicket, near the river." Robert looked at his father. "Do you have herons there?"

"They have a few nesting places, nothing much; it's not easy to keep them here. That thicket's the only place we have any of them."

"Without them I don't think I'd have ever reached the woods. I heard them before I saw them—I know the sound of their wings. I don't know how long I'd been lying on the riverbank. I had given up. And then I heard those wings and saw those two herons diving toward the thicket. I thought I was hallucinating, and I had to make sure. . . ."

"All this talking is too much of a strain," Skelnik said.

Daniel had come back into the cabin. He took three plates from a shelf and put them on the table, with a loaf of bread and a jug of wine. When he had finished setting the table, he removed the roasting pan from the hearth. The aroma of thyme and bay leaf went through the room.

"The birds are done," Daniel said. "If you want to stay," he said to Skelnik, "you're cordially invited."

40

Unexpectedly, winter had come, announced by freezing temperatures and an icy north wind. Frost covered the trees and bushes.

The north wind continued to blow, and ice began to form on the Delaware, beginning at the banks and expanding outward. Ice floes drifted in midstream. On the third day the temperatures rose by fifteen degrees to just below freezing and, toward noon, the snow began to fall. It came not in big soft flakes, but in driving, relentless sheets, and it continued for forty-four hours without a break.

Redford was buried in snow. At the encampment the men were busy from dawn to dusk shoveling snow just to keep the tents accessible. The guard patrols were finding it harder to reach the Delaware, but a single rider braved it every day despite the high snowdrifts and the wind, that, whistling over the river, seemed to have swept the heavy gray snow clouds from the sky.

It was eight miles by road from Redford to the Morris farm, which lay across the river from Trenton. But if you followed the windings of the Delaware, as this rider was doing, it was a good twelve miles. Freder Soerman had ridden that distance twice a day ever since Robert had been brought from the cabin in the woods to Redford. The ride had become a habit, and he set out again today, even though it was Christmas Eve. In his dark green coat with the fur collar, he had become a familiar figure to the river patrols. By now they knew when to expect him, and they took care not to cross his path. If they accidentally encountered him, they let him pass without a word; his story had made the rounds. He rode a chestnut Yorkshire out of Skelnik's stables and wore clothes from Skelnik's closet, but they hadn't forgotten finding him in that hated uniform, and when they saw him coming the word went around: "the Hessian."

Days of searching had brought no sign of the three who had gone down with the boat, and the likelihood of ever finding their bodies was fast diminishing, especially since the snow had covered the riverbank and the slopes alongside.

The first time Soerman had ridden to the Morris farm there had been no snow. He had left no stone unturned, no bush unexamined along the banks. He had spent almost the entire day at the river, without finding the slightest trace of anything. But the next day he had resumed his search, from the point at which Sergeant Haughton's patrol had fired on the boat all the way to the hedgerow of the Morris place. From that point he had a good view across the river to Trenton; he dismounted every time and gazed from the slight rise of ground over to the town, which was buried in snow so that it resembled a village or one of those sprawling hamlets so familiar from his Swedish home country. He had seen no troop movement; only once a platoon drilling in the snow, tiny figures coming to relieve the watch, and now and then a single rider, a special courier probably. The only place where there was constant activity was the solitary house near the riverbank. Soerman was particularly interested in the doctor's house. There were always horses there, sometimes droves of them, covered with blankets. Couriers were constantly coming and going. Even today, when most people would be indoors preparing for the holiday, there was a lot of activity around the house.

The wind was cutting at Soerman's face, making his eyes water, but he barely noticed. He stood there, on his favorite lookout, for a quarter of an hour, his hands buried in his pockets, staring against wind and sun across the river.

At last he started back, following the trail the horse had made on the way out. A half dozen times he stopped and dismounted, drawn by a faint bulge under the snow, branches broken from a bush, a root exposed by the wind. The slightest sign brought him out of the saddle to brush away the snow with his bare hands, but he found nothing.

He had left right after breakfast; now as he turned into the cedar drive leading to Redford, the noon meal was long over. He had been letting the horse set its own pace, the reins looped over the saddle horn. As he came in sight of the house, he picked up the reins and straightened up in the saddle, prepared to run a gauntlet of many curious eyes.

The courtyard in front of the house had been shoveled clean, but the wind had blown a thin powdery layer across it again. Mary stood on the porch, wearing a deep pink taffeta dress with vertical silver stripes that made her look especially tall and slim. As Soerman approached, she turned her back to him and handed some mistletoe to a man on a ladder, who fastened it to the top of the porch. Soerman wondered at her lack of curiosity—either she hadn't heard his horse approaching, or she had already seen who it was and was deliberately keeping her back to him. It wouldn't be the first time; he attributed it to his presence that her place at mealtime was always empty. Since Robert was well enough to be up and about, he and Soerman were included at the table, but Mary had found one pretext after another for staying away. It was the same with almost everyone at Redford, Soerman thought—like the river patrols, they avoided him. He touched spurs to his horse, anxious to get to the stables.

It was warm in the stables; after unsaddling the horse, he stepped outside, his jacket open. The stableyard was empty. Children had put up a snowman beside the well; there was a blue-and-white striped militia cap on its head. Clouds of steam billowed out of the open window of the laundry room. But the sound that had struck his ear was not the kind made by a washboard. He listened and, when he heard it again, he went in the direction it was coming from and found Robert in the yard of the feed storage barn, practicing with a bow and arrows. A narrow path had been shoveled through the snow to the barn; to one side there was a barrier of snow almost shoulder high. Robert stood in a spot protected against the wind, bareheaded, without gloves, his lamb's-wool jacket open at the throat, the bow in his hand. The target, a straw mat with a black circle painted in the center, hung on the barn door, about thirty yards away.

Robert was just fitting his last arrow to the bow; he tossed the hair out of his eyes, aimed, and released the arrow. There was a *thonk* as it struck the target.

"Aren't you being a little careless with that wound?" Soerman said.

"It's time I did something. There's no strength at all in my left arm."

"Pretty good marksmanship, for a totally incapacitated arm."

They walked side by side to the barn door. Robert began to extract the arrows from the straw mat; every movement cost him an effort.

"I can't stand this sitting around," he said, as they walked back. "I've never been sick before in my life. And never trapped indoors this way. This afternoon I'm riding with you."

Soerman lowered his eyes. "Anywhere you like, but not to the river."

Robert planted the arrows point down in the snow. The feathers at the other end were thin and worn. "You go first," he said to Soerman. "Five each."

Soerman took the bow and tested the resiliency of the wood and the string. He took the first arrow. For a while the only sounds were the crunching of the snow under their boots and the whizz and plunk of the arrows.

"Why not to the river?" Robert said. "I thought we'd talked it all out."

Soerman nodded, his head turned away. "We did," he said, "but there are some things you can't take care of with words."

He was glad Robert had brought it up and thankful that he had taken it the way he had—not holding it against him, but not trying to put a good face on it either. The one thing Soerman was afraid of was that he might forget what had happened, or worse, gradually falsify the truth in his memory.

Robert was reminded of what his father had said that first day in Daniel's cabin in the woods; it was true, Soerman was a changed man. It was not an outward change; his character had changed. The man who had once lived only for the moment, without ties, without an aim in life, that man suddenly had a center of gravity, even if it was only the festering wound of self-accusation.

"Sometimes I think it's not just hoping you'll find some trace of them that keeps you riding out there," Robert said. "That's hopeless, and you know it. There's got to be another reason. You've been to the Morris farm again, haven't you?"

"It's a strange feeling, looking over at it from this side. I can hardly believe anymore that there are Hessian regiments over there and that Rall's still sitting in the doctor's house and waiting for the Delaware to freeze over."

"Oh yes you can. You don't have any trouble believing that

at all. You don't think of anything else. Every time you open your mouth, you start talking about it. You can't get it out of your head, can you?"

"That's what started it," Soerman said. "It all started that night at the Weser River. . . ."

The wind was blowing over the rooftops of the barns, but down here in the yard it was quiet, especially where they stood, at the back of the stables, shielded by the snow barrier.

"Why don't we talk about it?" Soerman asked.

"About what?" Robert's voice was expressionless.

"This morning, on my way to the river, I noticed a platoon in the woods digging the boats out of the snow. Another platoon was on its way to the Morris farm, with their wagons and tents. They're being moved, I think."

Robert slung the bow over his shoulder and gathered up the arrows. "I think we've done enough of this for today."

"Wait a minute," Soerman said. "You probably know what's going on better than I do."

"All right, I know." Robert started back toward the house. "The Americans plan to surprise Rall in Trenton. It's already settled."

They crossed the yard past the stables. There was no one else about.

"You say that as if it doesn't concern you. Or me."

"Does it concern us?" Robert asked. "This morning an American officer came to see me. He asked me all sorts of questions. How many Hessians are there? How are their sentries distributed? How often do they change guard? Where are their cannon positioned? How much cavalry do they have? How do they keep in touch with their headquarters in Brunswick?"

"Well? Did you tell him?"

"I told him I didn't desert in order to support their war."

"You mean that?"

"Yes, I do."

"I wish you did. Or that I did."

Robert blew on his hands. "I really do. Maybe I'll change my mind. Maybe tomorrow, maybe a year from now. I don't know how long this war's going to drag on. Maybe long enough for me to forget I'm a Hessian."

"You're talking about the war," Soerman said.

"Aren't you?"

"Will you tell me when they plan to cross the river—if you hear about it?"

Robert stopped. "What are you going to do?"

"It'd be better if you didn't ask."

"If it's not the war, what is it? There's one thing you and I have to be clear about: you can't take care of any unfinished business of mine."

"That should be possible between friends. Besides, your unfinished business happens to be mine, too. You weren't the only man in that coach that never crossed the Weser; you weren't the only one in front of a firing squad; and Major Haynow didn't assign the kind of duty that meant certain death just to you."

"That's a long time ago," Robert said. "It's all over now."

"It'll never be over. Never. And you know it. This earth isn't big enough for the two of you. You've kept putting it off, again and again. This kind of thing doesn't start overnight, and it's real, and has to be dealt with."

"Stop it," Robert said, "I don't want to think about it."

"This time I'm telling *you* that you think about nothing else, that you can't get it out of your head. He wanted to kill you at the river. And he wouldn't hesitate to try again."

"When he finds out what happened to Mother. . . ."

"Then he'll really want to kill you. You know you can't forget. I can't—yesterday, when I was out riding, I realized that. There are foxes around here; they come out of the woods now, when the snow's on the ground. There are traps set up all over. I saw where a fox had got caught in one of them. He bit his paw off to get free. The paw was still there, and the bloody trail he left behind. He may die, but he had to bite his paw off to get free, so he did it. I want to be free too. . . ."

"Please," Robert said. "No more talking about it."

They went on without another word. They could see the main house ahead, windows gleaming in the pale winter sun. In the second story, leaning far out of a window, a man was using a long stick to knock the icicles off the gutter above him. Pine branches had been laid in front of the porch steps for wiping the snow off the boots of those coming in from outside. The red ribbon on the mistletoe hanging above the porch fluttered in the breeze.

41

When Robert had been moved from Jean Daniel's cabin to Redford, he was dressed in clothes belonging to Daniel. His uniform, tied up in a bundle, had been brought to the house, too, and Mary remembered having seen it in the vestibule, but when she looked for it later to have it laundered, it had disappeared.

It was a relief, after all, not to see it again, and so she did not trouble to search for it. Despite the absence of the hated uniform, however, she seemed unable to get on an easy footing with Robert. She left it to McGill to care for him as long as he needed nursing; when he was able to come to meals, she usually managed to absent herself from the table, did her best to avoid him, and avoided the library where he spent most of his time. She was annoyed with herself for behaving as she did, wished she could change, made earnest resolutions to take a different tack with him, but when put to the test, her defensiveness was always stronger than reason and good resolutions.

And so it happened again. Mary was just engaged in helping Henry Lee hang another sprig of mistletoe in the vestibule—it was one of the few concessions made to Christmas decorations at Redford—when Robert and Soerman came in. She handed the mistletoe to Henry, who was standing on the ladder, and hurried off into the big hall, where the huge table for the Christmas dinner was being set up, in the form of a horseshoe. The custom of the communal Christmas dinner was as old as the main house; it was held the first time when the walls barely stood, unfinished rough brick and wood, at a table consisting of planks laid on trestles. It was the memory of that first time that meant more to Skelnik and those who had been with him from the first than Christmas itself, and that distinguished this festival from all others celebrated during the course of the year.

Skelnik gave presents only to the children; simple things such as dolls for the girls, toy wagons with horses for the boys, little sacks of candies and nuts. He ordered these things from Philadelphia, and since Mary's arrival at Redford she had accompanied him each twenty-fourth of December when he went to pick them up. Their ride, by horse-drawn sleigh through the snowy landscape, had become Mary's most cherished Christmas experience. They went shopping together, then spent the night at the Hotel Francis, favored by all the sea captains who came to Philadelphia. Next morning they would start for home with a fully loaded sleigh. They would arrive at Redford after sunset, when the torches were already burning everywhere to light them home. All the families would be standing, with the children, in front of the main house portal, waiting for their arrival; and it was here, in the snow, in the light of the torches, that the children were given their Christmas gifts.

Mary was thinking of all this as she watched the men at their work, and she was also thinking of the new dress and coat hanging in her wardrobe, that she had intended to wear for this year's trip to Philadelphia. She opened the door to the hallway leading from the vestibule and listened; there was nothing to be heard out there, no steps, no voices. Hesitantly she went back to the vestibule. It was deserted; only the mistletoe hung from the center of the ceiling by its red ribbon. She went over to one of the windows that gave on the forecourt. The sleigh had not come to the front door yet, but she thought she could hear its bells jingling. Then she heard the step behind her that she would have recognized among thousands. She did not turn around.

His hand came to rest on her shoulder. "Why aren't you dressed for our sleigh ride?" he said. "Here I thought you'd be walking up and down out there, full of impatience."

Skelnik was wearing his brownish-black cloth coat with the Astrakhan collar. He had a wolf's pelt sleigh rug hanging over his arm. "Hurry and get dressed. I'll wait for you here."

Mary said nothing. The silence was broken by Jan Kellog, who came in the front door to announce that the sleigh was ready. "Whitcombe has put new runners on it," he said. "He thinks that'll get you there half an hour sooner."

Mary waited for Kellog to leave before she spoke. She wanted to be honest with Skelnik, but she did not want him to guess her true feelings either. Most of all she was afraid she wouldn't be able to hold back her tears. She spoke, at last, as casually as she could. "I think it would be better if I stayed here this time. There's still so much to be done. We seem to be behind with everything."

"They'll manage it all without us. And it's high time you got away from all this and had a change of scene. Come on now, get your things. And don't forget the list."

Mary reached into the pocket of her skirt and handed him a folded slip of paper. "It's all written down here. You won't have to wait for anything, they're supposed to have it all ready and waiting for you. And I've put it down in the right sequence, so you won't have to double back for anything."

Skelnik realized there was something wrong, but he didn't think it so serious that a word from him wouldn't straighten things out. "Surely you're not going to let me go alone, and spoil all my fun?" he said.

"I didn't expect you to go alone," she said.

"But we've always done this together, every year."

"That was before your son came."

From inside the house they heard girls' voices, laughter, doors opening and closing. Skelnik took hold of Mary's arm. "If that's your reason, why didn't you say so? Haven't we always talked openly about everything? Come into the library."

"You'd better get started," she said, "or you won't make it to Philadelphia before nightfall."

But he was already waiting at the library door. She walked inside reluctantly, with an apprehensive look at the table where Robert and Soerman usually played chess. They weren't there.

"It's true, Robert is here at Redford," Skelnik said as soon as he had closed the door behind him. "What difference does that make between you and me? I want an honest, open answer."

Mary avoided his eyes. She could think of no answer she could expect him to understand.

"It didn't start only with his coming here," she said. "Look at the scratches on the floors made by those officers' spurs. We'll never get them out. It's only a little thing, but it shows the change that's come over Redford. Nothing is the way it was anymore."

"I don't understand you. What has that to do with Robert?"

No, he couldn't understand. The soldiers had only taken her room—Robert was taking much more away from her. "I had you all to myself," she said. "Now I have to share you. With Robert, but not only with him; with the woman he brought with him, even though she's dead. They fill the house and take it away from me."

Skelnik did not answer. Had she really said he'd once belonged to her entirely? Or had that always been her greatest wish—to make it come true?

"I'll get used to it," she said, to break the intolerable silence.

"Are we riding to Philadelphia together the way we always have, or not?"

Mary didn't know why his words seemed so humiliating. Was it that he had spoken without looking at her? That he kept staring past her, frighteningly calm, frighteningly far away in his thoughts?

"You don't need any justification," she said. "Robert is your son, and I'm no relation at all, a stranger you took into your home. It is just as well for me to realize my true place in the scheme of things. Everything else was an illusion. It's not so long ago that you called me your daughter. I can still hear you say it, we were talking beside the fireplace over in the big hall. You were talking about my future, and it was Redford's future, too. I believed you, but now things are different, and I've realized it just in time."

Skelnik came closer and laid an arm around her shoulders. "Redford is home to many of us. It's as much Henry Lee's place as mine and it belongs to you no less than to Robert. How can you harbor such thoughts, living under the same roof with me? Nothing has changed between us, between you and me. . . ."

She felt his nearness, his calm and his strength, and with it a heightened fear of losing him. If he took his arm away from her shoulders, she felt, all was lost. She shut her eyes. Words came from her lips as though inspired: "Marry me."

He was hardly better prepared to hear these words than she had been to utter them. She didn't dare look at him. She was grateful for the lengthening silence; for an instant she had a mad hope that she hadn't really said those words, that she had only thought them. At last he said, "Since when have you had all this on your mind?" There was no irony in his voice, only a deep perplexity.

"Have you never thought about it?" she said.

He took his arm away. "What if I had? An aging man sometimes has silly ideas. Do you think that you love me then?"

Her eyes fell. "I'm afraid of losing you. Isn't that love?"

"The fear of losing someone may be a part of love. But the essential thing is wanting to possess someone."

She stood just where he had left her, unable to speak, or to move. She felt that if she just stood still long enough, his arm would come back to hold her.

"You're not saying anything," he said, "and that's a good thing, because nothing could be worse than self-deception. You don't mean me. Perhaps you mean Redford, perhaps certain memories we share—but you don't mean me. This isn't love."

She didn't want to understand him. She was afraid that if she understood she would no longer have the strength to fight for him. "Then why don't you tell me what love is," she said. "Is it love to wait for a woman for twenty-five years, as you did? You said, just now, that love is the wish to possess someone. But all you did was wait."

"It can turn into that. That's how crazy the world is, or how crazy we are, when we love. At least, it's what happened to me. And I have to believe it was right and good for it to happen. It's all I have."

"That's resignation."

"Possibly. But I'm too old to make more ambitious claims on life. And you, Mary, you're too young to be satisfied with so little. . . ."

"But what if it's true, what if I do really . . . ?"

He broke in. "Don't say that. Not to me. Save it, keep it in reserve for the day when you will say it far more surely than you can now; when it will mean so much more to say it."

"John said it to me, and John is dead. And she—she loved you, and she had to die before she could even see you again. It doesn't make sense."

He was tempted to take her in his arms as he had never done before, and as he was never likely to do if he let this moment pass. But he resisted the impulse. "It doesn't always have to end as it did with John," he said. "Or as it did with her."

"And how does it begin? How will I know?"

"You'll know."

"Can you forget what I said?" she asked after a while. "What I said about marriage?"

"Must I forget it?"

"Please. If you don't, I'll never stop feeling ashamed."

"Then I'll forget it," he said, "and I'll forget you made me feel young again for a minute. You were afraid of having to share me with someone. I know now I will have to share you with someone, some day."

For a long time she thought about his words and about the look he had given her when he had said them, but then she was caught up in preparations for the holiday and so busy she hadn't time for anything else. Not until evening, when she entered the library and found there the wolf's-fur carriage rug he had forgotten on a chair, did she remember what he had said.

At the rustling of her dress, Robert and Soerman looked up from their chess game; she hadn't noticed them before. The lamp with the green shade barely illuminated the chessboard. Robert and Soerman sat in the semi-dark, only their hands in the light as they reached to move a piece.

"Please come and sit down with us," Robert said, pointing to the third chair at the table.

Hesitantly she came over and sat down.

"I hope it wasn't your game we found here," he said. "I tried to finish it, but white's position was pretty hopeless."

When he had asked her to sit down, her old defensiveness had come alive again; she'd had an urge to find some excuse to leave. But as soon as she overcame it, her inhibition went away. "He always gives me white," she said, "and a two-piece handicap, but I always end up in a hopeless position."

Robert captured a rook. His figure was reflected in the black mirror of the window behind him. Outside another window, Mary could see the courtyard illuminated with torches. It had begun to snow again.

"Does my father play chess often?" Robert asked. Mary didn't answer. "I know how strange it is for me to ask questions like that, but I'm only beginning to get to know him. He's a good player, isn't he?"

"I'm afraid playing with me can't be much fun for him, but he simply hasn't anyone better to play with. He used to like playing with Doctor Banks, when he came over from Trenton."

For a while she watched silently as they made their moves. They took their time, wholly lost in the game. The clock on the mantelpiece struck four high notes, then nine low ones. Mary turned to the door.

"Don't go," Robert said. "We'll be finished pretty soon, and then you can play the winner."

"I have things to do."

"You always have things to do."

"It's a big house," she said.

"Does my father realize what he has in you?"

Mary said nothing. Robert was leaning forward a little, his face half in light, half in shadow. She couldn't see his eyes. He was wearing the old-fashioned green velvet jacket she had previously seen only on Skelnik.

The door to the library opened, and a man came in carrying a package. It was David Woodrock, the stable hand on the Hancock place; she hadn't seen him since the day Abigail Hancock had given birth to her new baby. It seemed such a long time ago.

"Come on in," she said. "I was beginning to be afraid the books wouldn't be ready in time. Here, you can put them down on this shelf."

"My father would have brought them himself." Woodrock said, "but his gout's gotten real bad since it's been so cold. Doing these bindings was just what he needed—it took his mind off his pain. I think he did a beautiful job, too."

"Thank him for me, please. And give my best regards to Abigail. How is the baby?"

"Fine, just fine. The baptism is day after tomorrow. Her name will be Roberta, but don't tell Mr. Skelnik. Abigail wants to tell him herself."

"Better come to the fire and warm up before you start back."

"I'd rather make sure I got home. There's a lot of snow in those clouds." At the door of the library he turned, gave a half-humorous military salute, and went out.

Mary loosened the cords around the book package and carefully picked up one of the narrow volumes. The green morocco leather was very cold. She leafed through each volume quickly before putting it in place on the shelf. She had discovered a box full of pamphlets, a collection of writings of the great astronomers, in the three rooms that had been locked up for so long and that were being cleared for Robert. The pamphlets must have lain there for many years. She said nothing about her find to Skelnik, but was planning to surprise him with them, newly bound in twelve volumes, at Christmas. Now the twelve volumes stood side by side. She patted the row till it was perfectly straight, then carried the cords and paper outside. When she came back to sit down once more at the chess table, there were only five pieces left on the board, three white and two black.

"Why don't you give up?" Robert said to Soerman.

"I don't understand it." Soerman shook his head. "It was my game, I had it in my pocket. I shouldn't have traded queens. That's how you got the advantage with your pawns."

Something banged against the window, like a big bird hitting the glass. Mary screamed. Outside the window a man was swinging in the air, a man in Hessian uniform—green coat, red lapels, silver braid, white trousers. Mary stared horrified at the ghastly body swinging back and forth in the dim light of the torches.

Then she saw the straw coming out of the sleeves, the trouser legs tied at the bottoms, and realized she was looking at Robert's missing Hessian uniform. The dummy's head, too, was a bundle of straw topped with the cocked hat of the Hessians.

Robert went to the French windows and threw them open. Outside stood a group of men carrying torches. When they saw him, they ran off across the yard, led by the man carrying the straw effigy at the end of a long pole; it waved behind him like a trophy.

Mary had closed her eyes as if she could in that way abolish what she had seen. From the open windows came an icy blast of air. Her fear suddenly turned to anger; she got up and ran to the door.

Robert caught up with her in the hall outside. She was just pulling one of the riding whips out of the rack near the door. "Don't," he said. "They didn't know you were in here. It was meant for me and Soerman."

She broke away from him and ran outside. He ran after her, across the yard toward the stables, where the men with the torches stood in a circle, the straw effigy dancing on its pole above their heads, illuminated in the flickering torchlight.

Robert took her hand, stopped her. "Let them be," he said.

But she kept going, walking slowly toward them.

One of the men held his torch up to the effigy. The flames licked up a leg, then the entire figure was on fire. The man holding the pole dropped it then, and ran, and the whole group scattered into the darkness. The effigy lay burning on the ground, seeming, in the twisting flames, to move, as if in pain. Robert and Mary stood watching it burn.

Finally only an outstretched arm was left, and the head in the Hessian hat. Then part of the arm caught and blazed up, and the hat, densely stuffed with straw.

"Come back to the house, Mary," Robert said.

She turned to him, shivering in her taffeta dress. He put his arm around her. For a moment her head lay on his shoulder.

"Why do they do such things?" She straightened up again at once. "Why does this kind of thing happen again and again? Why do people have to hate—why is the world like that?"

Robert knew no answer to this, none that would have satisfied her or himself. They walked back to the house in silence. Under the porch they stopped for a moment. It was snowing harder, and the torchlight on both sides of the door fell on Mary's face. It was the first time he had seen her so close, except for the time he had opened his eyes to find her leaning over him, at the cabin—the girl with the long brown hair.

"Why are you looking at me like that?" she said.

"I was thinking how you found me, wearing that uniform, and that you could have hated me, but you didn't."

42

The house stood on a small hill, just outside of Philadelphia, a two-story house with a portico of tall columns and a copper roof, the green patina of which was visible for a considerable distance. Two wagons stood at the main entrance; one was already crammed full of furniture. Wooden crates were piled on the ground. A board was nailed to the fence, bearing the legend: FOR SALE. Skelnik had not intended to delay his return home. There was nothing to hold him in town. It was a clear, sunny day, but the wind was cold and it would take him at least four hours for the return trip. He drew his watch out of his vest pocket. It would have to be a brief visit. He reined in the horses, set the brake, and climbed out of the fully loaded sleigh.

Two men were carrying a bookcase out of the house. They had made a fire in the garden out of packs of old newspapers and other trash. There stood Eph Tyler, Doctor Wyngard's manservant, with the inevitable sand-colored muffler that he wore winter and summer wrapped around his neck. He took his hands out of his pockets to greet Skelnik.

"The doctor is upstairs, sir."

"Then you're leaving Philadelphia, too?"

Eph Tyler shrugged. He seemed about to say something, but then bent down to the basket beside him and threw a roll of old newspaper into the flames.

Skelnik entered the house, made his way past the furniture cluttering the hallway, and up the stairs, a familiar climb in the years since his heart had been giving him trouble. When he opened the door to the doctor's study, he found the old man sitting on the floor, looking through piles of medical journals—there wasn't a table or chair left in the room.

When he heard Skelnik, he peered at him above his glasses. "I'd given you up," he said, "even though you've never missed a Christmas visit yet. Where's Mary? Didn't you bring her along this time? I may be an old geezer but I still like something young and pretty to look at."

"So you're giving up, too," Skelnik said. "I wouldn't have expected it of you, I must say. What's gotten into you? I've always loved coming here—Philadelphia's the finest, proudest city in the world, as far as I'm concerned. But after what I've seen here since yesterday, I don't know what to say. It can't be two weeks since my last trip, but the place is unrecognizable. My proud Philadelphia, Daughter of Liberty! And so you're leaving her in the lurch, too."

Wyngard took his spectacles off his nose. "It seems to me a man of seventy has the right to live as he likes, for what little time is left to him."

"I imagine everybody has a good reason. I'm sorry, but I wouldn't have believed it possible. Any other city, but not Philadelphia. I'm glad Mary didn't see this. Two weeks ago there was so much traffic you couldn't let the horses move faster than a walk; they very nearly had no room for me at the Francis. Crowds of young people discussing the latest news all over the steps of the Congressional building. And yesterday—not a sign of life. Nothing but empty shop windows, abandoned houses, doors and windows boarded up. I don't think I'd have been as shocked if I'd found the place burned to the ground. Not even the usual card game at the hotel; no fun at all. All anybody wanted to talk about was—who's sold out? How much did he get? Where should we go? Is Baltimore still safe? It was like a nightmare."

"I understand how you feel. But you can't expect people to stay after Congress itself packed up and fled. Everybody's scared. They all know three regiments of Hessians are garrisoned in Trenton, and nobody believes the general can stop them from crossing the river."

"They'll never cross the Delaware," Skelnik said. "Never. The only way those Hessians will ever cross the Delaware is as our prisoners."

"You certainly haven't changed." The physician put on his glasses again, and peered at Skelnik with an interest that seemed more professional than personal. "I wonder why you've been consulting me all these years. A waste of your money, I'd say."

"I've had another attack," Skelnik said. "The same symptoms, the same fear."

The old physician ran both hands through his white, wavy mane. "Want to be my last patient in Philadelphia?" He pointed to a side door. "They haven't moved my examining table yet. Shall we go in and look you over?"

Skelnik shook his head. "No, just tell me the truth. How much time have I got left?"

"Why? Are you thinking of getting married?"

Skelnik smiled for the first time since his arrival. "You're the second person to ask me that question. But don't worry, there's no danger of that." He grew serious again. "I want you to tell me the truth."

"The truth? What's your idea of the truth? You used to be interested in chemistry. So you know that the world, man included, consists of a certain number of basic elements—it's the same with the truth—a combination of various elements."

"You're being evasive."

"What would you like me to do for you, play oracle? Do you want to join the army? Do you feel like sacrificing yourself for a cause? And do you think it'll be easier to do that if I say, go ahead, it doesn't matter, you're going to die soon anyway? I've told you time and again: you are not a medical case."

"What, then?"

"Try miracle healers, astrologers, how do I know?"

"That's no answer."

Two long vertical furrows appeared on Wyngard's forehead. "Nobody likes to admit he can't find the answer to a question, least of all a doctor. The first time you came to me with those symptoms, I didn't expect you to last another six months. I was as sure as I could be. Ten years have passed since then, and I'm not a whit the wiser. I can't find anything wrong with your heart, but the symptoms keep recurring just the same. All I can say is, if your horse doesn't throw you one day and break your neck, you'll outlive us all."

Skelnik had been in a thoughtful mood when he left Doctor Wyngard, and he remained in that frame of mind for a long time on his way home. The new iron bands Jonathan Whitcombe had attached to the bottoms of the runners made the sleigh glide smoothly and lightly over the deep snow. Christmas packages were piled high at his feet and on the seat beside him, and gradually he began to regain a little of the festive mood that he usually felt on these Christmas trips to Philadelphia.

He did not encounter many people abroad this morning. He passed a few farmer's sleds on their way home from town; then he had the deep snow of the road all to himself, except for an occasional vehicle coming from the other direction.

The sun climbed higher in the sky. The wind turned southerly; a warm wind that made the snow cover moist and sticky, so that the horses had difficulty maintaining the pace. If this south wind held, the snow would be gone as quickly at it had come. He sat in the sleigh with his coat open, his fur cap beside him on the seat.

Shortly after one o'clock, dark clouds began to move across the sky. The wind had changed and came now from the west, bringing a driving snow before it. The sky kept getting darker, the snow thicker, and by the time Skelnik reached the fork 'n the road leading to Redford, he was in a virtual blizzard. The horses' blankets, the cover he had laid across the packages, were all white with snow. The sleigh moved soundlessly; the jingling of the bridle bells seemed to come from far ahead, as if from some other sleigh approaching through the snow.

In the distance, he could see the stand of trees that marked Redford's southern border, the gnarled old remnants of an oak forest. Through the snow, they looked like a single dark wall, a fortress of trees.

And columns of troops were emerging out of that fortress, marching toward him across the white plains.

They came three abreast, taking the easier path of the road

until they would have to turn across country, toward the Delaware and Trenton. Skelnik brought the sleigh to a halt and looked for a place to pull aside, but the snowdrifts beside the road were too high. He hadn't expected to see them so early; according to the plan, they weren't to have left camp until three o'clock.

The column had reached the sleigh. The men began to swerve out around it, trampling a path through the high drifts, the snow crunching under their boots, field packs cutting into their shoulders, ammunition cases slapping against their hips. Many of them carried two muskets, the second belonging to one of the men carrying the boats at the rear of the column.

Skelnik had tied down the reins. Hands deep in his pockets, he watched them pass. No two of them wore the same uniform. Every man wore what he had salvaged from the summer campaign, mended and patched, and supplemented by odds and ends—tight leather knee breeches alternating with long worsted trousers, tunics in the uncertain browns of tanbark dye, all kinds of jackets worn one atop the other. Their wool coats, too hot for marching, were rolled up and tied to their field packs. Their weapons, too, were a mixed lot; here and there he could see a musket that must have been left over from the conquest of Canada, or one of Spanish make, sometimes a French flintlock of the kind the English had captured in great numbers at the Battle of Louisbourg in Nova Scotia some years before.

The only thing uniform about these men was the expression on their faces. He watched them tramp past through the snow, expressionless, eyes straight ahead, an army with only one goal; and he suddenly wished he were going with them. He had made gunpowder for them, had rounded up wagonloads of arms and boots; the women of Redford had sewed coats and caps for them—but was that enough? He remembered the question Doctor Wyngard had asked so casually, and it was true: he had long struggled with the idea that his place, at this moment, was with the troops.

The long column had passed, the men with the boats bringing up the rear. He watched them recede through the snow until they were out of sight. The horses had grown restless; they shook the snow from their manes, jerking the sleigh forward. He untied the reins, and the sleigh moved out again; but his mind was still back there, with the troops marching toward the Delaware. He had been there when the general had briefed his officers on the plan of attack. He remembered the map, the blue line along the Delaware representing those eight hundred men he had just passed, the arrow cutting the Delaware ten miles south of Trenton, where they were to cross over—a small unit today, the rest tomorrow morning—in a feint to draw the Hessians away from the Delaware at Redford, where the main force of the army was to cross, march through the night to Trenton, and attack the town in the gray mists of dawn.

Looking at that map, he had believed the plan would work; but now, having seen that ragged, ill-equipped band of men tramping through the snow, grave doubts rose in his mind.

The wind had subsided, lulled by the falling snow; though it was still early afternoon, the day was sinking into a blue twilight. Skelnik had reached the bivouac area of the Continental Army. Despite the snow he could still make out the dark rectangles where row on row of tents had stood just yesterday. Charred circles melted in the snow, like miniature volcanoes, showed where the campfires had been; here and there a trickle of smoke still rose from one of these craters. He could almost believe a huge army had camped here. He flicked the reins and moved on toward Redford.

When he reached the cedar drive leading toward the house, he brushed the snow off his arms and shoulders, and urged the horses on. He saw a rider coming through the whirling snow on a white horse. Only when the horse drew alongside did he see it was Mary.

He stopped the sleigh, tied the reins fast, and got down to help her off the horse. But she was quicker than he was; by the time he touched the ground, she was in his arms.

Her hands were cold; her hair hung in wet, disorderly strands, and she was shivering. He cleared a place for her in the sleigh, lifted her into it, and wrapped a blanket around her. Then he tied her horse on behind the sleigh, and climbed back into his seat.

"What is it?" he said. "What's happened?"

She was huddled under the blanket, still shivering. She reached out and took his hand. "He's gone," she said. She looked grave, but more beautiful than he had ever seen her. "He's left us."

"Alone?"

"With Soerman."

The sleigh bumped across the frozen runner tracks in the drive until it slid into a track that suited its width; here, under the trees, there was less new snow, and the sound of the horses' hooves rang louder and sharper.

"Did he say anything to you?" Skelnik asked.

Mary shook her head. "Jan Kellog saw them taking their horses out of the stable. Robert told him they were going into the woods to hunt with Jean Daniel. But Daniel just now came to the house for Christmas. He said he saw them riding toward the river. I almost went after them."

"I'm glad you didn't," Skelnik said.

Mary moved away from him and stared. "You mean you knew about it?"

"He didn't say anything to me. But I could feel it coming, these last few days."

"And you said nothing to stop him?"

"I didn't think I could."

"What is this?" she said. "How is it that you men can think of nothing but the war? Are you so anxious to know what it was like for Compson to have to bring a dead son home? I don't understand you. Robert came all this way to find you. It's a miracle he made it alive. You were so happy—and now you don't lift a finger to stop him."

"Did you try to stop John?"

"That was different."

Skelnik looked at her, and it struck him how changed she seemed.

The sleigh turned into the left-hand curve of the drive just before it reached the main house. Snow was drifting down from the treetops. "Are the children waiting?" he asked.

She nodded.

Underneath the cedars, the light seemed almost violet, the

snow a subtle shade of rose; then the sleigh emerged from the arching trees into the blue of twilight and pulled into the courtyard in front of the house. The dark, low clouds seemed to be resting on the rooftops. In this light, the red brick walls looked black; the white of the veranda had an almost metallic gleam. A gust of wind swept the forecourt, and for a moment the torches threatened to go out; then they flickered and flared up again.

All the Redford people were standing in front of the main porch, the men in back, the women and children out front, all eyes on the approaching sleigh.

Skelnik reined in the horses and set the brakes. The little bells fell silent. The next moment the sleigh was totally surrounded by children, and everything was as it always had been at Christmas time at Redford.

Trenton

You have been sold, and for what? Jammed into foreign ships like cattle, you are being sent across an ocean! You defy cliffs and storms at sea in order to fight against people who have never offended you, and who are fighting for a just cause. Do you know what kind of people you are about to attack?

You are going into battle against men who are stronger, smarter, braver and quicker than you. You are abandoning your own homes, though you will not be fighting in your own cause! While they are carrying on their war in their own country, in a climate to which they are accustomed, supported by every assistance one's homeland offers, against a gang of men the ocean has spewed out upon their shores.

And you, betrayed, humiliated, sold peoples—flee the soil stained by despotism. Cross the seas, flee to America; but, once you're there, embrace your brothers. Learn from the Americans the art of being free and happy.

Extract from Mirabeau's broadsheet, "Appeal to the Hessians and other German Peoples sold by their Princes to England." Cleve, 1777

43

The storm had blown Robert's fur cap from his head; his long blond hair was so wet it looked dark. The wind was blowing from the northeast, bringing snow and rain and an occasional gust so strong the horses shied, but Robert and Soerman drove them on.

The closer they got to the Delaware, the fiercer the storm became, as if it was determined to bring the Continental Army to a halt at the river. On the rise above the ferry landing, Robert and Soerman reined in their horses. The process of transporting the army across had been underway for an hour now. It was a slow process: the fishing boats held only four men, five at the most; the cargo boats held ten or twelve, but there weren't very many of them. The reactivated ferry was transporting artillery, munitions, and horses. The river was high. The men in the boats were having to fight not only the storm but floating chunks of ice as well. The smaller boats hugged the downriver side of the ferry, which gave them some protection against the ice.

"We'd better decide what we're going to do," Soerman said. "We won't have any trouble getting a place in a boat, but that means leaving the horses behind."

Robert laid a hand on his horse's neck; he could feel it trembling every time a gust of wind struck. He felt intoxicated by the storm, exhilarated by the wind and the cold. In the middle of the storm-whipped river, he could see the ferry, laden to the gunwales with cannon, munition cases, terrified horses. Ice was piling up against the upriver side, grinding along toward the stern, bobbing away.

"There's no sense crossing without horses," he said.

Soerman wiped the rain from his face. "You changing your mind?"

Robert picked up the reins. "I'm just thinking about what happened here at the river, that's all." He guided his sorrel down the slope. A rider separated from the columns of men waiting for the boats and came up to meet them. Robert recognized Lieutenant Blyth.

The hat with the blue-and-white cockade sat low on Blyth's forehead; when he reined his horse to a halt, the rain in the hat rim spilled out over his face. He shook his head and wiped the water out of his eyes. "If this storm keeps up," he said, "we'll surprise them in their beds. Are you crossing over with us?"

Only yesterday Robert had thought Blyth an older man than himself. Now he saw the lieutenant was barely twenty. "Could you get us a place on the ferry?"

"With pleasure. We need every man we can get. Especially men like you, who know their way around over there."

"That wasn't the idea," Robert said. "You can't count on our help. Our errand over there is strictly personal."

Blyth pushed two fingers under the chin strap of his hat. "You plan to ride to Trenton?" he asked thoughtfully.

"That depends," Robert said.

"You might alert the enemy. Unintentionally, of course."

"You'll just have to trust us."

Blyth was silent for a moment; then he turned his horse and rode back down to the landing stage. Robert and Soerman followed. The ferry had delivered its cargo on the other side and was coming back; with the wind behind it, it was making good headway. Robert and Soerman had dismounted beside Blyth. They waited, holding the horses by the bridle, while the ferry docked and was tied up. The ferrymen in hip-high boots and canvas jackets were dripping wet. A group of soldiers started dragging two howitzers on board, followed by boxes of munitions, a troop of cavalry, and finally Blyth with Robert and Soerman. When the ferry started back, the horses panicked; it took both hands on the bridle to hold them down.

The water was dark green. Chunks of floating ice kept smashing the upriver side of the ferry; some of them were dragged under and scraped along the bottom, bobbing up on the other side as if alive. For the last hundred yards, the storm seemed to let up—they were in the lee of the opposite bank.

Robert and Soerman were the last to debark. Blyth had disappeared by the time they got ashore. They crossed the riverbank and started up the hedgerow along the river, upstream, away from the army.

It was impossible to move faster than a walk. Stretches of ice alternated with deep snow, and the horses kept plunging to their knees in unexpected holes and hollows. The wind came howling across the flat, as if gathering speed for a leap across the river. Soon the voices and sounds from the boats and the ferry were out of earshot. Every now and then Robert stood up in his stirrups and looked around; finally he saw it, half covered with snow—the sheep cart.

"Go on ahead," he said to Soerman. "I want to see what they did with the bodies of Niklas and Ploetz."

Soerman shook his head. "You won't find them."

They separated, and Robert rode slowly along the riverbank, searching. When he rejoined Soerman near the cart, he said, "They took them away."

"What did you expect? Did you think your brother would miss the chance to drag them out in front of the regiment, as an example of what happens to deserters? If I know him, he probably had them posthumously condemned to death. And us, too. What do we do next? What's your plan?"

Robert didn't know what to say. All he knew was that he had a night and a day ahead of him, and that it would have to be done in that time. "Let's ride," he said.

They soon overtook and passed the vanguard of troops marching toward Trenton. The rain mixed with the snow was almost as hard as hail. Soerman had wrapped his wide muffler around his fur cap and down around his chin to protect his face. They rode close together, side by side, constantly changing places so that only one at a time bore the full brunt of the wind. Every now and then they stopped to remove clumps of ice from the hair around the horses' eyes. The road stretched away across the wide white plain, and after a while they lost track of time. The day seemed to stand still; it was like riding through an eternal twilight. They encountered no one; the farmhouses that occasionally emerged out of the snow seemed deserted.

Not very long ago, they had marched up this road toward Trenton, part of a Hessian regiment, the drummers out front, under a blue sky and a hot sun. But nothing looked familiar; it was as if they rode through a freshly created world—and as if they were the only human beings in it.

Then, around a bend in the road, they saw a building on fire. Flames leaped up toward the dark, moving clouds; there was a smell of smoke in the air. But still the whole thing was like a picture, not like reality. It took Robert seconds to react; then he spurred his horse off the road and across the snow toward it. When he came closer, he saw it was a burning barn.

A tall ladder leaned against the roof. On it stood a man, and two women were bringing him pails of water from the well. It was a futile effort; in this wind, the fire was already out of control. Robert and Soerman tied their horses to an iron ring beside the door of the house and ran to the barn. The flames were already licking along the ridge-piece of the roof, and the man had taken the ladder down.

"You can't save it," Robert said. "Better let it go."

Flames came shooting out of the portholes under the roof, spreading with every gust of wind. Already the roof supports were beginning to sway. Finally the roof collapsed in on itself, sending up a shower of sparks. Wind swept a cloud of smoke across the yard. The younger woman started to cry. The older one put an arm around her and led her into the house.

"How did it happen?" Robert asked the farmer.

"You must not live around here," the farmer said. "Only a stranger would ask that."

"We're on our way to Princeton," Robert said quickly.

"They're in Princeton, too. They're everywhere." The farmer pushed his hands angrily into the pockets of his singed jacket. "Damn these Hessians! We left our slaughtering to the very last day before Christmas. I didn't think they'd come out of their burrows in this weather. I don't know how they found out, but suddenly there they were, three of them. Not only did they take the pig I'd just slaughtered, they set fire to the barn, too. I guess it's supposed to be a warning—to keep me from complaining to their commandant." His eyes went from Robert to Soerman and back again. "You mean to go on to Princeton tonight, in this storm?"

"Not if you can give us a bed for the night," Robert said.

"If you don't mind bunking in the kitchen. It's the warmest room in the house." The farmer walked with them to the house; at the front door he stopped to look at the horses. He stared at the brand in the chestnuts' hide, ran his fingers over it. "It's a long time since I've seen horses like this," he said. He turned hesitantly to Robert. "Not this side of the Delaware, anyway. If you want to keep your horses, you'd better not ride through Trenton.

Our horses were the first thing these damned Hessians took."

He had clenched his fists and was glaring out across the yard. When Robert turned, he saw the farmhouse was on a hill, and from here he could see down into the valley, to Trenton. There lay the town, its roofs white with snow, and the tents of the Hessians, yellow in the light of their campfires. And behind that, beyond a band of trees, a broad, deep green ribbon wound through the white landscape: the Delaware.

44

Colonel Rall had taken possession of the entire second story of the doctor's house, though he actually used only the large, wood-paneled room that had three windows looking out on the river. Thick logs were burning in the two fireplaces. The tall wax candles were curved out of shape by the heat. Tobacco smoke filled the room, mingling with the aroma of cinnamon, cloves, and red wine, from the punch container that was being kept warm on a little stove. It was getting dark outside; the windows began to reflect a red glow from the fireplace.

Rall sat at a large round table covered with maps, open atlases, stacks of reports. Rall was absorbed in his reading, his tunic unbuttoned.

Every time Sergeant Luib found the colonel like this, he could hardly believe it. In all his years with the colonel, he had never seen him read anything except the regimental lists. But since they had been in Trenton, Rall had rounded up three of his men who could speak English and was keeping them busy almost round the clock translating every newspaper, every pamphlet, that could tell him something about the Delaware, about Philadelphia and the surrounding countryside. He had had local citizens questioned and their reports translated, too; he had become obsessed with his subject. Luib was getting used to hearing no response to his knock on the colonel's door and to being greeted with a grunt of displeasure if he walked in uninvited. This time he stopped in the doorway.

Without looking up from his reading, Rall signaled him to come in. "Sit down here, and listen to this. The night watchmen in Philadelphia don't just call out the time; every hour they report the weather, the wind direction, falling or rising temperature, the time of sunrise and sunset—rain, hail, snow, drought, they predict everything. Think of that. They've got a bureau, twenty people, that does nothing but concern itself with the weather. I must say this Philadelphia of theirs is full of surprises."

Luib had resisted the invitation to sit. When Rall appeared to lose himself in his reading again, he said quickly, "There's a mounted courier who wants to speak to you, Colonel. Lieutentant Morgan, from Princeton."

"An Englishman? Send him to Major Haynow."

"The Major has seen him, and thinks you should talk to him."

"He keeps sending me these fellows who waste my time. Let the man wait. And you, sit down and stop being a nuisance."

Reluctantly, Luib approached the table. He had lost even more weight in the last two weeks, but no longer by choice; just seeing the colonel like this was enough to spoil his appetite for the rest of the day. His face, which had once been so round and optimistic, now looked drawn and troubled. He frowned as he surveyed the table. This damned reading! It had all started when they moved into the doctor's house. As the documents were translated they piled up on the table, then the chairs, the window seats, the sofa—it was like a progressive disease. To sit down, as the colonel had ordered, Luib would first have had to clear a chair of its stack of documents.

"The man has an urgent message," he began again. "His horse was steaming, he must have ridden like the devil. The English must have a pretty good reason to send a man to Trenton in weather not fit for a dog."

He stopped talking when he realized Rall wasn't paying the slightest attention to him.

"There's hardly another part of the country where the temperature fluctuates as much as it does here," Rall said. "In May of last year they registered temperatures in the eighties, and then at night they had a frost so bad they brought people with frozen hands and feet into the hospitals the next morning. They've seen the thermometer hit 120° in Philadelphia in the summer. There are days when people have to pour water over their roofs to keep them from catching on fire. You get a February that feels like July, and then comes a snowfall in May that makes the streets impassable. There are islands in the Delaware where banana and lemon trees are supposed to grow. The tropical warmth of the water is attributed to the hot springs in the riverbed there." Rall raised his eyes from the document. "Incidentally, Luib, did you know the King of Prussia is a citizen of Philadelphia? He's got a house there. They brought the lumber for it across the ocean; it was cut in East Friesland, and they say the house was built overnight. It's a hotel. That's where we'll stay when we get there, Luib."

Luib found Rall's obsession with Philadelphia and the weather alarming. "We're still in Trenton," he said, fully aware that the remark was out of line.

"Not for much longer," Rall said. "Not much longer."

A bugle sounded in the distance. Luib opened the window. The signal came again. "Three men stole a pig from a farm outside Trenton," he said, "and set the barn on fire. They were discovered on the way back. They're to get fifty good ones apiece, with the rod. The execution just started."

"Three men? Which regiment?"

"Linsing's, I hear."

Rall lost interest at once; they weren't his men. Here was another slackening of fiber Luib had had to adjust to. Whether a powder magazine got wet in the snow, a shipment of flour was delayed, a new chaplain arrived to hear confession and celebrate communion, a man came down with trench fever and had to be hospitalized—it was all the same to the colonel. Officers like Major Haynow were only too glad to take over. Haynow hardly bothered to ask for orders these days, he simply did as he saw fit. Thinking of this, Luib got angry. "For days you haven't made the rounds of the sentries," he said. "You no longer issue the order of the day. You let men like Haynow run things. All you do these days is hunch over your reading or play chess with the doctor. Do you realize we've had a heavy snow, and that the Delaware's full of ice floes?" It wasn't only what he said, but the way he said it, that constituted crude insubordination; but still, Luib felt he should have expressed himself even stronger.

Again the bugles sounded in the distance, and this time there was the sound of gunfire. It swelled up for a moment, then ebbed into silence. Rall leaned back in his chair and fumbled for his slippers with his feet; then, with an effort, he stood up. "What was that you said about an English courier?"

"A messenger from General Leslie."

"Does he speak German?"

"Badly, but you'll make out his meaning."

Rall slowly buttoned his tunic. "They're learning, at least," he said. Luib brought him his boots, but Rall waved them away. "He won't mind seeing a colonel in slippers, will he?"

"I remember a time you didn't take your boots off for days on end."

Rall laughed. "If I remember right, you weren't too pleased with me that way either." In slippers and no-longer-fresh white socks he walked out the door, followed by the anxious, embittered Luib.

The doctor's house had no veranda but only a flat wooden porch in front, roofed over but without a railing. When the weather was good, a bench stood there for patients who preferred to wait their turn outdoors. Two lanterns beside the front door provided light; the wind had covered one side of the porch with snow.

Lieutenant Morgan had been pacing up and down the porch, swinging his arms to get the stiffness out after his long ride. He saluted Rall, then handed him a paper drawn from the broad, upturned cuff of his scarlet coat. "From General Leslie."

Luib took the document, broke the seal, and stepped closer to the lantern to read it. "It's in English," he said. "Into the fire with it."

The Englishman wasn't sure he had understood. "It's most urgent," he said. "We have reliable and confirmed information that General Washington is preparing to cross the Delaware."

Rall was silent.

"Letters have been intercepted," Morgan said. "Washington intends to launch an attack on Trenton before the end of the year."

"Indeed. He wants to march on Trenton and is crossing the Delaware. Is he coming alone, or with an escort of troops?"

The English officer was about to answer, but Rall signaled for silence. From the direction of Assunpink Creek came the sound of hootbeats. A small troop of cavalry turned off the road toward the doctor's house. The officer in the lead was Adjutant Wardein. Two of the riders sagged in the saddle, evidently wounded.

Wardein halted his horse at the porch. He had been riding hard and he was still out of breath. "They're coming across the river!" he said.

Rall smiled. "General Washington with his army? Wardein, I've always thought of you as a man who didn't lose his head so easily. Now tell me, how many did you actually see?"

"Fifty, maybe a hundred."

"How did they cross the river?"

"In boats. They took the sentries at our Bordentown outposts by surprise. One man killed, two wounded."

"No casualties among the rebels?" Rall inquired coolly.

"Our men succeeded in beating off the attack. I happened to arrive on the scene with my troop just in time. The rebels had to leave five of their dead behind. We drove them back to their boats and across the river."

Rall listened with a mocking smile. "Are you satisfied now?" he said. "Now you've had the big battle you've been telling me about ever since we got to Trenton."

"Shall I give the alarm to our regiment?" Wardein asked. "In case the rebels come back with reinforcements?"

"Which regiment is on duty today?"

"Yours, Colonel, the Rall Regiment."

After a moment's silence, Rall said, "Send reinforcements to the outpost on the road to Bordentown, to bring them to full strength. The Rall regiment remains in quarters. You may give your men here a special ration of rum." With that, he disappeared inside the house.

Sergeant Luib had listened to this exchange with bitter satisfaction; he wasn't the only one to whom Rall was turning a deaf ear these days. "You may as well give up," he said to Wardein.

The men of Wardein's little troop had maneuvered up alongside the porch; two of them had dismounted, and were lifting one of the wounded men out of the saddle. The man was unconscious. His head hung down; blood trickled from under one sleeve.

"Where's the doctor?" Wardein said. "Can we get him to attend to these men?"

Luib shook his head. "Better take them to the camp surgeon. This doctor here won't move a finger for a Hessian." He was still holding the message from General Leslie; silently he folded it up and gave it back to Lieutenant Morgan. Then he followed Rall into the house.

The dislike Sergeant Luib had conceived for Doctor Noah Banks from the first had by now developed into open hostility. Luib forgot that Rall had insisted on moving into the doctor's house, despite the latter's protests. He regarded the move as a trap, initiated deliberately by the doctor to ensnare his colonel. He kept a fanatical watch on him, regarded his patients as potential enemy spies, and had him followed on his rounds.

Most of all, and basically, he resented the doctor's influence and blamed Banks for the profound changes in Rall's personality. The two of them sat hunched over their chessboard night after night, seldom going to bed before midnight, and sometimes going on into the small hours. On those mornings Rall—who had been toasting the doctor's more successful moves, and his own, with generous helpings of the doctor's punch—could hardly be gotten out of bed before noon.

Tonight, as usual, the game had been going on for hours. Every time Luib entered the living room he saw the same scene. The two men sat at one end of an oval table, the chessboard between them, illuminated by a movable lamp with a lacquered black shade. For hours neither of them said a word. They were an odd pair, the Hessian officer who spoke no English and the American doctor who never uttered a German word in Luib's hearing. Not even alcohol loosened their tongues.

It was long past midnight when they finally called it quits. Luib, who had been dozing on a bench in the hallway, helped the colonel up the stairs to his bedroom. Rall leaned on him heavily. In his room, he dropped on the bed as he was, and rolled over to face the wall, mumbling incomprehensibly to himself. His right hand reached out and closed around the bedpost; in a matter of seconds, he was fast asleep.

Luib had known his colonel for many years, and had seen him drunk often enough. But this seemed strangely different—a drunkenness that had little to do with the doctor's mild punch. He carefully snuffed the candles, placed more wood on the one fire that was still burning low in one of the two fireplaces, and cleared the maps and papers from the sofa where he had decided to spend the night, rolled in a blanket, instead of in the unheated room next door, which was his own bedchamber.

45

When Luib woke, a slate-gray sky framed by the three windows overlooking the river told him it was dawn. The blanket in which he had wrapped himself last night lay on the floor. His back hurt; he hugged himself to stop his shivering. Deep rhythmic breathing came from Rall's bed.

Luib's eyes fell on the heap of documents on the table and, without thinking, he reached for one, leafed through it absently. Suddenly he knew what he wanted to do. He spread his blanket on the floor and dumped all the papers and documents in the center of it, everything he could find on the chairs, windows, beside the bed. When he was sure that not one translation had been overlooked, he knotted the blanket together and lifted the heavy bundle to his shoulders. A last look at Rall showed him fast asleep, as though he had not budged once during the night. Luib carried the bundle down the stairs and did not set it down until he was inside the library. He looked at the pile of paper as if surprised at what he'd done, then turned and walked out. He found his coat on a hook in the foyer, put it on, smoothed his hair with one hand, tied the ribbon that held it together on the nape of his neck more tightly, and stepped through the back door out into the yard.

The storm had subsided overnight; the stone steps were free of yesterday's ice crust, and water dripped from the gutters.

He saddled his piebald horse and led it out into the yard. He still ached from the uncomfortable night he had spent on the sofa.

Down on the wide river plain, he gave his horse its head. What ice was left atop the snow was paper thin, and crackled under his horse's hooves. The land lay before him white and empty, not a mark on it, not a person in sight. He was the first to ride across it this morning, in a silence hardly broken even by the river which lay just beyond a dense stand of trees; it was muffled here under a wide sheet of ice stretching out from the bank. It was getting lighter; in fact, the clouds were getting darker and heavier. The light seemed to come more from the snow and from the sulfurous yellow stripe cutting through the dark blue wall just above the horizon. Luib was getting warm; he opened his coat. He had forgotten there was a sentry down here by the river. When he saw the shed, he was about to turn back. But the sentry was running across the snow toward him. "We had a boat drift ashore here this morning," he shouted.

"What about it?" Luib said.

"I thought I should report it," the man said. "It came downriver last night. We found it this morning. There was a dead man in it, wearing the rebel uniform."

"What time is your relief coming?"

"Seven o'clock—in an hour."

Luib looked at the sky. He understood his horse's restlessness now—the sulfurous strip on the horizon had grown wider; a bolt of lightning flashed from the dark blue clouds above. A few seconds later came a distant roll of thunder.

The sentry crossed himself.

"Haven't you ever seen lightning in winter?" Luib said. He turned his horse away from the river, and rode toward the woods, northward. He spurred the piebald on until it broke into a gallop. A strange light lay over the landscape, greenish on the snow. The tips of the firs and pines seemed almost to touch the horizon; they looked pitch black against that sulfurous yellow strip. Luib had never seen such a sky before. Though it was cold, the air seemed oppressive, like a humid summer day.

Lightning flared. Luib waited for the thunder, but there was none; instead, there were more flashes of lightning, one after another, all along the edge of the forest. The abrupt, cacophonous roar that followed was not thunder but the sound of cannon. And out of the forest came an army of men approaching across the open snow—an army that seemed to be dressed in tree bark.

Luib saw no red, no green, no gleam of metallic braid, no bright banners anywhere. The colors of this army were the colors of tree trunks, browns of every hue and shade. It was as though the forest itself were moving toward him.

The outposts had panicked. Luib saw them running toward him across the snow, fleeing the oncoming rebels. He wheeled his horse around so violently he was almost thrown from the saddle. He found what experience and instinct had told him he would: the woods to the east, stretching along an extended ridge of hills behind the town, were advancing too, and so were those to the south. The forests that surrounded Trenton in a wide semicircle were all suddenly converging on it.

Bugles were sounding from the direction of town. The dark storm clouds covering the sky had darkened the landscape, but Luib could make out the bivouac of the regiments in Trenton as clearly as if he were looking through a telescope. Everything seemed abnormally sharp and clear, as if somehow heightened by the eerie light occasionally flickering behind the clouds or by the brilliant white of the snow. Again a streak of lightning sliced across the blue-black sky.

Luib sank his spurs into the horse's flanks and raced back toward the doctor's house. He stormed up the stairs, afraid he wouldn't be able to wake Rall from his deep sleep—but when he entered the room, Rall was just getting up. His eyebrows were drawn together in a deep frown. "So they've really done it," he said.

"I don't know how they did it, but they're here. A whole army of them."

Almost gently, Rall pushed the sergeant out of his path, crossed the room, and flung the French windows open. Fresh air streamed into the room, bringing with it the sound of bugles and gunfire. Hands propped on the two open wings of the window, Rall leaned out, looking toward the river. "What's your guess, Luib, how many of them are there?"

"Two thousand men. Maybe more. They're pouring out of the woods, from all sides. Our outposts have been routed. I can't imagine how we can stop them."

When Rall turned around, Luib was holding his boots ready. Rall took them. "So you think we've lost this battle even before it begins. We'll see. Go and see to the horses. I'll be right with you."

He pulled on his boots, then picked up his gray wig from its stand. Hesitating for a second, he smoothed his dark hair back from his forehead and put on the wig, and on it, his three-cornered hat. Going down the stairs, he buckled on his belt and saber.

Luib was waiting outside. Rall swung into the saddle and they set off at a run in the direction of Assunpink Creek, toward the center of town, Luib leading two spare horses. Mounted messengers began to converge on them from all sides, but Rall didn't slacken the pace. Barely able to keep up, the messengers shouted their reports to him; eyes straight ahead, he heard them out. The information was a mass of confusion, but one thing was clear: the rebels' surprise attack had routed all the outposts. There was nothing standing in the enemy's way—no earthworks, no fortifications, nothing.

Luib listened to the reports with only half an ear. The only thing that mattered was that he was once more riding at Rall's side, that his colonel was again in command, interrupting the messengers to fire questions at them; and that it was taking all Luib's energy just to keep up with him. Last night when he had helped him upstairs to bed, Rall had seemed to weigh a ton—now, in the saddle, he looked weightless, as if he consisted of pure energy.

The crack of musket fire was almost constant now. The roar of cannons drowned out even the hoofbeats of their horses.

On the other side of the Assunpink they were met by Captain Kunkel. Kunkel was wounded; blood was running down the side of his head. "You can't get into Trenton. Your regiment . . ." he swayed in the saddle.

"What about my regiment?" Rall's voice had regained its old, hard, penetrating ring.

Kunkel was barely holding himself in the saddle. "Your regiment's been cut off, where the road to Princeton leads out of town. They're on the run—it's a regular rout."

"Do you hear that?" Rall shouted to Luib. His usually pale face had turned a vigorous bronze. "The Rall regiment on the run. Did you ever hear such nonsense? The world'll turn upside down before that happens." At the thrust of his spurs, his horse reared and leaped ahead. The group set off at a gallop toward Trenton.

Near the town, they found themselves in a cross fire—the staccato blasts of muskets everywhere, the whine of bullets passing overhead—but Rall charged ahead, leading them around houses, leaping fences, cutting across streets and pathways. They reached some kind of orchard, the trees trimmed into round shapes, their trunks wrapped in white cloths. Through the geometrically precise rows, Luib could see troops running across the snow—in the green uniforms of the Rall Jägers and the blue of the Grenadiers. The snow was scattered with discarded munition packs, grenadier helmets, even weapons.

A rider came toward them—Claus Haynow. "They won't stop!" he shouted to Rall, his voice breaking. "These idiots just keep running!"

Rall rode on after his fleeing troops. He drew his saber and slashed furiously at the trees around him, as if they were the enemy, dislodging snow that powdered his hat and his shoulders. In seconds he had himself under control again, and he spurred his horse out in front of his men. "A drummer!" he shouted "Where are my drummers? Drummers form on me!"

The stream of men flowed to a halt behind his horse, out of breath, haggard, but unwilling to risk running past Rall.

"Buglers form on me!" Rall shouted.

Gradually order was restored, the milling men formed into a semblance of ranks, the drummers and buglers at their head.

Rall raised his saber. "Forward! Follow me."

The bugles sounded; the drums began to beat in cadence. The remnants of the regiment moved out, Rall at the fore, leading his troops back into battle.

46

The storm had settled over Trenton, as if the Delaware were some kind of barrier the clouds could not cross. From the farmstead on the hill, Robert and Soerman could see the lightning flickering in the clouds above the town; it was as if nature had become a rebel ally, the lightning competing with the flashes of the guns, the thunder with the roar of the cannon.

The farm family stood in front of the house, watching with awe what was going on in the valley. The destroyed barn, the hay that was to have kept the cows fed through the winter, the threshing flails lying charred under the ashes, the stolen pig—all that was forgotten; an army had emerged from the forests to gain revenge against the Hessians, and even the heavens were taking part.

The two Yorkshire horses with the Redford brand stood saddled and ready. Robert and Soerman were sitting on a cord of wood stacked under the eaves of the house. From here they could survey the entire length of the valley.

They had hardly slept at all the night before. The farmer's wife had put down two stacks of straw for them in the kitchen, but neither of them had been able to go to sleep. Now and then one or the other had got up to stare out the window into the dark, and that was how the night had passed. And by morning it was too late to do what they had come all this way to do.

Soerman braced himself with his hands and let himself down

off the wood rick. "It looks like it's all over," he said. "How much longer do you want to wait here? And for what?"

Robert kept staring at the battle scene. There was still an occasional salvo of cannon fire. Here and there he could see a house on fire, a horse running across the snow, men scattering and seeking cover. From this distance they were only tiny figures, miniatures on a toy battlefield. "Actually," he said, "if we left now we ought to get there at just the right time."

He got down off the wood rick, and they went to get their horses. There was still a smell of smoke and ashes in the air, from the barn.

"We could be back at Redford by noon," Soerman said abruptly.

"You think we ought to go back?"

Soerman avoided Robert's eyes. "Why not? What can you do in Trenton, look at the dead? What makes you think he survived that slaughter? And if he did—would you kill a prisoner?"

Robert carefully tightened the saddle cinch. "If you want to go back, that's all right. Maybe it's a good idea. Tell them what's happened and that I'll be back tonight."

"What are you staying for? What are you going to do? We had all night and couldn't bring ourselves to go and do it. What makes you think it'll be easier in the daytime?"

"I don't know. I don't know what I'm going to do. All I know is, it has to come to an end. I have to see him. You may be right. He may be dead. But I'll have to see for myself."

"Come back with me," Soerman pleaded. "I'm the one who talked you into this. It's my fault we're here in the first place."

"If you want to go back, then go. Right now. I can't."

"I've brought you nothing but bad luck," Soerman said. "I couldn't bear it if I were the only one to survive again." He set his foot in the stirrup and swung himself into the saddle. "But you may be right. I'll go back and leave you alone. You've always been at your best alone." Without looking back, he turned his horse and rode away, slowly, as if to give Robert time to change his mind.

Robert watched till he was out of sight.

The road winding down the valley toward Trenton showed the signs of several horses preceding him. The roaring of the artillery and the musket fire had ceased, along with the worst of the storm. Suddenly it started to rain, a heavy downpour coming straight down. It lasted only for a few minutes, and stopped as suddenly as it had begun. The earth seemed to take a long deep breath, the clouds parted, and the sun broke out over the valley.

The snow-covered pastures and fields he passed were churned up by horses' hooves, boot tracks, the trails left by the cannon wheels. Here and there a large dark splotch stained the snow.

He dismounted when he reached the edge of town and led his horse through the clutter of discarded mustkets, bayonets, munition packs, trampled hats and blood-soaked coats—the debris of battle. A cannon with a damaged barrel blocked one side of the street. Soldiers of the Continental Army were herding little bands of prisoners before them at bayonet-point. Wounded Hessians lay against houses and fences, unshaven, the way they had been rousted from their beds. Their eyes were red from the smoke of battle. Nobody was paying any attention to their cries for help.

He remembered the way all this had looked from the hill above the valley—like a toy battle in a miniature toy town; even the musket and cannon fire had sounded tiny and unreal. Now he saw the dead, the wounded with bloody heads, bodies ripped by bayonets.

The snow in the road had turned to a muddy slush. Only in the yards was it still white. The fence was torn down around one of the yards. Inside was a wounded Hessian lying in a flower bed, another kneeling over him supporting the wounded man's head. As he came closer he saw that it was Sergeant Luib, and that the man on the ground was Rall.

Rall's eyes were closed; his tricorne lay on the ground, his wig inside it. The well-polished tops of his boots gleamed in the sun. His spurs were dug into the snow.

Luib looked up.

"How is he?" Robert asked.

Luib gave no answer. A layer of snow slipped from a nearby roof and hit the ground with a wet thud.

"I'll get you a doctor," Robert said.

Luib shook his head. "No doctor," he said. "It's too late for a doctor. And anyway, it would only make matters worse if he pulled through. To survive this would be the worst kind of punishment for him, much worse than death."

Robert looked down at Rall. His face was bloodless, but even now it hadn't lost its grim expression. The eyebrows were pulled together in a scowl. What made the mouth look so big and dark was the coagulated blood around it.

"What's happened to the others? Where is my brother?"

Luib straightened up. "Oh, it's you," he said, with distaste. "Where did you come from?"

"Where's my brother? Tell me."

"Your brother? He took thirty men to try to make Bordentown and get reinforcements." There was a moan from Rall, and Sergeant Luib bent over his colonel again.

Robert led his horse back to the street and went on. The road to Bordentown. It was from there, from the swampy plain between the Assunpink and the Delaware, that he had heard the last scattering of shots on his way into Trenton.

The marketplace in the center of town was swarming with rebel troops, and more were coming in all the time. The air was filled with the hum of voices and the clatter of horses on cobblestones. Captured weapons and equipment were stacked around the pavilion in the middle of the square. A new group of Hessian prisoners was adding its weapons to the pile. The captured Hessian flags were stuck in a high mound of snow in front of the building that had served as regimental headquarters.

Robert went on through town. The sun was getting hot, and he felt suddenly very tired; the lack of sleep the night before was catching up with him. He felt slightly dizzy and realized his wound had left him weaker than he had thought.

A rider came along the street toward him, reined in in front of him. It was Lieutenant Blyth. "Have you seen Rall?" he said.

"You've got to help me. I've got to find Rall. He has to be here in town."

Blyth's eyes were deeply circled, feverish, obsessed. Robert felt the lieutenant's face was a mirror held up before his own—could he possibly look like that himself? He thought of Soerman, probably almost back to the ferry by now. He couldn't understand why he hadn't gone back with him.

"How do you want to find him?" he said to Blyth. "Alive or dead?"

"You've seen him? Where?"

"You'll find him. If you don't find him now, you'll find him when you count the dead."

The land this side of the Assunpink was swampy. The howitzer that had stood at the bridge was sunk deep in the mud, buried by its own recoil. Rebels troops had hitched four horses to it and were trying to pull it out, without much success.

The bridge across the Assunpink was the southernmost point held by the rebels. Their next outpost was to the east of town; between the two, in the delta formed by the Assunpink and the Delaware, lay the swampy land crossed by the road to Bordentown.

The rebels wouldn't allow Robert across the bridge. About two dozen militia lined the bank, as if expecting attack any minute from an invisible enemy. To the right of the bridge stood a group of Hessian prisoners. Robert didn't recognize any of them; they weren't from the Rall regiment. One of them looked like an old veteran; the place where sergeant stripes had been removed was clearly visible on his sleeve. Robert went over to him.

"I hear a troop of Hessians tried to fight their way through to Bordentown," he said. "Do you know if they're still over there?"

The man gave him a disgusted look. "If they want to go on fighting, let them." He turned his head away and spat. "I'll be damned if I care. What I'm thinking about is the other side of the river. They're talking about four oxen and fifty acres of good land for every man willing to settle here. I'm not going to worry my head about a few madmen who haven't had enough yet."

Robert walked slowly back to the bridge. His shoulders had begun to ache with weariness; he felt weak. Again, he wondered why he was here, what purpose this was going to serve. In the distance, from the Delaware, came the sound of gunfire. The line of militiamen stiffened. Guns at the ready, feet widespread, they stared across the Assunpink. The creek was only about ten yards wide here. Robert joined the line of the militia. Beyond the brush on the opposite bank was the doctor's house, the Delaware, and far off on the white plain two small dots growing rapidly larger.

The officer in charge of the militia unit gazed through his telescope, adjusting the lens with an almost pedantic preciseness. A quiet clicking ran along the line as the militiamen pulled back the hammers of their flintlocks. The officer lowered the telescope. "They're coming to surrender," he said. But none of the men moved, no one lowered his weapon.

The two figures disappeared behind a clump of brush across the creek. Robert could see only snow glittering in the sun, shadowy movement. Then they emerged again, two riders in the uniform of the Rall regiment, coming at a trot toward the bridge.

The lead rider carried an upraised lance, a white cloth fluttering at the tip. He was young and slim and had lost his hair ribbon; his hair hung loose about his neck. Two or three lengths behind him came the second rider, hatless and without his wig. His dark hair was longer than Robert remembered it. His coat was draped over his left shoulder. A pistol was stuck in his belt, next to the hilt of his saber.

It was the pistol—a piece from the gun room at Haynow House—that suddenly, for Robert, made the whole thing real. For a long moment he saw only that one detail, the pistol, like a cut-out in a picture. His hand went to his own belt—but he had no weapon; no pistol, not even a knife. He had come this whole way unarmed. The discovery should have shocked him; but what he felt was only surprise.

The two riders had reined to a halt on the opposite bank, only a few yards away. The militiamen were silent.

Across the creek, Claus raised his hand. "Send me an officer I can negotiate with. We're willing to surrender—under certain circumstances." He sat very straight in the saddle; his words sounded like a challenge.

For the first time since he had left Redford Robert realized why he had felt compelled to make this ride to Trenton. It was a realization that came reluctantly, but it was the truth, sad as it was: for all these years what had been growing between himself and his brother was nothing less than hatred—a pure, deep hatred, nothing else. It had begun long before that night on the Delaware. He had refused to face it, right up through the moment he had left Redford—unarmed. But it was what he felt now, the hatred, and with it, because of it, a deep sadness—but a kind of relief, too. He saw that Claus had noticed him, had recognized him. Their eyes met; he thought he could feel Claus's breath catch, his heart skip a beat—it was an illusion, of course: it was his own breath catching, his own heart suddenly atremble.

Afterward, looking back, this instant seemed to have lasted an infinitely long time. Surely long enough for him to do something, if only to duck out of the line of fire. But he didn't move, suddenly flooded with weakness, suddenly very tired. The weapon he had with him—his hatred—was new to him. He didn't quite know how to handle it; but he trusted it.

The silver mountings of the pistol in Claus's hand glittered in the sun. Robert saw the flash of the gun muzzle. There was an outcry, and the man beside him went down, clutching his shoulder.

The militia's vigilance had been only sharpened by that fluttering white flag. Though Claus had spoken English, they had heard only the German accent, seen only the hated green uniform with its scarlet facings. There was no need to give them an order to fire; that pistol shot was order enough.

Robert was in a daze; dimly he heard the overlapping staccato fire of the muskets along the line to both sides of him, saw the lance with the white flag fall, the horse with the slim young rider bolting, followed by the second horse, riderless, galloping away across the snow. No one stopped him from crossing the bridge this time. Claus lay on his back in the snow, a few feet away from the fallen flag. His eyes were wide open; he was still alive for this one last second. Robert bent over him, saw those eyes; Claus's lips were moving—one final, painful whisper, ". . . bastard . . . you bastard . . ."

Robert felt all the weakness and tiredness well up in him, filling his brain; and then he was melting, slowly, into blackness.

47

He woke up in an unfamiliar room, full of unfamiliar objects. He remembered nothing; it was as if sleep had carried him across an ocean and washed him ashore on some foreign beach. He was lying, fully dressed, in a bed. Someone had pulled off his boots and unbuttoned the top of his shirt. He was hungry and thirsty.

Bright light came through the window. His boots stood at the foot of the bed. He got up and put them on. His coat was hanging on the back of a chair. He picked it up and went to the window, opened it, and drew the cold air deeply into his lungs.

A long column of prisoners was moving past the house; it stretched all the way down to the Delaware. The Hessians shuffled along three abreast, the uniforms of the different regiments looking very colorful in the sun—royal blue, green, brown, yellow, red, all the silver and gold braid on the cuffs and hat brims. It was strange to see such haggard, defeated troops in such spectacular uniforms being escorted by such vigorous but shabbily outfitted men.

The snow was completely melted off the road; only mud remained. Gradually, as if his sense of hearing were only just returning to him, he became aware of the tramping of boots on the muddy ground, the clatter of bayonets, now and then a shouted command.

He closed the window and went out into the hallway. He was beginning to remember being brought here. He opened a door and found himself in a library.

A man stood atop a ladder, arranging books on a top shelf.

When he saw Robert, he came down. "Every time I looked in on you," he said, "you were dead to the world. You've slept seven hours. I'm Doctor Banks."

There were no curtains at the windows; sunlight flooded the room.

"In Philadelphia, last year, they had a big popular attraction." Banks said. "A Hindu had himself nailed up in a coffin and covered with earth. You could probably do that as well as he did. Your pulse was down to forty, your breathing was barely noticeable. I believe I could have cut your heart out, and you'd never have noticed."

"Why didn't you?" Robert asked.

The doctor's eyes seemed to disappear under his heavy lids. "Do you think life would be easier without a heart? Maybe I could say that, I'm an old man, but you?"

Robert was beginning to remember the old man's face.

"Tell me what happened?"

Banks put down the book he had absentmindedly brought down with him when he descended the ladder. "Nothing much, you just fell over like a sawed-off tree. We carried you into that room, and there you lay and slept."

A door stood open at the back of the library. In the adjoining room, Robert saw a medicine cabinet and a doctor's high-legged examining table, covered with a white sheet. He could feel his memory coming back. "What have they done with *him?*" he asked.

"You mean the dead man?" Banks said. "I don't know why they bothered to bring him here. Unlike yourself, it didn't take a doctor to see that he was dead." He pointed to a round table. "You must be hungry," he said. "I've ordered us a snack."

They sat down together at a table, which stood in a corner alcove. "They buried him," Banks said. "After a victory, even generals relent a little. The Hessians were permitted to bury their dead. The Continental Army fired an honorary salute to their dead enemies. Not even the din they made could wake you up, though."

"Where are they buried?" Robert asked.

"They dug a big trench on the other side of the Assunpink Bridge."

"And *his* grave?"

Noah Banks slid a finger along the edge of the table. "In the Presbyterian graveyard."

Robert had started to eat. Now he put down his knife and fork and tried to read the doctor's expression. "What do you actually know about me?" he said. "You talk as if you knew me."

"Your escape across the Delaware was the talk of the town. A doctor's patients are a gossipy lot. And I knew your brother—he used to come here to report to Rall. I pieced the story together for myself. As for how I know you—" He looked up. "There's no mistaking that face. You look very much like your father, you know."

"Which side are you on, anyway?" Robert asked.

"Do you know which is the right side to be on, when the world's turned upside down?"

For a while neither of them said anything. Somewhere in the house a door or a window must have been left open; they could hear the marching column and the officers' commands.

"Do you know about the other grave?" Banks said.

"What other grave?"

Banks looked out the window to the snow-covered meadow. "It was the day after your escape. The sentry at the river found the body, and they brought it to me—the body of a woman. Your mother lay in this house until she was buried, in the graveyard of the Presbyterian Church, where your brother's buried now, too."

So the Delaware had carried her back to this side—that was Robert's first thought, and it brought with it not grief, but only a feeling of complete and final loneliness, like an armor isolating him from everything, from his mother, from her grave. Everything was suddenly drained of meaning. He would almost have preferred not learning about the grave, not yet, not today. He had seen too many dead people today. He suddenly longed to escape to Trenton, to return to the other side of the river.

He got up from the table. "How can I thank you?"

"I can't imagine how you could, unless you have the power to undo what's done." Banks accompanied Robert out of the house and waited until the Negro servant had brought his horse. They shook hands. "Tell your father our game's still the way we left it, locked up in a cabinet. Tell him to come soon. Who knows how much longer it'll be so peaceful on both sides of the Delaware."

The ferry lay deep in the water, moving sluggishly, weighted down with prisoners. All around it, small boats dotted the Delaware—some loaded with prisoners, moving toward the far bank; some empty, on their way back. The river was alive with spray and the rhythmic slap of oars on the water. Everything was etched in sharp winter sunlight.

Robert stood at the front of the ferry, wedged in between prisoners and guards, watching the bow cleave the water. They were moving much too slowly for him; the Delaware seemed three times as wide as it had when he had crossed it the day before. The prisoners stood closely packed beside him, but he felt no kinship with them. The time in garrison in Kassel, the swearing in at Bremerlehe, the crossing of the Atlantic, the battles here—none of that meant anything to him anymore. There was no one he wanted to look for among these prisoners, no one he wanted to talk with. Niklas, Ploetz, Louis—they were all dead.

The ferry docked with a lurch. He followed the prisoners ashore. The riverbank was lined with prisoners, three Hessian regiments, over a thousand men. They were beginning to form up into a column again. They had been quiet and somber on the ferry. Now, on this side of the river, they seemed to come alive; without waiting for orders, they arranged themselves in formation.

Robert rode along with the column until the road to Redford branched off from the main road to Philadelphia. He waited until the column had passed, and then turned toward home, looking back once or twice to watch them winding their way over the plain. For a while he could still discern the colors of the uniforms; then the colors blurred together and the single figures melted into one dark stream receding across the snow, growing tinier, and finally disappearing into the white altogether.

Now he was alone in the wide, silent country. The storm, the snow and the rain, had obliterated all the tracks from the road. The feeling he'd had when he woke in the doctor's house—that sleep had carried him across an ocean to a new shore—was still with him; nothing existed now except this new world.

The day before, twilight had begun in early afternoon, but today the light seemed to be lasting forever. The air only seemed to thicken a little and take on more color: shadows turned blue, and the trees in the distance seemed to soften.

The road was lined with bushes; then the bushes gave way to a fence, and behind the fence he could see the buildings of a farmstead. Paths had been shoveled through the snow—from the gate to the house, from the house to the well, from the well to the barn. When he saw the well, he remembered how thirsty he was. He rode into the courtyard. Pigeons sat around the chimney on the main house. He saw a child's sled leaning against a wall.

He dismounted, went to the well, and lowered the pail down inside. The chain clattered loudly in the old windlass when he brought the pail up. He set it on the edge of the well, dipped water up in his cupped hands, and drank deeply.

The door of the house behind him had opened. A red-haired woman stepped outside with a baby on her arm, a swarm of red-haired children behind her. The woman came running out to the well, still carrying the baby. "Look at her," she said. "I'm sure she's going to be the prettiest one of them all. And you helped bring her into the world." Then she stopped abruptly and blushed a fiery red that completely swamped the freckles of her face. She looked puzzled; then her face lit up with realization, the freckles emerged again, and she smiled. "You must be his son. We've heard about you. You really do look very much like him." She took another step forward. "I'm Abigail Hancock. And this is my youngest daughter. We baptized her yesterday. Her name is Roberta. Will you tell him?"

"I promise."

"And be sure to tell him how pretty she is." Abigail examined his face. "Have you just come from over there, from Trenton?"

He nodded.

"Is it true that we won?" she said. "Nobody believed we would, except your father."

Again, he nodded. He dipped up water from the pail again and drank. "You've got very good water."

"You'll have to come try it on a hot summer day," she said. "On a hot summer day after a long ride in the sun."

"I will. On the first hot day next summer."

A young man came out from the stables. "It's young Mr. Skelnik," Abilgail called out to him. "He's just come from Trenton. We've won a big victory."

Robert mounted his horse again. Abigail smiled and waved as he rode away. For a while he could still hear her and the children talking behind him; then he urged his horse on, anxious to get home. It was almost sunset, but the light seemed to linger. The brilliant blue was slowly fading from the sky, but in its place there remained a strange luminous light.

At last he turned up the cedar drive toward the house. There was no one in sight as he approached the stables. All the other horses were in the stalls, even Soerman's. He relieved his mount of saddle and bridle, poured fresh water into the trough and fresh oats into the feed bin. When he went outside, the yard was still deserted. Near the wall at the other end, an ice rink had been made for the children. The ice was dotted with puddles, and suddenly he realized how mild the air had become. The snow was melting from the roofs. Two men came out and began to light the torches that illuminated the yard in the evening.

The lamps weren't lit inside the house yet. The windows gleamed almost pink in the sunset. As he walked along the front of the house, toward the entrance, he passed the windows of the library; inside, he saw Mary. He went no closer, so as not to startle her. She was sitting alone at the chessboard, gazing down at the pieces of a game not yet begun.

Epilogue

As Abigail had said, Trenton was a great victory. It wasn't the importance of the battle itself, nor the number of enemy dead, nor the number of prisoners taken. What mattered was that Trenton had proved to the colonists that they could win.

The war was far from finished. It went on for five more years. Victories alternated with defeats, but the tide had turned. It began to carry the English and their German mercenaries back, out of the country and across the sea to Europe.

On October 17, 1781, at Yorktown, the enemy capitulated. The peace was signed in September 1783. The last of the returning Hessian regiments arrived at the harbor of Bremerlehe in April 1784, nine years after they had embarked there to cross the Atlantic. Thirty thousand in all had been shipped as mercenaries to America; seventeen thousand returned; three thousand had fallen. The rest stayed to become settlers in the New World.